Face
OF
Fortune

Also from *Phase Publishing*

by
Emily Daniels
A Song for a Soldier

by
Laura Beers
Saving Shadow

by
Rebecca Connolly
The Lady and the Gent

by
Grace Donovan
Saint's Ride

Face OF Fortune

THE SHADOWS OF ROSTHWAITE
BOOK TWO

COLLEEN KELLY-EIDING

Phase Publishing, LLC
Seattle

Phase Publishing, LLC first paperback edition
February 2020

ISBN 978-1-952103-02-5
Library of Congress Control Number 2020900529
Cataloging-in-Publication Data on file.

ACKNOWLEDGEMENTS

To Bonnie, and my sister, Kitty. Thank you for your encouragement from the beginning. Thank you for your love, for your faith in me, and for reading the first, very long manuscript.

To my daughters, Connor and McKenna, two incredible women and artists of whom I am so proud. Thank you for your love, humor, and encouragement.

And to the love of my life, my Paul. Thank you for your support, your love, and for sharing the poetry of your heart.

PROLOGUE

A dark figure threw sticks on the dying fire. Sparks flew towards the cave's ceiling a few feet overhead. Now, with the addition of two logs, the light began extending outward. Kicking at a rat emerging from the darkness for the warmth of the fire, the figure began exploring what the storm-flooded river had brought in from the outside. Sometimes there were pieces of wood that could be dried out; sometimes there were animals to be skinned and eaten; sometimes there was a dead body to be stripped for its clothes and valuables.

The figure moved closer to the mouth of the cave. Here, the river roiled in from the outside at a frightening speed, throwing up spray as it collided with the interior walls. There, in the dim light, many feet inside the cave, a body lay on a limestone outcropping. Sensing possible booty from the corpse, the figure scuttled forward.

Its hand reached out to clear away the mud and blood from the face of the dead man. The figure's hands quickly checked for coins, rings, daggers. Finding nothing, they began to work on removing the boots. The corpse's right leg jerked. The figure froze momentarily, turning its head, it found the corpse was awake and staring back with sea grey eyes.

The "corpse" was a man. He grimaced in pain before his eyes glazed over and closed. The figure moved silently on all fours and put its nose near the man's face. It sniffed his hair and, bringing its face very close, kissed him gently on his lips. He did not wake up. The figure sat back on its haunches and smiled.

CHAPTER ONE

Brilliant red petals filled her vision. A warm breeze brushed over her, causing her to sigh. A hand gently caressed the small of her back. A voice whispered, "I love you". He is here, she thought. She smiled. He is here in our garden, on our island. She kissed his lips, felt his body press down on hers, and she welcomed him.

Darkness. She called out for him. The wind howled, muting her cries. Thunder rolled. She opened her eyes and found she was alone in her bed, in her house in London. She lit a candle, trying to drive away the dread that threatened to possess her. James was dead. It had been three months since he drowned. She'd prayed for some word, some sign that said he still lived, but none had come.

Charlotte got out of bed and walked quietly to the nursery to look in on her young son, Jack.

He was fast asleep in his bed. His nurse, Annie, slept soundly in her bed next to his. Jack's thick, blond curls framed his face. His pink lips were parted, his eyelids smooth and shiny. His eyelashes followed the slight upward slant of his eyes. Jack was her world. The one earthly connection she had with James Clarke, her lover, though Jack carried her late husband's name, Pruitt. She treasured her son beyond all else and would do anything to protect him.

She thanked God that Count Cesi's men had captured Edward Hawkes, James's sworn enemy, who had threatened to kill Jack. She shuddered, remembering how Hawkes had murdered her husband, Audley, and made the world believe James was guilty. Count Cesi had Hawkes now and would extract a confession for that murder and the killing of the baby in Devon. The confessions came too late for James to enjoy, but at least his good name would be restored.

She kissed Jack on the forehead. He stirred but did not wake. As she walked downstairs, she thought about the decisions she needed to make concerning her late husband's silk business. Cottons from India were quickly becoming the fashion. There was not as much work now for the silk weavers in East London's Spitalfields. Until recently they toiled long hours to create the exquisite silks that Pruitt and Byrd Ltd. sold in England and abroad. It was time for her to choose which weavers and their families would continue under contract. Only yesterday, Mr. Sharp, the man who managed the day to day running of Pruitt and Byrd told her she must begin to make decisions on this most pressing matter.

As she crossed into the drawing room, she went to one of the windows facing the street and peeked outside. Since James's disappearance at Wookey Hole, Charlotte knew that Thomas Warrender, the powerful Earl of Chagford, was having her house watched. Warrender wanted to make sure James was dead. Charlotte wished she had not stopped James from killing his brother-in-law when Warrender had tried to rape her.

There were days in the three months since James's

death that Charlotte cursed her impetuous nature. She had fallen in love with James Clarke when she was sixteen, but he went off to war. At twenty, she married Audley Pruitt, her father's wealthy business partner. Charlotte found her wifely duties left her unsatisfied, especially when it came to her husband's quick and thoughtless lovemaking.

Three years into her marriage, she and James began an affair. He was a gentle and passionate lover, but she discovered that he suffered bouts of madness. Then Edward Hawkes, a vengeful enemy from James's past, entered their lives. Through it all, they loved each other and fought to be together and raise their son, Jack.

Now James was gone, and her world was cold and melancholy.

She peeked out the window again. Three men stood in front of the house directly across from her front door. Two were turned with their backs to her, but the third man's face was visible. She recognized him as one of the regular watchers, the men who came every day in small groups to spy on her. They were there all hours of the day. When they first began appearing, she thought they were idle apprentices. The idea of such a group loitering about filled her with dread. They could become violent, as they had in other parts of town. Then she noticed they would glance furtively at the house and move away if they saw her watching. She endured their presence. What other choice did she have?

Today was the day that she and Mr. Sharp, Pruitt and Byrd Ltd.'s manager, were to begin visiting the weavers. She wanted to see which of them produced the best work in the most efficient manner. The workshops that did less for her company would receive notice that their services were no longer required. Charlotte had not slept well. She hated having to make this decision, but she must think of her own economic situation. She was thankful that in the last few months production had been going well despite disturbances in Spitalfields. Some of the other silk merchants had lost thousands of pounds when angry workers came in the middle of the night, cutting work off the looms and smashing them beyond repair. Both sides were filled with rage. New laws, recently passed in Parliament, made taking wastage a crime. People were hanged for what had been a common and accepted practice the year before.

Charlotte left the window and went to ready herself for Mr. Sharp's arrival. As she chose the clothes she would wear for the day's outing, she thought about how the demand for silk was down, especially for ribbons. Ladies now wanted cotton for their dresses. She had her son's and her future to think of.

Charlotte dressed warmly as Mr. Sharp had bid her to do. The workshops were cold places this time of year he had warned her. Mr. Sharp called for Charlotte after the church bells rang the hour of nine. The weavers would have been at work since six in the morning, but Charlotte had no wish to go out that early. Sharp was not an unpleasant man, but he did lack a certain gentility.

"Good morning, Mrs. Pruitt," he greeted her, his tone clipped.

They spoke only about business. He had many facts and figures for her, telling her how ribbon sales had fallen off in the last week and that two of their London silk buyers had cancelled orders.

"Lady Overington wrote a letter praising the quality of

our fabric, but she stated that her dresses for the summer would be made of new cotton rather than silk."

On finishing his report, he stared at Charlotte awaiting her reply. She thanked him. He suggested they call for their sedan chairs and be off.

The weaver's house they were to visit first was only a few streets from Bellagio House where Charlotte lived. Audley, her late husband, had wanted to be close to them. His business had been his life, and he would never have agreed to move to the more fashionable and spacious west end. Now, as the chair men made their way along the narrow streets, Charlotte felt her chair bumped and jostled by the crowds.

At last they stopped.

"We are here," Mr. Sharp announced, as he exited his conveyance. He reached out and helped Charlotte down from her chair.

She looked up at the weaver's house, which was tall and narrow. Remembering the muddy puddles and other filth in the street, Charlotte looked back down and lifted her skirts to avoid soiling them.

Andrew Quail, the master weaver, met them with a hearty welcome and ushered them up the several flights of stairs to the top floor. As they entered the large room, his family greeted them and introduced themselves. Mr. Quail stood at Charlotte's side, nodding encouragement to each of them.

Susan, his wife, was a slim woman in her forties, her grey hair pulled neatly back and covered with a simple clothe cap. Charlotte was most impressed by her carriage. She stood straight, with self-assurance. Her six children ranged in age from the eldest son in his twenties to a little one about ten years old. Each described what they did and then returned quickly to their work. Andrew showed Charlotte and Mr. Sharp the work on each of his four looms and let them know that he oversaw five other workshops in the area. He had a total of twenty-five looms operating.

Charlotte was familiar with his silks. They were indeed beautiful and highly sought after. Most of his work was fabric for clothing, but some was for the walls and fine furnishings of the great houses of England and abroad. Count Cesi had several rooms decorated with Mr. Quail's silk. Charlotte was impressed by the industry of the Quail family. She complimented Mr. Quail and his wife for their fine children and excellent business.

At the door, Mr. Quail took Charlotte aside. "Mrs. Pruitt, I wish to say that you have been most fair in your dealings with us. My wife and I are proud to be in your employ. These are hard times for all of us, and there are many weavers that barely get by, skilled as they are. Please, be careful as you pass in the streets. There are some who are angry with their betters and would hurt you, given a chance."

She thanked him for his warning and told him that if her business prospered, he and his family would be generously recompensed for their fine work. They said their goodbyes; then she and Mr. Sharp were off to visit one of her warehouses in Wapping. It was next door, in fact, to the one in which James had hidden before his escape to France.

It was a clear, crisp day and the streets were crowded with people. Charlotte pondered Quail's warning. The incidents she'd heard about lately ranged from mischief to mayhem. Bands of boys would nail down a lady's skirts if she stopped to look in a shop window. Others would throw dye on dresses made of Indian cotton. More serious were the saboteurs she'd read about who raided workshops and destroyed property. There had been hangings, with more threatened. The number of soldiers billeted in Spitalfields grew larger as the violence increased.

As they passed Rag Fair, where the poor bartered and traded in used clothing, Charlotte realized how little she knew of life in London.

After looking over the inventory at the warehouse, they arrived safely back at Bellagio House. Mr. Sharp asked Charlotte if she wished to see the Widow Rourke's workshop tomorrow. Charlotte told him that would be to her liking, and he departed, promising to be back at Bellagio House again at nine o'clock the next morning.

In her grief over losing James, Charlotte found some solace in taking long walks with Jack and Annie. Most mornings, after taking care of the business at hand, she would call for them, and off they would walk towards Bethnal Green. The fresh air and exercise helped revive her flagging spirits. She loved to watch Jack toddle along, finding treasures wherever he looked. He would rush to her, or to Annie, to display them. This was not Charlotte's only reason for going out, however. She enjoyed throwing the men who watched her house into a panic. They tried not to be obvious about spying on her, but she'd gotten to know all their faces quite well.

When she returned from her meeting at the Quails' workshop, she noticed another figure across from her house. Perhaps, this lame beggar had been there before, but she did not recall seeing him. She could not tell his age because of the dirt covering his face and hands. His clothes were a patchwork of rags. He was stooped over and used a thick piece of wood with the bark still on it as a crutch. It held him upright, but just barely.

As Charlotte, Jack, and Annie began their walk, the beggar hobbled towards them. His face was covered by a ragged beard, and he had a patch over one eye. Charlotte was repulsed by his matted hair pulled haphazardly back into a queue. As he got closer, she could smell his dirty clothes and body. His approach frightened her, so she began to walk faster, attempting to catch hold of Jack's arm as she went.

Of course, being two years old and contrary of will, Jack veered away from her and ran right into the beggar, knocking him down. Jack began to wail. Charlotte quickly picked him up to comfort him. The man, in the meantime, clutched his ankle and groaned as he rolled on the ground.

Charlotte could not find it in her heart to abandon him altogether, even though he frightened her. She apologized from a distance for Jack's behaviour and asked how badly he was injured. The beggar did not look at her, mumbling he would recover, no thanks to her brat. She would have left him there, but her heart was moved to see him in such pain. Charlotte demanded he stay where he was and sent Annie to get the footmen. They would bring him into the house, Charlotte decided, where he could be tended to. All the while, the voices in her head were chastising her for caring about this odious man. She heard no word of thanks from him, only curses, which he muttered under his breath.

As she waited for the servants to come, Charlotte noticed that the watchers were enjoying this spectacle. They laughed and pointed to the poor devil as he writhed in pain. Finally, four of her stronger footmen came running out of the house, followed by Annie and Mr. Primm. After listening to Charlotte's commands to transport the fellow into the house and look after his leg, the men reluctantly hoisted him up and followed her orders. He fought them, but the pain appeared to be too much for him, and he slipped into unconsciousness.

Inside the house, they put him on a small bed in an unused servant's room, then they hurried off quickly to fetch what was needed for his leg and to clean him up. Charlotte looked in on him. He was badly in need of a bath. As she turned to go, she heard him say, "You have too kind a heart. You will get your throat cut one day."

Charlotte nearly fainted. "Jem?!" She turned. He had propped himself up on one arm and was smiling at her. "You're alive!" she exclaimed in a whisper.

"I am, my love."

The servants scurried back into the room, and he began to moan and grasp at his leg. He was the beggar once again. His voice was hoarse, and his language the cant of the streets. He pushed them away when they tried to look after his leg. Charlotte instructed them to leave him be, and allow him take care of himself. She told them to ask the cook to prepare the man some food, so he could be on his way quickly. When the servants left, Charlotte moved to where he lay. He looked up at her and smiled. His teeth were yellow and black. "My God, Jem," she whispered, "I thought you dead." She sat down next to him.

"My dearest, I nearly was. Here," he said. He took a dog-eared paper from inside his ragged shirt and handed it to her. "I've written down what happened these past three months. It's not safe to talk now, I think. Leave the garden gate ajar and your bedchamber window open. I will come to you tonight, with your permission. I love you." He kissed her.

"I'll be waiting for you," she said, barely able to believe it was him. "Jem, wait. I must tell you. I received a letter from Count Cesi just after you disappeared. His men caught Edward Hawkes. They were going to get him to confess. You will be a free man."

James appeared stunned for a moment. He looked at her, and speaking softly said, "Thank God, Charlotte. Perhaps fortune is smiling on us once again." There was a noise from the hallway.

He winked at her and began his ranting again. She tucked the paper into her robe's pocket and moved away from the bed. Mr. Primm came in, concerned for her safety. Charlotte reassured him she was fine an asked him to see that the beggar was properly fed and sent on his way with a small amount of money.

"He was a soldier, so he says, and so deserves to be treated with respect."

A few minutes later, she watched him hobble across the street and take up his place. He and Lord Chagford's spies exchanged curses. When one of the young ruffians started after him, James picked up his crutch and threatened him with it. The young man's companions held him back and laughed at the beggar. She took out the paper he'd given her and began to read its contents.

My Dearest Lottie,

I have spent three months in hell. I thought about you unceasingly. You are my salvation. To be in your arms is the heaven I have aspired to but thought I might never achieve again.

After leaving you at Scorhill Hall, my path was unhindered. I came so close to Squirrel's Inn, Charlotte, had I shouted, you would have heard me. It was then the soldiers appeared. I took on the seven of them. Rode right at them. I am sure they thought me mad, but it caught them off guard. I knocked three of them off their horses. The fog closing in, I was able to elude them for a day. My hope of meeting you gone, I prayed that you would continue on for London.

The next day outside of Cheddar, from a high vantage point, I saw that they had discovered my trail. I decided to take them through the gorge. My best hope, I thought, was to hide in Wookey Hole until they gave me up for dead. I remembered the caves. I felt they wouldn't follow me in too far, and I was correct.

My mistake was not reckoning on the rains that poured down as I took to the river. I was swept away from Lady Jane. I pray she was able to escape. I fought to keep my head above water as the torrent took me into the cave. Inside, I collapsed from exhaustion after crawling out onto the dry rock floor.

I awoke later as the water level inside rose swiftly. I was trapped. I crawled further in, thinking I saw a fire. There was none. I don't know how long I slept. I know I dreamt terrible dreams. When I woke this time, I took to the river Axe again, lost my footing and was swept into the underground rapids. It was so cold, Charlotte. I began to swim and to pray to God to let me live to see you and Jack again. I did not think I would survive to see you. I grew numb, my life ebbing away. I couldn't fight. My will was gone, and I knew I would die. Fate denied me that comfort, however. My leg caught and twisted between two rocks. The pain shot through me in an explosion of light. I fought being push under by the torrent. Wrenching my leg free, my body shot forward and out into the daylight. Getting free of the current, I came to the shallows. I dragged myself half out of the water and lost *consciousness.*

When I awoke, my leg was on fire. I saw nothing at first. Slowly, I realized I was lying on a pallet covered by a rough blanket, and it was keeping me warm. Light began to fill the room, and I saw beams above and a chair next to my bed.

Attempting to roll over on my side, pain surged through me, and I lay moaning. A face came into my view. It seemed to float above me. I heard a man's voice. I closed my eyes and felt myself float away. When I opened my eyes again, the sunlight was waning. This time, it was a woman's face I saw. She smiled at me. She was missing one of her front teeth. Her hair was pushed under a white cap and her cheeks were red.

"Are you back with us now?" she asked. I told her I thought I was. "Good, I will tell my husband. He was sure we'd lose you. But I told him you looked to be a strong man."

Her husband introduced himself as George Bunbury, a hedge cutter. He and his son had finished their day's work and had come to the river to wash. That's where they found me. I ran a high fever for several days and my ankle was broken. Mrs. Bunbury, with her knowledge of local herbs and plants, brought me back to life. I wanted to come to you, Charlotte, but I couldn't walk. The Bunburys treated me as family, and when I could walk again, I had nothing to repay them with but my labour. I stayed for several more days and helped them with their hedge cutting. I told them that I hailed from Devon, and my name was Will Cleveland. They gave me clothes to wear, and in the end, they sent me on my way with a full stomach.

I devised a plan to come to London as a beggar. Blind in one eye and lame, which I do not have to falsify, since my ankle still gives me pain. I came directly to Bellagio House, but after being across the street but a short time, I realized you were being watched. I have been here three days; three days of seeing you fleetingly and yearning for your touch.

I love you, my dearest, with all my soul. Kiss Jack for me.

Yours with greatest affection and regard,
Jem

Charlotte held the paper to her heart. James was alive! He had risen from the dead! Her joy was indescribable.

That night, after the household was asleep, she went into the garden and unlocked the gate to the mews. Returning to her room, she undid the latches on the bedchamber window. It was a moonless night, and the world was dark. She wrapped herself in a blanket and sat by the window.

As the candle burned down, she watched its flame dance in the draft. Her life, she thought, was like the candle flame, blown by breezes, as it shifted and moved in directions she could not control. From when she first saw James, she had been swept up into a course that her humours dictated. She loved him passionately and he returned that love. They reached out over distances of time and space, their fingers touching, only to be torn apart again and again. She ached to be with him, to look into his eyes, to touch the corners of his mouth when he smiled and to know that he desired her.

Charlotte's reverie was broken as one of the windows began to open. The blind-eyed beggar pulled himself up and into the room. He sat on the floor, and she slipped down out of the chair and crawled to him. They embraced, holding each other without speaking. He had come back to her! Tears in her eyes, she buried her head in his chest. She thanked God for his deliverance.

"Oh, Charlotte, how I have missed you!" he whispered.

"And I, you, Jem."

"I smell, forgive me."

"I don't care."

They made love, there by the windows. Their urgency to be one consumed them. Charlotte stripped off his ragged clothes. His scars from his battle with the caves were still red and stood out in the candlelight. She shuddered, imagining him bleeding and unconscious, by the riverbank.

His touch was gentle, but his hands had become rough and calloused. He held her face in his worn hand, and she watched his eyes as they moved in the candlelight. She loved his eyes. They held his soul, beautiful and loving.

"God has answered my prayers and brought you back to me. I know of no thanks great enough for this miracle. I love you, Jemmy, and will for all eternity."

The candle burned out at that moment, and they lay in each other's arms in the darkness. When Charlotte awoke, James was dressing in his beggar's clothes. "I cannot let anyone see me here, Lottie. I must go, but I will come again tonight, if I may."

"Please, come. Jemmy, take some money," Charlotte urged, going to the wardrobe to get some guineas for him.

"Just a few shillings, Charlotte. Thank you. I don't want to arouse any suspicions. I've been sleeping on the streets in abandoned houses near Rag Fair. Yesterday, I found a house in Rosemary Lane that I'll use as long as possible. I go by the name of Will Cleveland. Look for me across the street from your house later this morning. We'll talk tonight about the future. Please, be very careful. I don't know what Thomas may be planning. Hopefully, he'll keep his distance. If he thinks me dead, he may finally call off his men."

With that, he kissed her, climbed out the window, and was away just as the sky began to lighten in the east. Charlotte climbed into her bed. The bed linen was crisp and clean. She looked forward to James bathing.

CHAPTER TWO

Her eyes, it seemed to Charlotte, had only just closed when she was awakened by her maid, Betsy. She reminded Charlotte that Mr. Sharp would be calling for her soon. Today, they planned to visit the Widow Rourke's workshop. Annie, Jack's nurse, would be accompanying her because Widow Rourke was Annie's mother. Annie was already up and dressed as Charlotte began her morning toilette. After a small breakfast, they waited in the parlour for Mr. Sharp to arrive.

Both Charlotte and Annie dressed warmly. Outside was cold with a constant drizzle. The weather did not dampen Annie's spirits, however, as she told Charlotte how hard her mother and her siblings had been working since her father died. Charlotte asked if her uncle, Patrick Rourke, was taking over any of her father's business responsibilities. Annie sighed and seemed to be searching for the right words to describe her uncle.

"Uncle Patrick is not much interested in weaving. He spends most of his time talking with his friends about ideas."

"What sorts of ideas, Annie?"

"Well, I'm not certain, except that my mother says he uses the words 'equality' and 'liberty' a good deal. He has helped us. I don't want to sound ungrateful. My papa and he used to always have words about politics. They are, or were, different sides of the coin, my mother says. Where my father was quiet and never choleric, well, my uncle is the opposite."

When Mr. Sharp called for them, they boarded the carriage and were off. As they turned down Fleur-de-Lis Street, Annie could barely contain herself. She said not a word, but her smile grew broader and broader. When the carriage stopped in front of her mother's house, she looked to Charlotte for permission to move, which she gave quickly, fearing Annie might burst if she delayed. The girl had barely knocked on the door when her mother threw it open and took her daughter into her arms for a hug. After Mr. Sharp and Charlotte alighted from the carriage, Jane Rourke welcomed them into her parlour.

Though the room was small, it was well furnished and comfortable. With Annie's help, Mrs. Rourke served Charlotte and Mr. Sharp tea and honey cakes. Charlotte offered Mrs. Rourke her condolences for the loss of her husband. Mrs. Rourke said the same to Charlotte, adding that she hoped Mr. Clarke might be found very soon, alive and well. Charlotte smiled and thanked her.

As they ate, Jane Rourke explained that in her workshop above were eight looms. Six were single-handed ribbon looms and two were large floor looms. Her children were doing the quill winding and picking, the four journeymen worked on throwing and weaving on the ribbon looms while she and her daughter were weaving on the floor looms. All in all, it was a busy household. Mrs. Rourke also had piece work sent out to another forty weavers, plus more to several throwsters and spinners.

"I try, Mrs. Pruitt, to employ as many women as I can. We all struggle to feed our children. The men would exclude us, as you know. They've tried to pass rules forbidding us to weave, but we pay them no mind. They are a stupid and short-sighted bunch, present company excepted, of course, Mr. Sharp."

Mr. Sharp nodded, his expression never changing. Charlotte was amazed at what a phlegmatic person he appeared to be. In business he had a keen mind and was very helpful to her, still, his stony countenance left something to be desired.

"My husband worked with many beautiful patterns, Mrs. Pruitt, and I know how to create all of them. His broadcloth, as well as his ribbons, were admired by all who knew him. I've been working with a pattern maker in Diggon Street, to expand our selection. She has some exquisite flowers and birds. I'll show them to you, if you'd like.

Finished with their tea, Jane Rourke invited them to follow her up the stairs to the workshop.

Charlotte glanced out one of the windows and noticed a little garden at the back of the house.

"Mrs. Rourke, whenever do you have time to tend your garden?"

"In the spring and summer, when there's more light, Mrs. Pruitt. The children help me. It's important for them to see flowers and vegetables grow and to have a little colour of the country in our lives. Do you ever miss Coventry, Mrs. Pruitt?"

"Yes, I do, though I miss Cumberland more. You know, my mother's family home is there.

"Aye, my Annie wrote to me about the house and the

village."

Everyone in the workshop was hard at work. The journeymen and the children looked up when the group entered. Charlotte raised her hand in greeting. Mrs. Rourke introduced the journeymen first. After that, she gathered her children around her. Jenny was the nearest in age to Annie and tall like her sister but with a fuller face. She carried Duncan, the littlest, in her arms. He had ginger hair and a face full of freckles. He sucked his thumb and held fast to a small, square piece of blanket. Her other sons were the twins, black-haired Stephen and Luke who looked exactly alike, down to the same smile. And there was Michael, six, who appeared to be quite shy and hid behind Ralph, who was five and smiling broadly. They said their hellos and returned to their work.

Jane showed Charlotte and Mr. Sharp the new patterns that she and Jenny were working on, and they were indeed intricate and beautiful.

"I know many of the aristocrats and wealthy merchants will want these, Mrs. Rourke. Will you work up samples for us? If I might have them in a week, there are several people I would show them to immediately."

"It's as good as done, Mrs. Pruitt," Mrs. Rourke replied.

Charlotte noted the absence of Patrick Rourke. "Your brother-in-law is not in today?"

"I asked him to be present, but he said he had urgent business to tend to this morning and left in great haste just before you arrived. He has always been a man for causes, Mrs. Pruitt. My late husband and he had long arguments about Patrick's politics, but it did no good in curbing his activities. I just pray he will not bring the law on himself.

"As of late, he is most upset about the wage cutting.

19

When troops were lodged at Three Tuns Tavern, he was in a rage. Forgive me, Mrs. Pruitt, but weavers are in a sorry way. This winter when the river froze, two families on this street alone, died of the cold. I try to help who I can, and your generosity is praised throughout Spitalfields, Stephany, and Bethnal Green, but my brother-in-law is not a man to sit idly by when others are suffering."

On the pretence of looking at a pattern, Charlotte took Jane to a quiet corner, away from Mr. Sharp and the others.

"Is he a cutter, Mrs. Rourke?"

"I cannot say, Mrs. Pruitt. Truly, I am sorry, but I have no direct knowledge of him being involved, nor do I want any. I can say that some members of Bold Defiance have had a meal in my home, but as friends, naught else."

"Why does he ally himself with the journeymen, when he is a master weaver?" Charlotte asked.

"He's an Irishman, and as such, he fights for his rights and to aid his brothers."

"Are you and your family put in danger by these activities?"

"I hope not. Bold Defiance do their deeds at night, as you know, and in disguise. So far, we have not been bothered by the law, but Patrick does speak his mind more than I would have him do," Jane said ruefully.

"If I can be of aid, in any way, please, do not hesitate to call on me. I look upon you as my family," Charlotte said in all sincerity.

"Thank you, Mrs. Pruitt. We are ever indebted to you for taking in our Annie after that terrible accident."

"She's a hard-working girl and a great help to me, be assured. We should be going. My orders for broadcloth and ribbon will remain the same, at least until summer. The demand is down, and I have had to cancel orders with some weavers, but that should be of no concern to you."

Charlotte bid everyone in the workshop goodbye, and the group descended the stairs. Mr. Sharp and Charlotte boarded the carriage and waited while Annie kissed her mother.

They were soon back at Bellagio House. Annie went off in search of Jack. Mr. Sharp and Charlotte went over orders. Charlotte asked him to contact people he thought would be interested in Mrs. Rourke's new patterns. When they finished, she requested that he call on her the following morning, so that they could attend to other business matters.

After Mr. Sharp left, Mr. Primm, the butler, presented Charlotte with a small envelope. It had just been delivered, he said. She thanked him, and he left the room. On its front was written "Charlotte" in bold handwriting. She could not imagine who it might be from, but on opening it her stomach turned.

I have returned, Mistress Mawk. Is it possible that James Clarke is truly dead, at last? I beg to know the answer.

Oh, my God, Charlotte thought in horror, Edward Hawkes is back.

Her mind was racing. How had he escaped? Why had Count Cesi not warned her? She had to get word to James. How best to accomplish that, she wondered? Or was that what Hawkes was hoping? She did not want to be the one to lead him to James. She would wait and pray that James would come to her as he had promised. However, if she saw him across from the house, perhaps somehow, she could warn him.

She read the note again. The phrase, "I beg to know," struck her. Was it a coincidence, or did he know of James's disguise? Chills ran through her body. She could not wait. She had to find James.

Charlotte called for Annie. The girl came quickly, and Charlotte told her that she had need of some of her clothes, specifically a dress, shoes, stockings, and a cloak. Charlotte could see that she was bewildered by the request.

"It's a secret, Annie. Do not talk with anyone about this." The girl left and returned quickly with the clothes. Charlotte decided to tell her part of the secret. "Annie," she said, "I have reason to believe Edward Hawkes has returned to London. If that is so, we are in great danger. You must stay inside today and keep a very close watch on Jack." Annie's eyes grew wide. "I need go out in disguise, in case he's watching the house. I won't be more than a few hours. I need your help in this. I don't want anyone to know."

Annie nodded in agreement. "Please, take care, Mistress Charlotte."

"I shall, I promise."

After putting on Annie's clothes, Charlotte looked at herself in the mirror and was pleased with the transformation. She looked the part of a servant, especially when she pulled her hair back and pinned it up. The dress had been one of Charlotte's, but its style was out of fashion. Anyone bothering to notice her would assume she had received it from her mistress. James said he would be across from the house. If she did not find him there, she planned to walk through Spital Square and south towards Rosemary Lane and Rag Fair. If she kept a lively pace and appeared to be out on her master's business, she hoped no one would bother her.

Slipping out of her room and down the back stairs, she encountered no one. Soon, she was out the kitchen door, up the steps, and onto the street. Charlotte crossed first to the place where the watchers kept their vigil. They took no notice of her, and she smiled at her successful deceit. James was nowhere in sight. Please, dear God, do not let Edward Hawkes have found him, she prayed.

Spital Square was filled with people bustling about in the early afternoon. She first passed the victualler's shop then the butcher shop. They were both full of people beginning to think about their dinners. She had seldom been in such close contact with the people in this area. Usually, she travelled in her coach or her chair, avoiding the throngs that were about her now. It was like being at one of the West End routes. She found it difficult to breathe as she was bumped, pushed, and stepped on by those passing her. A lady was afforded some respect and space when she walked, not so a servant. Charlotte stopped from time to time to look in a window and turn to scan the crowd for James.

As she left Spital Square and headed for Rag Fair, the streets became dirtier and more crowded with people of a rougher sort. Charlotte tried not to make eye contact with anyone, but sometimes she could not help but stare at some poor wretch's infirmity. Just as she came onto Rosemary Lane, Charlotte chanced to see Patrick Rourke standing in the street, deep in discussion with a small group of men. A short man with a pendulous goitre and a bulbous nose was exhorting Patrick and the others to be careful in their actions. Charlotte was unable to stop and eavesdrop, though she did slow down her pace when she was close to the group.

"The common man must assert his right to liberty!" Patrick shouted, shaking his finger in the short man's face.

The short man turned on his heel and began walking rapidly away with Patrick following him, still talking. Charlotte shook her head and continued on her search.

Just before she reached Rag Fair, Charlotte thought for an instant that she saw James, but as the crowd closed in around her, she lost sight of him. She moved as quickly as she could in his direction, but she did not see him again. When she came to where she thought he had been, she noticed that the door of a decrepit-looking building was ajar. She glanced around. No one seemed interested in her movements, so she entered the house.

In the half-light that shone down from the holes in the walls and ceiling, she was only able to make out a stairway against the wall and some debris on the floor. Disappointed, she turned to go, but the door slammed shut, blocking her exit. She stood still, her heart racing. Her eyes strained to make out a figure standing in shadow by the door in front of her.

She heard a hissing whisper, "And who be you, Mistress Mary?"

"I'm a servant girl. My name is Annie Rourke," Charlotte said in a terrified whisper.

"Why have you ventured so boldly into our house, I wonder?" came the response.

"I thought I saw a man I knew. I was wrong. Please, let me go."

"What man be that?" the voice said, not moving from its place.

It was a woman's voice, but rasping and low.

"Will Cleveland. A beggar. I met him yesterday at my mistress's house."

There was a long silence. Then the voice came back, low and angry. "So, it was you he went to see."

"What?" Charlotte replied. She was confused and growing angry herself at this creature in the dark. "Who are you?!"

"His lover, you whore," the woman screamed. "I'll cut your throat!"

Suddenly, the woman lunged out of the shadows and jumped on Charlotte. They toppled over. Charlotte clawed and kicked at her tormentor. The woman's long hair had a horrible stench that gagged Charlotte. As her attacker's hands closed on Charlotte's throat, she grabbed the wretch's nose and twisted it as hard as she could. The woman howled and rolled off Charlotte, who got up quickly and made for the outline of the door.

As she flung the door open, the woman grabbed her by the shoulders. They struggled, and Charlotte managed to turn and hit her attacker in the face. The woman staggered back, clearly visible for the first time. She was small in stature and rail thin. Her long, black hair was matted, her clothes ripped and dirty. Her eyes were huge and dark. Their intensity riveted Charlotte. My God, Charlotte thought, she was the one who danced in my dream!

"What do you stare at, mawk?"

Charlotte backed out the door, keeping her eyes on her attacker. "I must see Will Cleveland. I must warn him. He is in danger. Where is he?"

"In my bed." The emaciated woman smiled wickedly. Her teeth were black and brown.

Charlotte wanted to scream but said again, "Please, he is in danger. Where is he?"

"Between my legs," the woman whispered and lifted her skirts suggestively.

"I am done with you." Charlotte turned and ran back towards Bellagio House, not stopping to see if the woman followed her. Her side ached. Where was James? Who was that woman? Charlotte felt as if she had fallen into hell and could not find her way out. She ran down the streets, tears stinging her cheeks in the cold wind. Just as her house came into view, she was grabbed and pulled into a stairwell. Charlotte struggled to break free.

In her panic, she heard a voice saying urgently, "Charlotte stop. It's me."

James! She threw her arms around him and would not let go. Words flew from her mouth, but nothing she said made any sense. Finally, she stopped and looked at him, terror in her eyes.

"Lottie," he asked soothingly, "what has happened? Why are you dressed like this? I only knew it was you when I saw your auburn locks flying as you ran."

"Jem, Edward Hawkes is back in London." She told him about the letter and her fear for his safety.

"So, he escaped. I'm not surprised. If fortune is with me, perhaps he will think me dead, and I can use surprise to catch him. Why were you running? Did you see Hawkes?"

"No, no, I thought I saw you go into an abandoned building on Rosemary Lane, but when I went in, I was attacked by the most awful, wild woman. I've seen her in a dream. I know I have. She knew you, Jemmy. She said Will Cleveland was her lover. Who is she? What is she talking

26

about?"

He held Charlotte tight and pressed her head to his chest. He did not answer immediately. His silence frightened her. She pushed away from him, so she could see his face.

"Jemmy, is that woman your lover?"

He took a deep breath and began, "When I was on the road to London two weeks ago, I had a night when I was in terrible pain, Charlotte. It was pouring down rain. I could not sleep, and I could find no relief. I lay there in the mud and the cold surrounded by all sorts of tinkers and beggars who took no interest in my suffering. I remember sitting up, rocking, and moaning. This woman sat down next to me and put a jug in my hand.

" 'Drink this,' " she ordered, and I did. The drink burned like fire, but it eased the pain.

" 'Poitín,' she said. We sat there in the mud and drank it all. I was on fire. I took her there, Charlotte. Never in my life have I done such a thing. I tried in the morning to pretend nothing had taken place, but she would have none of it. She is my shadow, and my shame."

Charlotte felt sick to her stomach. "James, I must go in. Take care. I'm very cold. I must go and wash. Please, excuse me." She stumbled away from him. He tried to hold on to her, but she pulled away. "I cannot talk to you now. I cannot!"

"Charlotte…"

"I cannot!" She looked into his dirty, tired face. She felt herself again in some hellish nightmare. James was back but utterly transformed.

"Be careful of Hawkes," she managed to whisper. She walked like a drunkard across the street, unable to control her body. A chasm of darkness yawned before her, and she looked into it, longing to fall into oblivion. She reached the servant's door and entered. She didn't care if anyone saw her. She made her way to her bedchamber and sat on the floor by the windows. All she could do was to stare into space.

There was a knock on her door. Mr. Primm spoke to Charlotte without opening the door, asking if she was quite well, and if there was anything she required. She attempted to hide her upset from him, telling him that she was just very tired and would not be coming down to dinner or supper. He wished her a pleasant sleep, and she heard his steps retreating down the stairs.

Her tears could not be held back now as she realized that James was lost to her. More, somehow, than when she thought he was dead. At least then, he still belonged to her. Now there was another woman who claimed him. A creature utterly foreign to Charlotte's experience.

Her skin began to crawl. She scratched at her arms until they bled. She must wash herself. She could feel the woman's greasy hair in her face and her dirty hands on her body. Charlotte imagined James inside the woman and then inside her. She would never be able to wash the filth out of her insides. She was defiled.

Charlotte could not move. Her body was too heavy. She felt as if she had drowned and was filled with water. She found herself in a dark, unknown, barren land. Falling asleep, under the window where the night before she and James had been joyfully reunited, her dreams began with a dark storm.

Far off in the black was a pinpoint of light. With heavy steps, she fought her way towards it. The wind blew in her face, mist clouded her eyes, but still she walked on. The light grew bigger, and she saw that it was a bonfire. Human figures were outlined in its blaze.

One, in the midst of the others, gyrated in a wild, abandoned dance. Stunned, Charlotte watched her. Her long, black hair flying in the wind as if her head was surrounded by crows and ravens. She followed the beat of drums and the keen of wailing pipes, sometimes slow, sometimes in double-time. Sweat glistened on her body, her clothes clung to her frame.

Only then did Charlotte become aware that the ring of people surrounding her was made up only of men. They stood transfixed and there, in the midst of them all, was James. Charlotte watched his lips part and his breath quicken. She tried to look away, but she could not. James rushed into the centre, grabbed the dancer, and threw her to the ground.

Charlotte screamed. She awoke, shaking and overwhelmed with sadness. It was very dark. No one had come to look for her. Her body ached from the cold and damp. She remembered the beating she had taken and wondered if she could move at all.

There was a sound at the window. Charlotte froze in the darkness. After a few moments, it came again. Small stones were hitting the window. It must be James. She was sure of it. He would go away. She did not want to see him. Hot tears came to her eyes and a pain burned around her heart. The bastard! I will kill him myself. She heard him outside the window. He had climbed the vines. I will kill him. Push him off. The son of a bitch! She jumped up and threw open the window. James was so startled that he let go, but he grabbed the vines with one hand preventing a fall to the ground. Charlotte leaned out the window and began to push at him.

"Charlotte, please, let me speak with you. Please!' he pleaded.

Had there been any light, Charlotte knew they would have made a comical show. Her beating at him wildly, and he clinging to the vines trying to fend off her blows. Finally, with one hit, she stunned him. He caught her arm just as he began to fall.

"Let go of me you bastard. You whoremonger!"

"I will come in!" he said as he gripped her arm.

"You will not!" She bit him.

He howled and let go. She slammed the window. There was silence for several minutes. She waited for someone in the house to come check on the noise, but no one did. An Irish whistle began to play softly. She tried to stop her ears, but its music transported her back to the island villa at Bellagio. She could not stand it. He would give himself away and wake up the household. He continued to play despite the danger.

She loved him still, though she hated him, too. Opening the window, she sat back on the floor. The music stopped, but it was a few minutes before he peeked his head in the room.

"May I enter, Charlotte?"

"Only briefly." He did not attempt to reach out to her after he climbed into the room. She did not light a candle. They sat in darkness and silence.

"Charlotte, I committed a terrible act, and I understand that you hate me. I do not hope that you will love me as you did, but I cannot simply slink away like a whipped dog."

"You've told me what you did. What more is there to

say?"

"I did not tell you the truth."

"You're saying you lied? Did you not fornicate with that creature?"

"Yes, but not as I told it. It did not begin that way."

"What! Did you woo her first?"

"She saved my life."

"I thought your hedgerow man did that."

"There was a Mr. Bunbury, but not quite as I described."

"It was pretence? All of it? That long letter was a lie? Did you go into Wookey Hole, or was that a lie, as well?"

"No, I went there."

"And then? No floods? No torrents? My God, James, what am I to believe?"

"Charlotte, I hid in the cave as I wrote. After what must have been two or three days, I was half frozen. I dreamt that I saw someone close by me. When I awoke, I was alone and determined to go out and surrender, but then I saw a fire."

"A fire? A fire in the cave?"

"Exactly. I thought I was losing my mind, but I crawled towards it, and she was there."

"Dancing?" Charlotte asked.

"No, she was praying."

"Praying! More like incanting, I should imagine."

"There was something holy about her, Charlotte."

"James, please! The woman who attacked me and lifted her skirts in such an obscene manner is hardly a saint. She is mad as a hatter, and I fear you are, as well."

"I was so cold, Charlotte. She gave me a warm drink and wrapped me in a woollen blanket. She fed me fish and bread. I fell asleep. When I awoke, my head was cradled in her lap. She was singing, and I couldn't move. I don't know if it was the drink or my fatigue, but I lay there feeling happy to be comforted."

Charlotte didn't say anything. She was burning with anger and jealousy. The picture of this woman and the cave was so palpable, she could have reached out and touched it. Taking a long, deep breath, Charlotte shut her eyes. She was determined not to cry.

"I cannot hope to make you understand the strangeness of the experience," James continued. "Perhaps I was mad again. I drank her potions every time she offered them until I had no desire to leave. She led me through the caverns deep in the earth. Time ceased to exist. She did not speak. Instead, she took my hands and urged me to touch the smooth stone formations, to run my fingers over their cool surfaces.

"After I was there for some time, she came, offering herself to me. I refused. She persisted, and finally one night, I awoke to find her astride me. I was bewitched and began to lust after her. She would come to me naked, and when I moved towards her, she would run. I gave chase, and when I caught her, I would throw her to the ground…"

"I've seen you," Charlotte whispered.

"What?!"

"In my dreams, earlier tonight. Perhaps she has bewitched me, too, but in a horrible way. I see her seductions, and I cannot reach you."

"But I'm here now, Charlotte."

"Perhaps, but she is with you, too. Are you still under her power?"

"No. There was a flood, as I described in my letter. We

were separated. I tried to find her and could not. I was swept into the torrent in the cave as the water rose. I thought I would die. In that cold, dark water, I came to my senses. My only thought was to be with you and Jack. The river carried me out of the darkness and the hedgerow cutter, Mr. Bunbury helped me. I started for London as soon as I could."

"When did you see her again?"

"Outside London, in the brickfields. She was quite mad. Out of nowhere in the pouring rain, she suddenly jumped on my back and knocked me down into the mud. She tore at my clothes. I pushed her away, but she came at me again. I tried to reason with her, but she was as you saw her at Rag Fair. She follows me, Charlotte. There is nowhere to hide. For all I know, she may be in the garden now. I am at a loss to know what to do. She brings me presents, like a barn cat, dead things that she lays at my feet. Charlotte, I have betrayed you, bewitched or not. I love you, but I know of no penance great enough to earn your forgiveness.

"Why did you invent all the lies? I don't understand, James."

"I'm ashamed of my actions. When I wrote the letter, I hoped you would never know the truth. Then, when you met her, I was desperate. Somehow, being drunk seemed more believable than what had happened. After you ran from me, I agonized over what I should do. Ultimately, I knew I needed to tell you the truth."

"Please, go. I need to sleep," was all she could think to say. When she heard him stand, she wanted to reach out to him, but she could not move. "Come again tomorrow," she said softly. She could not see his face because of the darkness.

"Goodnight, Charlotte," he whispered and climbed out the window. After listening to his retreat, she managed to close the window. Crawling into bed, she slept without dreaming for the rest of the night.

Chapter Three

In the morning, she awoke and wanted to bathe immediately. Betsy, her maid, organized the servants to bring in the water and the tub, so Charlotte could soak her aching body. After her bath, she went in search of Annie and Jack in the nursery. The toddler ran to his mother, and she gathered him up into her arms. He nestled his head into her neck and shoulder, and she felt his warm breath on her skin. He pulled his head away and looked at her. He grinned and threw himself backwards, nearly falling out of Charlotte's arms. She pulled him up and hugged him. She loved him so dearly. As she held him tightly, she prayed that God would grant him a long and healthy life.

Watching Jack play, she decided they would go to Rosthwaite for the summer. James could have what money he needed for his search for Edward Hawkes, but she wanted to be well out of it. Anger overtook her happy mood when she remembered the stories from the night before.

Perhaps, she thought angrily, Jack and I will leave secretly. James and his rag-picking whore may both be damned. Jack kissed her gently on the cheek. She looked at him and saw James's grey eyes.

"Go play with Annie, dear one," she whispered.

Fatigue overtook her again. She slept for the rest of the day, only waking for supper. Charlotte had little appetite, but she managed to eat some soup. After supper, she read to Jack and Annie took him off to bed. James did not come to her window that night.

The next morning, she sent a message to Jane Rourke asking if the pattern they had spoken about was ready to be shown to customers. Mrs. Rourke replied that it was, and that she would deliver it herself before dinner that afternoon. A bit later, Mr. Sharp arrived with news from Pruitt and Byrd Ltd. The silk shipment that embarked on the ship, Providence, that morning to Venice was the largest order yet. It included several thousand pounds of camlet, satins, and bombazine.

He also brought word of more cuttings. Pruitt and Byrd weavers were spared but Lawrence Grout's workshop was attacked, and nine looms were cut. The rumour was that Grout had cut wages as of late and also refused to pay Bold Defiance their so-called "commissions" on his looms. Grout was enraged, as were many other master weavers, Sharp told Charlotte. Constables and their deputies were dispatched that morning to hunt for the perpetrators. Trials and hangings, he said, were sure to follow.

Charlotte asked Mr. Sharp to stay for dinner, and as they sat down to eat, she received a tersely worded note from Jane Rourke, along with a package containing the promised material and pattern card.

Dear Mrs. Pruitt,

I have been detained due to urgent family business. Forgive me.

Your humble servant,
Jane Rourke

After reading the note, Charlotte showed Mr. Sharp the sample. They were both impressed with the intricacy of the pattern and the beauty of the finished fabric. Jane had woven a bombazine that was perfect for summer apparel, as well as for the clothes of clients in warmer Mediterranean areas.

"With your permission, I will make calls on all our best London clients, Mrs. Pruitt. I would suggest that we have the pattern cards done and sent abroad also."

"I agree, Mr. Sharp. Please, let me see the London list before you make contacts. There may be some people I should meet with personally."

"Very good, Mrs. Pruitt." They discussed a few other matters while finishing their oxtail soup. The meal over, Mr. Sharp excused himself and was off.

Charlotte then turned her attention to Mrs. Rourke. Calling Annie and Jack to her, Charlotte asked her if she had had any news from her mother in the last hour. She said she hadn't, so Charlotte sent her off to see what urgent family business had kept Jane from coming to Bellagio House.

Taking Jack to the nursery, Charlotte dressed him to go outside. The day was sunny, but a strong breeze sent clouds scudding across the sky. They went into the garden, so he could run and climb. After they played for a bit, Charlotte sat on one of the stone benches, watching Jack chasing after clouds. He would run, looking up to the sky then fall giggling onto the ground. Finally, he jumped up, spreading his arms wide and began to spin. As Charlotte reached down to pick up a brown, crumpled leaf, her eye caught movement behind a holly bush in the corner of the garden. Quickly, she rose, moved to Jack, and grabbed hold of him.

She did not stop to look behind but lifted Jack into her arms and ran into the house. Once inside, she called for Mr. Primm, the butler, and asked him to investigate who, or what, was in the garden. She watched as he walked towards the holly bush. There was no movement to indicate anything was there. However, as he got close enough to peer behind it, a figure jumped up, knocking him to the ground.

It was her! James's lover. Her wild, black hair covering half her face, she stopped just long enough to make eye contact with Charlotte. She bolted for the garden gate and was gone. Poor Mr. Primm did not have a clue as to what or whom had sent him sprawling on the ground. Holding Jack tightly, Charlotte went out to see if he was injured.

"I'm sorry, madam, it appears whoever it was got away."

"Please, Mr. Primm, it does not matter. Are you hurt?"

"No, Mrs. Pruitt. Do you have any idea who it was?"

"I believe a beggar or a rag picker. I've seen her before. She appears to be quite mad. I think we should employ some men to guard the house again. It's a dangerous time in London."

"It is, indeed, madam."

How, Charlotte wondered, would she set up guards to watch for this woman and Edward Hawkes, but leave the way open for James to come and go? She didn't have time to answer that question, however, for Annie came running into the parlour, out of breath. She managed to tell Charlotte that her mother and uncle had been arrested.

Trying to calm Annie, Charlotte sat her down on a chair and rang for some tea. She was sure half the staff of the house was just outside the door listening.

After a few minutes and many tears, Annie told her that Patrick Rourke had been taken off to the justice of the peace around midmorning. He was suspected of being the head of Bold Defiance and leader of the cutters. Jane Rourke, in desperation, followed after him trying to plead his innocence. She was pushed and beaten by the constables and left on the street. Several of the weavers' wives came to her aid, bringing her home and tending to her wounds. However, not an hour later, the constables were back, and this time, they arrested Jane.

"On what charge, Annie?"

"She is accused of harbouring criminals in her home and of stealing silver goblets from Lord Clanbrassil's house. The constables searched the house and found the goblets in the cupboard. But it's all lies! My mother has never done a wrongful deed. Never, Mrs. Pruitt. What will we do?" She began to cry, again.

Charlotte could not think clearly enough to put her thoughts in order.

"Annie, drink your tea. We must go and see your mother. These are false charges, and we will prove them so. No more tears, please." Annie tried to regain her composure. "What about your brothers and Jenny? Will they manage alone?"

"We have friends, mum. They will be cared for tonight, anyway."

"I am sure they will, but I would feel better if they were with you. Take some of the kitchen girls and go to your mother's house. Bring your family here. We will find rooms for them. I'll go and see your mother."

Charlotte called for Mr. Primm and explained the situation. He promised to organize the extra food that would be needed and the sleeping arrangements in the house. She then sent a messenger to Mr. Sharp to tell him what had transpired. Jack went with Betsy, the lady's maid, to play in the nursery. Charlotte's chair was called for, and she went to her room to ready herself for the ride to Newgate. She dreaded going there, but she could see no way around it.

When she opened the door to her bedchamber, she was hit with a cold blast of air. Someone had left the window open. Irritated, she went to close it. She crossed to the wardrobe to get her wool cape and her gloves. As she put them on, some instinct warned her that she was not alone. Charlotte turned slowly around and there blocking the exit was the emaciated witch. Her ragged, filthy appearance made Charlotte shudder. Not moving, Charlotte waited to see what the woman would do.

"Where is Will?" the witch asked in a soft, pleading voice.

"Who?"

"Will Cleveland. I want him. He's mine. What have you done with him?"

Charlotte could not take her eyes off the witch's dirty face. She looked like a sullen dog, her head cast forward and down, her lips pursed and pouting.

"You leave my house at once! I don't know any Will Cleveland. If you're caught here, they will hang you. Now get out, whoever you are!"

The woman shut the door and began to move towards Charlotte. "Hanging would be a pleasure. I live on your scraps. A little piece of silk's my cabbage..." Charlotte would have sworn that the woman's shape was changing. She was growing bigger and more menacing with each step. "Why, your dress alone would let me live like quality for two years. Should I cut your throat for it, I wonder? I bloody well knew you was no servant girl. What was my Will to you? That's what I wanted to know. But seeing that pretty little boy in the garden, I got my answer. So now I want to know who's Peg's Will? Oh, I rode him, I did. No pretty babies yet, but I'll ride him again. I'll spread my legs and make him beg to tell me all the answers. I'll let you watch Peg and Will. Would you like that, in all your silks, eh?"

She now stood very close to Charlotte, who recoiled from the smell of her rancid breath. Suddenly, a blind rage exploded in Charlotte and her fist smashed into the witch's jaw. The woman staggered, her eyes wide. Rushing forward, Charlotte pushed her over and jumped on top of her, pummelling her. The witch's nose bled. Charlotte slammed her head against the floor.

"If you ever come near my house again," Charlotte hissed, holding her there, "I will kill you. Do you understand?"

The woman managed to nod her head.

"I have no desire to see you hang," Charlotte continued, "so I will let you leave, but believe me when I say that this will be the only act of mercy you will ever receive from me."

Charlotte stood up, not taking her eyes off the witch, who was now small and pathetic to look at.

However, Charlotte did not trust this appearance. She allowed the woman to rise and shuffle quickly to the window, where she disappeared outside without a backward glance. Charlotte sat down, shaking. Never in her life had she felt such rage or been so violent. She could have killed the woman. Charlotte thanked God she had not. She realized her hand was throbbing, but she did not care, for deep inside a cry of victory was building. She gave out a squeal of joy and pumped her fist into the air.

It was not until she was in her sedan chair and on her way to Newgate that she began to think about what the witch had said. James was gone. To where, Charlotte wondered? Another hiding place, perhaps. Fear began to creep over her. Had he encountered Hawkes, or was he just trying to avoid Peg?

As her chair passed the slaughterhouses, the smell of death hung heavy in the cold moist air. She covered her mouth with her handkerchief.

Your dress alone would let me live like quality for two years. She heard the woman's voice in her head. Charlotte felt the smooth coolness of the handkerchief at her lips. I am not responsible for her troubles or anyone else's, she thought. That is her lot, this is mine.

As the men carried Charlotte's chair down the lane by the prison, St. Sepulchre's bells began to peel. Shivers ran down Charlotte's back as she remembered when James had been imprisoned in Newgate. What must Jane Rourke be suffering, Charlotte thought? She was bringing with her some items that might bring comfort. Annie packed a woollen coat and blanket, and some food all tied in a bundle. Charlotte hoped the guards would let her give these to Jane.

She needn't have worried, as before when she visited James, she found that enough money offered would allow her to do almost anything she wished. As a gaoler walked her down the long dark passages, screams echoed off the damp stones, arms extended from the cells reaching out to touch her. The stench was worse than the slaughterhouses.

All these lost souls, existing in fetid holes. Why hang anyone, Charlotte thought? This prison was truly hell.

At last, the gaoler pressed his key into a rusted lock. With a clang, the heavy door came open. There was only a little light filtering in from a small window high in the wall. The whole scene appeared as if it were underwater. Bodies huddled together for warmth. Dirty straw covered the floor.

Charlotte found the courage to speak and asked, "Jane Rourke, are you here?"

"Mrs. Pruitt?" a small, frightened voice responded.

"Yes, Mrs. Rourke," Charlotte called back, peering into the shadowed recesses. A hunched figure stumbled forward, holding on to her left side. Charlotte was taken aback by her battered face and torn clothing, and the manacles on her wrists. Jane stopped, seeing Charlotte's horrified expression.

"Dear God, Jane. What have they done to you?"

"The constables did not like me asking questions." She tried to straighten up with difficulty.

Charlotte remembered that she was holding Annie's bundle. "Here, please take this. Annie thought it might help."

Jane stepped towards Charlotte. She winced in pain as she reached for the bundle. There was no place to sit except the floor, but it was covered in all manner of insects. So, they stood, surrounded by staring eyes from the crowd. Curses, mumbling, and the clanking of chains began around them. Jane hugged her new belongings tightly.

"Of what do you stand accused?" Charlotte asked.

"They say I kept a house for the Bold Defiance, that Patrick was the Dublin-London leader, and that I aided him. Which I did not! But worse than that, they say I stole six silver goblets from Lord Clanbrassil's house. It is a lie. I went to his lordship's house, to deliver the silk we had woven for a new pair of breeches and a waistcoat. I was paid and went home. That was all! I am a God-fearing woman and have never done anything to be ashamed of!" She spoke this last loudly for the benefit of all to hear. The other voices were silenced momentarily. She continued more quietly, "The constables came to my house and searched everywhere, tearing up everything as they went. They came to me with the goblets saying they had found them in my cupboard."

"What of your brother-in-law?" Charlotte asked.

"I cannot account for his actions," Mrs. Pruitt.

"Jane, please, will you address me as Charlotte?"

"That would be unfitting my station, but I thank you for requesting it." She stood as proudly as she could, given her physical discomfort.

"On my direction, Annie is bringing your children to Bellagio House," Charlotte told her. "We will watch over them. You need have no worry about their safety and care."

Jane's eyes filled with tears at the mention of her family. "God protect them. They will be orphans in the streets."

"I will take care of them, whatever happens. They need never live in the streets. I promise you that. Please, do not despair. You are innocent. If justice is served, you will be freed."

"Mrs. Pruitt, I am a weaver, not an aristocrat. There is

no justice for the likes of me. You see the carts that roll to Tyburn and who sits in them."

Charlotte became aware of someone humming. As the tune grew louder, she realized it was *Charlotte Bird,* the song that assailed her in in the streets all though James's arrest and confinement in Newgate. She continued her conversation with Jane Rourke while attempting to spot the singer in the crowded cell.

"I know something of the system," Charlotte assured Jane. "I will see who may be moved by your plight."

"Thank you, Mrs. Pruitt. I have no way to repay your kindness and friendship."

"I consider you and your children part of my family. It is my duty and my desire to help. We are women in a world that does not favour women."

The voice in the shadows sang the words to the refrain, "Charlotte, Charlotte, pretty dove. On the tree you sit, so pale. Will they hang your falcon love? Charlotte, sing us your sad tale."

Charlotte located the singer. She was a thin, sallow-faced woman with a piercing gaze. Now she made her way through the crowd and stopped just behind Jane. A wicked smile grew on her face.

"Oh my, listen, ladies. Outta the goodness of 'er 'eart 'er ladyship's goin' to 'elp 'er friend."

Charlotte bristled at the woman's tone but held her tongue for Jane's sake as the woman continued her harangue. "Well, w'at about the rest of us, then? W'at are you goin' to do for us, eh? Do you know w'o we 'ave in our midst, ladies? It's Mr. Audley Pruitt's wife. She's a mawk, just like the rest of us, ain't you, dearie? O' but cover a tart in silk and she's a lady. 'Ow's your 'usband's 'ead? Do you keep it in a hat box, eh?"

Looking at the woman, Charlotte replied calmly. "I was not addressing you. You are not included in this discussion."

The woman arched an eyebrow and responded grandly, "O', I am sorry, now ain't I? Well, you 'appen to be in my parlour, dearie. So, it is my business, ya see."

Jane stood frozen during this interchange. Charlotte addressed her, attempting to ignore the woman behind her.

"I will be going now, but I shall see you tomorrow if I'm permitted."

"Thank you, Mrs. Pruitt."

The sallow woman peered over Jane's shoulder at Charlotte. "O', I will do my best to take care o' yer friend. 'Cause any friend of the dove's is a friend a' mine. Now ain't that right, ladies?" The crowd laughed and jeered.

Charlotte called for the gaoler, and he unlocked the door. As she glimpsed back, Jane stood illuminated in the single beam of light that shone from the little window in the wall. Charlotte's antagonist did not falter in her gaze over Jane's shoulder. Everyone else appeared as dark masses in the shadows.

Charlotte walked as fast as she could out of Newgate. The cold, wet wind hit her in the face as she stepped into the street. Riding back through the slaughterhouse row, she did not even notice the stench. Her thoughts were focused on her plan to help Jane. Charlotte would send word to Mr. Wooten, the lawyer who had helped with James's case, as soon as she returned home. He must see what jurors would be sympathetic to their side. She needed to find out who informed on Patrick Rourke and who was behind Jane's arrest. Who was it that convinced the constables to plant the evidence that incriminated Jane?

Certainly, many of the master weavers and merchants, as well, wanted the Bold Defiance brought to their knees. Charlotte had no love for their strong-arm tactics, but she understood their desire for power in the struggle against their masters. Jane's arrest for the theft of the silver goblets made no sense, though. Was it the Clanbrassils who planned this or someone else?

Charlotte's thoughts turned to James. She hoped that he might have some clue to Edward Hawkes's whereabouts. Please, dear God, be with him and protect him, she prayed. Searching the bustling streets, she saw no sign of him.

Arriving back at Bellagio House, Charlotte found Annie and Jenny, her sister, watching over all the children, including Jack. They were playing in the garden, despite the cold and damp. Jack was having a wonderful time trying to catch the older boys. Charlotte reckoned it was good for him to have playmates. Maybe someday, he will have brothers and sisters, she thought.

One of the maids brought Charlotte a letter, saying it had just been delivered by a ragged street boy rather than someone's footman. She absent-mindedly put it in her pocket as she watched the children play.

It was now nearly dinnertime, so she asked Mr. Primm to have the kitchen staff prepare a meal for all the children to be eaten in the kitchen. Charlotte told him she would have her meal in the parlour. She wanted time to collect her thoughts.

She wrote a note to be delivered immediately to Mr. Wooten. She asked if he might come around that evening, so they could begin their work on Jane's case. After the note was sent, she took a moment to look out on the street. Since the Lighting Act had taken effect, her street was well lit at night.

The watchers were nowhere to be found, which would make it easier for James to come and go, but where was he? Please come, Jem. I need to speak with you. I need to see you, Charlotte whispered.

Her hand touched something in her pocket. She realized it was the letter the servant had given her. The roughness of the paper's texture gave her a start. Not Edward Hawkes! Not now, she thought. It was too much to bear. She read the note.

Dear Mrs. Pruitt, or dare I call you Charlotte,

I find myself once again drawn to England. Is it to see you again and revive what we once had? Or is it to express my surprise that dear Jem did not appear in the sheriff's picture frame, as I most heartily hoped he would. It was an end to which I put forth so much effort.

Unfortunately for you, dear lady, Count Cesi's gaolers were no match for me, nor was his messenger.

What a place is London! You can get lost in its crawling mobs. Truly you could. So many lanes, so many alleys to inhabit.

I ask again. Is James truly dead? A pity, if it is so. I had more plans for him.

Watch after little Juck. He's grown so much in just a year. Your maid servant has a wandering eye and finds me appealing, I believe.

I bid you goodnight.

Your humble servant and admirer,
EH

What could she do? Where could she hide? Leaving the city was out of the question. The Rourkes' were not to be abandoned, but Charlotte felt exposed to this madman's whims. She called for Mr. Primm and asked him about the guards they discussed hiring. He reported that they had been employed and were eating in the kitchen at that moment. They were three strong, young men who came with the highest recommendations.

"I would speak with them when they are finished with their meal, Mr. Primm. Thank you." Mr. Primm nodded and left the parlour.

He soon returned with the men. They looked strong enough to ward off Hawkes's attack, but what would they do to James? She gave them instructions to patrol the halls downstairs and up. They were to check with her at midnight and at three in the morning. After saying that, she hit upon an idea.

"There is sometimes a lame beggar who sleeps in my garden. He is of no consequence, so allow him this refuge. I would speak with him tonight. He may have information from the streets that would be useful to me. Approach him gently and tell him that Mrs. Pruitt wants a word with him. It does not matter the time of night."

The three seemed puzzled by Charlotte's request, but they nodded that they understood.

With that taken care of, she spoke with Annie about where the children would sleep. Charlotte thought it best if they took over the nursery. Hopefully, there would be safety in numbers. Charlotte wanted Jack to be well watched. She had not yet decided how to question Annie on Hawkes's accusation of her wandering eye. It made her skin crawl to think he had been watching Annie and Jack.

A little later in the evening, Charlotte received a note from Mr. Wooten. He sent his apologies, writing that he was indisposed and could not meet with her that evening. He assured her he would be better in the morning and would come around at ten o'clock, so they could begin work.

Charlotte went to bed, a prayer on her lips for the protection of the children under her roof, and for James, wherever he was. She slept peacefully until awakened by knocking on her door. Groggily, she rose and opened the bedchamber door. The three young men were there.

"All is well, Mrs. Pruitt. It is midnight." She thanked them and returned to bed.

Falling into a deep sleep, she found herself walking amongst party goers. Everyone was dressed in fine yellow and orange dresses, wearing coats of bombazine. People stood in groups of twos and fours. It appeared that the music had just ended, and they were waiting for the next dance. The crowd parted and not far from where Charlotte was, James stood with his back to her.

Shyness overtook her, as it had at the ball where they first met. Determined, however, to meet him, she plucked up her courage and tapped him on the shoulder. When he turned to her, she saw that his face was terribly disfigured. It appeared to be melting from his forehead down and forming again all around his chin. He looked at her inquiringly. She back away from him, unable to speak.

At that point, she awoke, blinking her eyes rapidly and taking big gulps of air. The room was cold, and she had kicked off the bed coverings. She gathered them up around her and sat, trying to wake up fully. The shock of seeing his face so malformed would not leave her. She got out of bed, put on her dressing gown and crossed to her writing desk. Lighting a candle, she watched the flame burn. She decided to see what correspondence she might need to answer.

She found in the bottom right hand drawer the papers that Sir Rufus wrote just before he died. He had pressed them into James's hands that night, telling him to read them. She had carried the papers with her the day she fled from Scorhill Hall, two days before James disappeared. Sometime soon, I must sort through these, Charlotte told herself, but not tonight. She put them back in the drawer and closed it.

There was a knock at her bedchamber door. Opening it slightly, she discovered the three young men.

"It's three o'clock and all is well, Mrs. Pruitt."

She thanked them for their diligence. Returning to bed, she decided to ask them to wake her only if they had news of importance to tell her. She fell asleep and did not wake until the sun was well up in the sky.

Mr. Wooten called on Charlotte as promised. He was feeling much better. Charlotte asked him to investigate who might have paid the constables to plant and find the goblets in Jane's house. He said he would begin by trying to speak to the constables themselves and their deputies.

"Please, see also if there are any jurors who might be sympathetic to Mrs. Rourke's situation.

He promised he would send her word the moment he uncovered any pertinent information.

The children all slept well and were out playing in the garden. Mr. Primm reported that the young men patrolling the night before had neither seen nor heard anything unusual. Charlotte asked Mr. Primm to have the kitchen staff prepare a basket for her to take to Mrs. Rourke and to have her sedan chair sent around.

Her journey to Newgate was uneventful, and after paying the gaolers at the door to gain entrance to the prison, she was soon speaking with Jane. The sallow-faced woman was ill, so she did not bother them. Charlotte told Jane of her meeting with Mr. Wooten.

"Mrs. Rourke, is there anyone that you can think of who would want to do you harm?"

"No one, Mrs. Pruitt. I pondered on who I might have wronged. There are a few, no doubt, but none that have the cunning or power to pay off the constables and the justice of the peace."

The next few days, Charlotte sent either Mr. Primm or Annie to Newgate with notes of encouragement and small amounts of provisions for Jane. They reported back to Charlotte on these visits. Mr. Wooten was, unfortunately, unable to secure a better cell, but he had found two jurors sympathetic to Mrs. Rourke's side. Overall, however, most jurors and all the magistrates showed no compassion when members of the Bold Defiance were involved.

Mr. Sharp, of Pruitt and Byrd Ltd., let Charlotte know that several of their customers were eager to buy material with the new patterns. He contacted Mr. Quail to work with Anna-Marie Garthwaite, the designer, to begin production. Charlotte requested that Mr. Quail use Mrs. Rourke's journeymen, as well as his own, to do the work. The demand would justify this, and it was Charlotte's desire to keep Jane's helpers employed until she could secure her friend's release.

Charlotte's life took on a frantic pace with the additional children, the business, and the Rourke case. She found herself, when she had a quiet moment, looking out of the windows hoping to see James. She prayed he was not lying dead in a poor hole in some London graveyard. A week had gone by since she had seen him.

That evening, she received news from Emma that she and John had just returned to London. She breathed a sigh of relief that these trusted friends were home and nearby. Their note asked if they might call the following day. Charlotte sent back an enthusiastic yes.

She slept soundly. No strange dreams disturbed her rest. However, as she slumbered, she became aware, far off in the perimeters of her consciousness, of a knocking. Slowly, she realized someone was tapping softly at her bedchamber door. It was still very dark.

"One moment," she called out, then stumbled as she put on her bed gown. She opened the door and found one of the young men she had hired to guard her house standing before her.

"Begging your pardon, Mrs. Pruitt. Forgive me waking you, mum, but the beggar you spoke of is in the kitchen."

Charlotte stared at him blankly, so he repeated, "Mum, you said if he came 'round, you wanted a word with him. He was in the garden. We wrestled him to the ground so's he wouldn't run off. He's a strong 'un, too. He calmed down when we told him you wished to speak to him. Begging your pardon, Mrs. Pruitt, he's a foul smelling, bad-tempered old man. I hope he will keep a civil tongue for you, but I very much doubt it."

By the end of his speech, Charlotte was sufficiently awake to realize James was alive and in her kitchen. Thank you, dear God, she prayed silently, as she walked down the stairs. It was all she could do not to run, but she controlled her impulse.

When she entered the kitchen, she saw James sitting slumped over, his hands folded in his lap while the two young men stood on either side of him. They looked ready to catch him and throw him back in the chair if he dared rise. Charlotte thanked them and requested they return to their posts. She assured them she would call if she needed help. They left reluctantly.

Charlotte sat across from James. When the men were out of earshot, James raised his head. Smiling, he announced, "I have found Edward Hawkes, Charlotte."

"Is that what you've been doing, James, hunting Hawkes? I imagined you dead and in a pauper's grave every time I thought of you."

His smile faded. "Is that where you wish me to be?"

"No! But our parting was so unpleasant, I feared I would not see you again."

"Then, I have hope? You do still care for me?"

"Yes, I do."

"Charlotte, if you will allow me, I would say only one more thing about Peg, for that is her name."

"You may."

"When I saw her in the brickfields, when she knocked me down into the mud, I knew she had gone mad. I could not abandon her. I have been in that place and wandered in that darkness. I become her protector, Charlotte, not her lover, as she would have it."

He looked at Charlotte with pleading in his eyes. His face was covered in grime; his fine hair hung limp and dirty at his shoulders. The patch he wore was off his eye and plastered against his forehead. Was this a masquerade or not? Who, Charlotte wondered, was this man sitting before her?

"Peg came looking for you."

"When?"

"A week ago. She hid in the garden. Nearly killed Primm when he flushed her out of the holly bush. Then, she appeared in my bedchamber. We fought again, but I got the better of her. I've not seen her since. I have a fear that she may appear at any time."

"I'll be watching for her. I was hoping she had gone back to the country," James said.

"There's a doctor by the name of Francis Willis in Lincolnshire who deals kindly with lunatics. He has them farm, rather than locking them away. If I find her, perhaps we could get her into his keeping. I would pay for his help. I do understand your connection to her. I do," Charlotte said.

"Thank you," James said softly, as he looked into her eyes. They sat silently for a moment, then James spoke, "I plan to capture Hawkes. I will get a confession out of him if it is my last act on Earth. I will come back to you with my rightful title and ask you to marry me. Despite my lunacy and my stupidity, my one true and good sentiment is my love for you."

His gaze was earnest and vulnerable. Charlotte felt him looking into her soul and she offered him her heart.

"I love you, James."

"You are my life, Charlotte."

A noise brought them out of their reverie. One of the young men knocked on the door and entered.

"Is all well, Mrs. Pruitt?" he asked, scowling at James,

who returned his angry look.

"All is well. Thank you. I will call if I need you."

"Very good, mum," responded. Turning to James, he muttered, "Remember you're in the presence of a lady, you piece of filth."

"Please, that will be all for now," Charlotte said. When they were alone, Charlotte told James that Emma and John had returned to London. "Perhaps John can be of help. They are visiting tomorrow. What shall I tell them?"

"Have him meet me in your bedchamber. I will hide there after your guards escort me out. If I have your permission to do so."

"Of course, you do. May I get you some clean clothes, though? Your smell is overpowering."

"I will even wash for you, my dearest. Although the fragrance of the streets adds to my disguise, don't you agree?"

"Jem, I need your help. Jane Rourke, Annie's mother, was arrested a week ago. Annie's uncle was taken, as well. He, I believe, is guilty, but Jane is not. I must somehow prove her innocence. Mr. Wooten already attempted to offer money to the jurors but only two are mildly interested in our side. The authorities want to bring Bold Defiance to its knees and terrorize the weavers into accepting wage cuts. They can do both if they hang Patrick and Jane. I need to know who informed on them and why they incriminated Jane."

"When I was at Rag Fair," James began, "The talk of revolt was everywhere. The journeymen in Spitalfields and Bethnal Green are angry. Even the weavers are beginning to complain. They see their children hungry and ill. They have no hope and little to lose, they say. I will make inquiries and see if anyone has knowledge of what's behind the arrests.

"This last week I stayed in a common lodging house on Cowcross Street, inside Jack Ketch's warren. You could not find a place in the whole of London with more thieves and mawks. I was educated in the art of breaking and entering, and met several ladies who fence stolen goods. It's quite a business, and Edward Hawkes is in the middle of it. He's also involved with a certain doctor in Mayfair whose house he has visited during the day and the night. I don't think the doctor is a fence, though stranger things have occurred. He has some characters working for him. One is a big man. I'll wager he was a prize fighter, judging from his nose and eyes. The other is a copper-coloured mulatto."

Charlotte interrupted him, "He sent another letter."

"Hawkes?"

"Yes." Charlotte told James what it contained.

"So, the count did try to warn you. You must write to him and tell him that his messenger is dead. If you hear from Hawkes again, or if there is the slightest indication that he is near, you must be prepared to protect yourself and Jack."

"That's why I have the men here, Jem."

"You should hire at least two more. Speak with Emma about staying with her. The West End area is better protected. You should take the guards with you."

"Jem, I am terrified of Hawkes."

"My dearest, I want us to live long lives, so that at some point in all this chaos, we may have a quiet moment together."

"That is something I pray for daily, I assure you." Charlotte reached out and took his hands which had been resting on the table.

"Let your men escort me out. I will return shortly."

"You can get by them?"

"Yes."

"Then, so can Hawkes," she replied, shuddering. "Jem, tap on my window three times, and I will let you in. I do not feel safe leaving it open."

"I shall do that. Listen for me. I don't want to be caught hanging onto the ivy." He smiled and then grew serious. "You need more guards. Perhaps John will know some reliable, well-trained men."

Charlotte called for the young man who was waiting outside the door. James shuffled out, head bowed. Little did the man know, Charlotte thought, that in this lame beggar he faced a formidable foe. She walked back up the stairs to her bedchamber, made sure the window was latched, took off her bed gown, and crawled into bed. She prayed that James, not Hawkes, would come to her window that night.

CHAPTER FOUR

When she awoke, the sun was streaming in her window. The sky was an azure blue. She smiled and turned on her side, closing her eyes. As she did, her eyes caught something out of place. She opened them quickly. As if in a dream, she saw James, sitting, tucked in between her wardrobe and the corner of the wall. He was transformed. The beggar was gone and in his stead was the man she had first fallen in love with. He had bathed, washed his hair, and shaved his beard. He wore a white linen shirt, open at the collar, tan breeches, white stockings, and brown leather shoes. He gazed at her affectionately.

"You mentioned I needed a bath, so I obliged. It will take a few washings to get rid of the imbedded bugs, but overall, it's an improvement. What do you think, dearest?"

"You are beautiful, but how did you get into the house?"

"Before dawn, I hid by your kitchen door and waited until one of the maids opened it. I learned from the tribes I fought alongside in the Colonies to move very quietly through the forests. Getting up the stairs and through your house was an easier proposition. At least you don't need to hold your nose, eh? Although, perhaps I should have brought you a nosegay, just to be sure."

"Wherever did you get the clothes?"

"Rag Fair is the place for fashion."

"Are you hungry, Jem? Shall I have breakfast brought to the room?" Charlotte asked.

"I am famished. I've already hidden in the wardrobe once today, when the maid peeked in. I think I may have flattened a straw hat or two. Please accept my apologies."

Charlotte rang for the maid. James grinning at her, scrambled under the bed when the maid knocked. Charlotte made sure he was well-hidden, then turned and spoke with her.

"I am famished this morning. Please, let the cook know that I would like a substantially larger portion than usual."

The maid curtsied, and Charlotte closed the door. Peeking over the side of the bed, she found James lying on his back looking up at her.

"I love you, Lottie. I am sorry for all this."

"I am, too. Kiss me, won't you?"

He climbed onto the bed and took her in his arms. They pressed their bodies into each other. Their embrace grew more and more heated, but they had to stop suddenly when the maid knocked on the door, announcing breakfast.

James rolled off the bed, taking the bed cover with him. Charlotte smoothed her clothing and her hair and went to the door. Opening the door only as wide as she needed to take the tray, she thanked the girl and sent her off downstairs. James untangled himself from the blanket. Charlotte stifled a laugh and joined him on the floor. As they ate, they talked quietly about how best to get John and Emma to the bedchamber without arousing the suspicion of the servants.

"I need to go and check on the children," Charlotte said

at last.

"I'll be in there," he said, gesturing towards the wardrobe.

Charlotte dressed. As she got ready to leave, she stopped and looked back at James. His expression was exactly as it had been that first time she saw him in Bristol. She felt sixteen again and hopelessly in love.

"James."

"Yes." He turned to look at her.

"I love you."

He smiled and stood up. "Charlotte, we will see better times." He crossed to her, and they put their arms around each other.

"I wish I could hold on to this moment forever," Charlotte said, gazing into his sea grey eyes.

"I promise, I will deserve your love again," James replied. "In this calm respite, before the next storm, I tell you, you are my life. I will be a proper husband to you and a good father to Jack, God willing."

Charlotte watched his face as he spoke. She would always be fascinated by its beauty, its clean, thin lines, his intense eyes that could flash with anger or melt her heart, and his mouth, thin-lipped if he was angry or breaking into a glorious smile if he was pleased.

He looked at her. "What is it?"

"I could spend a lifetime looking at your face. As angry as I may become with you, when I stop and look at you, I am enchanted." Charlotte put her head on his chest. They held each other, and she thought of one instant of the island villa on Lake Como. She let go. "I'll return as soon as possible." She left without looking back, otherwise she knew she would stay.

Charlotte went first to the nursery. Jack ran to her, catching hold of her skirts. Picking him up, she hugged him. He began to recite all his new friends' names, as he pointed them out to her. Charlotte greeted them all by name as they looked up at her. Annie commanded the boys to stand and properly say good morning, which they did. Charlotte told her and Jenny that Lady Emma and her husband John Fuller would be visiting. They would look in on the nursery. She asked Annie to send a basket to her mother before they did, putting in it whatever she thought would raise her mother's spirits. Charlotte kissed Jack and sent him off to play with his friends.

Once downstairs, Charlotte reviewed with Mr. Primm the plans for the day. She sat by one of the front windows in the drawing room and waited with great anticipation for Emma and John to arrive. When she saw their carriage, she could barely restrain herself from rushing to the door. Mr. Primm entered and announced them. Charlotte moved gracefully and slowly as they came in the drawing room, but when she saw Emma's smile, she rushed into her arms. Charlotte was filled with joy at being reunited. Emma held tight to her friend.

"Oh, Charlotte, I am very sorry for your loss. You have suffered so much," Emma said.

"Emma, my dear friend, I have missed you beyond description."

When the women finally loosened their hold on each other, John extended his hands and took Charlotte's. There were tears in his eyes.

"I loved James as a brother, dear Charlotte. He was a good man and a true friend."

"Thank you, John."

Charlotte was trying to be the best of actresses. She knew she must be for James's sake. If any of the servants were informers for Lord Chagford or Hawkes, she would risk all by disclosing James's presence. She continued her performance and began to swoon. John caught her.

"Charlotte are you ill?" he asked.

"Forgive me," she said righting herself. "When I think of Jem, grief overwhelms me. Please, will you both help me to my room?"

"Of course," John responded.

John supported her, and Emma followed behind as they walked up the stairs. After opening the door to her bedchamber, they help her lie down.

"Please," she whispered weakly, "Close the door and lock it. I do not wish for us to be disturbed."

John did as she requested, and Emma sat on the edge of the bed. Charlotte looked at her and said, "I have a confession to make."

Emma looked at her, "What is it, dearest?"

"We are not alone."

The door to the wardrobe opened and James revealed himself. Both John and Emma stood, staring at him in disbelief.

"May I join you?" James asked, smiling.

"Dear God, you are alive," Emma gasped.

John moved to embrace his friend, then holding James at arm's length, he said, "Bastard! I should have known it would have taken more than Wookey Hole to finish you off."

A flood of questions followed from both Emma and John. James explained as best he could, making only a slight mention of Peg. He finished by telling them the details of

Edward Hawkes's whereabouts in London. Charlotte added her alarm caused by the two letters she'd received. John was eager to help in whatever way James saw fit.

"Come, let me tell you the plan to catch Hawkes as I have conceived it thus far," James said as he retreated to the window with John following him. Charlotte was not pleased at being excluded, but Emma took her hand and commenced telling her all about their tour in Europe.

John and Emma had spent September and October in Paris. Being fluent in French, Emma felt at home and had now returned to London with new ideas from her readings and discussions of Jean Jacques Rousseau's work.

"After Paris, we visited the count in Bellagio," she recounted. "He was the epitome of a gracious host. Oh, and my dear Charlotte, we purchased a villa on the shores of the lake! John thought it too much of an extravagance, but I tell you, Charlotte, I have never wanted anything so much in my life, except perhaps, to be married to John." She smiled coyly and continued. "I cannot tell you the glorious days and nights we spent there. Oh, and at the end of our stay, the count gave a banquet in our honour at his island villa. What an extraordinary setting. Do you remember it, my dear?"

"I most certainly do, Emma."

"Of course, you do." Emma laughed and winked at Charlotte. "Well, the evening was the most splendid I have ever experienced. Even John became quite romantic."

"Did I hear my name?" John asked, turning from his conversation with James.

"Yes, dear husband," Emma replied, blowing him a kiss.

Charlotte was moved to see how happy they were. Yet

a small, insidious voice nastily whispered in her ear at the same time. Look at them! What right have they to this blissful, uncomplicated love? Her own life was miserable. She was obsessed with this man who leaves her constantly in turmoil. Charlotte looked at James, the sun illuminating his golden hair and white silk shirt. He appeared as an angel, and Charlotte bit her lip to hold back tears.

"Charlotte, dear, is something troubling you?" Emma looked at her with concern.

"No, no. Life just seems overwhelming at times. I am so happy for you and John."

"I must tell you what happened after the fête. We travelled with Count Cesi to Venice where we met the countess. Well, of course, John had met her before, but I was introduced. We all became such good friends that we convinced them to travel with us to Paris and from there to London."

"The count and countess are here?"

"Not yet, but soon, I hope. When we first spoke about it in Venice, the count told us that they had a merchant ship scheduled to sail post haste for London. He said it would provide them with a floating home upon the Thames. Unfortunately, they left early from Paris and were not able to attend the opera with us. I'm sure we shall hear from them any day."

Charlotte turned to James, who was deep in conversation with John.

"Did you hear, Jem? The count and countess are expected in London."

"An excellent turn of events," he replied. "I should like Francesco to know that I have escaped the untimely end he predicted for me." James resumed his talk with John.

Charlotte became determined not to be left out of their discussion any longer. "So, what is my part in your plan?"

"To stay safe and well out of it, I would say," James replied.

"Well, I would *not* say that, James. Hawkes has made both our lives a living hell, and I will help in his capture."

"Charlotte," Emma broke in, "don't put yourself in jeopardy. Think of Jack."

"I can take care of myself, Emma, and of Jack." Charlotte faced James and spoke with a whispered intensity. "You must include me, Jem. I insist upon it."

James looked at Charlotte. He raised his chin slightly, his jaw tightening. He appeared to be choosing his words carefully before speaking.

"All right. John and I will teach you how to defend yourself. After that, I shall decide how best to include you. Do you agree?"

"I do."

"Good."

Emma and John looked from James to Charlotte. Attempting to break the tension, Emma said, "James, we must find a way for you to come with us. If you were in disguise at my house, you would have the freedom to come and go. No one should suspect anything out of the ordinary."

James took his eyes from Charlotte as Emma finished. "That's an excellent suggestion. I would welcome the opportunity to crawl out of the stink of Rag Fair for a brief time."

"Your friends there will not miss you?" Charlotte inquired innocently.

"They will survive, I think," he answered curtly.

"A Frenchman might be good." John said, "Someone we met on our journey. Perhaps a Parisian fop. I would enjoy seeing you in that guise, my friend."

"Then you shall have it, *mon ami*," James said, as he bowed low and took on an affected stance.

"Oh, be friend of Rousseau's, a writer or a poet. That would be *merveilleuse*," cried Emma.

"But you must tell me all I will need to know, please. Otherwise, I shall feel a fraud. A beggar I have no trouble with, but portraying an intellectual, I will be found out *très vite*," James laughed.

Charlotte felt herself detach from their merriment. She didn't want to let James out of her sight. She wished to keep him locked in her wardrobe, safe from all the dangers of the city. The three chatted on and Charlotte crossed to the window, to gaze out at the clear February day. She closed her eyes and felt the sun warm her cheek. A moment of calm, James had said.

Will I ever hold him quietly in my arms again, she wondered? A movement below in the garden caught her eye. Leaves out of place and rustling but there was no wind. Charlotte knew who it was. She froze.

"James!" she whispered.

The conversation behind her stopped. "Charlotte?" he asked.

"Peg is in the garden. I'm sure of it." He moved to the window and stood in plain view. Peg emerged slowly from behind the holly bush and stood, staring up at him. Charlotte saw the pain in her expression.

"You will die," Peg mouthed silently, pointing up at him. She bolted out the garden gate.

"Who was that?" John asked.

"Peg is her name," James said.

"You go, both of you," Emma said to the men. "Charlotte, please let me visit with Jack before I go."

Charlotte could not take her eyes from the garden. She wondered what curse Peg had brought upon them all.

"Charlotte!" Emma called to get her friend's attention.

Charlotte blinked her eyes and turned to Emma. "I'm sorry. What did you say?"

"Let the men return to our house. John can introduce James as our guest from France. I want to stay and see Jack. Will you offer me something to eat?"

"Of course, my dear. Give James and me a moment alone. After that, I must call the staff together." Charlotte turned to James and John. "That will give you an opportunity to slip out of the house. Have the coach pull very close to the door. After you're off, Emma and I shall dine."

John said his goodbye to Charlotte. He and Emma went out and down the stairs. Charlotte turned to James. "I love you. Please, be very careful."

"I don't believe in Peg's magic, Charlotte. I will not die because she says it. Not now, not so easily."

"I pray that God agrees." They stood very close. His scent filled her nostrils. She could not look at his face. Instead, her eyes focused on his neck and chest where his shirt lay open and a few golden hairs revealed themselves. She felt his cheek rest on the top of her head. Touching his hand, she mustered the courage to raise her face to his. Their mouths met, and they kissed softly at first, then long and deep. Charlotte closed her eyes and held him to her. Neither of them wanted to let go. Finally, she released him.

"Wait about ten minutes. I will gather everyone in the

kitchen." As Charlotte turned to go, he caught her arm.

"You are my life. I want to protect you and Jack."

"You are *my* life, James, and I will do my part to protect us all." She took a deep breath and walked out of the room and down the stairs. She located Mr. Primm and asked him to gather all the staff in the kitchen.

When they were all assembled, Charlotte warned them about Edward Hawkes. They needed to be mindful of strangers, especially anyone wanting information about Jack. She feared Hawkes might try to kidnap him. They all knew that the house was being guarded, but now they knew why.

On finishing, she left the kitchen and found Emma in the drawing room, who reported that John and James were out of the house and on their way to Grosvenor Square.

As they walked up the stairs, Charlotte explained Jane Rourke's situation to Emma. Her trial would be in one week. There were several people of good character from Spitalfields who were willing to speak on her behalf. However, Mr. Wooten had not been successful in moving any of the jurors to their cause. Being on the right side politically appeared to be of the utmost importance in this case. The magistrates chose the jurors and so, a juror being in favour was of prime importance in prolonging their tenure on the jury. Mr. Wooten had been unsuccessful in discovering who was behind Jane's arrest.

Charlotte told Emma that she planned to go to Newgate tomorrow. Annie said her mother's spirits were flagging. Jane's main concern was her children's well-being. Charlotte wished to assure her that they were being cared for. She planned to continue to do so, no matter what the outcome of the trial. However, Charlotte prayed daily it would be a positive one. Emma remained unusually quiet to this news, but Charlotte thought little of it as they reached the nursery.

It was noisy when they entered, but the children quickly stopped when they saw Charlotte, except for Duncan, who toddled forward and offered Emma his little square of blanket. Emma greeted him with a smile as Jenny came quickly to pick him up. Emma smiled with joy at seeing Jack and held out her hands to him. He responded by scurrying behind Annie's skirts and peeking out at her. In the end, he did begin to smile, but it would take time for him to make friends. She'd been away too long.

As they left the nursery, Emma turned to Charlotte. "Do you realize what you have undertaken with these children.?"

"I do. If Jane is hung, they will become my children. I plan to raise them."

"Charlotte, there are five boys."

"And Jack adores them all."

"What of Annie and her sister?"

"I will educate them and find them good husbands."

"I pray Mrs. Rourke lives, for your sake."

"I pray she does, too, Emma. She is innocent and has been dragged into this purely for retribution against her brother-in-law."

"I know you believe that, Charlotte, but perhaps she is involved. These people can be very deceitful when it's to their advantage."

"Emma, for heaven's sake, she is a woman as we are. She needs our help. I've known her since we were both very young. Please, do not let your fear of the less fortunate hinder your judgement."

"It's not fear, my dear. It's common sense and a knowledge of these people. They drink to excess. They will fight at the drop of a hat and in great brawling mobs. You have too kind a heart and a misplaced sense of loyalty, I fear."

"Well, then so be it, Emma. I will not harden my heart and turn from her. I have never experienced any of these things you talk about with her family."

"I will do whatever I can to help, Charlotte. Just realize not everyone shares your sentiments, and I foresee difficulties with these children."

"I am forewarned, dear friend." Charlotte said as Emma shook her head slowly at her friend's obstinance. Charlotte sent Emma home in her carriage after they made plans to see each other the following day.

As Charlotte rested that night after locking her bedchamber windows, she tried to sift through the emotions of the day. She was confused. She loved James more than ever, despite his betrayal. Emma and John's return filled her with joy, but Emma's distrust of Jane Rourke angered Charlotte. And what of Charlotte's own insistence on being included in the pursuit of Edward Hawkes? She felt justified in all her positions but not entirely at ease with them. At last, she gave up and fell asleep.

Charlotte dreamed of a white stag surrounded by purple heather on a mountainside. As it stood, she could see the velvet down hanging from one of its antlers. The white bone of the antler was exposed and one of the tips dripped with blood. She put her hand to her heart and, drawing it back, saw that it, too, was covered in blood. She gasped and fell to her knees. The stag looked at her with passive eyes, as life drained from her wound, and she lay down on the soft ground.

Charlotte awoke, bleeding. It was her time of the month. The bedcovers were soaked in blood. She felt faint, called out, and attempted to stand up. Charlotte fell onto the floor. Rising gingerly onto her hands and knees, she slowly stood up.

There was no blood. How could that be? She checked the bed covers and her night dress. Nothing. But it was so real, she thought to herself.

Fear began to grow in her. Was this Peg's doing? Was this dream, these hallucinations, a punishment on Charlotte for her part in taking James's love from Peg?

Suddenly, she desperately needed to see Jack. She needed to make sure he was safe. She wanted to grab him and flee to Whitestone. She wanted her refuge.

Taking a deep breath, she stopped herself. She had duties here. She could not leave James and would not abandon Jane Rourke or her family. Emma's words of yesterday tested Charlotte's resolve.

Perhaps Emma was the voice of reason, and Charlotte the fool for taking on the burden of this family. Stop it, she thought, you need to wake up and stop these ramblings!

She would check on Jack and get ready to visit James. As Charlotte approached the nursery, she heard loud crying. Her footsteps quickened. She entered and found Annie holding Jack, trying to comfort him. He was squirming and clutching at his stomach.

"He just woke, mistress. He is so hot."

Charlotte took him from the frightened girl. In Charlotte's arms, he threw himself forward, hitting her nose with his head. Stunned for a moment, she sat down and held him tight. Annie brought Charlotte a cold cloth and some powders they had used before for his ailments.

"I'll carry him to my room and see if I can settle him."

After more than an hour of screaming and vomiting, Jack quieted and fell asleep. Charlotte prayed to God to protect them both. Whether it was Peg's curse or simply coincidence, she did not care. She felt vulnerable and frightened.

Annie kept checking in on Charlotte and her son. When Jack fell asleep, Charlotte called Annie to her.

"You must go to your mother this morning. Your sister can watch your brothers. I need to care for Jack. Before you go, please, ask Mr. Primm to come and see me. I need to get a note to Lady Emma."

"Yes, mum." After Annie left, Charlotte went to her desk and wrote to Emma.

Bellagio House, Spitalfields
Dearest Emma,

My night was filled with troubling dreams. Jack has suddenly been taken ill, and I am very concerned. Please, give my best to your visitor from France. I hope he finds London to his liking. Perhaps you can find time to visit today.

With sincere regard and affection,
Charlotte

Mr. Primm knocked softly on the door, and Charlotte asked him to enter. He inquired as to Jack's health.

"I think we should be ready to call for the doctor, if necessary," Charlotte responded. She handed him the sealed note for Emma and asked him to take it personally. "I realize this takes you from your other duties, but it would ease my mind if you were to deliver it yourself."

"I will go directly, madam."

"Thank you."

Charlotte lay down next to Jack and listened to him breathe fitfully. His curls hung damp around his pale face. Exhausted, she closed her eyes. Sometime later, Jack's whimpering woke her. He had vomited in his sleep. It ran out of his mouth and covered the side of his face. She took a towel from the commode chest of drawers and dampened it with water from the pitcher. Charlotte gently lifted his head and cleaned him off. He did not wake.

After that, she moved him over, and he rested more comfortably. She rinsed the towel off in the bowl and hung it to dry. There was a knock at the door. Charlotte crossed and opened it. Mr. Primm stood with two notes in his hand. Charlotte thanked him and closed the door. Going to her escritoire, she sat down and opened the first note.

33 Grosvenor Square
Dear Charlotte,

We will plan to visit within the hour. We are all of us worried about Jack. You mentioned your fitful sleep. It is very odd; our guest, Monsieur Baptiste, did not sleep well, either.

Yours most faithfully,
Emma

So, James was troubled during the night as well, Charlotte thought. A shiver now ran down her back as she looked at the second note. The rough texture of the paper frightened her. She read:

Charlotte,

I am so close. So very close. Do you feel my breath upon your snow-white neck?

EH

Hot, angry tears were in her eyes. They must get out of Bellagio House and somehow escape this madman! James must show her what to do to protect herself and the children. She refused to stay a prisoner to such a demon!

Charlotte began to devise a plan of her own. She and the children would escape to Emma's house in Grosvenor Square. Her house was safer and in a much better part of the town. Charlotte would wrap up Jack. She would protect him from the cold, and once at Emma's, James and John could watch over them.

Oh, won't Emma be pleased, she thought to herself, but she had said she was willing to help. Charlotte prayed Emma would say yes to this idea. She felt Jack's forehead. His fever continued to rage. She took a small towel from the commode chest, dampened it and wiped his face with a cool clothe.

He let out a soft moan. A little while later, a servant knocked on the door, announcing Emma's arrival.

"And mum, there is a French gentleman accompanying her, a Mr. Baptiste." The girl was trying hard to suppress a smile.

"Please, ask them to come up. I cannot leave my son."

Charlotte heard them on the stairs but was not prepared for James's appearance. He was a giant. His head was covered with a large, white periwig brushed up smoothly to a mountainous height with curls cascading down the back. On the very top of the wig was perched a hat made to look like a tiny sailing ship. His face was powdered and rouged with a little black spot for beauty placed on his right cheek. His coat was emerald green brocade, and his waistcoat was gold and pink striped silk. His breeches matched his coat. White stockings and large buckled, high-heeled shoes finished off the ensemble.

With the servant girl still agog, he stopped and performed a deep bow, as Emma introduced him.

"Mrs. Pruitt, it is my pleasure to present to you, Vicomte Jean Emile Baptiste."

"Vicomte, I am charmed to make your acquaintance. Lady Bosworth-Fuller has told me so much about you, I feel that I know you already."

"Madame, how can I begin to express how honoured I am to be in your presence. *Mais votre fils*, he is ill? Please, what is wrong with him?"

Charlotte looked sternly at the girl who lingered at the door. She left quickly, shutting it behind her. Immediately, James took off the wig and tiny hat.

"Charlotte," he whispered, "what is wrong with Jack?"

"He awoke with a fever, had terrible stomach pains, and vomited."

James sat next to Jack and wiped his forehead gently with the wet towel. Emma looked on with concern. Charlotte hoped that Jack would not open his eyes. Otherwise, she reckoned, he might faint of fright on seeing Vicomte Baptiste by his side.

"Jem, Hawkes wrote again. I received his note along with Emma's." She gave James the note.

After he read it, he said, "I will kill him, Charlotte."

"He is a devil, Charlotte. A monster!" Emma exclaimed, looking at the note.

"No," James said with intensity. "He is a man, and I will destroy him."

Charlotte turned to Emma. "I have a request. You know you are my true friend and have stood by me in my various travails...."

Emma smiled at her attempted diplomacy. "Charlotte, please, what would you have me do?"

"I would feel safer if the children and I stayed at your house for a short time."

"All the children?" Emma said with a worried tone.

"I am responsible for them, Emma. I would not leave them here in danger."

Emma looked at James. "What a house full I will have, eh?"

"Now?" James asked. "Taking Jack out into the cold? I don't think that's a good idea, Charlotte."

"I'll bundle him up as best I can. I will not stay in this house."

"How will you get out of the house without being seen?" Emma asked.

"I'm praying Hawkes is watching only the front door and that no one in the house is reporting to him. My thought is that we go out through the garden and by the stables into the mews. If we all dress as weavers, we would be less conspicuous once we are out on the street. My coach could pick us up in Soho Square."

"Assuming no one sees you slip out the back, it might

work. Be sure to hide your auburn hair, Lottie. It gave you away before," James said.

"Vicomte, I would that I could dress as you are. What a truly marvellous ensemble," Charlotte teased.

Emma beamed. "We had it made for a masquerade in Venice."

"Perhaps I shall become a macaroni permanently," James said.

"You do, and I will give strict orders to have you thrown out of my house," Charlotte retorted.

"I am stunned by your narrow-mindedness, Charlotte. Are you not, Emma?"

"Truly, I am."

"James," Charlotte said, "what of your night? Was it your dreams that disturbed you?"

"I spent the night chained to a rock with my liver being eaten by an eagle. Not a pleasant experience."

Charlotte related her dreams of the previous night, ending with, "It's Peg's doing, Jem. I'm sure of it."

"No. I will not give her such power over me. They are dreams only."

"But Jack's sickness is real. What of that?" Charlotte asked.

"It is a coincidence," he replied.

"I pray that is so."

"It is." James said.

There was a knock on the door, followed by a mad scramble to get James's wig properly placed on his head. "Come in," Charlotte called out calmly, while trying to slow her pounding heart.

Annie entered and looked at the three of them. "Hello. Forgive me for intruding, but I must speak with you, Mrs.

Pruitt."

"Of course," Charlotte excused herself and went into the hallway. Annie's eyes were red, and her hair needed brushing.

"Mistress Charlotte, my mother is in a terrible state. That awful woman is hounding her day and night, filling her head with gruesome stories of hangings and what is done with the bodies afterwards. My mother is ready to go out of her mind for want of kindness and a civil word. I'm afraid she may do something desperate. Perhaps, if you have a bit of time, could you go to see her? Your reassurance would mean so much."

Charlotte took the girl's hand. "I promise I will go this afternoon, but first you must help me with something."

Annie listened attentively as Charlotte told her of the plan to move everyone to Emma's house. There was a noise on the stairs and Charlotte saw Mr. Primm coming up towards her carrying a small box wrapped in a silk pocket handkerchief.

"This was left on the doorstep, madam. It is addressed to you." Charlotte could tell Mr. Primm was concerned about what it might contain. He gave it to her.

"Thank you, Mr. Primm. I shall be careful in opening it." Charlotte turned to Annie. "Please, you and Jenny get your brothers ready. They should wear the clothes they had on when they came to the house. You should borrow one of your sister's dresses."

Annie hurried away, and Charlotte gingerly carried the box into her bedchamber. James and Emma looked up from watching Jack. Charlotte offered the box to James. Taking it, he examined it.

"I overheard what Primm said. I think it best if I open

it. May I?"

"Yes." Charlotte and Emma watched as he carefully took off the handkerchief. It was a simple wooden box. He opened the lid and inside was a scarlet ribbon with a small note attached. James read it silently. His face turned red.

"What does it say?" Charlotte asked, afraid of the answer.

"I don't think you need to read it," he answered.

"Please, let me."

Charlotte read it silently.

My Angel,

This is all you need to wear when I slit your throat.

She dropped it as if it had burnt her hand. Her vision blurred, and she felt hot and faint. Emma caught her arm as she staggered.

"I will find him. This torment will end," James said.

Charlotte nodded and sat on the edge of the bed unable to speak at first. Finally, she found words.

"Jem, you must teach me what to do, how to protect myself. If he were to come, and you were not here, I must know what to do. I will not be his victim a second time."

James took out his dagger. Charlotte imagined the sharp point piercing Hawkes's heart. "Keep this by you when you sleep. If he attacks you, then thrust it up quickly under his rib cage. Aim for his heart. Do not hesitate. If he binds you, you will be lost."

"I understand."

"Oh, Charlotte," Emma whispered.

"If he were to surprise you and try to drag you off, you

must put your legs wide and bend at the knees. Drop your weight low. It gives you a broad base, so it's more difficult to move you. If he comes at you, kick or hit him between the legs."

"Bite and scratch. Gouge his eyes," Emma added.

"Scream. Do not be silent, Charlotte," James said. "If he attacks you from behind, get your hand to your throat. Protect your airway. Grab him between the legs with your free hand and pull with all your strength. When he lets go, turn and kick him with your knee or use the heel of your hand to smash up and into his nose."

They began to practice quietly what James had described. At first, Charlotte felt ridiculous, but James encouraged her. When she imagined that he was Hawkes, she began to fight with more vigour. She decided she must wear only one petticoat under her morning dress. This would make her movement less cumbersome. They tried concealing a dagger on different parts of her person. The best seemed to be at her waist, slightly behind her back on the left side. She would conceal it with her mantua, and it would be easy to reach.

Annie returned to tell Charlotte that the children were prepared to leave. They all looked at Jack, who was still sleeping despite all the conversation around him. Charlotte hated to rouse him, but she knew she must. Annie brought Charlotte one of her mother's dresses to wear. Charlotte, with Emma's help, quickly changed into it. James and she looked at each other. He, the foppish Frenchman, and she, the simple weaver.

"We do make quite a pair, m'dear," James commented.

Charlotte wrapped Jack in a blanket. He looked like a pale rag doll.

"Jack," she whispered as she brushed the hair from his eyes. "Jackie, it's mama." He tried to open his eyes, but they rolled back in his head.

"Charlotte, let us take him," Emma urged. "We will wrap him like a bundle and take him in the coach. You cannot drag him through the streets in this condition. You simply cannot."

"I'm afraid he will scream if he wakes up without Annie or myself. However, I think you're correct. He should travel with you. Jemmy, sing to him if he's frightened. Hopefully, he will recognize your voice."

"We will take good care of him, Lottie. I promise," James said and kissed her gently. He wrapped Jack up carefully and carried him down the stairs. The women followed him, covering Jack's head and face before James took him outside to the carriage. Emma, James, and Jack were quickly away.

Annie went to get the children and joined Charlotte in her bedchamber.

"I have told them to follow closely," she said as she ushered them in, "and to listen for your instructions, Mistress Charlotte."

"Thank you, Annie." Charlotte turned to the children. "We're going to Lady Emma's house in Grosvenor Square. Hopefully, we will be there for only a few days. You will all be safe and comfortable." The boys looked frightened and unsure of what was happening. "Boys, there is a wicked man who wishes to hurt Jack and me. I believe that Lady Emma's house is a better place for all of us, because my friends will watch out for us there."

"Would the man hurt us, too, Mistress Charlotte?" Luke asked, holding onto Stephen's arm. The two identical faces looked up at her.

"I fear he might try. We must all be brave, Luke and Stephen. That's why as we walk along the streets, we must all stay together. We're going to leave the house through the garden, in case the man is watching the front door. I want you to pretend just for a little while that I am your mother. All of you must stay very close to me. Annie and Jenny will bring up the rear of our line, so no one will be left behind. Jenny, please carry Duncan. Are you all ready?" They all nodded. "Good. I must speak with Mr. Primm, then we will be off."

Charlotte rang for Mr. Primm, who came hurrying up the stairs and into her room. His eyes grew wide when he entered and saw all of them standing there. "Madame, forgive me for staring. I was surprised to see everyone here."

"Mr. Primm, we are in great haste," Charlotte said, explaining the plan. "Please, do not tell anyone else. The staff may only know that we are on an outing. If any more letters or packages arrive, please carefully open them yourself. If there is an urgent need to send me a message, please come to Lady Emma's yourself, but make sure you aren't followed. I fear it will be but a little time before Edward Hawkes discovers our whereabouts, but that time may save our lives."

"I will do exactly as you have instructed, madam."

Quickly and quietly, they left the house, slipping out through the garden gate. The rain was a constant drizzle falling from a cold, slate grey sky. Charlotte's little flock followed her obediently. Only little Duncan was unaware of the danger. He babbled away happily in Jenny's arms.

There were few people on the streets, most choosing to

stay dry inside. Charlotte glanced back several times to see if anyone was keeping pace with them. The third time she had occasion to do so, she ran into a man coming out of a butcher's shop. He caught her in his arms as she fell. She let out a yelp of surprise, startling the man so much that he nearly dropped her.

"Begging your pardon. I don't fink neifer of us was lookin' where was goin'."

His East London accent surprised her for he had the blue-black skin of an African. He was tall and broad-shouldered. Behind him stood a dour looking man who, Charlotte supposed, was his friend. She thought he must be a Jew, for he wore side curls and a wide-brimmed hat. Charlotte mumbled an apology and gathered the children about her. The African smiled and doffed his tricorne hat as he walked past them going in the opposite direction. His companion, scowling still, watched them as he passed following his companion.

"Come children. We must get to Soho." The group started off again.

Charlotte was more afraid than ever that they were being pursued, though she saw no evidence of this. Why, she asked herself, did I suppose that Soho would be a safe place to get into my carriage? She started thinking that they should walk all the way to Emma's. Her fear caused her to be distracted.

Suddenly, in front of her, the African man appeared, emerging from an alley and stepping into her path. Charlotte froze, and all the children nearly ran into each other. He was holding something under his jacket. As he moved towards her, she stepped forward and without hesitation shoved her knee as hard as she might into his groin. In an instant, his eyes grew big and he doubled over in pain. Duncan's small square of a blanket fell from his hand.

"My dear God!" Charlotte exclaimed seeing what her panic had produced. Duncan squirmed out of Jenny's grip and grabbed his precious blanket from the muddy ground. Annie and Jenny rounded up the boys who stood staring at the man in pain. Charlotte bent over to help the gasping man stand up.

"I am sorry, so sorry. Please forgive me," she said, forgetting to conceal her accent. He was in too much pain to notice, but Charlotte realized her error was not lost on his companion who had emerged from the shadows. The Jew's eyes were fixed on her. Charlotte retreated to where the children stood.

The man with the wide-brimmed hat stepped into the light and took his friend's arm.

"C'mon. I fink 'er ladyship's done 'er damage, eh?"

Trying to assume the correct accent, Charlotte said, "I'm sorry I 'urt you."

"No 'harm done," the injured man replied as he attempted to straighten up. He smiled weakly at her, his eyes watering.

Charlotte was moved by his forgiveness. "Fank you," she responded, as their eyes met and rested on each other for an instant. "Come dears," she said to her group.

With Annie and Jenny's help, she moved the children down the street and did not look back. The two men stood, watching them go.

CHAPTER FIVE

As they reached Soho Square without further incident, Charlotte decided that they would continue on to Emma's house even though she saw her carriage waiting. She felt all of them boarding would draw undue attention to the group. She knew the route. It would mean walking another mile and a half. So, on they went. The streets grew wider and she began to feel more at ease.

Then, the rain started pouring down in a hard shower as they hurried the last few hundred feet. They arrived at Emma's, wet, exhausted and footsore. Once inside in the kitchen, Charlotte hugged each child and praised them for their endurance. Emma's housekeeper took charge and, with Annie and Jenny's help, marched them to their room to dry off. Emma entered the kitchen and expressed her surprise that they came all the way on foot. Charlotte explained her reasoning as Emma led her upstairs to Jack.

James, who had changed clothes, was in the bedchamber watching over their son. The fever still raged, and Jack moaned in his sleep. Charlotte sat beside Jack on the bed. He appeared so small, so fragile.

"What have we done?" Charlotte said. "We should never have moved him."

James stood behind her, his hands on her shoulders.

"He is here now, and you and the children are safe."

Charlotte told James and Emma about the two men she had encountered.

"I'm afraid I hurt the poor man, and he was only returning Duncan's blanket."

"You had no way of knowing that, Charlotte. He could have had other intentions. You acted swiftly in what could have been a dangerous situation. I will remember to stand well back from you, from now on," James said with a small smile.

"He will not soon forget you, I would wager," Emma agreed. She noticed Charlotte shivering. "Change your clothes. You will be getting sick next, if you neglect taking care of yourself."

"They are only a little damp. Besides, I brought no clothes with me. I'll send to the house tomorrow for a few things," Charlotte said as she watched Jack.

The three adults stood in silence.

Finally, Charlotte spoke, "Emma would you send a footman to tell my driver to return to Bellagio House?"

Emma nodded.

"Also, I promised Annie I would see her mother. I must go out just for a bit. May I use your carriage, Emma?"

"Do you think it's wise after trying to hide from Hawkes to go to Newgate? He may have spies out looking for you," Emma said.

Charlotte thought of the two men they met on their walk but said nothing. James was quiet. Charlotte could tell by the set of his jaw he was not happy. She looked at him as she answered Emma.

"No, it probably isn't wise, but I promised I would go. If I may borrow one of your cloaks? I will hide my face as much as possible. Your driver can let me out well before the prison." Emma looked from Charlotte to James. "Emma, will you let me take the carriage or must I set out on foot again?"

"Of course, you may, dear. If you feel you must do this."

James stroked Jack's forehead. "I will be here with Jack. Please, use caution."

"I will. I promise," Charlotte said as she rested her head briefly on his arm. Much against her better judgement, she was off again. The driver found a quiet spot to let her out, and it was arranged that she should meet him in one hour's time at this same place.

Her spirits were as bleak as the weather. Her clothes were damp, and her feet ached. She took off Emma's cloak, folded it into a bundle and carried it in her arms before entering the prison. When she arrived at the cell looking like a weaver, no one took notice of her. Charlotte found Jane huddled in a corner, her head on her knees. She knelt down beside Mrs. Rourke.

"Jane?"

The woman looked up. Her eyes were red. "Yes?" she responded, looking confused.

"It's me, Charlotte Pruitt."

"Mrs. Pruitt?" she said, looking at Charlotte's clothes. "I don't understand."

Charlotte explained briefly why she was dressed as she was. It only seemed to confuse Jane more.

"The children?" Jane asked, tears welling up in her eyes.

"Be assured, they are fine. Duncan and Jack love to play side by side. Stephen and Luke include them in all their games and are as patient as can be expected. Michael and

Ralph play by themselves. Annie and Jenny are sweet to them all. The girls do make sure they say their prayers and keep themselves clean." Charlotte took Jane's hand. "They miss you terribly. All of them. Annie is very concerned about you. You must tell me what happened to make you so melancholy."

"It is her," Jane whispered, indicating the thin, sallow-faced woman who ridiculed Charlotte when she first visited Jane. "She will not leave me alone no matter how I turn away or beg her to stop. She tells me of the hangings and how one suffers. The ropes choke you slowly, so the pain is prolonged. Even after you're dead, certain doctors will try and snatch your body. They cut it up, as if you were a piece of meat. I am a Christian woman, Mrs. Pruitt. I wish to be buried as a Christian, not hacked to pieces. Sometimes, she told me, they even dig you up after your family thinks you're settled in your grave. They come in the dead of night. Oh, my God, I shall have no peace in the hereafter, and my little ones will wander homeless orphans." She began to sob.

Charlotte put her arms around Jane, who fell unto her bosom, weeping. The sallow-faced woman peered angrily in their direction but made no move towards them. Charlotte held Jane gently in her arms.

"Jane, I swear to you, if it comes to it, you will have a Christian burial. Your children will be safe with me. I promise they will not wander the streets bereft. I have been praying to God that He will deliver you from this terrible place, but if, in His wisdom He does not, I will do all I can for your family, even if I have to follow them to the ends of the earth to watch out for them. I swear it to you. Do you hear me?" Charlotte helped Jane sit up slowly.

"I do hear you. You are the answer to my prayers, Charlotte Pruitt." Her face took on a look of calm, and she rested back against the hard, stone wall. "I have heard," Jane said, "that they have put Patrick in a cell by himself. He was inciting the other Irishmen, in Irish, to riot. He will die fighting, I'm afraid. I wish he had stayed in Ireland. He and my dear husband, Donald, God rest his soul, were ever in arguments. I would walk by them and think to myself; praise be, I am not involved. My husband and he had words the night Donald died. I was so angry I wanted to throw Patrick out into the street, but Donald said, 'No, he is my brother. I will not treat him so. If something would happen to me, he will take care of the family.' Oh, hasn't he just taken care of us, indeed. For once, you should have listened to me, husband," she said looking heavenward.

Charlotte told Jane about the people who said they would speak for her at the trial. One was her neighbour, Sarah Southwell, whom Jane had fed and clothed when Sarah's husband was taken off by a press gang.

"They are all good, honest people, but I have little hope left in me," Jane responded.

Charlotte gave her presents from the children and a small bible she had brought for her. Jane took Charlotte's hand. "There is only one more favour I would ask of you. Donald gave me a locket on our wedding day. It was his mother's. I wore it every day until I came into this place. Annie has been keeping it for me. I would wear it now. Will you bring it?"

"Gladly."

"Thank you, Charlotte Pruitt. God bless you."

Jane seemed then to recall Charlotte's words from the beginning of the visit. "You are all safe?"

"We are. I will visit you tomorrow and bring the locket."

"Thank you."

Jane began to stand, but Charlotte bade her stay seated. The sallow-faced woman was looking in their direction and Charlotte wished to leave without incident.

"Tomorrow, then," Jane said and positioned herself back into her corner.

Charlotte left without a confrontation. She decided she must look as hopeless as the rest of the miserable crowd who inhabited the place. All her money and influence truly meant nothing in this case. She was not even able to get Jane away from her tormentor. Charlotte feared that Patrick and Jane, guilty and innocent, would be crushed together.

Throwing Emma's cape around her shoulders, she waited in a doorway for the carriage to appear. She watched the people of East London pass. The weavers, small in stature and bent in frame to fit their looms. The wretched beggars, many of whom had lived their lives as farmers, now thrown off their land by enclosures and forced into the city. Sailors who had lost their hands and soldiers who had lost their legs, haggard Jewish street sellers who had no country and no allies; how abandoned, how hopeless they all appeared.

Charlotte realized in that moment that she had floated above this life, had seen it from her windows but never felt it as she did now. She hastened to get into the carriage when it arrived and closed her eyes as it lurched forward on the drive to Grosvenor Square.

Once there, Emma insisted that Charlotte change into some of her own warm, dry clothes. Emma told her that Jack had been awake for a short time. He ate and drank a little. Now, he slept peacefully.

Feeling a bit relieved, Charlotte entered the bedchamber and saw James sitting in a chair next to the bed. He had a board on which a piece of paper rested, and he was sketching Jack's sleeping face with a piece of red chalk. The lines were soft and the child's face was beautiful. It caught Jack exactly as he was at that moment. Charlotte reached out and touched James's broad shoulders. She bent forward and kissed his cheek.

"It's beautiful, Jem," Charlotte whispered. He put the board and drawing to one side and pulled another chair next to his. Charlotte and James sat holding hands, not uttering a word.

There was a quiet knock on the bedchamber door. Charlotte opened it and went into the hallway where Annie inquired after her mother. Charlotte told her of the visit, but in her joy at Jack's seeming recovery she forgot about the locket.

"Jenny and I believe that Mama will be exonerated. How could the jury fail to see that she is innocent?" Charlotte did not have the heart to contradict the girls' belief.

"I promised your mother that I would go again tomorrow." Annie appeared gladdened by that prospect. It was only two days until the trial and the moment when judgement would be passed.

It was now James's turn to go out into the city. He and John were off to see how Edward Hawkes spent his days and nights. They hoped to find time when he was routinely alone. James kissed Charlotte on the cheek.

"I will return as quickly as I am able, I promise."

With night approaching, Jack's fever began to rise.

Charlotte watched him constantly and tried to comfort him. By midnight, she could hardly keep her eyes open. Thankfully, James returned, and they lay down on either side of Jack.

They were asleep for perhaps an hour when Jack suddenly sat up, let out a terrible scream and clutched his stomach. He gagged and coughed a dry, deep cough then fell back onto his pillow, whimpering.

Charlotte grabbed him up into her arms and held his limp body. James sat, watching them. Charlotte could feel Jack's body begin to cool.

"The fever is leaving," she told James.

"Leaving?"

"It is going from him. Feel his forehead."

"It is cooler. Dear God, thank you." He took Jack in his arms.

Jack looked up sleepily and reached out to touch James's face.

"It's Papa, my sweet Jack," James whispered.

They changed his wet clothes. Exhausted from his ordeal, he fell asleep quickly. His parents were not far behind.

The sunlight woke Charlotte. The storms of yesterday were gone, and the blue sky greeted her waking eyes. Stretching, she looked at the two figures next to her. Jack was sleeping peacefully, his breathing strong and normal. James lay next to him on his back with one arm over his face. Charlotte propped herself up on one arm and reached over to tickle James's chin with her free hand. He grunted and turned his back to Charlotte. However, his movement roused Jack, and the little boy opened his eyes and looked at his mother. Charlotte kissed his nose and he smiled.

Jack's energy had returned. He sat up and began his attack on his father. James, now awake, retaliated and grabbed his son, who laughed loudly at being caught. When Jack worked himself free, he pounced on Charlotte. The rest of the morning passed with play and rest interspersed. No one disturbed them, and they had no thought of the outside world.

At last, James said, "John and I need to go out again today. We lost Hawkes last night near Spital Square. He slipped into an alley, and there was no finding him. I was the beggar for that, but today I believe, the vicomte will make an appearance for a tour of the city."

It was then that Charlotte remembered the locket that Jane asked her to bring. "Watch Jack. I need to find Annie and ask her a question."

"What is it?" James asked.

"Mrs. Rourke requested I bring her a locket her husband had given her. Annie has it and I need to take it to the prison today. I shan't be a moment."

"Will you allow me to kiss you before you go?" James asked. Charlotte stopped and gazed at him. He sat on the bed, with Jack wrapped around his shoulders.

"It would please me greatly if you did." He stood, Jack still attached and giggling madly, took her in one arm with his other supporting Jack, and kissed her full on the mouth. Charlotte felt light-headed and took one step back.

"Thank you, sir," she said, her cheeks burning.

"My pleasure, madam." He smiled and the corners of his eyes wrinkled. Jack pulled his hair and he winced.

When Charlotte found Annie and told her what she needed, the girl turned pale. "What's the matter?" Charlotte asked.

"I left it at home."

"At Bellagio House?"

"Yes."

"Where?"

"In the chest of drawers in my room," Annie answered.

"I'll find a way to get it. You needn't be upset." Charlotte left Annie, who was looking very unhappy. Once back in the bedchamber, she reported the problem to James.

"Send for Primm to bring it," he suggested.

"No, I shall simply slip in the back and retrieve it. I need some other clothes for the children and for myself. I brought so little."

"Very well, John and I will accompany you. Dress in some of Emma's clothes. We shall go right to the front door as if we were visitors."

"My life is turning into a costume party, but I would prefer the carriage to going on foot again."

After a small meal and a quick explanation to Emma and John about what she needed to do, Charlotte, James, and John were off to Bellagio House. When they arrived, Charlotte threw the hood of Emma's cloak over her head and made for the door. Fortunately, Mr. Primm greeted them and quietly ushered them into the drawing room. Charlotte explained what she needed to get and left to go upstairs to Annie's room and the nursery. She found the locket in the chest of drawers and wrapped it in her clean pocket handkerchief. In the nursery, she gathered up more shirts, breeches and stockings for the boys. Her hands full, she entered her bedchamber.

Nothing could have prepared her for the grisly sight that lay before her. Charlotte dropped the clothes and screamed. The room began to spin. James and John came running in. James caught Charlotte's arm and supported her. John stood horrified.

Mr. Primm entered and let out an, "Oh my God!"

Others from the household came running after him, but he shut the door to prevent them from entering. Blood was smeared on every wall. On the bed lay a headless, naked corpse. It had been a woman. Her arms and legs were lashed to the bed, spread eagle, just as Charlotte had been. Her body was slashed from the neck down and her entrails pulled out and stuffed between her legs. Charlotte turned her head into James's chest.

"Who was she?" Charlotte asked.

"I don't know," James said.

He helped Charlotte walk over to where the other men stood. She stayed close to his side, like a small child. He cradled her in his arms. Closing her eyes, she tried to breathe. John, James as the vicomte, and Mr. Primm talked about what needed to be done next. They decided they must call for Constable Paine. James said he must excuse himself before the authorities arrived because of urgent business he needed to attend to in the city. John said he understood and would stay and help Charlotte through the ordeal. Charlotte realized she was in Emma's oversized clothes and felt suddenly ridiculous.

"I must dress in my own clothes to talk to anyone and there are a few things I need to gather up to take to Emma's."

James nodded. The men continued their discussion as Charlotte picked her way across broken furniture and blood-stained carpet to the wardrobe all the time looking away from the bed. As she began to open the door she was distracted for a moment, thinking she heard her name. She turned to the men, but no one was looking at her. Turning back, she opened the wardrobe door and stood face to face with the corpse's bloody head. Hanging by the mass of her black hair, Peg's face stared at Charlotte with horror-stricken eyes. A strangled noise came from Charlotte's throat and the world went black.

The next thing Charlotte recalled was the sound of voices. Slowly, she began to see faces in her field of vision. Her head ached, and she was sick to her stomach.

"She is back with us, I believe," Charlotte heard James's voice, but it seemed far away in the distance.

"What happened?" she whispered, having no idea how she got in the parlour.

"You had a nasty shock," John told Charlotte as James sat next to her on a chair by the settee where she lay in the parlour.

"I don't feel at all well," Charlotte managed to say before she gagged and vomited. After that, she lay back and closed her eyes, but in an instant, she saw Peg's eyes and it all came back to her. Charlotte sat upright.

"Oh, dear God! Her head!" she gasped. "Jem! Jem!" Charlotte pulled her knees to her chin and curled into a ball.

James reached out to her, putting his arms around her.

"Charlotte, I'm here. You're safe. I'm here."

"It would have been me. My head."

"But it was not," James said.

John spoke, "Charlotte, James must be away now. Primm has gone for Constable Paine."

Tears filled her eyes and her throat began to tighten.

"I understand. Please go, Jem. Go and watch Jack. Please, what if Hawkes...?"

"Jack will be fine. I'll be with him. John will stay with you. You're safe, Lottie. Thanks be to God. You're safe."

Charlotte held his hand tightly as he stood up.

"I will see you at Emma's. I love you, Jem." Her throat tightened more.

"I love you, Lottie." He kissed her hand and was gone.

Not three minutes after James's carriage pulled away, the constable appeared, huffing and puffing. Mr. Primm announced him. Mr. Roger Paine was his name. Charlotte wrapped herself in her blanket and received him. He was an extremely heavyset man with a red face, small squinting eyes, and tremendous eyebrows that had grown out in diverse directions. They completed the introductions and Mr. Paine, still out of breath, sat down.

"Mr. Primm informs me that a murder has been committed in your house, Mrs. Pruitt."

"That is correct, Mr. Paine," Charlotte responded but offered no more. She looked to John to explain, for the thought of having to describe the carnage in her bedchamber was more than she could bear. "Mr. Fuller will tell you what we have found, Mr. Paine."

John took the man aside and told him what they found. Mr. Paine's face drained of colour upon hearing how Peg was mutilated.

"Who was this woman? How did she come to be in Mrs. Pruitt's bedchamber, sir?" Mr. Paine asked.

John could not answer that, so Charlotte began, "She was a rag picker from the west country, I believe, who for some unknown reason, decided to plague me. She appeared first in my garden only last week, nearly knocking Mr. Primm over when he discovered her behind a holly bush. Soon after, she crawled through a window in my bedchamber. I discovered her there attempting to steal my silk robes. She escaped out the way she came in before I could call for help. I've recently thought of moving to the West End for safety's sake."

"But Mrs. Pruitt, where were you when this crime occurred?"

"I was not here. Besides dealing with the intrusions of this madwoman, I have received threatening notes from a man named Edward Hawkes."

"And who is he to you, Mrs. Pruitt?"

Charlotte took a breath. "He is an enemy, sir, of the late James Clarke." Mr. Paine did not comment on this information, but his left eyebrow raised slightly. Charlotte continued, "Hawkes is the man who broke into my house nearly two years ago and forced himself upon me in a particularly violent manner."

"The constable before me told me of that horrific attack," Mr. Paine said, looking at the floor.

"Last week," Charlotte continued, "Hawkes began sending me notes, each more threatening than the last. Yesterday's was the worst yet. He threatened to slit my throat. It was too much. I fled to Lady Bosworth-Fuller and Mr. Fuller's house in Grosvenor Square. Today, I returned for clothes and some other necessities, only to enter my room and discover that Hawkes had indeed visited."

"Is it possible to describe the man?"

"Mr. Paine, I never saw the man. He attacked me in the dark. However, he was once described to me by James Clarke, and I can relate what he said."

"Thank you, Mrs. Pruitt. It will be a beginning."

"He's about six feet, one inch in height, for James Clarke said they were of a similar height. Sturdily built, I believe, from his service in the army. Blond hair, which at the time, he wore long."

"Well, that could describe a good many men in London, I fear," Mr. Paine said.

"There is one more thing. His left ear is badly deformed. He wears his hair long to hide it."

"Do you have any idea where he might be in London?"

Charlotte stopped herself, for she could not tell him of Ketch's warren or the doctor in Mayfair without having to explain where she got that information. She shook her head.

"Mr. Paine," John interrupted, "we should allow Mrs. Pruitt to rest. I will show you what there is to see upstairs." They excused themselves and left the parlour.

Charlotte lay down and closed her eyes, glad to be alone. Yet there was no rest for her. She kept imagining Hawkes discovering Peg in her bed. Had his rage exploded when he found he was denied my throat, Charlotte wondered? What pleasure did he take from terrifying and torturing poor Peg? What curses had she spat at him in those few moments?

Charlotte fell asleep and drifted in a cool, grey mist. There was a pressure at her throat as the fog swirled and Hawkes materialized above her. The sharp point of his knife pressed at her neck. She tried to hold him off and begged him to let her live. Her skin gave way and the knife glided in, warm liquid pouring out and covering her chest. Charlotte struggled, wanting to stop the blood, but he held her arms. He watched her face, his expression loving, tender. She fought to keep her eyes open as he kissed her on the cheek. Crying out, she lost consciousness.

Someone touched her shoulder, and she opened her

eyes. Emma was kneeling next to her. "You were crying in your sleep. I could not bear to see you in such pain."

Charlotte sat up and looked around the room. "How long have I been asleep?"

"Perhaps an hour. James told me what happened, and I came directly here."

"Oh, my God, Emma," Charlotte said as she grabbed hold of her friend's arms. "He murdered her. Took her head off. I will never stay in this house again." Emma held her as she wept.

"I will instruct Mr. Primm to pack what you need for the time being. You will stay at my house indefinitely. I'll take you back there now."

The constable and John came into the parlour. The former was white as a sheet. "I have never seen so savage a crime, I can tell you, Mrs. Pruitt. We will do our best to find this man, Hawkes. I will come back directly and supervise the disposal of the body. Being as she was a vagrant, I don't suppose she has family in London?"

"I have no idea," Charlotte responded.

"Well, we will assume not, anyway. The parish will give her a Christian burial, though it's not truly our responsibility." He stopped and looked at Charlotte.

"I will help with that expense, if it eases the burden on the parish," Charlotte said.

"Thank you, Mrs. Pruitt. You are a kind and generous soul. I know the weavers who are in your employ appreciate your generosity, and Christ Church is proud to have you among its congregation."

He would have continued, but Charlotte's head was pounding now. She held up her hand for him to stop and he obliged.

"Mr. Paine, I leave my household staff at your disposal. I am returning to the Bosworth-Fuller house in Grosvenor Square. Please, do not tell anyone where I am. My life may depend on your silence. If you need me, please, send a message with Mr. Primm."

"Of course, Mrs. Pruitt, it shall be as you ask." He said his goodbyes and left the house. Charlotte suggested that Emma leave by the front door and have her driver circle the carriage around the block and come back to the mews. Charlotte and John would in the meantime slip out through the garden and meet her in the back of the property. Emma agreed. Charlotte prayed that Hawkes was not watching as she the John made their escape.

CHAPTER SIX

Upon leaving Bellagio House, Charlotte was struck by how foggy it was in the early afternoon. She could barely see three feet in front of them. The apprehension she felt in her dream swept back over her as the carriage pulled out of the mews. The fog swirled and lifted slightly as they rounded the corner onto Fort Street. Looking out the window, she saw the African and the Jew from the day before deep in conversation with a third man whose back was turned to her. Her heart stopped, for the man with his back turned was tall, sturdily built, his long, blond hair hung loosely at his shoulders.

"John, he is there!"

"Who?" John asked.

"Hawkes! I see him." Charlotte pointed out the window of the carriage,

"Where?" John who sat opposite Charlotte looked out his window. Emma sitting next to her moved so she could see out Charlotte's window. As she pointed to the group, they disappeared into a small side street and were lost from sight.

"Charlotte, what did you see?" Emma asked. She described the three men and reminded John and Emma of her encounter with two of them the day before.

"Do you think the Jew and African might have been spying on you yesterday?" Emma said.

"I don't know. It didn't seem so at the time. Yet seeing them now, I fear it was not a chance encounter." Charlotte thought for a moment. "If they knew I was at your house, why did Hawkes come to Bellagio House? Why did he murder Peg?"

"What if Peg and Hawkes came to your house together?" Emma suggested.

"And then he turned on her and hacked her to death?" Charlotte said, shuddering at the image.

"James and I will go hunting him again tonight," John said. "We'll find him and truss him up like an animal. He will confess to his crimes, and we shall be done with him."

"How is it possible for a man to be so evil?" Emma whispered.

In Charlotte's nervousness, she thrust her hand into the pocket of her cloak and touched her handkerchief.

"Oh, John, Emma, I have Jane's locket," she said, as she opened up her handkerchief. "I completely forgot about it. How shall I get it to her? The trial is tomorrow. She desperately needs it, along with words of encouragement."

"You cannot go there again, Charlotte," John said firmly.

"I'll take it," Emma volunteered. "Annie shall go with me."

"No, I couldn't ask you to do that. It's a foul place, Emma."

"You have no choice in this, Charlotte," Emma said. "You must stay safe and secure at the house with Jack. Anything else would be madness. Don't you agree, dear husband?" She looked at John with an expression that said, *you do agree and that's that.*

He smiled at Emma and nodded.

Charlotte could not argue with them. Secretly, she felt great relief at not having to go to Newgate, but then she was overwhelmed by guilt at abandoning Jane. Charlotte looked at Emma.

"Do not say another word," Emma told her firmly.

"I merely wanted to thank you both for all your concern and aid." Charlotte took Emma's hand and squeezed it. Emma turned her face away to hide her tears.

John spoke next. "I have told Emma, but I have not had occasion to tell you, Charlotte. James saved my life on my father's estate in Pennsylvania. He visited there when he was serving in the colonies. He and I were in the wilderness and were surprised by a Lenape hunting party. One had me down and meant to scalp me. James fought off his own attackers and appeared to me like an avenging angel, sword in hand, and dispatched the blackguard with ease. He is a man of tremendous courage, Charlotte. When I saw how he was broken after Portugal, I wept." John stopped to regain his composure. They rode some moments in silence. "Edward Hawkes is an evil man. I consider it an honour to serve Jem in whatever way I can to destroy this devil."

"Thank you, John," Charlotte said.

As they passed through Soho Square, Charlotte thought how much more menacing the world had become since only yesterday. She was glad when they reached Grosvenor Square and were able to sit down in Emma's parlour. James joined them, still dressed as the vicomte, though without the wig and make-up. He reported that Jack was safe and in Annie and Jenny's keeping. The boy's illness of the day before was gone, and he was running the older boys ragged.

John related their ride home in the coach and the sighting of Hawkes and the two men. James straightened in his seat, his eyes taking on an intense expression. To Charlotte, it appeared as if he wished to visualize every detail of their meeting in his mind's eye. Before she could question him about his thoughts, however, Emma broke in and told him of her decision to go to Newgate to deliver the locket. He agreed that it was best for Charlotte to stay hidden.

"I shall go with Emma, as well," John volunteered.

"Do you think that's necessary?" Emma asked.

"Yes!" both the men responded simultaneously.

So, it was decided that they, with Annie, would visit Jane in an hour. James and Charlotte would stay at the house and wait for their report. In the time they had before John and Emma were to leave, they tried to prepare Emma for the sights and sounds of the prison.

Charlotte knew in her heart, however, that it was too alien to Emma's world for her to truly be prepared. Emma went off with John, thinking of it as an adventure. Charlotte doubted that she would return with that same sentiment.

James and Charlotte looked in on the children. Jenny was watching them, and Jack was happily playing. So, they retired to their room to have a quiet moment to themselves. The room was larger than Charlotte's at Bellagio House. She lay on the bed and looked up at the sculpted ceiling.

James shed most of the vicomte's clothes, wearing now only the white silk shirt and the emerald green breeches. He sat beside her on the bed, and she felt him watching her face.

"Charlotte, are you at all recovered from what you saw

this morning?"

"I am afraid to close my eyes," Charlotte admitted. "When I try, I come face to face with her again."

James reached out and touched Charlotte's face gently. She held his hand to her cheek. "I hated her, Jem, and was afraid of her, but I never wished for her life to end like that. Never could I have conceived of such a horror. After I saw her body, I kept imagining what he said to her. How he tormented her. He is truly a monster. The joy he takes in inflicting terror and pain is unimaginable to me."

"That's the reason I chose to let the infant die with its mother," James said quietly.

Sitting up, Charlotte put her arms around his neck. He seemed suddenly so fragile.

"James, I'm sorry. I…"

He put his finger to her lips.

"I had no authority, Charlotte. He was in command. My moment of power came when I left him to die. My mistake was not killing him when I had the opportunity. I'm not a coward, but I value life, even his, or I did at the time. I will have my second chance, and I intend to see him dead.

"James, lie with me."

"Now?"

"We have so little time, and I'm frightened. Please, be with me."

They undressed as quickly as they could. There was no passion in it, only an urgency to be rid of their clothes and have their bodies touch. They lay between the crisp sheets, warm against each other. Charlotte's body shuddered as she realized they were the same kind of sheets on which Peg had died. She closed her eyes, trying to rid her mind of the bloody scene. She concentrated now on feeling James's skin on hers.

Lying on their sides, he encircled her in his arms and pulled her towards him. Charlotte kissed his neck and shoulders and moved up to face him.

"I love you," she said, her throat tightening.

"My dearest Lottie," he whispered soothingly. "I am so sorry for all this pain. From the moment I saw you, I loved you. I never wanted to hurt you. I only wanted to honour you, to bring you joy." They held onto each other, desiring only this quiet moment in which to close their eyes and feel each other breathe.

At that moment, Peg vanished from between them.

The time was passing swiftly. Emma, John, and Annie would be returning. They rose and dressed, but before they left to go to the parlour, he held her in his arms.

"I promise, we will have some time for happiness in our lives, Charlotte."

She laughed and looked at his beautiful face.

"I have you. We have Jack. I *am* happy, my love."

Emma and John were just entering the house as they came down the stairs. Emma looked ashen. John wore a stern expression, and Annie was nowhere to be seen.

"Dearest, whatever happened?" Charlotte asked, going to Emma.

"Oh, Charlotte, never could I have imagined a hell as horrible as that place, and that's not the worst of it." She looked to John to tell them the rest as she sat down heavily on the settee.

"We've had a message from Hawkes."

"What?!" James shouted.

"There is an evil, emaciated woman who rules the cell

in which Jane is kept. You know the one?" John asked.

"Yes," Charlotte responded. "She knew who I was from the first visit, and she's hounded Jane unmercifully."

"She called me aside when Emma and Annie were speaking to Jane. She could barely hide her glee as she delivered her message. She said, 'Tell Mrs. Audley Pruitt that a friend wishes her to know that the crows and hawks will have Mrs. R's remains, so do not bother with a Christian burial. She'll rise from the ground before midnight.' "

There was a heavy silence in the room. Charlotte's body grew cold, though she was perspiring at the same time.

"That's it, then," James muttered. "We'll take him in the churchyard."

"Oh, James no!" Charlotte cried. "He is the devil. He will kill you both."

"No, Charlotte, he is a man. A man who will confess and hang, I promise you. After that, I will personally see that the hangman tars his body and hangs it in the gibbet to rot."

Emma struggled to her feet and began walking unsteadily towards the door. "I must take to my bed, my dears. I do not presently have the stomach for this discussion." John went to her side to help support her.

"What of Jane's spirits?" Charlotte asked as Emma retreated.

"Low. Very low. She will live through the trial, I daresay. She thanked you for the locket. It was heart-breaking to see her and Annie part." Emma stopped and, supporting herself on the door frame, turned to Charlotte. "She is a noble soul. You are right to stand by her." She exited the room with John's help.

"What does Hawkes want with her body?" Charlotte asked.

"He will sell it to Doctor Urquehart in Mayfair, I imagine."

"They are abominable, all of them. They say they are doctors, but they are not human, James. I heard of one who, for want of a body, cut up his own child who had died. That is the act of a savage!"

Charlotte was in tears. She felt powerless. Jane was innocent and she could do nothing to protect her in life or in death.

"The doctor may try to claim her body after the hanging. You and Annie must be there to fight him. I want Hawkes to come to the cemetery." James spoke quickly and Charlotte could see him forming his strategy. His cold determination frightened her.

"Charlotte, I understand that you feel responsible for Mrs. Rourke's well-being. I share your frustration and your sorrow, but I must put all my attention into trapping Hawkes. His confession means my freedom."

"I will do what needs to be done," Charlotte answered and retreated to their bedchamber. She knew she must speak with Annie, Jenny, and the boys. What could she say?

There are men who want your mother and your uncle dead. There is nothing I can do to stop them. These men have the power to murder in the name of the King.

It all sounded so terrifying!

Charlotte walked slowly to the nursery. Annie was there. Charlotte thought she must have slipped in when she and James were talking to Emma and John. The children were gathered around Annie and Jenny. Ralph and Luke sat on Annie's lap, and she had her arms around them. Duncan was nestled in Jenny's lap, his head on her bosom. Michael and Stephen sat quietly on the floor, heads bowed. Jack sat next to Michael holding his hand.

Charlotte didn't have a chance to say a word. Annie spoke quickly and with determination. "We would all go with you tomorrow to the court session, Mistress Charlotte. All of us want to see Mama and Uncle Patrick. Do not deny us this, please."

"What is your mother's wish, do you think?"

"She asked me to bring the family when I saw her today," Annie said.

"Then we will do as she asked. We'll have to go very early to get in line for the courtroom. I don't know how long we will have to wait, or even if they will be tried tomorrow."

"It doesn't matter, Mistress Charlotte. We will be there until it is decided, if you will allow us," Betsy answered.

All eyes, save Duncan and Jack's, were on Charlotte.

"I will stand with you. You're my family." Charlotte indicated for them all to make a circle with her. "I would offer a prayer to heaven."

Except for the two little ones, they all bowed their heads. "Dear Heavenly Father, please hear our humble supplication. We ask You to give strength to this family. Jane Rourke is a faithful, true servant of Christ. Protect her in her hour of need. Please, spare her life if it is in Your infinite plan."

Charlotte paused when she heard sobs coming from the twins. She continued, "Be with us all. I ask in Your name. Amen."

"Amen," each responded.

They stood, holding hands in silence.

"I love you all," Charlotte said. "Please, eat and get ready for bed. We'll be rising early to go to the Sessions House."

They said their goodnights, and Charlotte kissed Jack, who was now in Annie's arms. Returning to her room, Charlotte said her own private prayer, asking for strength to be a good mother to these children and to Jack. She asked for a blessing on the tortured soul of Peg. Lastly, her most fervent request was for protection for James as he faced Edward Hawkes.

"Dear God, I pray for a legion of angels in this battle. Hawkes is a fiend and will only be vanquished with Your divine help. I pray in Christ's name. Amen."

Charlotte and James held each other as they fell asleep.

Peg's head swung before Charlotte's eyes in her dreams. She sat bolt upright, awake now. As she lay back down to rest, she saw Jane standing at the gallows. Please, give me peace, she beseeched the darkness.

James slept soundly beside her. Finally, with no more than an hour before she needed to rise, Charlotte fell into a fitful sleep.

The noise of the bedchamber door opening woke her. There was a strong smell of dirt and perspiration. It was dark, and terror gripped her.

A voice very near her spoke, "Charlotte?"

"James?" She was barely able to mutter his name, her throat was so constricted.

"Forgive me if I frightened you. I am going out disguised as the beggar."

"Where? Why like this?" she asked groggily.

"It is the best way for me to blend into the crowd outside the Old Bailey and to make the final preparations to meet Hawkes." He lit a candle by the bed so they could see each other.

She was awake now. "I don't believe they will do the hangings so quickly. It's just not done that way," she said, sitting up.

"The government wants to make an example of them. I believe it has been their purpose from the beginning. If I'm wrong, then we'll have more time. Don't acknowledge me in the crowd as you go into the trial. I am sure Hawkes will be there, but I shall be watching. Goodbye, my dearest Lottie." He was out of the room before she could respond.

The trials always began at 6:30 in the morning, so they were all up and dressed by 5:30. Charlotte left Jack and Duncan in the keeping of Emma's housekeeper, Miss Middleton. The other boys, with Betsy and Annie, met Charlotte at the front door. Charlotte thought they must have looked a bleary-eyed group as they loaded into the two carriages that would take them to the Old Bailey.

They met little traffic as they made their way to East London. People were already up and bustling about, however, delivering coal, vegetables, milk, and other goods on this brisk March morning. As they drew close, they passed Fleet Prison and Bridewell. The boys' eyes grew wide at the buildings' brooding exteriors. The carriages turned down the alleyway off Ludgate Street and drew into the Sessions House yard. It was already filled with many of the people who were involved in the day's trials.

Charlotte, Annie, and Betsy herded the boys towards the door to the court. Charlotte paid the doorkeeper the money for them to enter, and they took their seats towards the end of the second row. The jury for the city of London sat on one side of the courtroom and the jury for Middlesex on the other. The judges sat on a high dais in the front of the room.

Prisoners were brought in one by one from a passage connecting Newgate Prison with the Old Bailey. They were placed in the dock where they stood answering questions and listening to the evidence against them. The cases moved quickly with no more than a few minutes for each person accused.

The juries huddled after each case and gave their verdicts without hesitation. Food and drink could be withheld from them if they did not decide with speed. The morning wore on until there was a break for dinner. Charlotte and her group went out into the sessions yard.

Luke, who had been agitated all morning, broke from Annie and ran towards a woman in the crowd calling out, "Mother! Mother!"

Before Charlotte could act, he was hit on the head by a soldier and went sprawling on the cobblestones. She hurried forward to protect him from further attack. She dropped down to shelter him from further blows and to see how badly he was injured. Other soldiers gathered and began shouting at her to move away. She refused to let go of Luke.

The soldiers fell silent and Charlotte looked up to see Thomas Warrender standing over her. He smiled.

Charlotte struggled to help Luke to his feet. "Is the boy hurt, Mrs. Pruitt?"

"No, Lord Chagford. Only stunned and bleeding, I believe."

"Good. Please, try to keep him and the others under control, or I fear Justice Eyre will have you removed from the proceedings."

"Thank you, your lordship."

"Your servant, madam." He turned and walked through the line of soldiers and the crowd, who were gathered to see what was happening. Charlotte held on to Luke's shoulders and guided him in front of her as they returned to their group. Annie wiped blood from the side of his head.

Charlotte watched Thomas as he was joined by several dignitaries from the King's Party, as well as a group of rich drapers and cloth merchants. Taking centre stage with Thomas was Lord and Lady Clanbrassil and Mr. Grout, the master weaver whose looms and silks had been destroyed. It was becoming evident to Charlotte who was behind the rounding up of the Bold Defiance and the framing of Jane Rourke.

Once everyone was almost back in the courtroom, Charlotte looked behind her and saw Thomas enter grandly with his group taking up the last row. She turned forward and focused on the Honourable Sir Thomas Parker, knight and Lord Chief Baron of his Majesty's court of the Exchequer. He was a stern and impressive looking figure as he sat on his high-backed chair and overlooked the room.

Several more trials were heard. Some moved so quickly Charlotte barely had time to understand what the crime was before they moved on to the next. The children were tired and hungry by the time the cases of the seven accused with Patrick and Jane were heard. Each was found guilty of the destruction of Mr. Grout's looms and materials. The monetary amounts established in all seven were just enough to make them hanging offenses. In the absence of the recorder, Sir Thomas read each verdict in a deep and booming voice.

Patrick's case took longer because of the number of charges against him and the evidence that was provided. Letters were produced that linked him with a radical group in Dublin. There was no doubt that money collected by the Bold Defiance from the master weavers was sent on to Ireland. The witnesses against him spoke of his hot temper and his hatred of English authority. When Patrick was allowed to speak, he accepted his guilt with dignity.

"The winds of change are upon us gentlemen. The men and women who toil in East London deserve more from their masters. The rich grow fat off the industry of the poor. My people have a right to decent wages. They have a right to feed and clothe their children from the labour they give you. The colonists in America understand this. Mr. Wilkes understands this. It is time that you, gentleman, understand this as well, or you shall be swept from the face of the earth when those who toil for you rise up and demand their rights."

When Justice Parker realized what was being said, he motioned for Patrick to be taken from the dock. He was pronounced guilty without the jury even making a pretence of deliberation.

The court adjourned for supper to the upper floor of the building. These banquets, Charlotte had been told could go on for some time. Annie and Jenny decided it was best for Jenny to take the boys back to Grosvenor Square. They were all exhausted and hungry. Annie found the carriage waiting nearby and the children with Jenny were soon on their way. Charlotte and Annie decided to head towards a narrow side street in search of a nearby inn and something to eat.

As they walked, Charlotte's eye was drawn to a motley

looking group who had assembled around a man who was repeating Patrick's speech and exhorting the crowd to revolt against their masters, for judgement day, he said, was surely at hand. One beggar leaned on his crutch and listened intently to the speaker until he turned and looked at Annie.

Charlotte realized it was James. She wondered what he thought of Patrick's sentiments, especially now that he himself had fallen from grace and walked among the discarded people of London. Will we, she thought to herself, all be swept away? Will a great flood, not of water, but of people, sweep us from the earth because we refuse to see them as human?

James's gaze fell on Charlotte, but she averted her eyes. She was sure Edward Hawkes was somewhere close at hand and did not want to chance giving James away.

Just as she and Annie began to walk down the side street, Charlotte felt a hand on her arm. She gasped, attempted to pull away, but was held fast. She turned to the aggressor.

Thomas began addressing her. "Excuse me for startling you, Charlotte. I simply wanted to catch you before you left."

"Please, let go of my arm, sir." He did not release her.

"First hear my invitation, dear lady."

"Your invitation?" Charlotte stood tall and did not relax her arm.

"The justices, the Chaplain in Ordinary, a few selected guests, and I are dining together during the recess. Please, I would consider it an honour if you would join us."

"Do you think that quite appropriate given my inclination in this case?"

"Your inclination?" Thomas feigned ignorance and

released his grip.

"Oh, please, Lord Chagford, I'm sure it has not escaped you that I am a friend of Mrs. Rourke, whose case is to be heard presently."

"All the better. Come state your case during supper when everyone is in a jolly mood. Much better to do it there than in the courtroom, I would wager." Charlotte noticed that James in the beggar's guise had moved close to Thomas's back where he began a conversation with an old woman in ragged clothes. She was sure he was listening to Thomas.

"Where is this feast taking place?" Charlotte asked.

"At the Old Bailey, upstairs. It will save you going in search of your meal. Your nursemaid can join the other servants upstairs."

"Annie Rourke accompanies me as my ward and my friend, or we will not be accepting your invitation, Lord Chagford."

He responded disdainfully. "Your ward? My, Mrs. Pruitt, you do make interesting choices in the company you keep."

"So, shall we both be included, or shall we seek our supper somewhere more amenable, your lordship?"

He tilted his head to one side and laughed a little too loudly.

"You will not always get the better of me. You do know that, do you not, dear Charlotte? Come both of you, then, let us raise some venerable eyebrows."

Charlotte glanced over her shoulder at James. His face was full of rage. Had he been a lion, Charlotte imagined, he would have leapt on Thomas and torn him to pieces. He looked at Charlotte, and his expression softened. He gave no warning sign for her to stop, so she proceeded into the building with Thomas leading and Annie at her side. The stairway was dark and narrow, not what she'd expected from such a grand building. Her nostrils were assailed with the smell of roasted meats, strong wine, and ale. Annie followed close behind, not saying a word.

At the top of the stairs, they entered a brightly illuminated great hall. The justices and their invited guests were already eating. Charlotte had rarely seen such a sumptuous feast. It was served *à la française*. There were so many different dishes that the servants were finding it impossible to bring them around the table fast enough for the guests, who were impatiently pointing at the ones they wanted.

When Lord Chagford and his guests entered the room, quiet descended and heads turned in their direction. The ordinary chaplain from Newgate Prison, a well-fed man with a great bulbous nose and thick lips was speaking with Justice Eyre, the Clanbrassils, and another gentleman. He stopped when he noticed Lord Chagford, excused himself from the company, and moved towards the three of them in haste.

"Your lordship, we have been awaiting your arrival. Who are these charming ladies you bring with you?" the ordinary said, smiling at Charlotte and Annie.

"Come, come, Reverend Whitgate, you must know Mrs. Audley Pruitt from her many visits to Newgate," Thomas said.

"Mrs. Pruitt, I am charmed to make your acquaintance. I have had numerous reports of your faithful ministrations to Mrs. Rourke, but sadly for me, I have not had the pleasure of meeting you before this," Reverend Whitgate said as he moved closer to Charlotte than she cared for.

Attempting to step back, Charlotte trod on Annie's toes. The girl quickly moved back to give Charlotte room.

"You are most kind, reverend," Charlotte said. "Yours is a perilous calling. Doing God's work in such a place as Newgate is to be commended."

"Oh, it has its earthly rewards," he said, patting his stomach.

Charlotte took a step to the side and brought Annie forward. "Reverend Whitgate, please let me introduce my ward, Anne Rourke."

"How do you do, Reverend Whitgate," Annie responded quietly.

"Hello, my dear. These are difficult times for you and your family," he said. Annie looked down at the floor.

Charlotte interceded. "Reverend Whitgate, we are here in hopes of persuading the judges of Jane Rourke's innocence." The reverend raised an eyebrow as he turned to Thomas.

"Perhaps, Mrs. Pruitt, you should start with the Clanbrassils and the gentleman speaking with them, or to Mr. Grout over there," Thomas suggested, indicating the master weaver at one of the other tables. "They all, I fear, feel differently about Mrs. Rourke and her compatriots." Thomas smiled at Whitgate as he spoke. The reverend turned from them, trying to hide his amusement.

"My mother is innocent, sirs!" Annie declared, glaring at both the men. Charlotte took her arm.

"We were wrong to come here. Good evening, gentlemen. We will see you when the court resumes." Charlotte turned to go, guiding Annie before her towards the door. Thomas moved quickly to block their exit.

"Please, Mrs. Pruitt, Miss Rourke, do not go. It is awkward, I grant you, but I promised to provide you with supper, and I would not have you go without some repast." He led them to seats at the end of a long table, some distance from Lord and Lady Clanbrassil, who were both watching their progress intently.

Charlotte sat between Thomas and Annie. Reverend Whitgate, who'd skittered away at Annie's outburst, joined them again, sitting next to the girl and engaging her in conversation. Charlotte's anger made her unable to look at Thomas.

Finally, he spoke, "It saddened us all to hear of James's death. Elizabeth was heartbroken." When Charlotte did not respond, he continued, "I owe you my life. He would have killed me, but for your intercession."

"He would have."

"Often in these last few months, I have wondered why you stopped him."

"I wanted no blood on his hands. I wanted him free to prove his innocence."

"Ah, I see. I hoped it was perhaps because you wanted me to live," he purred.

"No, that was not the reason," Charlotte said flatly.

"I'm not the monster you suppose me to be, Charlotte."

"Your behaviour, sir, has led me to believe otherwise."

"I would atone for that, if I could. Perhaps, if you want it, I can help your friend, Mrs. Rourke."

"You would help her, Thomas?" Charlotte looked at him, trying to decide if this was the truth or a lie.

"Let me intercede with the judges. I will even speak with the Clanbrassils. They are not unreasonable, and I am not without influence. I know that Mrs. Rourke is suffering. The gaolers told the ordinary of her piety and kindness to other prisoners. She must miss her children terribly. And to think of never seeing them again, it must be unbearable." His earnestness touched Charlotte. "As you are well aware, I have no children of my own, but I care deeply for Elizabeth's boys. To imagine myself separated in such a way from them is unthinkable."

He was a consummate actor and Charlotte knew this, but still she was moved by his seeming sincerity. His face drew very close to hers. She looked into his eyes and drew back, remembering his attack on her.

"Are you suddenly so selfless that there is no price for your offer?"

He laughed out loud, stood up, and offered Charlotte his arm. She took it and he escorted her to a window overlooking the courtyard. Their backs were to the dinner guests.

"Charlotte, were you taught no manners befitting a lady? You are too blunt, I dare say. But you are beautiful and still young enough to be of interest to me. Since you ask, I will tell you. My offer is this: come to my bed willingly for as long as I want you, and I will give you Jane Rourke's freedom." He smiled and waited for Charlotte's reply.

Her knees went suddenly weak, and her face grew exceedingly hot. He held her by the elbow and whispered in her ear. "Supper will be done quite soon. I need your answer quickly if I am to act."

Sir Rufus's bloodied face flashed into her mind's eye. Momentarily, she was back in the bedchamber at Scorhill Hall. The old man dying on the floor, James, in a rage, lunging at Thomas, wanting to kill him, her clothes torn and a searing pain in her side. Charlotte looked at Thomas, now in this room and it became clear to her that this proposal was the culmination of his plan. He had fabricated the case against Jane Rourke, so he could force her into his bed.

"No, I will not do it," Charlotte said without emotion.

He moved closer to her, holding tightly to her arm. "Give me the daughter, then."

"What?" she asked, not understanding his meaning.

He looked towards Annie. "She is a virgin, is she not? Give her to me, and you can have Mrs. Rourke's freedom."

Charlotte was sickened by the thought of his body pressing down on Annie's frail form. The air around her became permeated by his lust. Pulling away from him, Charlotte lurched towards the table as if in a nightmare. Grabbing Annie by the hand, she did not even acknowledge the ordinary who was in the process of advancing on the girl. Charlotte pulled Annie behind her like a small child. They met no resistance as they fled through the door and down the stairs. The cold air hit them as they opened the door to the outside. Charlotte's eyes searched in vain for a glimpse of James.

Annie's confusion matched her own. "Mistress Charlotte, what is it? What has happened?

"Thomas Warrender is an evil man, Annie. He and the people in the room mean to murder your mother, and I am powerless to stop it." Charlotte took her by the shoulders and looked into her brown eyes. "She is innocent, I know that. We must pray to God for her deliverance."

"We should go to the church," Annie suggested. "Do we have time before Judge Eyre and the others come back, do you think?" The corners of Annie's mouth turned down and tears came to her eyes.

"We do. They have just begun to eat. They will take their time, I warrant." They walked from the courtyard and covered the brief distance to St. Sepulchre's door in a matter of minutes. Thankfully, the sanctuary was open, and candles were burning. They were alone as they sat and prayed silently. Charlotte put her arm around Annie's shoulders while the girl wept.

"I will take care of you, Annie, and your sister and brothers. We will be a family. I promise you."

"Oh, Mistress Charlotte, I would do anything for my mother. God took my father, and I tried to accept it as His will, but this is too horrible. My brothers need their mother, especially Duncan. He's still a baby. You are so kind to take us all in, but what will we do if Mama dies?"

She got up and walked to the front of the church. Kneeling on the steps to the altar, she closed her eyes and began to pray. Charlotte sat in the pew, unable to think. Out of the corner of her eye she caught movement in the shadows to her left. She looked more closely and saw James behind a pillar, out of Annie's view. She walked quietly over to him. Speaking in the softest of whispers, Charlotte told James what transpired with Thomas. He listened, stone-faced.

His reply was simply, "I should have killed him."

"Please, do not bring God's wrath down on your head. Perhaps I should tell Annie what Thomas wanted from her."

"No! He will have you both, and then murder Jane Rourke for spite. He is a madman, Charlotte, exactly like Hawkes, but with money and power. Listen to me, protect yourself and the children. He has Mrs. Rourke trapped in his net. Do not be swept up into it as well. Take the children and flee to Cumberland. I will follow as soon as I dispatch Hawkes."

"I will not abandon Jane. I cannot." Charlotte looked up at James's face, her eyes pleading for some better answer.

Annie started to stand but did not look in Charlotte's direction. James backed into the shadows. Charlotte was bewildered. She had not finished her exchange with him. His inability to understand her loyalty to Mrs. Rourke angered and frustrated her.

Charlotte and Annie returned through the courtyard and entered into the courtroom just as the jury was filing in. Charlotte recognized the man who had been talking to the Clanbrassils at supper. He was introduced to the court as Sir Thomas Harley, Knight Lord Mayor of the City, and presiding justice for Jane's trial. He was joined by Sir Richard Aston, Knight and Justice of his Majesty's Court of the King's Bench, other justices and James Eyre, the recorder.

The trial took all of ten minutes. People were tired, and in a hurry to get home. The court read out the charges. "Jane Rourke stands accused in the theft of eight silver goblets from the house of Lord and Lady Clanbrassil on the date of February the fifth of this year, as well as harbouring members of the Bold Defiance in her own house."

Witnesses from Jane's neighbourhood told of the comings and goings of the Bold Defiance members. They told of seeing Jane bid them goodbye, sending them away with packets of food after late night suppers. Then, the testimony on the theft of the silver began. The downstairs maid in charge of the goblets was the first to give evidence. She began her testimony.

"I am Mary Penny, servant to Lord and Lady Clanbrassil. I was at my master's house the day Jane Rourke came with the fabric for her ladyship. I brought in the eight goblets and set them on the table to put them away. Lovely, silver goblets they were, just newly polished. I was called to do another chore just as the butler, Mr. Newby told Jane Rourke to wait for her ladyship in the dining room. When I came back, not a half an hour later, the goblets were gone and so was Jane Rourke."

The butler was the next to speak. "I am Richard Newby, butler to Lord and Lady Clanbrassil. I live at their residence and have been in service there for fifteen years. On February fifth, Jane Rourke came with a delivery of silk fabric for her ladyship's approval. She came to the servant's entrance, but her ladyship asked me to bring her into the dining room because she was busy preparing for a dinner party that evening. Lady Clanbrassil had no sooner sat down to look at the fabric when she was called away to check another detail for that evening. She asked me, as she went into the hallway, to tell Mrs. Rourke to wait in the dining room. I did so and, having other duties, went about my business."

Mr. Newby went on to say that Mary Penny reported the missing goblets after Mrs. Rourke left. He gave the value of the goblets which was very dear.

The two character witnesses for Jane were called. Both attested to her honesty and charity, but Charlotte noted the jurors were yawning. Justice Harley shifted in his seat. The jurors brought in a quick verdict of guilty on both counts. The court did not adjourn as was normal. Instead, Justice Harley called for Patrick Rourke and the other members of the Bold Defiance already convicted to be brought back to the courtroom. They had been kept in the hallway during Jane's trial, so they were readily handy. All stood with their wrists and ankles shackled as the Justice Harley sentenced them to death by hanging at Tyburn two days hence.

Annie hastened to the bail dock where Jane Rourke stretched out her shackled hands to touch her daughter. Charlotte caught Reverend Whitgate before he exited the courtroom.

"Sir, please, I beseech you to allow Jane Rourke to stay in the keeper's apartment for the night. Do not allow the gaolers to take her to the cell for the condemned."

"Mrs. Pruitt, as much as I would like to oblige, I have no power…"

"I will pay whatever is asked, Reverend Whitgate, though I understand it is out of your hands."

"Mrs. Pruitt, you are truly a saintly woman to care so deeply for Mrs. Rourke. I shall attempt to make arrangements."

"Thank you, Reverend Whitgate, you are too kind."

In no time and for a goodly sum, Charlotte, Annie, and Jane found themselves in one of the keeper's rooms. Mother and daughter sat by the fireside, holding onto each other. Charlotte crossed to the four mullioned windows that looked out onto the street in front of Newgate. There was a knock at the door and Reverend Whitgate entered.

"Mrs. Pruitt," he began, "Lord Chagford would see you if you have a moment to spare."

"Where is he?"

"At the Sessions House, in chambers off the banqueting hall."

"I will go to him. Please, look after Mrs. Rourke's needs."

"I shall."

Charlotte turned to Annie and Jane. They sat side by side. Jane's head rested on her daughter's shoulder. They were rocking ever so slightly. Annie's eyes were closed, her mouth tight. Jane stared straight ahead, her cheeks wet.

"I must leave for a short time. The ordinary has promised to see that you have what you need."

Jane's eyes rose to meet hers. "My freedom?"

Reverend Whitgate spoke. "Let us pray for that miracle, Mrs. Rourke. Please, will you pray with me?" She looked at him and nodded her head.

Leaving the room, Charlotte was able to exit the prison through the keeper's door. It was a short walk to the Sessions House in the cold spring night. St. Sepulchre's bell rang the hour, causing a shiver to run down Charlotte's back. The cold fog surrounded her as it rolled over the city. Perhaps James would see her, she thought, and stopped to look around. She saw no one. The crowd from the trials had dispersed. The smell from Smithfield Market assailed her nose as it came in waves. It was a sharp, fetid scent of dung and rotting meat.

"Please, let me close my eyes and be at Whitestone," she prayed.

Reaching the dark staircase, she had run down only a short time before, she saw a dim light at the top. She knew Thomas was up there, waiting like a spider. She imagined him sitting, smiling to himself about how he had caught her. Yet the verdict was pronounced, and the sentence given, what could he do now? A heaviness overtook her feet. The thought of his touch reviled her, but how could she watch Jane hang, knowing she had the opportunity to save her?

When Charlotte mounted the last stair, she peered into

the dimly lit hall. It was empty, but there was a door ajar to an antechamber beyond where a light was burning. He would make her come to him. Beginning to shake, she halted, feeling unsteady and hungry. She desperately needed time to close her eyes and think, but there was no time.

No one came out from the other room. There was no sound. Perhaps he is gone, Charlotte thought.

"Sir Thomas?" she called in an unsteady voice. "It is I, Charlotte Pruitt, come to see you."

Still there was no sound, no answer. Her stomach growled, and she realized the extent of her hunger. She smelled food, roasted meat and potatoes. Her mouth watered. Charlotte's hunger drove her forward. She moved towards the door. Peeking in, she saw the table was set for two. She turned to leave but stopped.

A small voice in her head told her, *"No one is here, eat a bite and then you can go."* The voice won, and she went to the table. Standing, she began to eat. It was delicious; roast duck, pudding, and potatoes. She heard an intake of breath and froze.

He spoke from a dark corner of the room, "I was so sorry to see you go earlier, but I'm glad you have reconsidered. Will you do me the honour of sitting down at my table, Mrs. Pruitt?"

Charlotte stood with her mouth half full. Thomas laughed softly. Charlotte felt ridiculous.

"Do swallow, or you will choke. I would hate to be accused of murdering you."

Charlotte turned to leave.

"Stop!" he commanded. "You will not run away again."

She managed to get the food down her throat. "I will leave, if I wish," she said defiantly.

129

"If you do, there will not be another opportunity for reprieve."

"Is there one now?"

"I would like to talk to you about the possibility of it over supper, in a civilized manner. Will you join me?" he asked as he lit a candle, illuminating the table where he sat. His eyes were fixed on her.

She turned to face him but did not move to sit down.

"Thomas, why are you doing this? Why destroy Jane Rourke? She means nothing to you."

"She's your friend."

"I don't understand."

"For some reason, you feel a loyalty to her. Why, I do not understand. Be that as it may, my aim is simply to make you feel as powerless as you and James, God rest his soul, made me feel in Devon. An eye for an eye, as they say."

"You attacked me."

"You needed to be more accommodating. Perhaps father and son would still be with us if you had not chosen to put up such a fuss. You are much too wilful, Charlotte, but then, that presents a challenge, I suppose."

Charlotte's stomach twisted in a knot. His self-assurance was detestable, but she needed to know if he could still aid Jane.

"What can you do at this late hour? The verdict is passed. She is found guilty and will hang."

"A royal pardon is still possible, albeit more difficult to attain. The price now will be much dearer."

"What you ask is already impossible."

"Why did you return then?"

"Thomas, you cannot be such a monster. You cannot destroy Jane Rourke simply for spite."

"Her life or death means nothing to me, except, of course, how they affect you, dear Charlotte."

There was little else she could say to him. What price he meant to extract she would ask, but she thought of James. If she gave herself to Thomas would James ever forgive her, she wondered?

Would he understand that Jane's life was the prize she sought to win? She wanted to believe that once Thomas got what he wanted he would give Jane her liberty. How could it be otherwise?

"Now that the task of freeing Jane is more difficult, what would you ask of me?"

He let the silence fall for several seconds. He leaned forward, beckoning her to come closer to him. She did not move.

"I would suggest that you begin by obeying me."

"I am not yet under your command, sir. Speak your terms, and I will make my decision."

He sat up, clasped his hands in front of him on the table. His tone was perfunctory. "Very well, you will begin by giving yourself to me now, freely and without hesitation. I want you to do whatever I ask. If you do, I will obtain a stay of execution for your friend and request a royal audience.

"During that time, you will come and be a guest at my house. You will attend to my needs there, and when I go out publicly you will accompany me." He finished and sat back to see her reaction.

"What about Elizabeth?"

"She is in the country. You should be overjoyed that I want to be seen with you. It will bring you a good bit of royal business, I would wager. Both for Pruitt and Byrd and for you, personally."

Charlotte's stomach tightened on hearing his terms. She did not know if she was capable of intimacy with him. How could she not cry out, caught up in his arms with his flesh against hers? St. Sepulchre's bells tolled the hour and Charlotte saw the image of Jane Rourke torn from Annie's arms and carried through the mob to Tyburn's gallows.

With this in her head, she almost spoke out and agreed to his terms. She stopped short when James's face appeared before her. The look of betrayal in his eyes stabbed her in the heart. To give herself to this man, to go about publicly with him would drive James from her forever. She could not delude herself about that.

"What stops you, Charlotte? Is it such a difficult decision? I am a gentle lover when not driven to take what I want. Your beauty first attracted me, but your wilfulness is your most alluring quality, like a fine horse to be broken." He sensed that he was winning. He stood up, his shadow looming behind him. He was wearing a long, quilted, dressing gown. It made him appear tall and more ominous as he reached his hand out to her. "Please, do sit down. Enjoy the meal before it grows cold."

Charlotte came and sat at his command. She looked into his face. His wig was off, and his dark hair fell over his forehead. His dark eyebrows gave him a brooding look, but his face was not unpleasant. Charlotte could not help thinking of him as a spider. She was becoming entangled in the web he was spinning, and she couldn't think beyond the mouthful of food she took to her lips.

He poured wine for them both and sat down. Raising his glass, he proposed a toast. "To your acceptance of my proposal. It will definitely be to our mutual benefit."

She touched the stem of her goblet but did not lift it to her lips. The silver caught the candlelight gleaming in the darkness. I am lost, she thought. Only the shining surface kept her from losing consciousness.

Finally, she managed a whisper, "To our agreement." She could not bring herself to meet his eyes. She waited for his advance, but none came. Instead he laughed a long, low laugh.

"You will waste away to nothing if you do not eat, dear Charlotte. I have some arrangements to tend to if I am to hold off Jane Rourke's meeting with the sheriff's picture frame. I shall not be long. Do make yourself at home. I took the liberty of sending word to Lady Emma that you will be detained. I am sure she will be relieved to know that all is well when she bids goodnight to your brood. Come now, stand and kiss me for my services."

Charlotte stood, and he moved to grasp her around the waist with one arm and with the other hand reached down her dress front and cupped her breast. His tongue thrust in her mouth and he pulled her towards him. She was unable to move, her body frozen. He let go, appearing to be satisfied with her acquiesce.

"That's a good girl," he purred and bit at her neck. He put on his wig, his cocked hat, and his coat ready to go out into the chill night air. "I do expect that you will be here when I return. I would hate to have gotten dressed for nothing. It would make me most unhappy." He smiled and touched the tip of his hat and left through the banquet hall.

Charlotte heard his steps echoing down the stairs.

He had sent a note to Emma. What a fool she was to imagine she had power in this game. Her appetite was gone. She took a mouthful of wine and spat it back into the goblet. She shuddered to think of his hands on her. In a melancholy humour, she sought refuge at the window seat, pressing her forehead against the cold glass of the window. I could throw myself to the cobblestones below, she thought. She imagined herself falling onto some passer-by.

What a horrible muddle I have made of my life. Her eye was caught by movement in the torch lit courtyard below. It was James! She was sure of it. She threw herself onto the floor. Oh, dear God, what have I done? I will lose him forever when he finds out what I have agreed to.

Wild with panic, she grabbed her cape and descended the stairs. She must hide. That was her only thought. She did not know where to go, but she could not let James find her.

As she hit the last step in the darkness, just before the exit outside, she felt herself grabbed from both sides and a hand clasped over her mouth. Struggling was pointless, as she was dragged outside and into an alleyway. She saw three men, the two that held her and one who walked ahead with a torch. She was dwarfed in their midst and their rough clothes chaffed her face. Pushed against the side of a building, her head smarted where it hit the stones. She looked up into James's angry face.

"What the hell are you doing here, Charlotte?"

"Jem?" was all she could manage to say. Her head was swimming. The other two men had dropped her arms, but they remained looming next to her.

"Why are you here with him?" James spit his words at her. His eyes held a madness she had not seen since Devon.

"I needed to talk to him. Jane is desperate. I must help her, or she will hang. Please, Jem, you have to understand." Out of the corner of her eye, she realized the man to her left was the African she had seen before. She turned to the right and there stood the Jew. She could not make sense of it. They were friends of Edward Hawkes. She had seen them with him and now they were here, companions of James. Her James, she thought, who presently appeared to be a madman.

"James, you must let me go. Yes, I have made a bargain with Warrender, but I have to do this. I cannot let Jane hang. Giving him what he wants is the only means to her freedom."

"And what is he demanding?"

"I think you can imagine," she said looking at him for understanding.

"If you do what he demands, you are a whore, madam. You will have thrown away your honour." He took a step back from her. His disdain for her was palpable.

"Jem, do not say that, please. Save me. Save us all. What would you have me do?"

"Honour is all we have to separate us from animals. Honour, madam."

"No, we have our lives. Jane Rourke has her life, but she will lose it, if I do not act. You can offer me nothing more than the word 'honour'? Where was your honour when you slept with Peg?"

James said nothing. She looked from the African to the Jew. "Who are these men to you? She stepped towards James, trying to touch him, but he moved away. "James, listen to me. I saw them with Hawkes. I told you that."

The two did not come at her as she expected them to do. They said nothing in response to her accusation. James appeared not to have heard her words. He began to walk away.

"Did you hear me?" she cried to his back. "They were with Hawkes. I am sure of it."

James turned to her. "These men are my friends. I have no doubt of their loyalty." He continued walking away.

"James, please, do not go. I do love you. Do not abandon me!" she pleaded, but he did not turn to look at her. The two men passed by her without a glance and joined up with him.

"You have made your choice, Charlotte Pruitt. I am not your saviour," he said, as he threw the torch to the ground, and they disappeared into the gathering mist and the dark.

Stunned, she leaned against the rock wall. What to do next, she did not know. Suddenly, shouting and scuffling was heard from the far side of the courtyard. A man's loud screams pierced the air. Terrified, Charlotte inched along the wall and peeked out in the direction of the fray. She could see little, only forms in the fog illuminated by the few torches. Quickly, she ran back up the stairs and into the antechamber. Looking down, out of the window, she was able to make out two men lying prone and unmoving, a third was writhing in pain on the ground.

This last was attended by another man, while two more stood, swords drawn, ready for another attack. They were peering out into the darkness beyond the small circle of light. Charlotte opened one of the windows a crack to see if she could hear the voices more clearly.

She was unable to suppress a cry when she heard one of the men say, "Sir Thomas, do not move. You bleed, sir. We will move you as soon as we are sure the brigands have retreated."

Oh, my dear God, Thomas, she thought. Charlotte shouted out the window to the men below, "What happened? Who is down there?"

The reply came swiftly. "The Earl of Chagford was attacked. He is badly wounded."

"Bring him upstairs, if you are able. I will attend to him," Charlotte said. They hesitated, not sure what to do. "Quickly, bring him! Do you hear me!?"

The urgency in her voice roused them from their stupor, and the three gently lifted Thomas and carried him inside and up the stairs. Charlotte met them and saw they were wearing the earl's livery. She guided them into the antechamber. They lay him on the settee in the dark corner and stepped back. The arms of the man who supported Thomas's shoulders and back were covered in blood. Thomas groaned; his face distorted by pain.

"Go summon a doctor," Charlotte ordered the one who had answered her from below. To another, she said, "Quickly, get the ordinary from Newgate. He is a friend of Lord Chagford and will know what should be done." When they were gone, she turned to the third to ask him what happened.

"Lord Chagford sent a man ahead to call for the carriage. We went out to meet his lordship, but just as we got to him, he was turning back. Said he had forgotten something in the Sessions House and would get it himself. We all accompanied him because of the lateness of the hour and the rogues that are about. Just as we got to the courtyard, we were set upon by a dozen men, at least. It was as if they'd descended out of the air. We never heard them until they were upon us. Like avenging angels out of the sky, they were."

Charlotte shuddered, thinking of the look of madness in James's eyes, only moments before the attack. Thomas began to moan. She sat beside him in a chair and held his hand. Suddenly, his eyes opened, and he looked at her.

"Charlotte," he whispered, "may God have mercy on my soul. The boys…" His grip tightened on her hand as a wave of pain washed over him. He lost consciousness and his hand relaxed. She held it still.

The ordinary hurried in, and on seeing Thomas, exclaimed, "Oh, my dear Jesus! Mrs. Pruitt, they told me he had been attacked, but I did not come expecting such a scene of carnage. Who could have done this?"

"The footman swears it was angels, Reverend Whitgate."

"I beg your pardon." He looked at her, wide-eyed.

"They neither saw nor heard anything before they were set upon," Charlotte explained.

"Oh, I see," he paused to put his thoughts in order. "The lord mayor is summoned. We shall put every effort into finding the perpetrators. I must send a messenger to Lady Chagford directly. I know she would wish to be at her husband's side at such a time." He stopped, not quite sure of Charlotte's relationship to the earl, and smiled weakly. "Though, I am sure Sir Thomas feels well cared for with you present, dear lady."

"Thank you, sir. I think I shall retire to pray at St. Sepulchre's, if you will excuse me. After that, I shall be at Lady Emma Bosworth-Fuller's house if you need to send word to me." Charlotte gently released Thomas's hand and stood. He groaned and opened his eyes.

"Charlotte, the fire in my back, make it cease. I am so cold, but the fire burns." He became more agitated. "Do not let me burn in hell, Charlotte. Save me!" He grabbed her arm and pulled her down. She nearly fell over on top of him, but the ordinary caught her and helped her sit in the chair next to Thomas.

"The doctor is coming. Please, try to stay quiet," Charlotte urged. She rested her hand on his cheek, and he closed his eyes. His breathing was shallow and fast. Charlotte noticed her fingers looked dark next to the pallor of his skin.

As the ordinary began to pray, "Almighty God, the giver of all things…" Charlotte said her own prayer, asking for the strength to face the next two days. She beseeched the Lord's guidance in helping the children with the loss of their mother. As she finished, so did the ordinary. Not long after, the doctor arrived, a self-important man who wanted all to clear away so he could assess the earl's condition.

Charlotte took her leave just as Thomas Harley, the lord mayor, and several other well-dressed gentlemen entered the antechamber. She was sure her presence would not be missed.

Slipping out into the cold night air, she took a deep breath. Now, she could smell the river instead of the stockyards. The wind was shifting, but the fog still clung to the ground.

Charlotte was filled with rage. Who else but James could have attacked Thomas? She hated James, hated him completely. Her face contorted with rage, and she slammed shut the heavy wooden door to the Sessions House courtyard with all the strength she could muster. The sound echoed off the walls and up into the dark night air.

As she walked past the place where Thomas was attacked, she felt for one awful moment that she was not alone. She looked behind her quickly and from side to side, but there was no one. It did not stop her from moving with great haste back to the keeper's door at Newgate. Her pounding of the door knocker soon brought an answer, and she was admitted without argument.

Charlotte found Jane fast asleep with her head in her daughter's lap. Annie sat looking down at her mother as she stroked her hair.

On seeing Charlotte, she asked, "Mistress, is there any news?"

"Annie, all hope, I am afraid is extinguished. Lord Chagford, who might have given us some aid, has been badly wounded. Even if he recovers, it will not be in time to help."

"Poor Sir Thomas. I am sure Mistress Elizabeth will be very distressed."

"Yes, she will. I need to return to Lady Emma's and see how Jenny and your brothers are faring. I will bring them all first thing in the morning. Will you be comfortable, do you think?"

"Yes, Mistress Charlotte, I'm just so cold. I cannot seem to get warm." Almost inaudibly, she said, "I don't know how to comfort my mother." Seeing Annie touching her mother's face tenderly gave Charlotte the answer.

"Hold her fast in your arms, Annie. Rest assured, your being here is the greatest comfort you can render."

Charlotte left in despair. What comfort could be given? They were all trapped now as the hours rolled on. Charlotte roused the carriage driver, and they headed back to Grosvenor Square. Arriving at the house, Charlotte entered her bedchamber without encountering anyone from the household. She intended to sit on her bed for only a few minutes. Once seated, however, sleep overtook her.

She was in the sessions yard. The night mist swirled

around her. Torches still burned. Charlotte approached the entrance to the building. Going up the steps, she stood for a moment. Anger overtook her. She opened the heavy door wide and in a blind rage she gave the door a furious swing shut. It shattered, breaking from its hinges. The sound echoed off each stone in the courtyard. She covered her ears and rushed down the steps and across the yard. But now, it took much longer than before. The dark alley at the end of the block took on the shape of a giant, black cave that grew and diminished in size. Finally, reaching it, she was engulfed in its darkness as if imprisoned in a cage.

A whisper came from behind her, "Is the earl dispatched to heaven?" Her stomach sank, and her flesh became ice cold. She took two steps forward, trying to get her back against the wall. She could see nothing in the darkness. The cold mist covered her face and ran into her eyes. "I missed you at your house. You have no idea how anger feeds violence. You are a gentle creature, or at least I thought you were."

Charlotte said nothing. At last she pressed her palms against the cold stone and turned to face the voice. She was trying not to lose consciousness.

"But perhaps you do know something of anger. You certainly put a great deal of power into destroying the door. I have not given you a chance to show your real strength. Perhaps now is a perfect opportunity."

Charlotte still chose not to speak.

"I can see you. The darkness is not your ally. Are you angry because I interfered with your tryst? The earl is a greedy man. He does not like to pay his debts. I was tired of asking. If your passion is seeking an outlet, I will avail myself. I have lodgings over in Cow Cross. I insist you join me."

Charlotte began to inch along the wall towards the Old Bailey Street. If she could reach the keeper's door at Newgate, he would not capture her. She prayed for deliverance. There were three footsteps behind her and a loud crack that resounded off the walls. No words, no further sounds came forth from the darkness. Charlotte ran. There was no pursuer. She crossed the street and knocked madly on the keeper's door. A sleepy gaoler could not seem to get it unlocked. At last, he managed to get the door ajar. On seeing who it was, he motioned for her to enter and returned to his resting place without any further acknowledgment.

CHAPTER SEVEN

Charlotte woke with a start, and was confronted by a small, smiling face.

"I love you, Mama," came the sweet voice. "You wake now?" He laid his head on her pillow and looked into her eyes.

"Yes, Jackie, Mama is awake." She put her arms around his little body.

He pointed out the window.

"Sun!" he shouted as he escaped from her and threw himself off the bed.

He rushed into the light. The warm spring sun streamed in, and Jack's hair burst into a brilliant gold. She forgot every care as she watched him. When she could stand it no longer, she leapt from the bed and grabbed him up in her arms. They danced; his arms held tight around her neck. He laughed with abandon as they circled the room. Charlotte paused only to wind the music box, as Jack stood on the desk, still clutching her around the neck. A mad tarantella began to play, and she hopped, skipped, and bounced him around the room. Finally, out of breath, Charlotte was forced into a slow glide as the music wound down and died.

There was a knock on the door. It was Mrs. Middleton, Emma's housekeeper. Charlotte bade her enter. Jack, she said, had begged to come in earlier, and after crawling into her bed, had fallen asleep at her side. She asked Charlotte's pardon for allowing him in. Charlotte thanked her for honouring his request. She inquired about the other children. They were all sleeping, she said, except for Jenny, who had been up for some time, pacing the parlour.

"They came home last night, wet and tired. They looked like street urchins, Mrs. Pruitt. They are well-behaved children, but so sad and confused."

"And tomorrow will find them much sadder indeed, Mrs. Middleton. The jury found Mrs. Rourke guilty, and she is sentenced to hang."

"Oh, dear sweet Jesus!" she exclaimed. "Begging your pardon, Mrs. Pruitt."

"Please, Mrs. Middleton, I share your sentiment." Charlotte grabbed up Jack as he trotted by and held him, though he struggled to break free. "If you would be so kind as to send Jenny to me, I must get our morning organized. Please, allow me to tell her of her mother's plight."

"Of course, Mrs. Pruitt, I do not wish to be the bearer of that news."

"Nor do I, Mrs. Middleton, but unfortunately, I shall have to be the one." Charlotte held Jack and rocked him. He became restless, so she released him to explore the corners of the room.

Jenny knocked and Charlotte asked her to enter. Her eyes were red, and Charlotte soon determined she had already heard the news. It seemed the carriage driver told the maids who passed it on to Jenny as soon as she came downstairs.

"Is there no hope now, Mistress Charlotte?" she asked as she sat down next to Charlotte at her desk.

"None, dear Jenny," Charlotte said, taking hold of her hands. The girl looked away, her eyes wide and blinking. Freeing her hand from Charlotte's grasp, she stood slowly. Walking with unsteady steps, she reached the curtains, buried her face in the fabric, and began to sob.

Before Charlotte could reach her, Jack, hearing her distress, looked up and ran full speed to her aid. He threw his little arms around her knees and held fast. She nearly toppled over with this embrace. Charlotte pried him loose as Jenny slid down the wall and sat, crying. Jack began to howl, trying to get to Jenny.

Charlotte was nearly ready to join them both when Mrs. Middleton knocked. Quickly assessing the situation, she took Jack and exited the room. Charlotte coaxed Jenny to her feet and got her to sit on a chair. After a few minutes, the girl attempted to control her tears. Charlotte decided they must move forward.

"We will go to see your mother today. Will you go get your brothers dressed and fed? We should leave as soon as possible."

"Yes, mistress."

Before Jenny could rise, Charlotte took hold of her hand tightly and looked into her eyes.

"Jenny, I shall do my best to take care of you all, I promise. However, I need your help if I am to succeed."

"You shall have it, Mistress Charlotte."

"Thank you, Jenny."

As the girl left, Charlotte thought to call her back. She wanted to ask Jenny to address her as Charlotte, then she stopped, confused. What should they call me the day after tomorrow, she wondered? I will be their guardian, but no replacement for their mother. God help me with what is to come. And what of Annie? Jack adored her, but she was to be his sister now and not his nursemaid. Charlotte wanted to give all of them proper education, so they might flourish in their new lives. They would not suffer want; she knew that. Yet, these next few months would be sorrowful.

James could suffer the torments of hell for all Charlotte cared. He had taken away the only hope for Jane's salvation. Honour be damned, Charlotte thought. Her dreams wished it to be Hawkes, but who else but James could have perpetrated the attack on Thomas? Yes, he had walked the other way with his new friends, but he could have assembled a gang of rogues to attack Thomas when he returned from the King. Thomas simply walked into the trap early.

After she readied herself, Charlotte asked Mrs. Middleton to arrange with the cook for both a dinner and a supper that might be taken along to Newgate. Jenny got the children dressed and downstairs, where they were fed breakfast, while Charlotte called for the carriage. These next few days, she thought, would be devoted to Jane and her children. Jenny carried Duncan and rode inside with Michael, Ralph, and Charlotte. The two older boys, Luke and Stephen, rode solemnly on top with the driver. Two of Emma's footmen rode outside on the back of the carriage. Everyone looked pale and tired. No words were exchanged along Oxford Street and High Holborn. They crossed the Fleet Canal, and as they neared Newgate, St. Sepulchre's carillon rang the quarter hour. Charlotte closed her eyes and bit her lip. Tomorrow, the bells would ring for Jane.

They found Annie and Jane just outside the keeper's entrance with a goaler guarding them. Jane was walking in circles. Annie stood, her arms crossed, watching her mother. As the group approached, the boys broke from Charlotte and raced to their mother. She held them to her and sank onto the cold cobblestones. They piled onto her, unable to satisfy their desire to touch her body and smell her scent. Annie and Jenny joined in on either side of their mother. Their behaviour was more subdued than the boys', but their need was as great.

When at last she was able to catch her breath, Jane looked at each of their expectant faces, "My angels, I have done nothing wrong. Of this, I want you to be certain. Please, tell Duncan this when he is old enough to comprehend."

They interrupted her with, "Mama, please," and, "of course."

She continued on, "I can do nothing now to save my life. But, please, all of you pray that our Lord will be waiting at the gates of heaven to take me to his bosom. Papa will be there, and we will watch over you, each of you. I love you all, my dear ones."

Here, she broke down, and with Duncan in her lap, she grasped all their hands. Her head rested on the great pile of little hands. At last, she raised her face towards the heavens. "I fear I may be a little mad, my dears, but I have decided that tomorrow I will carry Duncan with me to Tyburn."

They stared at her, faces reflecting their shock.

She continued on, "The rest of you must stay at Lady Emma's house. I do not wish you to remember me in the midst of this bloodthirsty spectacle. My last wish, Charlotte, will be that you retrieve Duncan from me as we arrive at the gallows."

Charlotte looked at Jane, realizing that she already had passed over. Tomorrow, her body would fight for its last breath, but her spirit was already on its homeward journey.

"I will speak with the ordinary and make all the arrangements necessary," Charlotte replied.

"I have spoken to him already, and he has agreed. I will ride in the cart and sit on my coffin, but I will go to my death with my head held high. I am innocent. All of you, my dear ones, when you are old enough to leave London, I pray you do so. Go far away, to Ireland, to France, to the Colonies, to the wilderness. Find a place, a far outpost, where only God will be your judge."

The clouds began to gather overhead and threatened rain. Charlotte urged Jane to move everyone back into the keeper's room. She agreed. The family moved as one group. Charlotte followed behind. Each child had hold of their mother and would not let go. When they were inside, they again sat on the floor and held tight to one another. Charlotte knew they would be getting hungry, so she excused herself and went to the coach where the food was waiting. She instructed the footmen to take the basket to the keeper's room and wait for further instructions.

Needing to be alone and put order to her thoughts, Charlotte walked down Old Bailey Street. She turned left on Ludgate and faced St. Paul's Cathedral. Her eyes were always drawn to its great dome when she passed near. Sometimes, she would try and imagine the fire that swept the city and burned this great edifice to the ground. It arose from the ashes, more beautiful than before, like the legendary phoenix.

Tomorrow, Charlotte thought, will be my conflagration. Standing at the bottom of the steps of St. Paul's, she began a silent prayer. Dear God, help me to rise from the sorrow and terror I face in the morning. Help me to serve these children of Jane Rourke well. Please, take her soul unto Your bosom. Charlotte could not continue, her throat began to hurt so badly, as if someone unseen was pressing their thumbs into her windpipe. She walked up the steps and into the church where she sat down and wept.

When Charlotte returned to the keeper's room, Annie told her that the family wished to stay together that night. She asked Charlotte to come for them in the morning before the sermon the ordinary would deliver to the prisoners bound for Tyburn tree. Charlotte promised she would be there. As she was leaving the building, Reverend Whitgate caught up with her and asked her to come with him to Sir Thomas's bedside. He remained at the Sessions House, being in too grave a condition to be moved.

Charlotte dreaded seeing Thomas but agreed to go with Reverend Whitgate. They walked in silence through the sessions yard, their footsteps echoing off the stones of the street. Charlotte's dream came back to her, and she shuddered at the thought of Edward Hawkes. Was he truly a human being or a force from hell? A flock of crows were in the yard and took flight with a great cawing and flapping of wings as the two passed through.

They reached the door and went up the stairs. She followed Reverend Whitgate, her feet once again getting heavier and heavier with every step. The antechamber was dark when they entered, the draperies had been drawn. The doctor attending Thomas greeted the ordinary and Charlotte with hushed tones and bade the servants to let a little daylight in the room. A bed had been brought in for Thomas to lay on.

He moaned and Charlotte crossed to his bedside. He was feverish, his brow wet with perspiration. His dark hair matted on his forehead and stood in stark contrast with his pale face.

"The blade fell very near his heart, I fear. It did not reach that vital organ; else he would not be with us now." The doctor told the ordinary, who listened intently and responded with small intakes of air to show his concern.

Charlotte took Thomas's hand and held it in both of hers. Would he slip away, she wondered, or would his desire for power and mastery keep him in this life? He seemed so fragile now that she could not help but care for him. He stirred a little and moaned again.

"Thomas," she whispered. "Thomas, I am here with you. Please, stay with us. Elizabeth needs you so much. The boys need you. They will be here soon. You must not leave us."

Charlotte imagined she felt some small movement of his hand. Looking closely at his face, she tried but could not see any acknowledgement of her words. Charlotte closed her eyes and held his hand to her lips. To her surprise, when she opened her eyes Thomas was looking at her through half open lids. He smiled slightly and drifted off again.

"Doctor," she called, "I do believe Sir Thomas was awake briefly."

"Perhaps, dear lady, but I hold only a small hope that he may recover."

"You must let me know his progress, sir. Please, send any news to Lady Emma Bosworth-Fuller at 33 Grosvenor Square."

"I shall do so, madam." She bid the doctor and the ordinary goodbye, after confirming with him the time of his sermon the following morning. The ride back to Emma's was upsetting. All along High Holborn and Oxford Streets people were gathering. Great anticipation was in the air. To her dismay, Charlotte realized these were the first of thousands who would gather to cheer on the procession to Tyburn tree. Arriving back at the house on Grosvenor Square, Charlotte was greeted by Emma.

"A disreputable looking man called not half an hour ago to give John news that he would not share with me, except to say that it was of a serious nature. He left with this fellow, telling me not to expect him back for at least two days."

"What was the man's appearance, Emma?"

"He was a Jew, no doubt about it, very thin, with distrustful eyes and a downturned mouth. His clothes were disgraceful."

"He was a messenger from James," Charlotte said.

"He was? Oh, my lord, was he one of the men you saw with Edward Hawkes?"

"The same, I'm sure of it. I saw him again last night."

"Last night?"

"My dear Emma, I cannot begin to tell you the events of the last twenty-four hours."

Emma took Charlotte by the hand and insisted she sit next to her.

"But you must. Now, please, what has happened?"

Charlotte related it all: Jane's trial, Thomas's part in the whole affair, his indecent proposal, Jane's despair, Charlotte's going to Thomas a second time, James's outrage, and the attack on Thomas.

Emma sat spellbound at every new turn in the story.

"And now this," Charlotte said. "James has undoubtedly called on John to help in the capture of Edward Hawkes. Would that I could jump three months hence, so I might not have to face tomorrow!"

"My dear, you should make plans to go to Rosthwaite. Take your new family and leave London for an extended period. I will come with you, if you think my presence might be of aid. I am sure John would not object."

"You are so kind, Emma. I wish I could escape."

"What holds you here?"

"Peg's murder, I am afraid. I don't know what will be required of me, but I am sure the authorities would not look kindly on my leaving so soon. When that is settled, I will sell that house. I've grown fond of Soho. Perhaps I can find something on the Square. We could be neighbours."

Emma smiled and patted Charlotte's hand. "It is all very complicated, is it not?"

"I'm done with James, Emma."

"You think so?"

"Yes."

"It's a beautiful day, despite all. We shall take tea in the garden," Emma said. She led Charlotte out of the house. A spring thaw had begun. The clouds parted, and the smell of the warming earth brought Charlotte to an awareness of her surroundings. She took note of the day and bird song.

"Death, whether it is fast or slow, is not kind. I don't understand suffering, Emma. I don't understand why humans are made to suffer."

"It is God's will, Charlotte, for whatever His reasons may be."

"My father was angry at his end, my mother seemed to be at peace. They both were in pain. I could do so little for them."

"Charlotte, in what way may I help you with the arrangements for tomorrow?"

"Dear Emma, thank you for asking. I will go very early with two carriages to Newgate. I'll send the boys back with Jenny. Annie will ride with me in the second carriage at the end of the procession. Jane insists on taking Duncan with her in the cart."

"What!?" Emma exclaimed.

"It is her desire to hold him until the end."

"I see."

"I think I would wish to carry Jack. To be with my little one…" Charlotte could not finish. She looked down into her lap and tried to regain her composure. She hurried on to ask her next request, not sure she would be able to speak the words. "Will you ask John if he would help me bring Jane's body back here afterwards? We can place it in her coffin and carry it on top of the coach."

"As soon as I see him, I shall ask," Emma said.

Charlotte felt faint. "Forgive me, Emma, I'm suddenly exhausted. Please, allow me to forego tea. I need to rest for a short while."

"Of course. I'll look in on Jack and call you when dinner is ready." Excusing herself, Charlotte retired to her bedchamber. She lay down and tried to rest. The events of the last few days and those that lay ahead vied for her attention.

What slowly made its way to the forefront of her thoughts was her experience of Tyburn when she first came to London. The noise of the crowd had been deafening. She'd never before been in the midst of such a huge number of people. They pressed in on all sides of Audley, her father, and her as they made their way to a friend's house with a good vantage point of the scaffold.

Her mother had refused to go and was much against

her daughter being involved. Her father, however, insisted that she should see the spectacle just once. William Byrd thought of it as a moral lesson, one that would reinforce for his daughter what end awaited those of bad character.

It was a notorious highwayman that day who mounted the scaffold full of bravado and ale. A multitude of ladies had come to watch. They called his name, and he in turn did the most elegant bows. It was theatrical to say the least, but in the end, it was a horror show.

They hadn't covered his face, so when the trapdoor dropped, he made the most awful grimace and gagged loudly. His legs flailed, and his body jerked. She had become ill and needed to remove herself from the window. She was shocked that Audley and her father did not stop talking business for one instant.

Now, she rose and paced the bedchamber. There was a knock and Emma appeared with Jack. He raced to his mother and grabbed her skirts.

"He has been giving the housekeeper and maids a race," she reported. "Mrs. Middleton has gone to bed exhausted."

"Mama, stay with Jack!" he shouted up at Charlotte.

Kneeling, she put her arms around him. "I'm here, my dearest. Right here."

He pulled away and slapped her across the face. "No!" he shouted at her.

Shocked, Charlotte dropped her arms and her hand went to her stinging cheek. She stared at him. His face was drawn tight into an angry scowl. Something over her shoulder caught his attention. He headed off to investigate. Charlotte sat down on the floor and closed her eyes. Emma, who was sitting in a chair against the wall, cleared her throat. Charlotte glanced up at her.

"Would you mind if I study how you deal with this behaviour? I may have children someday, and I want to be prepared."

"Having a sense of humour helps, and a nurse to take him away when he is like this are the two things I would recommend. Unfortunately, I seem to be lacking both at present," she replied wryly.

Charlotte turned her head just in time to see Jack reaching for a Chinese vase that stood atop an oak pedestal. The next moment, saw the vase falling and shattering into pieces while Jack just managed to escape being hit by the pedestal as it crashed down. Charlotte did not remember getting to her feet, but she must have, for she found herself picking up the crying child from the debris. Clinging tightly to her, he buried his face in her neck. Charlotte tried to soothe him, but he continued to howl. Only after getting back to the bed and sitting down did she realize she had cut her foot on the shards from the vase.

Emma saw that Charlotte was hurt and came to her aid. She took Jack out of the room and gave him to one of the upstairs maids to look after. She called for water and cloth and soon had Charlotte's foot taken care of.

"Keep it up, on the pillows and close your eyes."

Charlotte, thankful to be cared for, agreed and fell asleep without another thought.

Sometime later, Emma summoned her to tea. Charlotte could barely keep her eyes open, but the desire for Emma's company got her out of bed and limping down the stairs and into the parlour. Upon entering, she was surprised to see a person unknown to her deep in conversation with Emma. The stranger was equally surprised and rose so quickly that he caught his coat pocket on the arm of the chair. A ripping sound followed, and the fellow closed his eyes in embarrassment.

Emma smiled at Charlotte and offered her a seat. "Oh, Charlotte I am so happy you are joining us. How wonderful! Please, allow me to present Mrs. Audley Pruitt, this is Mr. William Burke-Scott. Mr. Burke-Scott, Mrs. Audley Pruitt."

"I am most pleased to make your acquaintance, sir," Charlotte said, sitting down.

"Madam, thank you, as am I."

"Mr. Burke-Scott is my cousin from Oxfordshire. He recently graduated Oxford as a classics scholar, quite brilliant."

The young man sat and cast his eyes downward. He was in his early twenties at the most. Tall and exceedingly thin but with broad shoulders. The most extraordinary feature about him was the prodigious number of curls on his head. He had tried to pull them back in a queue as was the fashion, but they appeared to be in rebellion, charging out from the top and sides of his head, falling in torrents around his face. His eyebrows, too, were remarkable. Each arched to a point above his large, brown eyes. His was a comical, but not altogether displeasing, countenance.

"My cousin is looking for employment, Mrs. Pruitt. He enjoys the company of children, having been the oldest of nine boys."

"Ah, I see," Charlotte responded, not understanding Emma's point.

Emma pursued the matter. "He is a tutor, Mrs. Pruitt."

Suddenly, Charlotte woke to her meaning. "Oh, of course. Mr. Burke-Scott, I am about to become the guardian of several children, as well as having a son of my own, although he is quite young."

"Never too young to begin," Emma interjected. "The Earl of Richmond's son was reading Plato at three, in translation, of course. He did not master Greek until he was seven."

"Perhaps in a few days' time, we could discuss your qualifications and your ideas on education, Mr. Burke-Scott," Charlotte suggested,

"That would be quite fine, Mrs. Pruitt," the young man responded.

"Cousin William, please, go to the library and see if you can locate Virgil's *Aeneid*, so that we may intelligently discuss that passage you mentioned before Mrs. Pruitt joined us."

William looked at her, as if trying to recall what passage to which she might be referring. Then, his expression brightened, as though he'd successfully remembered.

"Yes, of course," he responded. "Excuse me, Mrs. Pruitt, Cousin Emma." He rose too swiftly and tore his pocket a second time. Grabbing at the dangling material, he made a quick bow, walked out of the parlour only to re-enter, bow again, and leave by the opposite door. Once he was out of earshot, Emma burst out laughing.

"Emma, please, he will hear you, poor boy."

"Forgive me, Charlotte. He is extraordinarily bright, but his social graces have always been lacking."

"And you would have me add him to my already chaotic household! Honestly, Emma, we are falling over each other as it is."

"Charlotte, William is truly a different person with children. I promise that you will be amazed."

"I am amazed already, dear."

"Truly, he will be an asset to you. It will also be a great

help to me."

"How so, Emma?"

"His mother is eager to find him a position. I fear because of his awkwardness that may prove difficult. He was originally to inherit a large estate in Oxfordshire, along with a yearly income of several thousand pounds. Unfortunately, his father, my cousin, gambled most of it away. He then had the effrontery to die. I never cared for him at family gatherings. His wife is a dear friend of mine, however. Why she married him, I will never understand. It is her influence alone that has saved the boys. They are all well-mannered and intelligent, but with little means of support. What do you say? Give him a try, will you, for a short period of time, anyway?"

"My dear Emma, how could I refuse you anything? I am so unnerved by these last few days and what is to come tomorrow, that if you suggested your horse, Nattie, as a tutor, I would accept."

"Well, I assure you Mr. Burke-Scott will prove invaluable to you in the end. So too, your gentle influence will aid him. I am sure of it."

A crash resounding in the hallway, William Burke-Scott came backing through the door carrying a large book which he had opened. "Cousin Emma, I found it and truly it is the most beautiful of translations."

Seeing Charlotte, he faltered.

"Forgive me, I have blundered in on your conversation."

He grasped the book to his chest, closing it on one of his fingers and twisting it painfully. He let out a howl. His distress caused him to drop the heavy tome on his foot. He screamed again as the book hit his toes. Clasping his hand over his mouth, he looked at both the ladies. He waved to indicate that he was not mortally wounded.

His eyes watering, he managed a hoarse, "Excuse me," after which he retrieved the book from the floor and left the room, closing the door behind himself.

Charlotte turned to Emma. "Do you think perhaps Nattie would be available to tutor?" Before her friend had a chance to answer, there was a knock at the door, which Mr. Burke-Scott had exited so recently.

"Please, enter," Emma called out.

The door opened slowly. Her cousin stood in the entryway. "May I come in?" he asked nervously.

"Of course, Cousin William, please do and sit down." Holding the book still, he entered with great care, choosing a chair as far from both of them as possible.

Silence fell in the room.

Finally, Emma cleared her throat and began speaking, "Mrs. Pruitt and I discussed the possibility of your employment as a tutor to her son and her wards. I highly recommended you, based on your superior academic achievements and your abilities in dealing with children, especially boys."

William raised his head slightly and looked at them shyly.

"Are you interested in the outcome of our discussion, cousin?"

"I am most decidedly interested, Cousin Emma."

"Mrs. Pruitt has agreed to a six-month trial period of employment."

Charlotte shot Emma a glance, but the latter continued, choosing not to notice Charlotte's surprise.

"After this time, she will evaluate your performance

and decide whether you will remain as her children's tutor. The two of you may discuss your wages after dinner, but I assure you, Mrs. Pruitt is known for her overly generous nature."

"Emma!" Charlotte protested.

"Please, let me finish. Tomorrow will be particularly trying for all of us. I took the liberty of explaining to Cousin William your situation in regard to Mrs. Rourke."

Here, William attempted an interjection. "Mrs. Pruitt, I am so…"

Emma stopped him mid-sentence. "Thank you, William," she continued. "So, dear cousin, I expect you to jump right in and help however you are able. You will accompany Mrs. Pruitt to the gaol in the morning, and she will direct you in whatever she needs to be done." Emma turned to Charlotte. "No task is too menial or too abhorrent for William tomorrow."

This time William did the interrupting. "I am up to it, I assure you, Cousin Emma. Mrs. Pruitt, I am at your service." Standing without mishap, he chose to emphasize his commitment to Charlotte by slamming the copy of *The Aeneid* on the table, which sent both the ladies' teacups overturning with a crash. Charlotte's stayed intact. Emma's did not. It shattered in several pieces. Emma looked from the broken cup to her cousin and raised an eyebrow.

"Dear William, perhaps you should take a walk in the out of doors for a few minutes before dinner."

"I think that's an excellent idea, cousin. Thank you for thinking of it." He started to leave, stopped and turned to Emma. "Forgive me." She dismissed him with a thank you.

After he'd gone, Emma looked at Charlotte. "He will be helpful, I assure you. However, if too many things are broken too quickly, you have my permission to find a new tutor."

The evening passed quietly. Cousin William broke nothing else. After dinner, they discussed his services and his wages and came to an agreement. He was a shy, but charming, young man. His countenance was serious, but when he occasioned to smile, his face had a pleasing appearance.

Charlotte looked forward to his meeting the children, even in such unhappy circumstances.

CHAPTER EIGHT

Charlotte's dreams that night brought her no peace. She found herself standing in a crowd of people all dressed in clothes of brilliant hues, like the Mediterranean sun and sky. A man approached her and stood quite close. He pressed himself on her. His hands touched her, and though she was fully clothed, she felt his fingers move up the insides of her thighs. The harder she pushed him away, the more he insinuated himself on her. Enraged, she lashed out. Pounding on his chest, pushing him until he fell. His manhood lay exposed. She began to beat it more and more fiercely. At last, the man lay lifeless, faceless. The flesh between his legs was a bloody mass.

Fighting to wake up, Charlotte opened her eyes. She was chilled and soaked in perspiration. A shiver overtook her, and she pulled the blanket over her shoulders. Dawn was just beginning to lighten the sky as she looked out the windows. There were no clouds. The new moon was a pink sliver in the brightening heavens.

After a hurried toilette, she chose clothes that she could move in with ease. She walked softly into Jack's room and gave him a gentle kiss. Downstairs, she met Mr. Burke-Scott. He had attempted to subdue his hair and had managed to get most of it into a queue. He was serious and attentive to her directions. She was glad to have his company. Emma came to breakfast a few minutes after Charlotte. She brought a message from John. He planned to meet Charlotte at Tyburn and help her retrieve Jane Rourke's body.

"Emma, did you ask John about Jane's body and her coffin last night?"

"Yes. He came in quite late. We talked, and he agreed to what you want to do. He is already up and gone."

"Did he say anything about James?"

"Only that he would be at Tyburn, he thought."

William looked up from his breakfast. "James?"

"James Clarke," Emma responded.

"Cousin Emma, is he from the Clarkes of Devon?"

"Yes, William."

"Oh, my, mother has spoken of him. Quite mad, she says. Is that the one?"

"He has had some difficulties, yes," Emma said.

"Oh, yes, indeed. From what I've been told…"

Charlotte interjected, "He is my son's father."

"I beg your pardon?" William questioned.

"Cousin William, I think it's best to speak of other subjects."

"Of course."

"There are baskets of food to take to the Rourkes'. Would you see that they are ready to be loaded onto the coach?" Emma asked William.

"Very good idea." Burke-Scott hurried off towards the kitchen.

Charlotte and Emma looked at each other. Emma broke the silence. "What would you have me do today? How may I help best?"

"Be here for the children when they come back. I must make sure that I'm there to take Duncan from Jane when they reach the gallows. Also, I must claim Jane's body. John's help will be invaluable in this."

"And James?"

"Emma, I have no idea what he may be thinking. He believes he can catch Edward Hawkes if he tries for Jane's body. The whole situation is so grotesque I cannot bear to imagine it. I pray only for the strength to get through it."

William returned to announce that all the food was loaded, and the carriages were ready. Emma put her arms around Charlotte. After goodbyes, Charlotte and her companion stepped into the carriage. It was a quiet ride at first. The route led them from Grosvenor Street to Great Marlborough Street. Only a few early morning souls were about, but when they turned down Wardour Street and onto Tyburn, the city came alive. Crowds jostled and shoved to get a seat with a good view of the procession to come. People leaned out windows and shouted to the street vendors.

Charlotte closed her eyes and put her hand to her mouth to keep from sobbing. William looked at her with alarm.

"Mrs. Pruitt, are you ill?" She shook her head, trying to breathe without crying.

Finally, she spoke. "Forgive me, I was not prepared for the crowd and its gaiety. Please, do not bring the children back this way. Make sure you go back by Fleet Street and the Strand."

"I will instruct the driver."

"Thank you."

To take her mind away from the scene outside, she

related stories about the boys. William listened attentively. As they neared the prison, Charlotte saw the early morning light touch St. Sepulchre's steeple, illuminating the cross at its top. Newgate Prison across High Holborn caught none of the light, its dark edifice seeming to prove too impenetrable even for the sun.

The carriages came to a stop in front of the keeper's door. Candles burned in the windows of the rooms above.

"They are awake, I think," Charlotte said, turning to William. His eyes grew wide as he surveyed the prison's façade. "Come, let us see if they're hungry."

Charlotte's words broke his trance. He rose, stepped out of the carriage, and turned, offering his hand to Charlotte as she alighted.

While Burke-Scott organized the footmen to carry in the heavy baskets of food for the Rourkes, Charlotte presented a special one made up of breads and jams for the gaoler at the door. He seemed pleased to receive it, nodding his head and thanking her.

Leading the procession up the stairs, Charlotte knocked at the door of the keeper's room. Annie answered. She looked exhausted, her face pale with dark circles under her eyes. The inside of the room revealed the children in a tight circle around their mother. Charlotte could see the desperation in their faces as they attempted to protect their mother from her fate.

William entered, and all eyes went to him.

"Everyone, this is Lady Emma's cousin, Mr. Burke-Scott," Charlotte said softly.

The children responded almost in unison with their hellos. Jane rose wearily and came forward. "How do you do, Mr. Burke-Scott?"

He replied quietly, "Madam, how do you do?"

She acknowledged his greeting and turned to Charlotte. "Reverend Whitgate has visited this morning to inform me that I must go to his sermon in a short while. He also tried to dissuade me from carrying Duncan to Tyburn, but I told him I am determined, and he argued with me no more."

Charlotte reached out and took Jane's hand. "I will wait with Duncan at the door where you must..." She could not continue. Her throat constricted. That it must come to this, she thought, I cannot bear it.

Jane's expression was full of compassion for her friend. Holding tight to her hand, she said softly, "...which the condemned must pass through. I have imagined that walk. The sound of my steps echoing off the stones of the passageway from the chapel. The ordinary will tell us all to pray for our souls' salvation. God knows that I have not broken His commandments. I do not understand why I must die, but He calls me, so I go. I will pray for you and for my children. That is what I will be doing in the chapel. And when I am on the scaffold, I will stretch out my hands to my children so that my fingertips, even if only in my imagination, will touch them until the very moment of my death."

She closed her eyes. The room was silent. Duncan began to cry. Annie picked him up and held him tight. He would not be consoled until Jane took him in her arms. She smiled at him, turning to the boys.

"Gather your belongings," she said. "It is time for you to go. Mr. Burke-Scott and Jenny will take you to Lady Emma's. Be very good. Listen to what they say." She stopped, biting both her lips together. "I love you, my sweet ones."

The boys ran to her, grabbing hold wherever they could. She kissed them all and pulled them to her as much as she was able, since Duncan still clung to her.

"Go now. Go," she said softly. "Go"

Charlotte and Annie made their way from the keeper's room to the door from which Jane and the others would emerge. Charlotte was struck by the unremitting grey of the building and courtyard. Even the gaolers who waited by the carts appeared grey and lifeless.

Red-headed Duncan held tight to Charlotte. His arms wrapped around her neck. Annie tried to relieve her, but the little boy would not let go until he saw the horses that were harnessed to the carts. He began to point and call out. One big black horse in particular fascinated him. He urged Charlotte towards the animal by rocking back and forth in her arms and reaching out for it.

"Horse!" he called out, his voice rising at the end of the word with sharp insistence.

Charlotte, surprised by his outburst, laughed. Embarrassed at the inappropriateness of her laughter, she handed the struggling Duncan to Annie.

Jane came outside after listening to the ordinary's sermon. Reverend Whitgate followed her out and now swept over to Charlotte.

"Please, Mrs. Pruitt, you must dissuade Mrs. Rourke from this course of action. It is most ill advised."

"I will not, sir," Charlotte answered.

"Madam, please, I understand your attachment to the

woman, but it will do no good for her to incite the crowd, I assure you."

"I cannot help you, sir." He appeared disappointed at her unwillingness to be of aid to him. She continued. "Is there any word of Lord Chagford's condition today?"

The tension around the ordinary's mouth grew tighter. "He is gravely ill, Mrs. Pruitt. He remains at the Sessions House, unable to be moved. If you wish to see him, I will make arrangements."

"Is he awake to visitors?"

"No, but your gentle ministrations could not but help him." He paused, perhaps to renew his suit for help with Mrs. Rourke, but before he could begin, he was called to the head of the procession. Charlotte watched him hurry off, his heavy frame nearly toppling over as he shifted from foot to foot.

James came into Charlotte's thoughts and she chided herself. Thomas lay dying. James, who meant to murder him, was a madman who had destroyed her life. Yet she could not remove him from her thoughts. She saw his eyes, his lips, his hands, his long fingers. She longed for him to be there, to hold her and help her. But he was not there! Take a step forward on your own, she scolded herself.

Moving through the crowd that filled the yard, Charlotte walked to Jane and embraced her. As they held each other, Charlotte became aware of Jane's inhalation and exhalation. Soon, she will not breathe, Charlotte thought.

"I love you," she whispered, pulling Jane closer. "I am so sorry."

Jane buried her head in the soft wool of Charlotte's cloak. She did not speak.

Duncan came running to his mother. Annie was close

on his heels. However, before he could reach his goal, he was swept up into his uncle's arms. Annie stopped, stunned to be suddenly in her uncle's presence. Charlotte's back was to this reunion, but she felt Jane's body go rigid. An instant later, Jane rushed towards Patrick and Duncan. She stopped very close to them.

"Give him to me, Patrick Rourke. He is an orphan because of you. You have no right to a tender goodbye!"

Patrick did not relinquish his nephew. His temper flared now.

"Calm yourself, woman. I am not the cause of your misfortune, and you know it. The Crown wants us dead. All of us!" He looked at Charlotte. "You guard my brother's children well, Mrs. Pruitt. They are the children of revolutionaries, and as such, their lives will always be in peril."

"I am no revolutionary, Patrick Rourke. I am an innocent woman who has the misfortune to have a rebel for a brother-in-law!" Jane lunged at him, but Annie interceded, trying to calm her mother.

The show of emotion between the two opened the floodgates for the other condemned prisoners who began to shout and jostle the soldiers and gaolers. A riot erupted.

Jane grabbed Duncan. Charlotte took hold of Annie's arm. The four stood in a tight group against the cold, stone wall, hoping to avoid cracked heads.

The struggling and cursing did not last long. Bleeding and subdued, the condemned men were hastily loaded onto the carts by the gaolers. Jane and Duncan, too, were gathered up and unceremoniously hoisted onto the last cart in the procession. Annie ran alongside them for several minutes, holding on to her mother's hand when possible.

Charlotte took her place in the carriage just behind the group. Her heart was racing. Slowly, she became aware of the tolling of St. Sepulchre's bells as her carriage came out onto Newgate Street. Nothing could be done now to stop the horrors to come. It was a nightmare circus. The bells were its music. The throngs in the street were its audience, wildly cheering as the performers came into view.

The procession took two hours down High Holborn, across Fleet Canal, and on to Tyburn Road. Several times, they were stopped while the crowds surged forward to offer up mugs of ale to the condemned. Patrick shook hands and offered a toast to the health of his benefactor. Jane sat holding tight to Duncan. Her face had taken on a serene look. At each stop, the crowd nearest her ceased their shouting and grew silent. The silence moved outward through the throng, but then the procession lurched forward, and the shouts of encouragement rose again.

Annie left her mother's side and boarded the carriage. Her face was drained of colour. She sat with her face in her hands. Charlotte watched from the carriage as Jane closed her eyes and stroked Duncan's red hair. Her lips touched his head.

Finally, after travelling from the poor sections of East London, through the city and past the fashionable new squares of the west end, the carts jostled up to Tyburn Hill. There, surrounded by thousands of onlookers, stood the gallows with their multiple nooses.

Charlotte's carriage came to a halt. Panicked that they would be unable to retrieve Duncan unharmed, she roused Annie and told her to run to her brother. The crowd surged in towards the gallows, the soldiers trying to hold them back. Annie's path was blocked. Charlotte, looking from the carriage window, could see the condemned men being pulled from the carts in the front of the line. Some walked without hesitation while others cried out as their legs collapsed under them. Jane stood in her cart not twenty feet from them. Duncan's small arms and legs wrapped around her. She was not ready to give him up yet.

Charlotte stepped down into the throng. She felt faint from the press of people all around. She grasped hold of the open door trying to steady herself. The deafening tattoo of the drums began. She felt the beat throughout her body and closed her eyes. When she opened them, pinpoints of light danced before her eyes, obscuring her vision.

Suddenly, a hand touched her shoulder and she tried to move away. James's voice called to her. Her vision clearing, his face came into view. He was in the guise of a beggar. His greasy hair hung limply around his dirt-smeared face.

She heard Annie call her name. Charlotte looked to see the soldiers moving towards Jane's cart. Before Charlotte could get to Annie, James was already moving through the line of soldiers. He reached Jane and, getting her attention, he took the terrified child into his arms. Charlotte watched as James and Jane exchanged a few words. Jane appeared calmed by whatever was said. As he moved back through the soldiers, Jane stepped unaided from her cart. It was to be Charlotte's last glimpse of her friend's face. Her view was obscured as Jane mounted the gallows and a bag was placed over her head.

James fought to keep Duncan in his grasp. The boy stiffened and threw himself back in an attempt to get free of the stranger who had taken him from his mother's arms. He was screaming and crying. The crowd gave way so they could pass. When the boy saw Annie and Charlotte, he reached out for Charlotte's neck, cutting her face with his sharp nails as he clamoured into her arms.

Without a word, James was absorbed back into the mob of onlookers like a man overboard swallowed up by an angry sea. Duncan held onto Charlotte, whimpering in fear. She patted his back to calm him, but her own agitation was mounting.

On the platform, Patrick was being allowed to address the throng. She could hear very little. He was speaking in both English and Irish and those who did understand his words greeted them with applause and cheers. No doubt there was a large contingent of Irish journeymen and labourers who had waited all night for the opportunity to hear their man speak his final words.

Charlotte feared they might be caught in the middle of a riot, for now the cheering was offset by jeering and boos.

The hangmen came forward and pushed Patrick to his spot to join the others. A bag and a noose were placed around his neck, his hands tied behind his back.

The condemned appeared like a group of faceless dolls on a shelf. Some were upright, some were having great difficulty standing. The drums rolled. The floor under their feet gave way. Suddenly, their feet were flailing in the air, their bodies convulsing uncontrollably.

Charlotte cried out, Duncan covered his ears and closed his eyes, and Annie stared, motionless. Time seemed to stand still.

Suddenly, three men bolted from the crowd and grabbed hold of one of the hanging men. They pulled down on him with all their combined weight. It was not an act of cruelty, but of mercy. Their wish was to dispatch him quickly to heaven, rather than let him writhe in agony any longer than necessary. In a few moments, his body hung limply while others around him still moved. The three fell to their knees, praying.

Charlotte could not move. Should she try to run to Jane? Should she try to relieve her suffering? But if she lived, she would be pardoned. It was the last thread of hope. From the mob, a bearded man with long, dirty, blond hair rushed forward and took hold of Jane's legs.

"NO!" Charlotte cried out. At that same moment, she realized it was Hawkes.

Another form literally flew out of the crowd and began to fight with Hawkes. It was James. The crowd parted to avoid being drawn into the melee. James and Hawkes beat each other as Jane's legs thrashed above them. The onlookers cheered loudly, incited by the violence in front of them. Others from behind began to push for a better view. Punches were thrown, and another fight and then another broke out.

Alarmed, the soldiers around the scaffold fired their guns into the air. There were screams and the crowd surged backward. People fell and scrambled to get away from the crush of the mob. Charlotte, holding on to Duncan, boarded the carriage. Annie followed behind. The carriage could not move with people all around it.

Blood streamed from a cut over James's right eye, but he fought on. He landed a blow to Hawkes's jaw, sending him sprawling. As James caught his breath, Charlotte saw the African approach him from behind. Too late, she shouted a warning, as the man raised a cudgel and brought it down on James's head. He fell heavily to his knees and dropped, face down, on the ground.

Hawkes rose. He nodded a thanks to his compatriot.

Moving to James's body, he kicked him savagely in the stomach. Soldiers began to clear the area. Hawkes and the African dissolved into the crowd. Fights began flaring up in other areas. The soldiers dispersed in those directions and did not bother with James's inert body.

Charlotte stood and leaned out the carriage door. She became aware of the black man standing near her. "He's not hurt. Except for a cracked rib maybe."

She recoiled into the carriage and sat down as he leaned in the door.

"What happened to your Cockney accent?" she challenged.

"My dear Mrs. Pruitt, you name me a place in the British Empire, and I be from dere, oh yah." He smiled at her. "Clark was crazy to go after Hawkes. But you know that, eh?" Seeing someone approaching from his left, he departed without another word.

Charlotte's gaze was drawn to the hanging bodies. She closed her eyes and prayed for Jane's soul. Annie was crying and Duncan crawled into Charlotte's lap, resting his head on her breast. John Fuller appeared outside the coach.

"May God have mercy on her soul," he said quietly as he stepped up into the carriage. "I am so sorry, Miss Rourke."

Annie managed a nod, saying, "Thank you, sir."

Charlotte's concern for action overrode her desire to respect the solemn moment. "We must get her body, John, quickly. Hawkes is here. He and James fought. Did you see them?"

"Yes, Charlotte, I did." He pointed out the window to the scaffold. "Young Scott-Burke came with me and is beside Mrs. Rourke now. He will guard her. I shall join him directly."

Charlotte looked in the direction of the scaffold. Seeing William eased her anxiety. She looked to where James had been moments before. He was gone.

"Jem has disappeared," she said, her voice filled with a mixture of relief and sadness.

"He must have gotten safely away, then," John said.

"That black ruffian hit him, and Hawkes kicked him. The African came to the carriage to say he was all right. I don't understand what's happening. What if they have taken him somewhere?"

"Jem is fine, Charlotte, I'm sure of it," John said, cutting off her questioning. "When the hangmen give the word, we will retrieve Mrs. Rourke's body. I will return. Stay here. Do not get out of the carriage."

John had difficulty making his way through the large group of women, some carrying pock-marked infants, who had gathered at the base of the scaffold. Each one was desperate for the touch of Patrick's hand, sure that a miraculous cure for their boils would take place. This superstition of the gallows cure was usually reserved for dead highwaymen, but Patrick was considered enough of a criminal to render healing possible.

As John came to stand by William's side, he saw that the hangmen were busy prodding the bodies to determine if any life was left in them. None was, so they began cutting the ropes and letting them fall like so many sacks of potatoes. Other, more unsavoury types came behind them to take those left unclaimed.

The fight that Charlotte feared did not come to pass. Jane's limp body was let down into John's arms. Scott-Burke cut the rope that bound her wrists, and John carried her away from the scaffold.

Charlotte knew from Emma that John had agreed to put Jane's body in the pine coffin and carry it back to Grosvenor Square atop the carriage. However, as Charlotte saw them approaching, she could not abide the thought. She called for William, who hurried over to her window.

"Please, stay with Duncan. I wish to be with Jane's body."

Annie indicated that she wanted to come as well. After helping both women alight from the carriage, William hopped in and stopped Duncan from following. After the excitement of the morning, Duncan settled on to one of the carriage seats and closed his eyes.

They moved quickly through the crowd of people, Charlotte leading the way. They met John as he arrived at the cart where the coffin lay. Charlotte spoke with him, telling him she and Annie wished to ride with Jane's body. He did not disagree.

The women took down the back of the cart and he hoisted Jane's body onto the floor. He helped Charlotte up, but Annie did not wait, choosing to scramble up by herself. John came up last and closed the back of the cart. The noose was still around Jane's neck and the bag over her head.

Charlotte closed her eyes, fighting off the urge to faint. Her head swam. She felt John holding her arm to steady her. The sound of the crowd became increasingly distant and muffled.

"Charlotte, open your eyes and take a deep breath, if you can. It will help." John's voice was quiet and soothing.

"Thank you," she said.

She never imagined herself in any situation so horrible.

She did as he instructed and felt herself more in control. Opening her eyes, she thought she saw James's face in the crowd, but it disappeared. Her composure regained, she realized Annie lay prostrate over her mother's body. Charlotte wanted desperately to remove the wretched bag from Jane's head.

John got Charlotte's attention.

"We must try and make our way out of here. The more the crowd drinks, the more dangerous it is for us."

Charlotte nodded. She knelt down and placed her hand on Annie's back to comfort her. The girl's body was wracked by sobs. John spoke with the cart driver and gave him some money.

Returning to Charlotte, he said, "The man will drive the cart to Grosvenor Square. I will guide him." He moved to the front of the cart and took his seat on the bench next to the driver.

The man clucked for the horse to move. The driver of the carriage, seeing the cart begin to go, followed without hesitation. The celebrating onlookers shouted drunken toasts to the departing cart and carriage.

Charlotte watched over Annie and Jane, fearful that Hawkes or some other body snatcher would try and attack them. None did. The crowd began to give way. People on Tyburn Road were moving off towards the surrounding taverns. Charlotte looked back at the scaffold.

Patrick's body was the last left hanging. The Crown was not done with him yet. He would be gibbeted and left to rot, so all could see the fate of those who challenged the King's authority. However, the canting songs would spread the news of his last words, and in that way, he would get some small revenge on the authorities.

As the cart made its way down Tyburn Hill, Charlotte could not help thinking of Patrick's warning. Jane's children were marked from this day forward. She must get them north, away from the furore. For just a moment, she smiled as she thought of Whitestone.

It was short lived. John guided the driver to the mews behind Grosvenor Square. Annie looked a pitiful sight as she cradled her mother's body. When the cart stopped, Charlotte spoke soothingly to the girl.

"You must go inside, dear, and rest. Emma will be with you. John and I will see to your mother."

Annie looked at her blankly at first. Gently, she laid her mother's head down. Charlotte helped her to stand on unsteady legs. William carried the sleeping Duncan in his arms.

"Allow me to help you, Mrs. Pruitt." He trotted towards the house and gave the boy to one of the maidservants with instructions to take him to Jenny. He returned to the cart. John, having thanked the cart driver, came to Annie's side and helped her down. She held the side of the cart to steady herself and took William's hand as she climbed down. He put his arm around Annie once she was on the ground and guided her towards the house.

When they were out of earshot, John turned to Charlotte. "We must get Mrs. Rourke inside."

"John, I must take that dreadful cover from her head."

"Let us do that inside."

"No, I will do it now."

"Very well, if you must."

Charlotte knelt and removed the bag. Jane's eyes were wide open, and her mouth contorted in a last gasp for air.

"Oh, dear God!" Charlotte closed Jane's eyes and tried

to close her mouth. Her fumbling fingers pulled at the rope. The rope had cut deeply into Jane's throat.

Seeing Charlotte's difficulty, John helped loosen the noose. Charlotte held Jane's head and he took the loop off. She rested Jane's head in her lap while she took her handkerchief from her pocket. Carefully folding it, she wrapped it around the wound that ringed Jane's neck. She cradled Jane's head and shoulders in her arms.

"No, no, no…" she murmured, rocking. The reality of Jane's death crashed over her in waves.

After a few moments, exhausted, but knowing that there was no time to rest, Charlotte followed as John carried Jane into the house, where she oversaw the preparing and dressing of Jane's body. When these were done, John and several of the servants placed her body in the coffin.

Charlotte found Annie and Emma in the parlour. Annie stared at the coals in the fireplace. Emma sat beside her on the settee. Charlotte crossed to Annie and knelt.

"It will be time very soon to go to the churchyard. The vicar will be awaiting our arrival. I must speak with the boys first. Do you wish to go with me, or would you like a moment alone with your mother?" She waited for an answer. Annie bit her lip, trying to gain control of her emotions.

Finally, she responded, "I will go with you."

Emma interjected. "Charlotte, the boys are already dressed. I spoke with Jenny earlier. She said she would tell them about going to Christ Church. All you need to do is call them down. Duncan and Jack should stay here. Do you agree?"

"Yes, of course. I am afraid poor Duncan has suffered a terrible shock. You must be gentle with him, Emma. Poor little soul."

Annie stood up, straightening her clothes. In a quiet, monotone voice, she said, "I will gather up the boys and my sister, Mistress Charlotte."

Charlotte and Annie looked at each other. Both felt awkward with the shift in their relationship.

At last, Charlotte spoke, "Annie dearest, I am your guardian now, not your employer. Please, you have my consent to use a more familiar form of address."

"Should I call you Charlotte?" Annie asked.

"Yes, I think you should. That sounds quite good. Do you agree, Emma?"

"Yes, yes, I do," Emma responded, attempting to restrain her desire to laugh. Unable to rein it in, she broke out in a loud guffaw.

Suddenly, all three were laughing, which quickly turned to weeping. John Fuller entered the parlour in the middle of this explosion of feeling and looked at them as if they had all gone mad. On seeing his expression, they attempted to regain composure.

Charlotte spoke. "Annie, please, go and ask Jenny and your brothers to come to the parlour."

Annie left the room, stopping to do a small curtsy as she passed John.

"The carriages are ready. The funeral coach has just arrived. With your permission, Charlotte, I will send one of the footmen ahead to inform the vicar that we are on our way."

"Yes, please do. Thank you, John, for all your help."

"You are most welcome, Charlotte." As he turned to leave, Emma excused herself, stood, and took his arm. They left the room together.

Alone, Charlotte raised her eyes upward. Please, dear Heavenly Father, speed my friend's soul to Your side. And on this night to come, help me protect her earthly remains from those who would do them harm. Amen.

Charlotte went to her bedchamber to ready herself for the funeral.

The boys came down the stairs, followed by Jenny and Annie. Charlotte was the last to leave the house. No one spoke as the carriages began the slow journey east. When the procession arrived at Christ Church Spitalfields, the vicar was waiting.

The service was to be brief, but word of its happening had spread throughout the area. Master weavers, who had closed down their shops because of the hangings, now gathered with their families and journeymen to honour Jane. The church filled with silent and weeping mourners. When the vicar finished his words for the deceased, everyone filed out into the churchyard, where the earth waited to embrace Jane in what would be, hopefully, her final resting place.

The sky turned grey and threatening as they gathered around the graveside. The vicar prayed and the children one by one threw small handfuls of dirt onto the coffin after it was lowered in the ground. Jenny was so distraught that William helped support her. Annie, though her eyes were red and her face pale, stepped forward with dignity and tossed in her handful of earth. Charlotte bid a silent farewell to Jane and took Annie's hand. The new family moved through the crowd.

People reached out to touch an arm or place a hand on the head of one of the boys, gestures they extended to the children to reassure them they were not alone, and perhaps to expiate the guilt they had for not being able to save one of their own. When Charlotte made sure all the children were safe in the carriages and on their way back to Grosvenor Square, she sought out John. She had determined that she would be part of the watch in the churchyard, though she knew it would not meet with his approval.

"No, Charlotte absolutely not! You know the violence of which Hawkes is capable. I would not place you in such danger," John said.

"John, I will stay. I must be there to protect Jane." She touched the sheath of the knife that she had placed in her pocket before she left Emma's house.

"Has the murder of that woman in your house so quickly gone from your memory?"

"It has not. Do not forget it was my throat he meant to cut, sir."

"I do not, madam. That is exactly my point."

"John, Hawkes's voice haunts me. His shadow pursues me. I still feel the touch of his fingers and hands. He inhabits my nightmares. If necessary, I will kill him myself. Tear out the eyes that have looked at me. Cut off the hands that touched my body. He will die, John! I will kill him, and may God damn his eternal soul!" Her face contorted with rage, she stepped back from John. The power of her hatred shocked her. "Forgive me," she whispered.

Turning away, she walked back to Jane's grave side. Her shoulders were slumped forward. She pulled her cloak around her. She knew John thought there was no place in James's plan for her tonight, but she hoped he understood now how deeply she felt.

More Spitalfields families began to gather at the church.

Slowly, the carts came carrying their dead. A battle has been fought for the rights of man, John thought, and these are the defeated, but glorious, dead. History would not record it so, he knew that, but it was true. Lost in his thoughts as he moved back towards the church, he did not notice a figure watching him from the shadows.

After John passed him, the man silently approached Charlotte. She did not hear him coming until he whispered in her ear, "Jem wants to see you. Will you come?"

She knew the voice. It belonged to the African. Her abrupt turn startled him, and he took a step back. She advanced, her jaw tight, her face hot. "I will not tolerate this behaviour for the likes of you. Tell me now, rogue, what master do you serve?"

"Clarke will tell you," he said.

"No!" Her shout turned heads. She lowered her voice. "*You* tell me!"

He stood and stared at her, saying nothing. This only served to further enrage her.

"You, with your ingratiating smile, how dare you approach me as an equal. I saw you with Hawkes! I saw you strike James Clarke, whom you so lightly call 'Jem'. He may be a fool, but I am not."

Putting her hand in her pocket, she grasped the weapon hidden there. She came up very close to him and drew the blade. He held his ground, realizing too late that she had a dagger held just under his rib cage. She looked coldly in his face.

"Speak the truth to me now or you will not speak again."

The surprise of her attack shocked him. Her vehemence held him still. "I am a friend of James Clarke. I serve him, though Hawkes counts me as one of his own."

"What?"

He hesitated, deciding not to tell her more. "Come with me, lady. Clarke will tell you."

"No. You inform him that if he wishes to speak to me, he should come to me in the garden at Bellagio House. I shall be there in a quarter of an hour."

"I will take your message, lady. But watch out for Hawkes. He is in Spitalfields. He will be here tonight," he said, indicating the churchyard.

The man stepped back, looking down at the dagger. Charlotte waited until he moved away and then put it back under her cloak. She did not take her eyes from him until he turned and walked away towards the east side of the church.

Slowly, she made her way through the muddy churchyard and out onto Pater Noster Street, which ended directly at the churchyard gate. It was a short walk to Bellagio House. After she unlocked the front door and slipped in, she rang for Mr. Primm.

He came, startled to find his mistress in the parlour. "Mr. Primm, I will only be here for a short while. Please, do not let anyone disturb me in the garden."

"Of course, Mrs. Pruitt."

"Thank you. Is all in order upstairs?" she asked.

"Yes, Mrs. Pruitt. The undertaker and constable have taken away the unfortunate woman's remains. The room has been scrubbed and painted. The constable said he would be speaking with you at Lady Emma's."

"Thank you, Mr. Primm."

"Madam," he replied, and left her looking up the staircase. She did not know if she would ever find the strength to mount it again.

She passed through the silent house and out into the garden. A light rain was falling. The late afternoon seemed darker than usual, so thick was the mist. She sat down on the stone bench nearest the back wall and the mews beyond. The world was quiet. James would come, she assumed, but what if he did not? Anger began to build inside of her. The voices in her head started their shrill complaints. How could you have been so stupid to love such a man? He is a weakling and a fool. Are you blind to the trouble he has caused? Wake up, Charlotte Byrd!

As the cacophony raged in her mind, she didn't notice that James had silently stolen into the garden. She stiffened involuntarily when he softly called her name. Closing her eyes, she tried to quiet her warring emotions.

"Charlotte?" he called again.

"I wished you to know that I will be in the churchyard tonight," she said flatly, not turning around.

"I do not think that's a good idea," he responded, his tone angry.

"Nevertheless, I will be there."

"You will need protection. It will take away my effectiveness in dealing with Hawkes."

She stood slowly and turned to him. "I will protect myself, thank you. You are somewhat lacking in that area already."

"I see," he responded, suddenly sounding cold and distant. "Very well. I will devote myself to the capture of Hawkes."

"I believe you have already been doing that for some time." Unable to stop herself, she continued, "I must tell you that after tonight I will not see you again. The feelings

I once held for you and so unwisely acted upon, are no more. Your presence in my life has brought me only pain. Your dark melancholy has enveloped me for too long, and I am done with it."

She watched as a war of emotions played across his face. Shock. Anger. Despair. Then, a moment of hope.

"And what of our son, has he brought you no joy?"

"Is he our son?" she said with an overwhelming desire to hurt him as he had hurt her. "Perhaps he is Audley's and mine. I am not so certain of his paternity."

His words came out in a cry, "He is my son!

Letting her anger reign, she struck again, "I do not know that, sir." She stood like a statue; her words cold as stone, despite the tight lump that formed in her throat.

"This is not the end, Charlotte Pruitt." His face was flushed. Tears glistened in his eyes. "You will not cast me out like this."

"James Clarke, I think it best if you leave my garden. I have nothing more to say to you."

"Do not dare dismiss me, strumpet!" He advanced on her, in a rage. "Tell me, why did they hang Jane Rourke? Did Lord Chagford feel your charms were not worth the trouble of obtaining a royal pardon?"

Now it was Charlotte who was confused. "What are you talking about? You nearly killed him. He lies dying in the Sessions House from your attack."

"I did not touch him. Your accusation is ridiculous."

"Well, one of your avenging angels did it then, but you are to blame. Who was it? The African?"

"Charlotte, I know nothing of this."

His voice held confusion, but she would not be swayed.

"Get out! Because of you, Jane is dead. Thomas is

dying. My family is pursued by Hawkes and now by the Crown. I will not hear your lies any longer. You left me two nights ago. Left, not caring what would happen. You showed me no love or understanding. You attacked Thomas. You are a fool to think I would believe anything you ever say again. I am done with you!" She turned from him and ran towards the house.

He leapt onto the stone bench. "Charlotte!" he screamed as she reached the door to the house.

She looked over her shoulder at him. He stood facing her.

"I am innocent," he pleaded.

"And I am done with you," she whispered, carefully keeping her countenance unchanged. She turned and walked into the house, shutting the door firmly behind her.

In the parlour, she finally released her emotions. Kicking at the furniture and breaking several small vases, she raised her voice in an angry harangue. The outburst came to a sudden halt when she heard a tentative knock on the door. She tried to compose herself by wiping her eyes and smoothing her hair, which she realized was an unruly mass on her head.

"Yes, come in," she said.

The door opened slightly. Mr. Primm's head appeared. "I am sorry to disturb you, Mrs. Pruitt, but Mr. Burke-Scott has come to call."

"Thank you, Mr. Primm. Show him into the dining room and have tea brought to us, please. And would you have one of the maids tidy up in here?"

"Yes, madam." He turned to her unseen visitor in the hallway. "Sir, please follow me to the dining room."

Charlotte attempted to straighten her stomacher and

smooth her hair before she crossed the hall.

William was seated at the table when she entered. He stood immediately upon seeing her.

"Madam, forgive the intrusion, but Cousin Emma and Cousin John sent me to inquire after you. Is there any way that I may be of service?"

Charlotte was about to dismiss him. His offer irritated her. She thought, do they all imagine that I am a child? James, Emma, John, they all feel the need to watch over me. She stopped short.

There was tonight.

There was Hawkes.

"Mr. Burke-Scott, thank you. I would ask something special of you. It is not a task we included in your duties, but it would be of tremendous help to me."

"Madam, any duty you assign me I shall endeavour to fulfil." He spoke earnestly. His innocence moved Charlotte and brought her out of her choleric state.

"Are you aware of Edward Hawkes's threat to disinter Jane Rourke's body?"

"I am; Cousin John told me about it."

"Very well. I am determined to be part of the watch in the graveyard." She pressed on, disregarding his expression of concern. "Everyone has advised against it. It is dangerous, and I understand the risk. However, Hawkes has plagued Jack and me, and I will have a hand in his capture. I would ask you to be with me in the churchyard."

An image of William falling head over heels and breaking all the china in the vicinity interrupted her thoughts. She tried to banish it as quickly as it appeared, but mentally, she could still hear Emma saying, "no, No, NO!" She blinked and forced her focus to return to William.

"Your strength and youth would be great assets," she said sincerely. "I am asking for your aid, not requiring it."

"Mrs. Pruitt, I shall be there with you. I promise I will help in whatever way possible."

"Thank you, William. Please, do sit down. Tea should be here momentarily."

Charlotte watched out the window as nightfall came with deepening gloom. She and William talked about people they knew in common. He told her about his upbringing. Yet all the while, her thoughts were on James's face, his lips and his long fingers. What had she done?

At last, it was time to go to the churchyard. Charlotte decided to wear her scarlet cloak. It was the warmest outer garment she owned and one that had protected her from the Cumberland gales. Thankfully, the rain had ceased as they began walking at a brisk pace down Pater Noster Street.

William was careful not to walk too fast, realizing his long strides would quickly leave Charlotte behind. However, he was impressed by her energy as she surged ahead of him, bound for the dangers of the night. The churchyard loomed ahead of them. The light from the oil street lamps shone down on the entrance gate; beyond was darkness.

Charlotte stopped just inside the gate, trying to sense if anyone else was there. She heard no sounds; not a crack of a twig, nor a breath from someone hidden. Turning right, away from the front of the church, she moved with cautious steps in the direction of Jane's grave. There was a slight rustle of bushes to her right. She froze.

Unfortunately, William was distracted by a twig that had gotten stuck in his stocking and did not realize

Charlotte had stopped. His next step caught the back of her cloak. He fell into her with a loud expulsion of air. He desperately tried to right himself without knocking her over.

She lurched forward, falling painfully onto her knees. Her head jerked back from the pull of the cloak. William struggled to disentangle himself. Charlotte shook her head and felt the sting of her knees.

Abruptly, she was lifted off the ground by unseen hands and deposited several feet away by the side wall of the church. A moment later, William joined her, protesting in a loud whisper at being pushed about in such a manner. She grabbed his arm and pulled him towards her. Their assailant slipped into the shadows without a word.

As their eyes became accustomed to the darkness, they searched to make out some human figures amongst the tombstones, but there were none, only the tops of the taller stones slightly illuminated by the lights from the street. Occasionally, some passer-by would be seen hurrying down the street, but mostly it was quiet for many long minutes.

Charlotte's eyelids began to droop just when the churchyard gate squeaked. Standing bolt upright, she reached for William's arm. He touched her hand to acknowledge that he, too, was aware of the sound. They watched intently and made out the silhouettes of six individuals moving towards Jane's grave. One had a lantern whose metal side did not quite shield the light. Charlotte watched as it swayed. The lantern stopped moving and the shutter opened. Its light was directed at a grave not far from Jane's. Two other lanterns were lit, and it was possible to make out faces of two of the men.

Charlotte shuddered. One of the men was the Jew. His

face contorted as he screwed up his eyes to see the surrounding area better. The voice that Charlotte had heard only that afternoon called out in a loud whisper. "Over here, Mr. 'awkes. It's 'er we're looking' for. I am sure of it." The African shined his light on the freshly turned earth.

Bastard! Charlotte thought.

Hawkes went to the man's side. "Are you sure?"

"I saw it this afternoon. I know it's 'er. Look closer. I put three big stones at the 'ead so's we'd know for certain."

The black man revealed his markers. Hawkes bent over to see. Charlotte wanted to kill them both.

Unexpectedly, the scene before her became a terrifying spectacle. Muddy arms shot up from the grave and grabbed Hawkes's throat. A head and body followed, covered with earth. Mad eyes shone out, illuminated by the lantern light. It had to be James. Charlotte was sure of it.

The African drew his cudgel from his belt and knocked Hawkes unconscious. At that instant, five other spectres rose up from their new graves and rushed with knives drawn at three of Hawkes accomplices. They were dispatched in no time. Their bodies were thrown in a newly dug hole and quickly covered up.

The African and the Jew helped James tie Hawkes's hands together. They put a gag around his mouth. A coach drew up in front of the churchyard. Four men carried their prisoner to the coach door. A large, wooden chest was inside. They threw Hawkes into and closed the top, padlocking it for good measure. James wiped his face and turned to look in Charlotte's direction. She could not make out his features. She knew he was searching for her. Finally, he turned and got into the coach.

John spoke from the darkness, near enough to cause

Charlotte to jump. "You must leave. It is not safe here. Go home. Jane will be disturbed no more."

Seeming unsurprised at John's presence, William answered, "I think that is an excellent suggestion, cousin. I shall accompany Mrs. Pruitt."

Charlotte listened to John's retreating steps. She noticed that there were bells ringing. Unable to say from which direction the sound came, she asked William, "Do you hear that?"

"No, I hear nothing of note. What am I listening to, Mrs. Pruitt?"

"The church bells. You do not hear them?"

"No, I am afraid not."

She felt odd. They were so clear to her.

"Shall we go, Mrs. Pruitt? I think Cousin John is correct. It is best to be out of here."

"Yes, of course."

They walked slowly along the side of the church, not sure of what was in their path. Reaching the gate without incident, Charlotte stopped to make sure Pater Noster Street was deserted. She noticed in the light of the streetlamps that snow was falling. As she turned, she found Burke-Scott preoccupied with pulling up his stockings. The top of his head was covered in large snowflakes. Tears welled up in her eyes.

"Thank you, William, for your assistance."

Burke-Scott stopped picking at his stockings and looked at her. He straightened up quickly and replied, "You are most welcome, Mrs. Pruitt."

"You have snow in your hair."

He touched it with his hand and began to brush the flakes away. "I most certainly do. It has turned very cold all of a sudden."

For an instant, Charlotte found herself charmed by this innocent man.

William caught the look that crossed her face.

She turned away, suddenly light-headed, her ears ringing. "We shall go to my house."

"As you wish, Mrs. Pruitt."

Gathering her cloak around her, Charlotte led the way to her front door. The bells grew louder with each step, and now her head ached. Unlocking the front door, she went in with William following.

Once in the parlour, she rang for Mr. Primm, who appeared quickly. She asked for tea and biscuits. "I am done with the city, William. I shall sell Bellagio House and have Mr. Sharp care for my late husband's business more fully than he already does. The mountains of Cumberland are wild and rugged. The weather sometimes has a violent nature, but I am not afraid there. Here, fear has ruled my life. Man's cruelty overwhelms me. My great-grandfather fled to the hills of Rosthwaite to be safe from the plague. I will take the children away from the madness that rules this supposedly civilized place. I will watch from my hill and not let violence touch my family again."

She was unable to continue. Pain shot through her temples and nearly blinded her. She pressed her hands to the sides of her head and groaned.

Concerned, William moved towards her. "Mrs. Pruitt, are you ill? How may I help you?"

She barely heard him. A sound like the wind rushing through the trees overtook her senses and swept her away into unconsciousness. She found herself peering into a wall of water. Lodore Falls, she wondered?

The thunderous torrent crashed down in front of her. She scuttled further back into a protected nook of the cold Borrowdale cave. A knife's blade of pain slid down through the top of her head to the base of her neck. A brilliant light shimmered. She saw her grandfather standing before her. He was speaking. She strained to hear his words. The pain shot through her head again, and darkness overtook her.

CHAPTER NINE

The coach with James, his men, and the chest containing Hawkes, arrived at the dock where Fleet Canal emptied into the Thames. A bargeman with his boat awaited them. Allen Peters, a long-time friend of James's, directed the loading of the chest into the boat, making sure the air holes that had been drilled into the top were not covered. James thanked three of the men who had helped with the capture. They left, disappearing into the foggy streets.

James and the remaining men climbed into the boat. It glided quickly through the water towards Wapping, where a Venetian ship waited to take them on board. Arriving there, the chest was unloaded and taken to the hold. James went to his cabin, where, with the help of Count Cesi's servants, he rid himself of his muddied garments. He bathed in warm water, surveying his cuts and bruises received during the battle in the churchyard. His hair was washed, combed with difficulty, and dressed into a queue. New clothes, a fine linen shirt, silk breeches, waistcoat, and coat were brought in his cabin. He began to look like himself again.

All the while, he made a list of Hawkes's transgressions. Each wrong done to Charlotte, to Peg, Countess Cittidini,

Charles Bonnie, Jacob Golder, the Okehampton innkeeper and his wife, and to himself. What he required, however, were Hawke's confessions to the infant's murder in Devon and to Audley Pruitt's killing in Hampstead. He would see Hawkes hang for those crimes.

He smiled to himself. I have you, trapped like an insect. The thought of Hawkes possibly escaping made him pause. He is too much like Jack Sheppard. I will double the watch and double his irons. So much of James's experience with Hawkes was in heightened circumstances, the battle in Portugal, his madness on the moors, the fight at the gallows. Hawkes's acts of evil were outside of James's civilized experience. He could not fathom why a man would act as Hawkes did.

Now perhaps I will have an opportunity to find out. My challenge is to not let my hatred overtake me and kill him in the process.

James's plan was to gather a group of influential gentlemen on the ship who would hear Hawkes's confession of the crimes for which he, James, stood accused. This group of men would understand that he was innocent. They would have the authority to clear his name and take Hawkes into custody. Hawkes would undoubtedly be convicted and hanged.

The chosen gentlemen had been approached through various channels and told of the plan. Each agreed to take part. The invitations they received announced that said they were to be treated to a weekend fête, sailing down the Thames from Wapping to Sheerness and back again. William Murray, Earl of Mansfield; Sir John Fielding, the blind magistrate; General John Campbell, Earl of Loudoun; John Wilkes, the politician; and Robert Adam, the architect, arrived at the ship separately in the early evening before Hawkes was captured.

Once settled into their quarters, the gentlemen met the count and countess for a sumptuous supper. During the meal, Lord Mansfield proposed a wager with General Campbell on how long it would take before Hawkes confessed. Wilkes asked to be included in the betting. The terms of the wager settled, the group fell to discussing the state of politics and art in Europe. Full of drink and food, they retired for the evening. Only the count and countess were aware when James and his group boarded with their captive.

The countess was pleased to learn of Hawkes's capture. She was the first cousin to the present doge, the ruler of Venice. The wealth of the Cittidini family was legendary. Hawkes had made a great mistake when he stole from her.

"You know, of course," she had told James when she'd met with him two weeks earlier, "that horrid man took from me some small, but priceless *objects d'art*, some of which have been in my family for two centuries. We attempted to discover what he had done with them when he was our prisoner in Venice. He would admit nothing no matter how he was tortured. Please, do your utmost to divine the whereabouts of my treasures. For this, I would be most grateful."

James learned at that time that she would be bringing with her a beautiful slab of marble from the quarry at Carrara. Its intended use was for the floor in the grand entrance way at Kenwood House, Lord Mansfield's mansion in Hampstead that Adam was remodelling. The countess suggested in the interim that it might be used to press the answers from Hawkes that they sought. Later, she would broach the subject with Lord Mansfield.

Now, Count Cesi greeted James warmly when he was announced. Countess Cittidini entered the cabin upon hearing their voices.

"Signor Clarke," she said, as she extended her hand grandly to James.

"Countess." James took her hand and kissed it lightly. "You do me a great honour by allowing me the use of your ship."

The grand lady smiled. "You are looking well, signor, much better than when you came to see us two weeks ago."

"I fervently pray, countess, that I shall not have to return to life on the streets. It is most unpleasant."

"How is dear Mrs. Pruitt?"

There was an uncomfortable pause, during which time James attempted to compose his thoughts. "I fear we have parted company."

"Ah, but not at your behest."

"No, countess."

The lady looked directly into James's face, trying to discern his sentiments.

The count, sensing his cousin might be overstepping English sensibility, enjoined James to have some repast before he retired. James ate, and endeavoured to converse but he was eager to get below. A heavy guard of both the count's men and his own watched over the chest and its contents. No one, he told them, was to open it but himself.

After James excused himself from the table, the count took him aside.

"I know, my friend," he said, "you hope to secure a confession tomorrow. The noise of the docks and the traffic on the water should hide any screams. We shall sail into the estuary as we planned and if necessary, take to the open sea if more time is required. Hawkes has tormented us all. We may be allowed to enjoy his pain, I dare say."

"I will not fail to take advantage of the opportunity you have afforded me, Francesco," James replied, "I am, as always, in your debt."

"I simply wish to see you returned to your ancestral seat so that I may come and take advantage of your hospitality, my friend." The count smiled. "James, I intend to send an invitation to John Fuller and Lady Emma as we planned. I would still like to invite Mrs. Pruitt with your permission. I believe that she should be here."

"As you wish."

"Do you love her?"

"I shall always love her, Francesco." James left the cabin, trying to prevent his friend from seeing the pain on his face and in his heart.

On deck, Charles Bonnie and Jacob Golder waited for James. This evening had been a long time coming for both of them, and they felt great satisfaction that it was here at last.

The three men, Clarke, Bonnie, and Golder walked together now to the steps leading to the dank hold where their captive lay. Bonnie was not convinced that Hawkes was human. His gruesome acts appeared to be the work of a demon in league with evil forces. Perhaps he would rise out of the chest in another form, kill them all, and make his escape into some nether world. Bonnie shuddered at the images swirling in his head.

James did not envision that fate, but he did not want to chance Hawkes's escape. As they descended into the hold of the ship, they passed the countess's slab of marble. It rested among the chests of exquisite Venetian glassware, silks from Lake Como, and other treasures that were to be sold in London.

At the far end of the hold, illuminated by oil lanterns, equipped with mirrors, four men stood watch over the wooden chest. The three newcomers greeted the others. Jacob Golder whispered to James that he would wait in the shadows, then he moved away silently. James asked Allen Peters to open the lid of the chest while all the rest stood ready with pistols drawn and cutlasses at the ready. Peters undid the padlock and slowly opened the top.

There was no movement.

James peered into the chest, asking Peters to hold a lantern closer. The man obliged, and James saw Hawkes's mud-covered body. Blood oozed from his mouth and nose.

"Remove him from the chest," James said.

Two of the men leaned over, each taking hold of an arm. His inert body was heavy and slippery from the mud. They struggled to lift him. Peters and another man grabbed his legs. Together, they hoisted him out. Once clear of the chest, they dropped him on the deck. He lay there on his back, legs akimbo, showing no signs of life.

Allen Peters bent over to see if he could detect any breath. James reached out to pull his friend back just at the moment that Hawkes made his move. Grabbing Peters by the neck, Hawkes bounded to a squat. Apparently, he had freed his hands in the chest and only pretended to be bound. He held his hostage with one arm and grabbed Peter's dagger from its sheath. As he held the dagger point between his captive's shoulder blades, he glared at James.

"You'll need to kill me or set me free to save your friend," Hawkes hissed. "You're an honourable man, eh,

Jem? You won't let him die. Either way, I'm free of you."

He stood up, forcing Allen Peters to follow. Using him as a shield, Hawkes circled around towards the steps. He got past the chests with the silks and glass.

From out of the shadows, Golder appeared. He brought a large piece of timber squarely down on Hawkes's head. Allen Peters jumped to the side as Hawkes fell on his face. In short order, the men dragged Hawkes back to the area with the chest. This time, they chained his arms behind his back and shackled his ankles.

"Bring some water, would you? Clean him up for bed," James said, allowing himself to smile at last.

CHAPTER TEN

At Bellagio House, Charlotte's eyes opened. Her headache had subsided, but she was disoriented. The glowing embers from the fireplace gave off only a bit of light by which to see. She realized she was on the settee, still fully clothed. Someone had covered her with a blanket.

As she sat in the near darkness, she became aware of little spurts of snoring. Raising herself onto her elbows, she turned to look over her shoulder. William Burke-Scott sat upright in a chair, sound asleep, his hair going in every direction, and his mouth wide open. Suddenly, he began snoring loudly until an enormous snort caused him to stir, shifting his position. Then, the spurts of snoring resumed.

In a rush, the day's events returned to Charlotte as she lay back down and drew the blanket up around her neck. Fear gripped her until she recalled James taking Hawkes away.

"He's gone," she whispered, her mind in confusion. They are both gone, she thought; Hawkes, who brought terror into her life, and James, who brought both joy and sorrow.

She felt cold, her throat tight, as if she were swinging from a rope. A long, dark future lay before her. Jack and all of Jane Rourke's children were her reason for living now. It was her love and care that would shape their futures.

Her grandfather's voice echoed from the waterfall. This time, she heard his words. You have great strength within yourself, Charlotte. You may draw strength from the land, as well. Look to the rugged beauty of the fells, the power of the water as it rushes down the ghylls, the howling voice of the wind in the mountain passes. Take heart and find solace in these gifts. Heft to the hills like the flocks of sheep. Do not be moved by fashion and frivolity. Your passion for life is deeper than these.

She heard her own voice adding to her grandfather's advice. And James Clarke will always be a part of my life. These words startled her. She answered herself, yes, he will, but my path is not with him. The rest of her night was spent fitfully. She would fall asleep, only to be roused suddenly by a clock's chime or one of Burke-Scott's snorts. When she finally did sleep, early morning light was beginning to brighten the sky.

She awoke to find William gone. On the table beside her lay a silver tray which held a newly delivered letter. The envelope was made of gold paper lace. Her mood brightened as she read it. Countess Cittidini and Count Cesi were requesting her presence at dinner that afternoon on board the countess's ship anchored in the Thames at Wapping. The ship would then sail leisurely on the Thames for two days. She was invited for that, as well. They apologized for the lateness of the invitation but begged her to come.

She was thrilled. However, realizing she must respond and get to Grosvenor Square to prepare for the evening, she nearly fell off the settee calling for the servants.

After quickly freshening up and eating a small

breakfast, she was off at a fast pace in her sedan chair. When she arrived, she found the house in an uproar. Emma and John had received an invitation, too.

"It is short notice. You will go, Charlotte? We must respond directly, don't you agree?" Emma asked.

"Yes, I shall go, Emma," Charlotte said. "How could I not? But I must see how the children are faring."

"William took them to the park. He has some expedition planned for them this morning."

"He is a very kind young man, I think. He helped me immensely in the churchyard. It was a horrible night, Emma."

"He said nothing to me, though he may have spoken of it to John."

"I don't feel able to speak about it now. Please, forgive my reticence. James did capture Hawkes, that much I can offer."

"You are free of Hawkes!"

"Of both of them, I think."

"What happened, Charlotte?"

"James and I argued in my garden. I will never be able to forgive him."

There was a great commotion in the front entryway and William came bounding into the parlour. He did not see Charlotte as he approached Emma. "Dearest cousin, you will never imagine who I met in the park."

"William, I…" Emma began.

"You will not guess who. So, let me tell you. Theodore Brinsley Hall. Do you remember him? He was engaged to Miss Henrietta Rawlings, our cousin Lavinia's dearest friend, but then she ran away with an actor from York. Teddy was bereft and went off to India for two years. He is back and living in a very nice house in Hampstead. He asked if the boys and I could come for a visit. Two or three days, he said, at least. It would do them a world of good to get out of the city. Do you think Mrs. Pruitt would approve?"

Charlotte laughed at his enthusiasm. The unexpected sound behind his back startled him. He jumped and nearly knocked over one of Emma's Chinese vases.

"William, please try to control yourself," Emma cried.

Charlotte caught his arm, trying to help him regain his balance. His hand touched hers. She felt her face flush and quickly stepped away from him. He hadn't noticed, she was sure, nor had Emma.

"I'm sorry, William," she said. "I didn't mean to startle you. I think it's an excellent idea to go to the country. Will you take Annie and Jenny with you? They will help keep an eye on everyone."

"You might consider staying for two days," Emma added. "We've been invited to stay for the weekend on a Venetian ship anchored at Wapping. We shall be staying two nights at least, I venture."

"Cousin Emma, how exciting! Will you be attending also, Mrs. Pruitt?"

"Yes, I shall."

"This outing to Hampstead will be perfect. I shall begin all their studies in an idyllic setting. Will you excuse me? I must go prepare my charges." He bowed to Charlotte and to Emma. Turning, he left the room without mishap. They watched him bound down the hallway.

Charlotte was the first to speak. "Is it odd that I find him quite charming?"

"Not in the least. Puppies are quite dear also, but then

they ruin your furniture. However, there is no time for new romances. We have to prepare for our outing." Emma grabbed Charlotte's hand, pulling her along to the dressing room where they spent the rest of the morning deciding on their wardrobes and having their hair dressed.

CHAPTER ELEVEN

Preparations had been underway aboard ship since dawn for the weekend's festivities. Fresh produce had been ordered and was being delivered. Game and poultry were being rowed over from the docks. Flowers and greenery needed three boats and several boys each to hoist it all on to the deck.

James slept longer than he planned. His dreams were vivid and upsetting. He wrestled with Hawkes, who swiftly changed into a heavy, dark beast. The creature weighed heavy on James's chest. He could not breathe. His arms had no strength. The hot breath of the beast filled his nostrils. James himself began transforming into the creature, his claws tearing at some prey he held. Looking down, he saw the prey was himself in human form. In a rage and unable to stop himself, he killed the writhing man.

Desperate to be out of the nightmare, James tried to call out. Finally, a small sound born in his chest crawled painfully up his throat and slipped out his mouth. It was enough to break the bondage of sleep. His eyes flew open, and he was free.

He dressed and made his way to the hold. The watch greeted him. There were two Venetians and two Englishmen. Hawkes was asleep, his body covered only in a dirty rag around his loins. He rested upright, chained to a squat, rough, timber pole. James sat down on a wooden box in front of him. He stared at Hawkes, thinking to himself, why, dear God, have you sent this man to plague me? What lesson is it that You would have me learn? He looked down at the floor, lost in thought.

"You are a bloody weakling," a rasping voice hissed. James's head shot up. He saw Hawkes staring at him. "My father was a fucking weak sot like you. He's dead and so will you be."

The four men who were guarding Hawkes came close ready to follow James's commands. He held up his hand to indicate that they should stand their ground. He sat quietly, trying to comprehend who this creature was that sat chained before him.

The image of Charlotte's room in the aftermath of Peg's murder flashed into his mind.

"And you are a man of such strength that you butchered that poor, madwoman in the Pruitts' house," he mused aloud.

Hawkes turned his face partially away from James. A small smile played on his lips.

"Oh, aye, I drank her blood. Did you know that? But what did you do? You fucked her. But what else are lunatics good for?" Now he smiled broadly. "Eh, brother?"

"I am not your brother! You vile, inhuman filth." Repulsed, James stood and moved away from Hawkes.

"No, true enough." Hawkes responded, ignoring the second part of James's statement. "No brother would have left me to die like you did."

"You slaughtered the Portuguese boy for no reason, you bastard."

"What boy?"

"When we took Vila Velha de Rodao. You do not remember? He came out of the shadows. You called him out. Offered him safety and food. You slit his throat. Have there been so many you have no recollection?"

"Perhaps, or maybe he never existed."

"What?" James said.

"Your mind, Clarke, is your weakness. You cannot deny that."

"He lived, and he died by your hand. That is the truth."

"Truth is written by the winners. I am in no position to argue." He turned his face to James. "I remember no boy."

"You have neither honour nor compassion."

"Nor money for either. My life is about survival. I've had nothing handed to me. I never was dressed in lace skirts and coddled like you. My father got caught poaching a rabbit in Land's End. That earned him seven years in Georgia picking cotton. In year six, he saw the butt end of a bitch in a field. Invited or not, he fucked her there. She dropped me where she stood nine months later and went off after a big black buck on the plantation. I was passed from one wench to another until I bit the nipple off a whore at three. From then on, my father figured I could take care of myself. He gave up looking for a ma for me and went back to lookin' for a good fuck for himself. We were always close, old dad an' me."

"Without honour or moral constraints, you are a wild animal," James spat.

"Oh, aye. And with 'em you become a dried-up hypocrite like yourself. Where was your morals when you invited yourself to Pruitt's wife?"

Hot rage filled James. With two steps, he stood in front

of his prisoner and the back of his hand hit Hawkes's face full on. The man's head shot back, but his eyes did not close. He righted himself and rested against the timber. A gloating laugh rose from his throat.

"I gave her a better fuck than you ever will. Did she give you all the details brother? How she spread her legs…"

"Shut up!" James shouted, unable to control his rage. He grabbed at his enemy's throat. The Venetian guards, surprised by this turn of events, pulled him off Hawkes. "I will kill you!" James spat out. He pulled free of the Italians. Falling on his knees, he put his face close to Hawkes's face. "I will hack you to pieces. I will slice off your private parts!"

"Too late, boyo," Hawkes hissed back. James looked confused. "You, brother, left that to the Portuguese. You, man of honour, abandoned me after I begged for your help."

James sat back on his haunches. "No, no." He shook his head slowly. All of his anger gone.

"Oh aye, they held me down, two stinking, cadaverous, old women. One of 'em sat on my broken leg, the other took her time with a dull knife, while I screamed for mercy." James needed air. He could not breathe. Staggering to his feet, he lurched towards the steps.

Charles Bonnie stood in the shadows and watched the interchange. All doubts were gone. Hawkes was the devil, and he would cut out Hawkes's tongue before killing him.

CHAPTER TWELVE

Charlotte was in the last throes of preparation. She'd spent an hour having her hair dressed as Jack played happily at her feet. Her body ached from the previous day's ordeal, but she was determined to ignore it. Jack crawled into her lap and looked up into her face. The grey of his eyes caught Charlotte off guard. They were James's eyes in the garden at Bellagio that morning when the sunlight bathed his face, and he'd caught her up in his arms. She pulled Jack close to her. For an instant he responded and relaxed against her body, but then he pulled away and struggled to be free.

She let him go. He galloped wildly around the room. With Jack whooping in the background, her hairdresser held up a mirror, so Charlotte could see his creation. She was satisfied after the few strands were rearranged from a curl on the top to a loop on the side.

With the hairdresser gone, Betsy, Charlotte's maid, was ready with her robe, skirts, and stomacher. Charlotte chose the dress the countess had made for her. She had worn it only once, on the island in Bellagio. The light, liquid feel of the silk made her want to dance. Jack seeing her take a little sidestep, came running and crawled under her petticoats.

There was a knock at the door and Betsy hurried to answer it. Whispers were exchanged at the door.

"Begging your pardon, mum, but Mr. Burke-Scott would like a word with you."

"That's fine, Betsy. Allow him to enter."

Coming in, William thanked Betsy, who smiled broadly at him. He turned his attention to Charlotte. About to speak, he stopped on seeing her, his shyness overcoming him. He looked like a lost little boy.

The awkwardness was broken when Jack bolted out of his hiding place and threw himself at William's legs. The unfortunate man, being taken completely by surprise, lost his balance. Legs flying up into the air, he toppled over backward onto Betsy. Charlotte screamed as she saw Jack hurled heavenward. He fell with a thud just short of a large, Delft vase. His wind knocked out of him, he could not catch his breath. Charlotte sat on the floor and took him into her arms.

Using the most soothing voice she could muster, she cooed, "You will be fine, Jackie. Mama is here. Try a little breath, my sweet one. Mama is here." She rocked him gently.

After what seemed ages, he drew a breath. Clinging to Charlotte, he cried pitifully. William rolled off of poor Betsy. Not bothering to get to his feet, he crawled on hands and knees to Charlotte and Jack.

"Jackie, I am so sorry. What a fright you had." Jack stopped briefly to look at William and then began to ball uncontrollably.

Exasperated and shaken by the breach in her calm, Charlotte spoke sharply to William. "Take the other children and go! Jack will come with me. And for heaven's sake, be careful!"

Still on his hands and knees, William felt the rebuke.

212

"Yes, Mrs. Pruitt, I shall do my best." He stood, trying to regain some dignity. "Please have a good evening, madam. Goodbye." Turning, he saw Betsy. "Please, excuse my clumsiness, Betsy. Good day." He exited without mishap.

After about ten minutes, Jack calmed down. Betsy took him while Charlotte got to her feet. Jack stretched out his arms and tried to grab at her, unhappy to be in the maid's arms. Charlotte sat him on her lap while the hairdresser, who had been summoned back, did his best to repair Charlotte's hair.

There was a timid knock at the door and Charlotte stiffened, imagining it was William, come back again. She bade the person enter and to her surprise, Annie appeared.

"Excuse me, Charlotte, but William said that Jack was going with you. May I come along and watch him while you are on the ship?"

"Annie, you are the dearest girl," Charlotte replied, truly touched by her thoughtfulness. "Yes, please, you should come with us. I would like the count and countess to meet you and Jack. I think you would enjoy sailing the estuary. Will you come?"

"Oh, yes! Thank you!" Annie replied.

"Let me see what clothes we can arrange. Here, sit down and have your hair done." Annie obeyed, and Charlotte, with Jack in her arms, went off to find Emma and make plans.

CHAPTER THIRTEEN

Standing on deck, James attempted to calm himself. Though it was a fine day with a warm wind, the weather did not cheer his spirits. His shame and guilt at what he saw as his part in Hawkes's mutilation overtook him. Hawkes, he'd thought from the first, threatened all he held dear. He was a man who, having nothing, was willing to risk everything. James wondered how many more like him there were in the world. He understood that his code of honour was imperilled by men like this.

When James was a child, he understood who he was and where he belonged in Society. Now, ambition seemed to allow anyone to create their own destiny. James thought back to his youth. His world had changed when his brother died. All assumptions and expectations were nullified. He had Thomas Warrender to thank for that. Another man of ambition, but one with wealth and a title.

The only joy I have had, James thought, is in loving Charlotte and Jack. He is my son no matter what she says. Anger and confusion overtook him, and tears came to his eyes. He prayed silently, dear Lord God, help me. I am an arrogant, foolish man. Please, guide my hand and my heart. I would have revenge on Hawkes. I am full of fury and hatred. I would love Charlotte and care for my son, Jack, but they have slipped away from me, because of my stubbornness. I humble myself before You. I ask Your forgiveness and Your guidance. I pray in Lord Jesus's name, Amen.

He looked out towards Wapping and noticed the countess's gondoliers were transporting visitors to the ship. Obtaining a spyglass and putting it to his eye, he saw that it was Charlotte with Jack held tight in her arms.

His joy and confusion collided. She was coming. He might have one more chance. Oh, but ye gods, do not make more mistakes. And what to do about Hawkes? He felt giddy and sick at the same time.

Jack, thrilled by the closeness of the water, struggled to be free of his mother's grip so he could touch the smooth surface as they glided along. Annie watched carefully, sitting next to him and ready to catch him if he succeeded in obtaining his freedom. Charlotte and Emma were deep in conversation about the countess and count. John Fuller sat, seemingly indifferent to all the excitement around him. Betsy sat near the boatman, endeavouring to get the swarthy fellow's attention.

As their boat came alongside the ship, Jack made one more attempt to break free. Pushing forward, he caught Charlotte off balance as she began to stand up. She fell backward and would have landed on Betsy had not the surefooted boatman caught her with ease. Jack hopped over John Fuller and was nearly in the water before John grabbed his coat tails. He held the struggling child under one arm.

"I've a mind to throw you in the Thames, Jack. Do you think you could make it to the bank? Shall we try?"

"Mama!" Jack screamed.

Charlotte sat with Annie at her side, trying to compose herself.

"Thank you, John. I shall take Jack now."

John Fuller got hold of Jack in both hands and let him down gently. "Go to your mother, Jack but mind your manners or you will find yourself swimming, I warrant thee." The tearful child crawled slowly into his mother's arms.

From up above a voice, from the main deck greeted them. "Would you care to join us, my friends?"

It was the count.

"We would be honoured, Count Cesi," John called up to him.

Soon, they were all aboard. The count introduced everyone to Signor Gabriele Bella, a slightly built, but quite handsome, young man. He, Count Cesi explained, had been a student of Canaletto's and had been invited on this journey to record memorable scenes for his patroness, the countess.

Greetings and introductions done, they proceeded to the Countess Cittidini's cabin. As the count ushered them in, they were surprised to find five gentlemen in a heated discussion. The men stopped and turned their attention to Charlotte's group. Before Count Cesi had the opportunity to begin introductions anew, John Wilkes stepped forward.

"Mrs. Pruitt, I am delighted to see you." He smiled, and taking Charlotte's hand, kissed it with a great flourish.

"Mr. Wilkes, what a pleasant surprise to find you here,"

Charlotte replied.

"Mr. Wilkes," the count said, laughing, "seldom have I seen such a genteel greeting from an Englishman."

Now introductions began in earnest. Lord Mansfield, being well acquainted with Emma and her family, stepped forward and greeted her and John. Finally, the count bade the ladies be seated in comfortable chairs. Charlotte and Emma did so while Annie looked after Jack as he explored the room. Servants appeared with wine in goblets, and just as the count was about to make the first toast of the evening, the countess made her grand entrance. The door opened wide, and she stepped in and chided the count.

"Cousin, would you begin toasting without me?"

All the seated gentlemen quickly rose to their feet. Count Cesi responded seriously.

"Dear lady, never. I, like the sun and moon, live solely to do your bidding." He finished with a flourishing bow.

"Oh, he is the greatest liar alive, dear friends," Countess Cittidini said as she crossed the room, nodding acknowledgments to the gentlemen whom she had met the night before. She stopped in front of John Fuller, and offering him her hand, said with a girlish laugh, "But I do love his lies." She smiled at John, removing her hand after he lightly touched it with his lips. "Lady Emma, welcome. I am so happy to see you again and so glad you all could come on such short notice." She stopped when she saw Annie chasing after Jack. "Who is this young beauty?"

Charlotte rose and spoke, "Countess Cittidini, may I have the pleasure of presenting my ward, Miss Anne Rourke." Annie did a curtsy, her eyes remaining downcast.

"Dear child, please, look at me. You have beautiful eyes. Do not hide them." Annie looked up and smiled, charmed by the great lady.

The countess's gaze fell on Jack as he came close to her.

"Charlotte, this is your son? How handsome he is! His hair is like spun gold. Truly, he is an angel."

"In appearance only, I assure you, countess," Charlotte laughed.

"I see the mischief that plays around his eyes. He is his father's son, I suspect." The countess smiled innocently and sat down. Charlotte returned her smile, choosing not to comment, and took her seat again.

A knock at the door broke the silence. A servant stepped over to open it. In the entrance stood James. His hair was duly powdered, his stockings straight, his silks fitting most handsomely. Countess Cittidini looked up.

"James, I was wondering if we were to have the pleasure of your company this evening."

"Countess, I am most grateful for the invitation. Good evening everyone, Lady Emma, John, Miss Rourke, Mrs. Pruitt, gentlemen."

His eyes rested on Charlotte's face. His expression held both sadness and desire. He did not speak, but his face reddened.

Charlotte was also speechless. Her first reaction was to attempt to flee the room, but she forced herself to sit stiffly at attention. Her anger mounting, she tried to affect an indifferent air. Yet now, seeing James's heart so exposed to all, she was filled with longing. She hated herself for loving him so uncontrollably.

During the introductions, Jack had been quiet, but when James entered, he ran to Annie, where he stayed peeking out from behind her. He did not recognize his father with his wig and formal attire. Now he ventured close to his mother, trying to get her attention.

"Mama! Jackie hungry now!"

The count was the first to reply. "Young Signorino Jack, you speak for all assembled, I believe. Let us dine, else we miss watching your beautiful English countryside when we set sail."

"An excellent suggestion, cousin," the countess agreed as she stood up. Lord Mansfield came forward, "May I accompany you, Countess Cittidini?"

"Thank you, your lordship," she said, smiling. She turned to Emma. "Lady Emma, please come sit on my right. You must tell me all your news since last I saw you in Paris."

Emma arose and took John's arm. Count Cesi crossed to Annie and offered her his arm. She smiled shyly and gladly accepted it. Turning to Jack, she took him by the hand and the three of them went in to dinner. Jack tried to resist, but Annie chided him, and he came along beside her.

Mr. Adam and Signor Bella left the room chatting, in Italian, about art. Mr. Wilkes took John Fielding's arm and led the blind magistrate to his seat. General Campbell followed after them.

James, regaining his composure, moved to Charlotte. "Madam, would you do me the honour of accompanying me to dinner?"

She looked up at him, "I would, sir." Standing, she took his arm. She felt a rush of pleasure as her hand touched him. However, the events of the past few days crashed in on her. James took a step forward, but she was still.

"Charlotte?" he inquired. He turned to look at her, a question in his eyes.

Her head was bowed, and her eyes closed.

"Do you feel ill?" he asked and touched her hand.

She opened her eyes but did not look at him. "I'm fine, thank you."

They proceeded into the dining room with no more words spoken between them. As soon as the ladies were all seated, the gentlemen sat, and dinner commenced. Dish after dish was set upon the table. The servants moved busily to give the guests servings of all the dishes they requested. One wished to try *le fricassee de poulets à l'Italienne*, another *le côtelettes d'agneau a la Toulous*, and still a third demanded *le saute de faisans aux truffes*.

It was an excellent feast, and their glasses were never empty. The servants poured bottles of wine, ale, or port depending on each guest's desires.

The count led the discussion and soon everyone was laughing at the tales of the Venetian court. At last, Count Cesi turned to Charlotte, asking, "What are your plans for the future, dear lady?"

"I have had too much of London and most of the people in it as of late, excepting, of course, Emma and John, who have been exceedingly kind through all my difficulties, and Mr. Wilkes, with whom I always enjoy speaking. I shall retire with Jack and all my wards to Rosthwaite in the north where I plan to live a quiet, peaceful life."

"We will miss you terribly, Charlotte," Emma said, "but we will come and visit. Will we not, John?" Turning to the count, she continued, "I was quite charmed by Rosthwaite when I visited."

"You enjoy the rustic life, do you Lady Emma?" the countess asked.

"Within limits, countess. Whitestone, Charlotte's home, is charming. It made me believe that Arcadia was possible, but the surrounding mountains, or fells as they call them locally, are terrifying. Their peaks are wild, unattainable heights that make one believe in the most fantastic spectres. It will never be a place for holiday outings, of that I am quite sure."

"Oh fie, Emma," Charlotte retorted. "If I were a painter or poet, I would find endless inspiration there."

"You are one of a kind, my dear," Emma said, laughing.

"And what are your future plans, James?" Count Cesi asked innocently.

"If I have my way, I shall return to Devon and regain what little is left of Kirkmoor."

The count smiled. "I believe, James and Mrs. Pruitt, you are destined for one another." He continued, though he saw Charlotte's mouth tighten at the suggestion. "One loves rainy mountains, the other dark moors, if I understand my English weather and topography correctly. I believe you should both come back to Lake Como. There, you have mountains and rain, but you also have warm nights and the myriad scents of flowers. And wine," he said, looking around the table. "Everyone, please, have more wine."

With his stomach full, Jack fell asleep on Charlotte's lap. Annie took him, at the countess's urging, into her bedchamber and laid him down on the bed. A servant was left in charge to watch over him as he slept. When the feast finished, the count invited all the guests to take a walk on the main deck.

Charlotte, Annie, and Emma first shared a spyglass in order to observe the comings and goings on the river. After that, Emma and Charlotte entertained the countess, Annie, and Signor Bella with the latest gossip and scandals of the city. The count, James, John, and the other gentlemen moved apart from the ladies to discuss subjects of interest.

The afternoon light was beginning to fade. One towering cloud obscured the sun for a few minutes. Looking up, Charlotte saw its top edge begin to glow. This glow transformed into silver rays shooting out into the sky as the sunlight broke through the cloud. Her reverie was disturbed when one of the countess's servants came running on deck from her cabin. After a low bow to the countess, he began speaking so fast in Italian that Charlotte could not understand what he was saying.

Abruptly, the countess rose to her feet and dealt a swift, hard, blow to the cowering man. He fell whimpering to the deck as she called out, *"Imbecille!"*

The count went to his cousin's side. They were whispering heatedly as Charlotte approached them.

"What did he say?" she asked. "What is the matter?" She suddenly knew that the man was speaking of Jack. "What has happened?"

"The idiot left him unattended for a minute," Count Cesi said. "When he returned, Jack was not in the cabin. He will not have wandered far. We will all look for him. I will organize the servants to search as well. We will find him quickly, Mrs. Pruitt."

The deck began to spin under Charlotte's feet. The image of Jack's little body falling deeper and deeper into the murky water surrounding them filled her vision. She grabbed Emma's arm, but looked to James who was approaching her.

"Jem, it's Jackie!" she managed to say.

He turned to the men and quickly gave instructions to all present on where they should search. They dispersed in a matter of seconds. Annie and Signor Bella went as well.

With her body growing cold, Charlotte struggled to stay conscious. She willed herself to move, to join the search, but her body fought her. Both the countess and Emma attended her, speaking encouraging words and stroking her arms and her back. After bending her head forward, she began to think more clearly.

"I must find him," she said.

"Are you quite sure you're not lightheaded?" Emma asked, still holding on to her arm.

"I shall be fine." Emma let go but continued to stand close to her friend in the event she needed help.

"Mrs. Pruitt, allow the men to search, *per favore*," Countess Cittidini said. "My cousin and James, I am sure, have instructed everyone on board to search for little Jack."

"Countess, thank you, but I must join them." She looked past Emma.

Her eye was caught by the dark hatch. The grate, which normally would cover it, was askew. Without stopping to explain she ran to the steps that led down into the ship's innards and descended into the darkness of the decks below. Several steps down, she reached the first deck. There were no lanterns alight. Her eyes, even when adjusted, could make out very little. She heard footsteps overhead. There were no sounds of a small child exploring or fretting. The steps continued downward, past two more decks to where there was a dim light in the hold. She heard voices below.

"Hello," Charlotte called out, going down the stairs to another deck. "Have you seen a small child?"

"A small child?" a voice responded. "Is that what you said?"

Charlotte realized the absurdity of the situation and

moved further down the steps to explain that Jack was missing. She came to the bottom of the stairs and began to speak before she could make out who was there.

"My son has wandered away from where he was sleeping. We are all searching. Please, if you find him…"

She stopped mid-sentence as one of the men came towards her, trying to block her from coming any further. What was it she saw before her? She could make out three men standing, but what was on the floor? She heard moaning.

"We have seen no one, madam," the man in front of her replied in a too loud voice. "But rest assured, if we see the lad, we will bring him to the main deck. Please, let me escort you back up now."

The man speaking was dressed in a dark, woollen suit. He was gentle in his tone, but firm in not allowing her to pass. She turned to go but heard the sound of someone retching and vomiting. Her stomach turned. There was something wrong here, but she was afraid to ask, feeling herself in danger.

She mounted the first step but stopped dead when a raspy voice yelled.

"CHARLOTTE PRUITT! BITCH!"

She turned and was now able to see over the guard's head behind her. She found herself looking at the deathly pale face of Edward Hawkes. Spittle dripped from his chin, and he was nearly naked. Chained to a pole, his wrists and ankles were shackled. After their eyes met, he was struck down by a powerful kick to his side.

Terrified, Charlotte flew up the steps, all the while stepping on her skirts and hitting her knees on the stairs. On reaching the third deck up she saw the sky above her.

She moved like a drowning man striving to reach the water's surface. She burst out into the air. The man behind her tried to reach her with words of comfort, but she tore away from him as if he were the devil himself.

There in front of her, where she had left Countess Cittidini and Emma only a few minutes before, stood a crowd of people, and in the centre was James holding Jack. The little boy laughed as he was bounced up and down by his father.

Charlotte, overcome with relief at seeing her son, rushed into the crowd and embraced both Jack and James. The latter's arm pulled her close. She covered the boy's face with kisses, her tears causing his nose and cheeks to shine. In the midst of so much joy and with their three faces so close together, James and Charlotte kissed. Jack grabbed both their necks and pulled himself into the middle. Reluctantly, Charlotte and James parted.

"Who found him?" Charlotte asked.

"James did," the count answered. "Found him crawling up onto the railing aft. He is very taken with the water. You should bring him to Venice. Our canals would please him. Do you not agree, cousin?"

"I do, indeed," Countess Cittidini replied, smiling.

"Thank you, James." Charlotte took Jack into her arms and buried her face in his hair. The little boy hugged his mother, unaware of the commotion he had caused.

In that moment, James saw Allen Peters standing at the edge of the assembled group, his plain woollen suit contrasting with the gentlemen's finery. James went to him and the two men talked quietly. When they were done, Peters returned to the hold while James turned back to Charlotte, his face now sombre.

Managing to get the count's attention, James pulled him aside to have a private conversation. "I have so much that needs to be said to Charlotte, my friend, but I am afraid. I do not want her to turn away from me in anger because of my bumbling. Please, help me. Ask her to join us in my cabin. Be my interpreter. Tell her I am an idiot if you must but get her to listen to me. Help me to keep my temper and let go of my pride. My God, I am nearly forty, and I find myself knowing less and less each day. I want to marry her. Tell her I will give her all I have, if I ever get back what is mine." James stopped to take a breath. His face was red and small beads of perspiration formed on his forehead.

"My dear English friend," Count Cesi began, "calm yourself. You are a hero, a brave soldier, an intellectual of sorts, and yet you become a schoolboy when faced with talking to this woman. Tell her what is in your heart, please. I will help, but I believe she wants to hear it from you. Come, I will extend the invitation. What do you plan to tell her of our guest in the hold?"

"She has seen him."

"When? How?" the count asked.

"Peters told me. She came looking for Jack. They tried to hide Hawkes, but he made himself known by screaming her name, accompanied by profanity. I will be honest with her. That is all I can do now."

"I think that wise."

"You will ask her to come?"

"Yes. Go and prepare yourself. John shall entertain the gentlemen while we weigh anchor and get under sail."

The count returned to the group, and James paused briefly. Why, he wondered, was he unable to have reason and logic rule his life? He found no answer, but it appeared to him that his task now was to come to terms with the opposing passions of love and hate. They were both here for him on board the ship in the forms of Charlotte and Hawkes. Please, dear God, guide my words and actions this day. Please. Amen. He left to go to his cabin and await Charlotte's arrival.

After her initial relief at Jack being returned safely to her arms, Charlotte thought about what she'd witnessed below decks. She shuddered and hugged Jack once more as all those around her continued to celebrate his safe return. She realized James was missing as she surveyed the deck. The count's voice in her ear called her attention away from her search.

"James has gone to his cabin and requests you join him there."

She gave Jack to Annie with a strong admonition.

"Please, watch him carefully. I need to attend to business for a short while."

Annie took him willingly and Jack hugged her neck. Signor Bella spoke to him in Italian, and Jack laughed. Seeing her son well cared for, Charlotte turned to the count, who was waiting patiently.

"I am ready, if you would be so kind as to lead me to the gentleman's cabin."

As she followed the count, Charlotte tried to put her thoughts in order. Her initial terror at being confronted with Hawkes was subsiding. She found herself relieved that he was in chains. He must be killed, so that he will never torment us again, she thought. She carried no forgiveness in her heart for such a monster. How could she be expected to?

They arrived at the cabin and the count knocked on the door. James called them in and offered them seats around a small table.

"Thank you for coming, Charlotte. Thank you, my friend, for escorting Mrs. Pruitt." James turned to Charlotte. "I will come directly to the heart of the matter."

Before he could continue, Charlotte interrupted him. "I have seen Hawkes. You are aware of that, of course. Your man told you. Thank God, you've captured him. What a horror in the churchyard! Seeing you covered in mud, I felt myself in a nightmare. When I saw Hawkes below in the hold, I was overcome with fear. However, I cannot express the joy I feel that he will no longer threaten any of us."

James's face was a study of conflicting emotions.

"Charlotte," he began again, "there are other subjects which I would like to discuss first. They are of the utmost importance to me. Will you hear me out?"

"Of course, but I cannot rest until I understand why you brought Hawkes here. What are your plans for him?" she asked.

"Hawkes must confess to the murders of the child on the moor and of Audley," James replied patiently.

"And then?"

"I plan to see him tried and hanged."

"What if he refuses to confess?" Charlotte asked.

"I do not believe he will in the end."

"How can you keep from killing him, James, after all he has done? I would torture him." She stopped short of describing the acts she imagined herself performing on Hawkes.

"Dear Mrs. Pruitt," the count interjected, "there are several individuals on this ship who have suffered at the hands of our captive. There would be little left of Hawkes if it were not for James wanting him alive."

"Who are the others?"

"My cousin, the countess, to begin with, who has lost family treasures and wishes them returned."

"Charles Bonnie, the African, is on board," James added. "Hawkes raped and murdered his sister, as well as performing acts of abomination upon Bonnie himself when he was only a lad."

"Oh, dear God," Charlotte whispered.

"Jacob Golder, the Jew, saw his family killed by an angry mob that Hawkes incited so he would not have to repay a loan. You are here. I am here. The count was made a fool of by Hawkes, who pretended to be friends with both he and your late husband. The last who have been invited to the ship are the innkeeper and his wife whose child's murder was laid at my feet."

"On what pretence did you get them to agree to come here?" Charlotte asked.

"A friend of mine in Devon, a justice of the peace by the name of Richard Fletcher, whom I served with under Wolfe's command in Canada and who believes me innocent, knows them and has invited them to come to

London. They have no idea that it is at my behest that they come. The wife suffers from severe melancholy since the child's death, and her husband agreed to the trip in hopes it might lift her spirits. They arrived in London two days ago. Today, Fletcher received an invitation from an old friend to come and view the Thames from this ship. We will stop to have them come on board at Tilbury tomorrow morning. I will begin in earnest tonight to extract a confession from Hawkes. If he refuses, the countess has brought along a large piece of marble that we will set on his chest to help loosen his tongue."

"You will press him? What if the stone crushes him?"

"We will watch him carefully. He will not leave this life until we are done with him."

"I shall be part of that watch," Charlotte said.

"It will be most unpleasant. You saw how he is."

"I loathe the man. He is a monster, and I would see him suffer."

James hesitated, seeming to gather his courage before he spoke.

"There has been a revelation of which I am most ashamed. I wish you to be aware of it, though whether a woman should be privy to such a secret I do not know."

"James, I am not sure," the count interjected, but James held up his hand.

"Hawkes will reveal it, I am certain. I would rather Charlotte know and be sickened by it beforehand."

"What is it?" Charlotte asked.

"I share culpability in Hawkes's desire for revenge."

"How?"

"He told me today that after I left him to die in Portugal, he was castrated by scavengers in the battlefield."

Charlotte stared at James. She heard Hawkes hissing in her ear, "I went to your garden shed and found a pitchfork. Nice, big, thick handles on pitchforks. I cut the handle off...."

There was the sound of rushing water in her ears and she felt lightheaded. From far away, she heard a voice.

"Charlotte?" James was calling, but she could not make out from which direction. James moved to her when her face lost colour. He held her shoulders and called softly to her. "Charlotte?"

Finally, her eyes opened, and she turned to him.

"Yes?"

"Are you feeling ill?" he asked, knowing the answer, but needing to say something.

"Forgive me. I am dizzy," she replied as if in a dream.

The count moved a chair next to Charlotte's and urged James to sit with her. He did and put his arm around her so she could rest more comfortably. When the room stopped spinning, she looked into his face.

"Seeing him, it brought back that night, Jem. I knew he would kill me. Kill Jack. The pitchfork...." She began to sob.

James held her shaking body which gave her a bit of comfort.

The count turned away from the table. At last, he put his hand on James's shoulder and indicated he would leave them alone. James nodded and the count left quietly, closing the door behind him.

Slowly, Charlotte's crying subsided, but she held onto James. The soft touch of his silk waistcoat comforted her. She had no desire to move.

James stroked her back as he spoke. "We have been

through quite a bit together, my dearest, the very good and the very bad, eh?" He took her chin in his hand, and she looked up at him, her face streaked with tears. "I know you have hated me of late, and with reason. Yet I would ask you now, though I have no right, to forgive me for the difficulties I have brought upon you." He hurried ahead, hoping she would not stop him, for she had sat up now and was looking at him. "I have not forgotten you said you never wanted to see me again. I felt a fool standing and shouting at you from the garden bench. I am hoping that with some reflection, you will reconsider. I understand that my behaviour has been at times…" He searched for the right word.

"Pig-headed and detestable." The words were out of Charlotte's mouth before she could stop them.

"Yes, it has. I will not defend against it." James looked at her, waiting for her next attack.

None came. She, too, was trying to control herself. "Forgive me, Jem. That was uncalled for, but so much has happened, I cannot begin to express what my feelings are. I mourned your death and rejoiced at your return. You lied to me about Peg. The thought of you and her together still sickens me. But the worst is that you attacked Thomas when he was my only hope of saving Jane Rourke." Her voice was beginning to rise.

James leaned towards her.

"Let me begin again, please." He took her hand in his. "I am not responsible for the attack on Thomas, I swear to you. Though all evidence may point to me, I had nothing to do with it. Yes, I was blind with jealousy at the thought of him touching you. He tried to rape you. Have you forgotten that? And then for you to go to him, to make such

an arrangement, even if it was the only way to help Jane
Rourke. I could not bear it." He paused in order to regain
some composure. "I am sorry she is dead."

"So am I." Charlotte ran her fingers along the rough
grain of the table, studying it intently as she fought back
tears.

James looked at his hands. "Charlotte, I wish you to be
my wife."

She looked at him in astonishment. "What?!"

James smiled in his disarming way. "Will you marry
me?"

Charlotte laughed until she was breathless. Gasping for
air, she answered, "I will consider it, but first you must
admit you are an absolute madman."

"Never!" James shouted.

"Say it, or you will grow old without me," Charlotte
demanded.

"Oh, very well. I am an absolute madman!" he cried out
and added quickly, "And I am in love with an absolute
madwoman by the name of Charlotte Byrd."

"Pruitt," Charlotte corrected. "Oh dear, poor Audley,"
she said.

James took her in his arms and held her. "Charlotte, I
promise I shall somehow make this all right. We will regain
Kirkmoor and my title and start again; you, me, Jack, all the
children. I will be a country squire, and you shall be my jolly
wife, and no one will ever believe that we lived through
such a time as this."

"But first you must deal with Hawkes."

"Yes, it all hinges on his confession. I need to go and
see to it. Have you recovered sufficiently?"

"I have, and I shall hold you to your proposal, my

dearest madman."

"Fair enough." He stood and helped her to her feet. "We shall seal the bargain with a kiss," he said and pulled her to him. She did not resist.

CHAPTER FOURTEEN

They walked, arm in arm, back to their friends on deck. Emma was the first to see them.

"There you are!" she exclaimed, then grinned. "Hm, I see ruddy cheeks and broad smiles. May I infer that a reconciliation has taken place?"

Charlotte looked at James, then back at Emma and nodded.

"Oh, I am so pleased for you both," Emma responded. "I hope for happier times ahead for you. Charlotte, the countess was just telling us the story of when she first met you."

"Ah, my dear, yes, Francesco did not reveal to me until much later why he called you away so urgently to Bellagio." The countess looked at Charlotte. "This was the dress you were going to wear for the masquerade, was it not? I remember it well. My mantua maker has a special style all her own. Is it not beautiful, Lady Emma?"

"It is indeed. I must make her acquaintance when my husband and I next visit you in Venice." Emma smiled at John, who rolled his eyes playfully at her mention of more travel. He was distracted by James tapping him on the shoulder and pulling him aside to talk about their plans for Hawkes.

Charlotte guessed the subject of their discussion and crossed to join them.

"I will be included in these plans. Please, make sure of that."

"I shall, madam," James replied.

Satisfied, Charlotte went in search of Annie and Jack. She found them in the countess's cabin, which was aglow with lantern light. Signor Bella was in the process of doing a sketch of them together. He had given Jack a small golden ball with a bell inside. The boy moved it from hand to hand, mesmerized by its tinkling sound. The drawing was exquisite, catching Annie's melancholy beauty and Jack's innocence.

With a few added strokes, Bella finished and indicated, in Italian, that it was a gift for Charlotte. She replied in Italian, thanking him for his beautiful sketch. One of the countess's servants entered and invited them all to the main deck where musicians were assembled and ready to play as the ship cast off and moved down the river.

"Thank you, Isabetta," the countess responded. "We shall come immediately."

As they ascended to the main deck, the countess turned to Charlotte.

"They are the most talented of the court musicians. All loaned to us by the doge just for this voyage."

Des petites souffles au chocolat were served, and the ladies and Signor Bella watched as London disappeared. Great homes and flower-filled meadows began to appear along the banks.

A short time later, just as the musicians ended a lively piece by Vivaldi, a scream of pain no one could ignore came from below. The countess smiled pleasantly.

"I suggest we retire inside and play cards if anyone is so inclined. The cold night air on deck will do us no good."

"An excellent idea," Emma agreed.

Charlotte understood that Emma must have been informed of Hawkes's presence, else she would never have remained so calm. Annie, however, looked troubled and glanced from woman to woman for some clue as to why no one took notice of the scream. Charlotte reached out and took Annie's hand as if to say, all is well. She released her hand so the girl could hold tightly onto Jack as he fell asleep on her shoulder.

"Countess, would you mind greatly if Annie and I take Jack to my cabin?" Charlotte asked. "It is past the hour when he should be abed."

"Of course, my dear. Please, you both will join us again?"

"I think it best if Annie stay here and watch him, given our experience today."

"But you will return, yes? The night is just beginning," the countess insisted.

After a hesitation, Charlotte responded, "There is some business below decks which I must attend to, with your permission, Countess Cittidini."

The countess's expression grew serious. "Do you truly think that necessary? Men are hardened by experience and inclination to perform such tasks. For a woman like yourself, such images of violence would only cause bad dreams, of that I am sure."

A small smile played across Charlotte's lips. "I have the nightmares already. It is my desire to banish them that leads me below. The men feel as you do, but I desire to be a part of it. Please, indulge me, if you will."

"Very well, but do join us when you can." The countess took Charlotte's hand, holding it for a moment. Letting go, she shook her head, but said nothing more.

"Please take care, Charlotte," Emma added. Both the ladies moved towards the countess's cabin. Annie looked anxiously at Charlotte.

"There is nothing to fear, truly, Annie. James Clarke, Mr. Fuller, and Count Cesi are speaking in a most serious manner with Edward Hawkes who has plagued us so. It is a lively discussion, and I would add my own word or two, as well. You need not fret about it. Please watch over Jack as he sleeps." She looked at the girl. "Have I reassured you at all?"

"Yes, Charlotte, but do be careful. Hawkes is a horrible man."

"I shall. Now, let us go and get you settled."

Charlotte's cabin was below deck on the port side of the ship. The room was small, but well-appointed with beautifully crafted Venetian furniture. There were two small beds, a table and chairs, and a small wardrobe. Each piece was made of mahogany and glowed a rich, deep red.

Charlotte helped Annie put Jack to bed. After kissing him goodnight, Charlotte slipped out of the cabin. Out on deck as she crossed to the stairs, Charlotte's footsteps grew slower. Perhaps all those who attempted to dissuade her were correct. Why should she feel compelled to face Hawkes? What purpose did it serve? She stood listening at the open hatch door. All was quiet until she heard someone coming up the steps.

Count Cesi appeared and greeted her with a smile, "My cousin will be pleased I think, for we have gained the location of a house Hawkes keeps in Ios, in the Greek isles.

Many of our family's treasures are hidden there, if he is to be believed."

"Has he been forthcoming with a confession to either of the murders?" Charlotte asked, hoping perhaps she would not have to face Hawkes after all.

"No, of these, he refuses to say a word. I have never seen a man so consumed by hate, and I have experienced much in the world. I think he may die willingly, rather than give James what he desires." The count watched a sadness come over Charlotte's face, her shoulders slumping slightly. "You, perhaps, are having second thoughts about proceeding with your plan to go below?"

"I have such a hatred of the man, Count Cesi. Many times, in my fantasies, I have taken revenge on him, but now when it comes to truly seeing him suffer for his crimes, I find myself squeamish. I must face him, however. Otherwise, I fear my mind will never be rid of him."

"Shall I be your escort into the underworld, Mrs. Pruitt?" the count asked.

"I should think myself privileged," Charlotte responded with a sad smile. She paused and looked at the count. "Thank you for your friendship."

"You are most welcome."

They descended the steps, Charlotte going first. As before, her skirts made it difficult to manoeuvre, but she slowly made it to the bottom without mishap. This time, however, she did not rush forward. With the count at her side, she stood well back, trying to understand what was taking place. Her view was obscured by the gentlemen who were standing in a tight circle, Hawkes apparently in the centre. He made no sounds. Was he dead, Charlotte wondered? She took a few tentative steps forward and stopped again.

The sound of her footsteps made several of the men turn in her direction. The circle parted, and Charlotte gasped. Hawkes hung by his wrists, suspended off the ground. He was naked, his mutilated groin in full view. A few paces back, but in the centre also, stood James, a cat-o'-nine tails in his hand. Perspiration covered his face and neck. His coat was off and his shirt open.

Sickened, she turned away, putting her hands to her face. She heard James's voice. He had come close to her.

"I told you before it would not be pleasant. This is not the place for you, Charlotte."

His tone angered her, and though she desired to flee, she refused to give in.

"I will not go," she said. "I need only to regain my composure, sir."

"Very well. Stay then, madam." James walked back into the circle of men. He said something to one of them who left at a quick pace, passing Charlotte as he went. Hawkes made no movement. His head was slumped forward on his chest, his mouth slightly open. Bloody spittle dripped from his mouth.

"Water!" James demanded, exploding the quiet.

One of the onlookers picked up a bucket and, stepping forward, hurled the contents on Hawkes. His body jerked, like a marionette whose strings were suddenly pulled by unseen hands. The irons on his ankles clanked as his legs moved spasmodically. His head shot up and his eyes opened.

"Let me down, for Christ's sake. My arms! Oh, Christ!" His cries caught Charlotte off guard. She felt pity for this wretched creature. It made her stomach turn to see him suffer. She found herself taking a step back into the shadows. As she did, she nearly collided with the man who had so recently left.

" 'Scuse me, mum," he whispered, passing her.

She watched as he gave James a piece of cloth. He called for two of the guards, passing it to one of them.

"Put it round him. We have a lady present. Cover him up." Hawkes, becoming aware of the two men approaching him, rallied and began to struggle. Two more men were needed to hold his legs quiet and apart, so the cloth could be passed between them. Hawkes swore and spit at the four of them. Another man was deployed to put a leather band across his mouth and hold his head still.

After experimenting with knots and wrapping the cloth three different ways around Hawkes's waist, they were satisfied it would hold. The men stepped away. Hawkes stopped struggling and closed his eyes, perhaps to preserve his strength for the next battle.

It was not lost on Charlotte that Hawkes's body, dressed as it was, looked much like the body of Christ she had seen in a chapel in Venice.

James caught Hawkes by a greasy forelock of hair and pulled his head up. "Admit now that you were the man that beat and tortured me on the moors two years ago."

"I am that man," Hawkes replied in a whisper, without opening his eyes.

James waited as a man off to the side, quickly wrote down what had just been said. On seeing he was finished,

James continued.

"There was another man also, an old man. Who was he?"

"No other," came the almost inaudible reply.

"What?"

"There was no other." This time, Hawkes opened his eyes.

"You masqueraded as the old man?"

"Maybe it were me, maybe a dead man." Hawkes managed a smirk before pain overtook him and he closed his eyes again. The men surrounding Hawkes grumbled at his insolence.

James stood silently for a moment, eyes narrowed.

"It was you who gave me the child's body," he finally accused.

"No."

"It was the dead man?" James moved close to Hawkes's side and spoke in his ear.

Hawkes, grimacing, tried to move his head away. "Don't remember no baby."

A look of triumph crossed James's face. "I did not say baby. I said child."

"What difference?"

"Because it was a baby."

"I don't remember no kid. Let me down, Clarke, sweet Jesus, my arms!"

"What mercy did you show me, you son of a bitch!" James took a few steps back from him and let the strips of the cat-o-nine tails fall. "Perhaps this will aid your memory."

He pulled his arm back and swung it forward with great force, hitting Hawkes's back with a loud thwack. Hawkes screamed. Blood ran down from where the lashes struck. James hit him a second time and Hawkes screamed again.

"Is your memory any clearer?" he asked.

"NO!"

James flogged him again. "Now?"

"NO!"

Charlotte was unable to take her eyes away from the scene. It both repelled and fascinated her. To her shame, she realized it aroused a sensual passion in her. Looking at James, his face glowing with perspiration, his hair unkempt, his shirt undone, she felt a stirring in her loins. She turned away, determined to rid herself of this sensation. This was not the place for such feelings, she told herself. Justice was being served. Punishment meted out. Her thoughts were disturbed by James's voice.

"Put him down."

Charlotte turned to see Hawkes's limp body being lowered to the floor. He was unconscious.

"Douse him with water." Two men with buckets were dispatched to go above.

While the group surrounding Hawkes waited, Charles Bonnie appeared with a drink for James. They talked quietly, James nodding approval of some proposal of Bonnie's. The African exited, passing very close to Charlotte. Their eyes met, but no words passed between them.

As before, Charlotte was affronted by his boldness. What life has this man had, Charlotte wondered. She had given it scant thought before. For that matter, what about the lives of other blacks that were so omnipresent in London?

There was the friend of Garrick's, Ignatius Sancho,

whom Emma and Charlotte met recently. He seemed a kind and pleasant man and was considered by many to be a man of learning and letters. He was also the valet to the Duke of Montague.

Bonnie, on the other hand, was simply bold beyond his station. Charlotte wondered why James tolerated this behaviour.

The men with water arrived and poured it unsparingly on Hawkes's prostrate form. Groaning, he tried to raise himself, but fell again into a stupor. He curled up onto his side. James indicated for two men to roll him over on his back. After doing so, one of the men took hold of the rope tethering Hawkes wrists and pulled his arms over his head. The other man stood on Hawkes's ankle chains, so he could not move his legs.

James knelt near Hawkes's head. He spoke now in soothing tones.

"Edward, all I desire from you is the truth. Confess to the babe's murder in Devon and Audley Pruitt's killing, and this interrogation can end. Please, I have no wish to torture you to death. However, if you resist, I will put you in the hands of others on board who will use you much worse. I cannot stop them unless you confess. What is your answer, Edward?"

Hawkes did not move.

James indicated for two more men to join those holding Hawkes's bonds. Now with two at his arms and two at his feet, they began to pull and stretch Hawkes as if upon the rack. His eyes shot open, and he spat in James's face.

"FUCK YOU!" Hawkes cried.

James wiped away the dripping saliva and stood up.

"I take that as your answer. Give our guest a moment

to breathe, gentlemen." The men pulling on Hawkes relaxed, but did not let go.

From behind her, Charlotte heard footsteps. She turned. It was Golder and Bonnie. The latter was carrying a pike and some sort of apparatus she had never seen before. Seeing Bonnie, James spoke again to Hawkes.

"Edward, may I introduce a gentleman to you who was recently in your employ but whose true identity was kept a secret from you. I think he had a different name when you first made his acquaintance. Is that correct, Mr. Bonnie?"

Bonnie, standing beside Charlotte, responded to the question.

"It is, sir. My sister and I had African names when Edward Hawkes took ownership of us on the slaver, Little Pearl. We were partial payment for his duties on board. But you know, sir, Mr. Hawkes liked the demon rum, and he had an eye for my sister. It is an evil combination, drink and the desire to rape a child, sir."

Hawkes turned his head towards the voice, but he could not see who spoke, Bonnie being in the shadows. A look of terror spread slowly over Hawkes's face.

"He committed unspeakable acts upon my sister," Bonnie continued. "She bled horribly, being young and small. He laughed at us. He put live cockroaches in my mouth, sir. If I swallowed them or spat them out, he would rape her again and blame the attack on my lack of love. After days of torture, my sister lay dying. In front of her eyes, he took me in the most disgusting way. Hawkes stuffed us into a small, locked hold on deck. I lay with my sister, singing songs of home to comfort her. Exhausted, I fell asleep. The rats descended. My sister died. I have never forgotten Edward Hawkes. Indeed, the memory of his face is my constant companion. I have here the first of many presents for him. Would you care to see if it fits correctly, sir?"

James nodded. Bonnie handed the pike to Golder. He walked into the circle of men. Hawkes began to struggle. He was quickly stretched out again. Bonnie handed James the iron contraption, saying to the men who watched.

"It is a mouthpiece, a mask, or a muzzle, call it what you will. This flat piece rests tightly down upon the tongue and the plate fits in front of the mouth. If the sun were hot, the iron would heat up and burn his nose and chin, but we'd have to transport Hawkes to the West Indies for that. It was designed for sullen negroes, but it will serve for Hawkes."

James and Bonnie placed the mouthpiece on Hawkes. He gagged. His eyes watered, but his struggling ceased as his attention was taken up in trying to breathe. James instructed the men who held Hawkes to chain him again to the pole.

"Gentlemen, I think it is time for a drink and some pleasant conversation," James suggested. "Let us retire above deck."

As the group left, he took note of their quiet. Before they had urged him on, but now they did not look at him. What was it that disturbed them? He would find out, he thought, but not down here. He needed air and time away from this business.

Charlotte took two steps to the side to clear a path. James stopped to ask her if she would accompany him above deck.

"I shall be there directly. I will take my time mounting the steps, as my skirts are burdensome."

The count, who had stayed by her side all this time,

spoke. "I shall accompany Mrs. Pruitt, if she wishes." James looked to Charlotte for her answer.

"Thank you, Count Cesi, your aid would be most appreciated."

"I shall see you both presently." James nodded his head. He left, accompanied by Wilkes and Adam.

Charlotte turned back to where the circle of men had stood. Two of the count's men stayed to guard Hawkes. They stood some distance from him, speaking quietly to one another. Hawkes sat chained to the post. His head, made heavy by the iron muzzle, slumped on his chest. The contraption obscured his face. His breathing was laboured. Spittle dripped from his mouth as the iron piece pressed on his tongue.

Hawkes was a man who had seen physical labour, Charlotte noted. His body was muscular, with scars as well as the wounds from the past two days. One scar in particular caught her eye. It cut a straight, white, diagonal line from above his left breast to below his right. She looked at his hands. They were small, with stubby fingers and enlarged joints. Hands made for pummelling. Shivering, Charlotte felt again the leather strap Hawkes had pushed into her mouth before he violated her.

She approached him, coming close enough for him to hear her whisper, "Now it is you who has no voice, Edward Hawkes."

He inclined his head slightly in the direction of her voice and opened his eyes. From where she stood, Charlotte could only see one eye, and in that one small area of his face was expressed such sorrow that she found herself moved to pity him.

"May God have mercy on you," she found herself

saying to the eye, as though it were a repentant soul she was watching fall away helplessly into the pits of hell.

"Mrs. Pruitt, shall we go above?" The count's voice broke the spell of Hawkes's eye.

"Yes, thank you, Count Cesi. I am ready to quit this hellish place."

Charlotte now prayed that her legs would support her as she climbed the steps. They felt soft and wobbly, as if her bones were melting away. Her shoe caught in her petticoat, nearly toppling her down upon the count.

Catching herself, she took a deep breath and called out, "I apologize most humbly, Count Cesi, I fear this experience has made me lightheaded and not quite in control of my legs and feet."

"Mrs. Pruitt, this has been a most unpleasant experience for all of us. However, for one of your gentle nature, I am astounded at your strength."

Charlotte smiled, thinking of her rough and tumble childhood. Would the count think her such a lady if he had seen how she climbed the fells above Rosthwaite? Perhaps she would invite him to visit Whitestone someday.

When she emerged on deck, the breeze from the river caressed her face. She stopped to let it wash over her. The last hour seemed a nightmare from which she was now awakening. Her thoughts were troubled by the savagery she had witnessed. Realizing that the count was at her side waiting quietly, she turned and addressed him.

"Thank you, Count Cesi for accompanying me. If you will excuse me, I shall wait a bit before joining the others."

"Of course, signora, you need time to collect your thoughts. There is a side to men that is dark and violent. Our rational mind attempts to deny its existence. We build fine buildings, compose beautiful music, and paint exquisite pictures, but in the end, it is there, waiting in the shadows, threatening all we have created. Hawkes is the embodiment of that side. In him, the dark is given form and life."

"Yet now he is a pitiable human being. Did you see his eye, Count Cesi? Is he merely a trapped animal? A mad dog muzzled? I am befuddled. I cannot help but feel the desperation he is experiencing. Why should that be? I would banish it if I could."

"But you cannot, Mrs. Pruitt. Therein lies the difference between the two of you. If you were to reverse your roles, do you suppose Hawkes would pause to consider your suffering?"

"No, the very opposite. He would revel in it." A thought came to Charlotte. "Count Cesi, I have been told on good authority, and I hope I do not offend, that Venetians enjoy intrigue and deception."

"Dear lady, I take no umbrage, but the subject of our discussion has altered. I wait to see where you would lead me."

"I'm thinking that perhaps I might employ my genuine feelings of empathy in a devious manner."

"How so?"

"By making Hawkes believe that my sentiments for him have changed. I would have him believe that his suffering has wiped away my hatred for him, that I am his friend and would beg mercy on his behalf. By doing so, I might offer him some hope."

"What is your purpose, Mrs. Pruitt?"

"He has not confessed to the murders. Through all this torture, he seems ready to die rather than give James what he wants. If Hawkes was shown some gentleness, some kindness now in his weakened state, perhaps it might give him a desire to live. If he had some hope of escape and life beyond today, would he be willing to confess?"

"It is within the realm of possibility."

"I shall broach it with James. Come, let us find him," Charlotte said.

They made their way to the countess's cabin where they found the gentlemen assembled. Allen Peters directed them to an antechamber just off the dining room where James and John Fuller were deep in conversation.

"The gentlemen are dismayed with my including Charles Bonnie in Hawkes's interrogation," James told Charlotte and the count. "They have expressed their concern at his overstepping his place in this matter. His place, indeed!"

James turned to John.

"Were they deaf to the horrors that Hawkes inflicted upon his sister and himself? Would not any one of them seek revenge as he has done?"

"But they do not see the man. They see the colour of his skin," John said.

"This is England, John! He is a free negro, with the same rights to liberty as any Englishman."

"In theory, perhaps. But you know as well as I that there are slaves in England. Not only do the planters bring them from the West Indies, but negroes are bought and sold on English soil."

"It is a gross injustice, and one that must be righted," James snorted.

"I think we would all agree, but you must deal with how the gentlemen are reacting to the African's involvement in this matter."

"John, I will not exclude Charles Bonnie."

"If not, you risk losing these men as witnesses to Hawkes's confession."

Charlotte spoke, seeing her opportunity to interject her ideas into the discussion. "If I may, sirs, I see a way perhaps of guiding you out of this sticking point."

John Fuller looked relieved to be out of the confrontation.

James turned to her with his jaw set and his eyes hard.

"Yes?" he asked.

"I believe that we might have more luck getting Hawkes to confess if I were to act as his angel of mercy." Charlotte was unsure if this was the best way to introduce the subject, but she decided to go directly to the heart of the matter.

"What!?" James exploded, his face red.

Charlotte, turning choleric herself, responded, "Sirs, what hope does the man have if you simply beat him to death? Why would he confess, given his hatred of you? Better to die knowing that you will rot a beggar, or better yet, be caught and hanged. Are you such fools not to see that?"

"I am no fool, madam."

"Perhaps not, James Clarke, but you are an arrogant, single-minded man, if you refuse to let others help you."

"And how will your show of compassion soften Hawkes's resolve?"

"By allowing him a hope, however small, that he may live to see tomorrow. He thinks all women stupid. Let that be to our advantage. He may believe that he can use my softheartedness to escape your wrath and perhaps even evade the gallows. By giving him some hope of life, he may think it worth his while to confess his crimes."

"What is your plan for implementing this deception?"

"I would start by removing the muzzle." Seeing James's face darken, she hurried on to recount her experience below deck and her subsequent conversation with the count. "It was the look of despair in his eye that moved me so. If Hawkes was at all aware of my feelings, it would make sense to him that I might come to you to plead for the mask's removal."

John added, "This would help ameliorate the grumbling by the gentlemen."

"How?" James asked, still looking steadily at Charlotte.

"Because I shall be the one to rid you of the mask, the symbol of the African's involvement."

"Charles Bonnie's involvement," James corrected her.

"Yes, Charles Bonnie. And it shall be done without direct confrontation with the gentlemen, allowing us all to get on with the business at hand," said Charlotte.

The count, who had been listening, spoke. "In this drama, you should perhaps heighten the conflict. May I suggest that you, James, lead Hawkes to believe that Mrs. Pruitt is removing the mask without your knowledge. So moved is she by Hawkes's desperation, that she cannot help but rush to his aid. Then you, sir, upon discovering her treasonous act, fly into a rage. Mrs. Pruitt, wounded by your words, flees the room. Thus, Hawkes's belief that he has an ally is cemented."

"But what of the guards?" Charlotte asked.

"They could be ordered away. Hawkes is bound and muzzled. He is not going to escape."

"Perhaps not," James said. "He is weakened, but he remains dangerous."

"Post guards in the darkness. Take no chances. He is a

man. He cannot simply disappear," the count urged.

"Charles Bonnie believes he is a demon. It has crossed my mind that he may be correct."

"You, who gave no credence to Peg being a witch, are saying this?" Charlotte said.

"I fancy myself an enlightened, reasonable man, but perhaps my knowledge of the world is too circumscribed. I am tired, Charlotte."

As James said this, the colour drained slightly from his face. There were lines she had not noticed before. He appeared to have aged ten years in a matter of minutes.

Charlotte took his hands in hers. "I believe I can help you. Please, let me try."

"As you wish, my dearest. I will play my part as best I can. I hope that God is with us, for Satan is surely with Hawkes."

He kissed her hands and smiled. Charlotte prayed that this heaviness would lift. Together, they could fight Hawkes, but if James fell into his melancholic humour, she feared all would be lost.

"Jem, after this, perhaps we should speak with Garrick. You may have a promising career as an actor. You most certainly have a talent for it. Remember the Scotsman? I certainly do. And what about your French fop? Would you not agree, Count Cesi?"

"*Si, signora.* I have always thought James a consummate thespian."

James brightened. "I will consider it. I do like Shakespeare, especially the way Garrick has changed the endings of some. They were rather dreary in the original plays. I am a bit old for Romeo, but Hamlet would suit me, don't you agree? My life is rather like his with all the madness, death, and revenge."

"Please, do not dwell on *that* for any length of time," Charlotte laughed, "or we will never get on with our own drama."

John voiced his disapproval of the plan.

"I am unsure that having Hawkes here on the ship, whether treated cruelly or kindly, is for the best. I have supported you in all of this, James, but perhaps we should turn him over to the authorities."

"Then, in fairness I should surrender myself, too, and let the law decide which of us is guilty of the murders. I am afraid that with the circumstantial evidence, I would be the one they would hang. I must have his confession, John, or resign myself to live my life a fugitive."

"You could come live in Bellagio. You have always enjoyed it there. You might live in Lady Emma and John's villa," Count Cesi added. The two men turned to him with serious faces. He smiled. "It is only my humble suggestion."

In the end, it was decided that they would have to see how Hawkes accepted Charlotte's aid.

"Time is our enemy," James said. "The gentlemen are here for, at best, only another twenty-four hours. The innkeeper and his wife will join us in the morning. Hawkes must stay alive and confess quickly, or we might as well throw him overboard and sail for Venice."

"We had best get started," Charlotte said.

Suddenly, she felt frightened at the thought of facing Hawkes. She chided herself. I have placed myself here, and it is for the best. I can do this.

"Charlotte?"

She heard James's voice. When she looked up, he was standing next to her.

"Are you questioning your decision in this?" They were alone. John and the count had left the room. She had been so lost in thought, she had not heard them go.

"I am frightened, James, but I believe it is the right course of action."

"Your strength astounds me," he spoke softly and with great tenderness. "I do not have your courage, Charlotte."

"I love you, Jem. I want this nightmare to end."

"And I love you, Charlotte."

Embracing, they held onto each other with great urgency, as if expecting in the next moment to be torn apart by some terrible storm. It did not materialize. Instead, Charlotte felt her body relax into Jem's. Her cheek rested on his chest, and his chin touched the top of her head.

"We should go." His voice vibrated in his chest.

"Yes."

She took a step back, not letting go, and looked up into his face. He looked younger now. She touched the wrinkles at the corner of his right eye. He was smiling. He took her hand and kissed her fingers.

"We must go, or we will not go," James said, looking at her.

"Yes," she whispered in agreement and reluctantly loosened her grasp on him.

A short time later, James climbed down the last few steps into the hold. He was followed soundlessly by several men who would stand guard in the darkness.

"Gentlemen," he called to Hawkes's guards, "how is the prisoner faring?"

"He breathes still, sir. I can grant that much only," answered one of the men.

"Good," James responded as he entered the circle of

light where Hawkes sat motionless. "I think it safe for you to go above for a breath of air and some food. Do you agree, sirs?"

"Aye, indeed, we do," the two Englishmen replied.

"*Si, per favore!*" added the two Venetians. The men exited quickly up the steps, leaving James and Hawkes alone.

"It would be a terrible fate to be thrown overboard with that muzzle on. Lord, to think how fast you would sink to the bottom of the Thames. A quick death, I'd say, what with the muddy water filling your lungs. But it may end up that I give you to Charles Bonnie. He wants his revenge, and I think he deserves it more than any of us. A slow and painful death, to be skinned alive. I will give you a bit more time to think about your choices, Edward."

There was no audible response from Hawkes. James thought perhaps his breathing quickened at the mention of Charles Bonnie's name, but he could not be sure. He walked into the darkness and up the steps without another word.

Charlotte made her way down to the hold. The pounding of her heart sounded in her ears. She did not attempt to pick out the guards in the darkness. She only hoped they would come quickly if she needed their aid. Kneeling beside Hawkes, she fumbled at the catches of the muzzle, attempting to undo them. Hawkes gagged, trying to raise his head.

"Do not struggle, I will remove it." She cursed herself for not asking Charles Bonnie how to unlatch the catches. Finally, two of them gave way, and she was able to pull the muzzle off Hawkes.

His eyes were wide, his tongue protruding. He spat and

tried to curse, "Bastards!"

It was unintelligible to her ear, but Charlotte knew what he meant.

Then, he managed to croak, "Water."

Charlotte rose, retrieving the bucket used to throw water on Hawkes. There seemed enough to soothe his parched throat. She held it up to his mouth, and he drank clumsily. When he finished, Charlotte moved away from him.

Resting his head on his bent knees, he began to sob. His face contorted as tears streaked his cheeks.

"Why?" he asked at last in a hoarse whisper.

Not sure that she'd heard him correctly, Charlotte said nothing.

He asked again, this time more emphatically. "Why have you helped me, Charlotte Pruitt?"

"I was moved by your desperation. I, unlike you, have compassion for those who are suffering. The mask was too much for anyone to bear. Though, of anyone alive, you deserve it most, Edward Hawkes." She knew she must leave quickly. Her anger was mounting. She turned ready to go and heard James's footsteps, knowing he would burst upon them.

At that same instant, she also heard Hawkes saying, "Thank you, Charlotte Pruitt, for your kindness." This caught her so off guard that when James came out of the darkness, she looked at him dumbfounded.

"What have you done, Mrs. Pruitt?" James demanded. He held his whip in his hand. She did not answer at once. "I asked you a question. I expect an answer," he said sharply.

"I could not stand to see Edward Hawkes suffer so,"

Charlotte answered back in kind.

"You, of all people, know his crimes. How can you feel any pity for such a monster?"

"I do not say he should not be punished, but the muzzle is too much, sir. I demand you not abuse him in this way."

"You demand? How dare you, madam!"

"Do not speak to me in such a manner, sir."

"Madam, you have gone too far!"

"Sir, look to yourself. If you show no pity, no mercy, you will turn into that which you claim to loath. Pray, have some compassion."

"Out of my sight, treacherous woman!" James raised the whip as if to hit her. Instinctively, she covered her face.

"Stop, Clarke!" Hawkes called out. "Don't touch her."

James lowered the whip and turned to Hawkes. "What did you say?"

"You puke-faced son of a bitch aristocrat. She had a little pity on a man in pain. A thing you wouldn't understand. Leave her alone, or I will get free and fucking kill you."

James lashed out with the thick handle of the whip, bringing it down of Hawkes's cheek. Blood spilled out from a deep gash. Charlotte moved in between the men. Falling to her knees, she put her handkerchief to the wound.

"No more, James, please," she pleaded.

"Out of this place, madam!"

Charlotte placed her blood-soaked handkerchief on Hawkes's bended knee. After rising, she faced James with her chin raised and a defiant look in her eye.

"I shall take my leave now, sir." Walking through the darkness she climbed the steps to the next deck. A single lantern burned, lighting her way. Exhausted, she sat down on a wooden box and put her head in her hands.

Below, James had not moved. He stood watching Hawkes, praying that in the next few hours he would break and confess. Had he been foolish in letting Charlotte attempt this game? He was unsure. He wanted to speak to her now, to ask her why she had greeted him with such an odd expression on her face.

Hawkes groaned. James looked down to see him resting his bloodied cheek on Charlotte's white handkerchief. A cold shudder ran through James's body. He left at a quick pace to speak with Charlotte. He found her resting on the box. She had not moved since she sat down. Her head rested on her hands. He knelt beside her and stroked her hair. She moved her head slightly, acknowledging his touch.

Speaking softly, he asked, "Charlotte, why did you look at me so strangely? I had no desire to fight with you when I saw you. You appeared lost, forlorn. What was it that affected you so?"

"Jem, Hawkes thanked me for my kindness in such a gentle way. It was confounding. He was a human being speaking to me as another human being in a polite and civilized manner."

"Or was it the monster pretending? I do not trust him. Nor should you, Charlotte. In the end, he must die for his untrustworthiness as well as his crimes."

"Untrustworthiness?"

"Yes, because his life is all deceit. He has no honour. Even if his thanks were sincere, what does it matter? He has broken the covenants we all agree to in order to live in society. I am who I say I am. You can trust me to obey the rules of society. I will not hurt you, nor should you hurt me. In our society, we care about others as well as ourselves.

Christ is the highest example of that selflessness. Hawkes is the antithesis. His world centres totally on himself. He uses everyone around him as tools to further his own ends. So, when he says thank you, be very careful to keep your distance, else he may pull you in and eat you alive."

"Allow me to go and talk to him one more time. I will beg him to confess. I will point out the instruments of torture that Charles Bonnie has promised to use on him. Dying by hanging must seem a better prospect than what has been promised him here. I believe he has some feeling for me. You heard how he defended me when you raised your hand against me."

"He most definitely fancies himself your champion." James laughed without smiling. "I would suggest you let him sleep on this first encounter. You may visit him in the morning before the gentlemen gather, and the innkeeper and his wife arrive. See then if he has softened at all."

Charlotte nodded in agreement. She closed her eyes and wished she could sleep where she sat.

James kissed her on the cheek. "Allow me to accompany you to your cabin," he asked quietly.

"Would you carry me there? I do not believe I can walk another step." Charlotte smiled at him sweetly.

"Madam, in lieu of my advanced years and your youth, I will agree to carry you to your cabin, but first you must climb up the steps. If I attempted to hoist you up, although you are light as a feather, I would most likely break my back."

"Very well, sir, since I am a spry lass and you an old man, I will race you to my cabin."

Charlotte quickly stood up and lifted her skirts. She ran to the steps and up she went, with James right behind her.

They were both laughing and panting when they came out on deck.

Charlotte did not stop to look around but took off at a fast pace towards the steps leading to her cabin. Only after she reached the stairs did she turn around, expecting to find James behind her. He was not. She was alone. She began to walk slowly back towards the hold. As she passed the main mast, he reached out from his hiding place and pulled her to him.

"Old man indeed! There is a little life left in me yet, madam," he said as he held her against the mast and kissed her. She yielded willingly and returned the kiss.

"Shall we retire to your cabin?" Charlotte asked, aching to be with him.

"No, not tonight, Charlotte. I desire to be with you more than anything in the world, but I am tired. Tomorrow is most important. We should rest."

"Of course," she agreed, but could feel herself drawing away from him.

"Have I angered you?" he asked.

"No, no, I shall say goodnight. Please, wake me when you rise. I would be done with this business as quickly as possible."

"I will call for you quite early."

"Excellent. Goodnight." She turned and moved away from him. She hoped he would call her back, but he did not.

Before she descended to her cabin, she looked and saw James standing straight and still where she had left him. He stared out at the riverbank, his face illuminated by the moonlight, pale and unmoving. He could have been made of marble.

Charlotte entered her cabin and found Jack fast asleep in Annie's arms. Whispering a thank you to Annie, she kissed Jack on the forehead and picked him up gently. No sooner had she placed him to one side of her bed than he rolled into the middle and stretched out his full length. She smiled, watching him.

The image of Jack chasing birds at Kirkmoor came to her. His joy and laughter as they all took wing was infectious. He had charmed his grandfather, ill as he was.

"His papers!" Charlotte said out loud. All the papers the old man had given James. She had completely forgotten about them.

Where had she put them? She remembered seeing them recently. It slowly came to her. They were in her desk and had been there for over three months. I must look at them when this business is done, she told herself.

After changing for bed, she scooted Jack over and lay down. Exhaustion overtook her, and within a matter of seconds she was asleep. She did not dream.

The next thing she knew, she heard a soft tapping at her door. Groggily, she rose and answered the knock. James stood there, a bemused look on his face.

"Good morning, Charlotte, you asked me to wake you, and apparently I did."

She looked at him, barely comprehending that the whole night had passed. She tried to sound coherent, but her attempt failed.

"I... the time... I need... where?" She stopped and looked at him.

Taking her hand, he kissed it. Pulling her close, he put his arms around her. She rested her head on his chest and wished for all the world she might return to bed.

"Wake up, my angel," he whispered, stroking her hair. "Meet me shortly in my cabin. We shall breakfast together."

She stepped back from him, managing to reply, "Yes, good."

He smiled and left.

Charlotte closed the door. Leaning against it, she began to recall all that happened the day before. And now I must face Hawkes again, she thought, yearning to be anywhere but on this ship. She readied herself and went out into the early morning dawn. As she neared James's cabin, she saw a figure standing by the door.

"James?" she called out.

"No, Mrs. Pruitt, it is Charles Bonnie."

"Mr. Bonnie, may I pass?"

"I would ask a word with you."

"What is it? James Clarke is waiting for me."

"Edward Hawkes has been calling for you all night. I sat with the guards and watched him. He moaned and ranted in his sleep. Often, he called out your name. You are his saviour, it would seem. Taking the muzzle off let him be a man again. I've known wretches who deserved such resurrection, but Hawkes should not have been spared."

"Mr. Bonnie, I only desire to give him some hope so that perhaps he will be motivated to confess to the two murders for which James has been blamed."

"I wager my thumb screws will quicken his tongue faster than your kindness. Just be wary in dealing with the devil."

"And do not forget that you are a black man and Hawkes is white. If you put thumb screws on him, you put thumb screws on every man that stands in that circle, to their way of thinking. I do not say that you do not have a right to justice. I have also suffered from Hawkes's cruelty. You and I are bound together in that. However, you must consider your role in this."

"My sister says that he will suffer in heaven."

Charlotte, not sure she heard him correctly, asked him to repeat what he said.

"My sister speaks to me often. She told me that I need not seek revenge in this life. Hawkes will be tormented in heaven."

"In heaven? You mean hell, do you not?"

"No, he is a devil. Hell is his home. It is God and all the angels who will judge and punish him."

"Hawkes thanked me for my kindness, Mr. Bonnie. What do you make of that?"

"That you moved him by acting as a Christian, or that he has become a gentleman, or perhaps he sees your gullibility as a means of possible escape. Which is more likely, do you think?"

Charlotte felt herself turn red with anger. She was glad that it was still dark enough that Bonnie was unable to see her face well. Perhaps she was a fool. Perhaps Hawkes bested her at her own game. It certainly sounded so when put in such a way.

"Mr. Bonnie, I shall consider your words. Is there anything else?"

He took a step closer to her. "Just do not allow your tender sentiments to cloud your judgement or make you forget his crimes, Mrs. Pruitt. Hawkes will be mine in the end. Despite what my sister advises, I shall have revenge on him in this life. Good morning to you." With that, he disappeared into the shadows.

Charlotte turned to James's door. She did not stop to

knock, but entered rapidly, throwing open the door. Startled by her entrance, James jumped to his feet.

"Charlotte, good morning. I thought perhaps you had gone back to bed."

"I should have," she replied heatedly. "I just had a conversation of sorts, with Charles Bonnie. He all but called me a damned fool."

"He did? Why?"

"He believes me naïve in my dealings with Hawkes. This from a man who thinks nothing of talking with his dead sister." She stopped and looked at James. "I know you agree with him."

"About his sister?"

"NO! About Hawkes. You would both torture the man to death. Well, see what he confesses when he's dead."

"Charlotte, remember, it is I who agreed with you that we should pursue the course you proposed."

"And we shall. This instant, as a matter of fact. Come to the hold when you are ready." She exited as quickly as she had entered.

When Charlotte reached the bottom of the steps, her anger began to subside. She walked quietly towards the light. The guards lay asleep on either side of the prisoner. Hawkes slept sitting up, chained to the post. His head rested on Charlotte's handkerchief, which covered his bent knees. The square of cloth was dirty and blood-stained.

He is a wild animal, beaten and chained, Charlotte thought to herself. She wanted to tear the handkerchief from him and rip it into the smallest of pieces. She was a fool, she thought, for her feelings of charity. And yet, as she watched him sleep, she could not help but wonder how he was capable of committing such horrible acts. Did he wake feeling his life was a nightmare from which there was no escape, as he made others feel? Or did he wake with no remorse? If it was the second, he was not human.

"Mrs. Pruitt," came Hawkes's hoarse whisper. "What is the time?"

"Very early, first light."

He groaned as he tried to sit up straight. The guards slept on, undisturbed. He put his head back on his knees. He retched and spit a bloody gob on the floor. Charlotte looked away.

"I'm dying. Fucking bloody Christ, the pain is worse than when those old bitches hacked me up," he moaned.

"Do you want water?" Charlotte asked.

"Aye. Get it. Will you?"

"I would just as soon slit your throat," Charlotte responded.

Hawkes sat up as straight as he could, glaring at her. The white of his eyes contrasting with the dirt and blood on his face made him appear fierce and strange. He spit a bloody gob in her direction.

"So why the hell did you come back? Did you want to watch me groan and puke? Be kind to the stupid bastard then let him suffer, is that what you thought? Or did Clarke knock some sense into you, eh? Women are all fucking cowards."

"I am no coward. You are. The way you butchered Peg in my bedchamber, the way you sent your threatening letters, the way you prey on the weak. Do not trouble yourself to imagine I have any sympathy for you. You are a foul murderer and a damned soul. You'd best confess soon, or Charles Bonnie will use his devices on you as you deserve. He's already talked of thumbscrews. I do not doubt that he will skin you alive, if you become his property."

Hawkes closed his eyes and dropped his head onto his knees. Charlotte thought perhaps the pain had caused him to lose consciousness. Walking back towards the steps, she saw James standing to one side in the shadows. Their eyes met.

"Do not go, Mrs. Pruitt," Hawkes called softly. "Please, come back."

She looked at James. He indicated for her to return to Hawkes. As she walked back slowly, Hawkes lifted his head and watched her.

"You are a fine-looking woman, even a dying man can see that." He managed a smile with his swollen lips. "Please, Mrs. Pruitt would you give me a drink of water?"

Charlotte felt herself grow cold at his words. They propelled her back to her bedchamber, to his voice in the darkness, to her helplessness. She refused to allow him to see her fear.

"I will," she said flatly. She crossed to one of the sleeping guards and, kneeling, touched his shoulder. He opened his eyes.

"I am going to give Edward Hawkes some water. Wake your partner. You should go and get some food. Tell the men who are replacing you to come. I will watch the prisoner for a short while."

The man did as he was asked. Standing stiffly, he crossed to the other guard and roused him from his slumber. They whispered to each other, looking from Hawkes to Charlotte. They thanked her and ascended the steps.

Bringing the water to Hawkes, Charlotte tried to

position the bucket so he could drink with reasonable ease. He took a sip and began to cough. He groaned, and his body twitched as his bruised chest and stomach muscles spasmed. Tears ran from his eyes.

"Mrs. Pruitt, I am dying. I am a lost soul as you say. Please, relieve my misery."

"How?"

"Free me from this life," he begged.

"What?"

"Kill me."

"No!" Charlotte, horrified, stood up and backed away from him.

"Please, help me," he pleaded. "Fucking, Christ, please! You said you wanted to slit my throat. You said you aren't a coward. Prove it!"

"Confess, Edward. I will make them promise to turn you over to the authorities for sentencing."

He did not appear to hear her. He stared into space, pain contorting his face.

"Bonnie is insane, a devil," he whispered hoarsely. "He will torture me, cut me up, piece by piece."

"Hawkes, listen to me. Confess that you murdered the child and my husband."

"Will you help me then?"

"Perhaps." The moment was interrupted as the new guards descended into the hold.

"Do not abandon me, Mrs. Pruitt," he pleaded in a rasping whisper.

Charlotte did not answer him. As she turned to leave, the two men passed her, wishing her a good morning. She thanked them for coming so swiftly and bid them good day. She made her way towards the steps, knowing that Hawkes watched her go. James was not to be found in the shadows. Had he heard this last exchange, she wondered? Wearily, she ascended the stairs.

As she climbed awkwardly up to the last deck before the hatch, she heard James's voice.

"He begs you to be his executioner. That is quite a turn." James bent down and put his hand under Charlotte's arm, helping to steady her as she pulled her skirts up to clear them from her feet. She stepped onto the deck as best she could.

"He says it only because he knows you are incapable of such an act," he continued.

"Perhaps he is wrong," Charlotte answered.

"Charlotte?"

"I hate him, James, as you do."

"Enough to kill him?"

"Perhaps, if he confesses. He deserves to die a thousand times, each worse than the one before. However, if I were to promise, and he were to confess, I would feel it my duty to fulfil my pledge. Just as you would, would you not?" Charlotte felt herself standing on the edge of an abyss. What was she capable of doing? She wasn't sure.

James held her hand. "Come, you promised to have breakfast with me. You should honour that first before we make any decisions."

Once more, Charlotte made the cumbersome ascent. The eastern sky presented itself in pinks, reds, and greys as they came out onto the main deck. A strong breeze rippled the water and broke the colours into a thousand fragments. Charlotte and James bid good morning to John Fuller and Lord Mansfield, who were admiring the dawn sky and watching the sailors set sail up and down the estuary. A little further on, they met Robert Adam, who was describing the scenery to John Fielding.

"Adam has a great eye for detail and a gift for words. I believe I am seeing more of the landscape than if I had my sight," Fielding marvelled.

Moving on, Charlotte suggested they stop to see if Jack was still asleep. He was, and they drew together, whispering admiringly of his golden hair and his full pink lips. They moved noiselessly out of Charlotte's cabin and up to James's where they had tea, spiced muffins with butter, and fresh fruit. They ate in silence. Charlotte gazed intently into her teacup. She looked up and found James gazing at her.

"I would never have imagined when I first saw you in Bath that our lives would have entwined as they have," he said, smiling tenderly at her.

"Nor I."

"You are a remarkable woman, Mrs. Pruitt."

"My mother always called me wilful."

"I believe I said that myself not long ago."

"I do not doubt it, Jem." Charlotte was suddenly cold. She closed her eyes. Fear gripped her.

"Charlotte, what's the matter?" he asked, coming to her side.

"I am afraid, James, of the future. Suddenly, it seems cold and empty."

"It will not be. We have each other, and we have Jack. I do not want to be apart again."

"I now have eight children. Will you be able to open your heart to all of them, do you think?"

"I shall do my very best to a father to them all, Charlotte."

"I love you, James. I always will, in this life and if

possible, into the next." Charlotte rested her head on James's shoulder as he kneeled beside her.

The calm did not last long. There was a knock at the cabin door. James got up to answer it and found Count Cesi's smiling face greeting him.

"Good morning, my English friend. The gentlemen await you on deck." Before James had a chance to answer, the count spied Charlotte over his shoulder and greeted her merrily, "*Buongiorno, signora*, I hope I did not disturb your repast."

Charlotte rose and crossed to the door. "Good morning, Count Cesi. You did not disturb us in the least. Quite the opposite. It is a pleasure to see you."

"What a delightful lady you are," the count remarked.

"We should attend to the gentlemen. If either of you would care to join me," James said, raising an eyebrow at their interchange.

"An excellent idea," the count said as he turned to lead the way.

The breeze had died down, but the clouds were gathering in the west as they walked towards the gentlemen gathered on deck. After greetings were exchanged, General Campbell was the first to get to the business at hand.

"James, you have seen the prisoner this morning, do you reckon that a confession will be forthcoming?"

"I believe it will, General Campbell."

"How can you be sure?" Lord Mansfield questioned. "He seemed mighty determined yesterday to hold his ground."

"The man took a horrible beating," Adam broke in. "Are you sure he is the murderer?"

"I am, Mr. Adam," James said.

"And what of the mask, sir?" Wilkes broke in, red-faced.

"The muzzle has been removed," James answered.

"When?" asked Fielding. "And by whom?"

"Mrs. Pruitt took it off him last night with my permission." There were exclamations from the gentlemen, some approving and some not. James pressed on while Charlotte stood silently by his side. "I shall answer any questions you may have on our plan of action. First, however, I would want you to know that we will be joined this morning by Mr. Richard Fletcher, and Mr. and Mrs. George Norton of Okehampton. The latter are the parents of the murdered child. The former is a friend of mine and a justice of the peace from Devon. To answer your query, Lord Mansfield, it is my fervent hope that prior to their arrival, or soon after, we will extract a confession from Hawkes."

"If that is the case, I shall win the wager, gentlemen," Wilkes said with a smile.

"What is your plan, sir?" Mansfield asked, annoyed at Wilke's gloating.

Charlotte touched James's sleeve. "May I explain what we have done?"

"Of course."

"I sensed, gentlemen, your disapproval at the mask being employed. I, too, felt a certain compassion for Hawkes's situation, which, frankly, surprised and disturbed me. I wondered how I could feel kindness towards such a creature? It made me wonder if treating Hawkes with sympathy might help loosen his tongue. We are, I admit, at a standstill, but he is considering confessing, I believe."

"And I believe Clarke's more forceful approach is the

only way to proceed," broke in Mr. Fielding.

"You are of the gentle sex, madam, and so it is understandable that your heart would lead you when you see suffering. Contrary, Hawkes is a man, and a cruel one at that. He will better understand and respond to the lash."

"I agree," said Lord Mansfield.

"As do I," added General Campbell.

"My vote is with the cat-o-nines," agreed Mr. Wilkes.

"I would side with Mrs. Pruitt," argued Adam. "I believe gentle persuasion can be quite convincing."

"You just want him to hold out longer, so you will win the wager," said Wilkes.

"Honestly, how can you say such a thing, Mr. Wilkes?" responded Adam hotly.

"Oh, have a sense of humour, Adam, you are too damned serious, man," Wilkes said.

The count spoke. "My friends, please, I would offer the services of our fine slab of Carrera marble, if you feel it is required."

"To press him? The countess was not saying that in jest? I did agree, but, really, that is the piece intended for my hall at Kenwood!"

"Exactly, sir."

"A bit macabre, I must say, but I might seriously agree to it, if it would speed the process," Mansfield said.

The storm from the west was moving closer. A light mist fell, but heavier rain was on the horizon. Those assembled decided to move the conversation inside. Charlotte held James back until the others were gone.

"Does this mean I am done with Hawkes?" Charlotte shivered as a gust of wind found its way under her cloak. Her auburn hair flew in all directions as she attempted to put her hood on her head. James moved to shield her from the blast. He squinted as the mist flew in her face.

"I will test him this morning and see. If he resists us, you may have one more opportunity with him."

"James, I believe Hawkes would rather die than give in to you, but I also know that he has a tremendous fear of what Charles Bonnie would do with him given the opportunity."

"I agree, Charlotte, I was there in the shadows when he spoke of it."

"If Hawkes stays true to course and refuses you, threaten him with Bonnie and let me speak to him one last time."

"You have the strength for it?"

"I do. Your group thinks me gentle, but had they ever seen me run up the fells, petticoats and all, chasing my grandfather's sheep and yelling at the wind, they might have a different opinion."

"You are mad, my angel. Do you know that?"

"Of course, I do. I am in love with you, am I not James Clarke? It follows that I would have to be mad." Charlotte smiled and kissed his cheek. "I should look in on Jack and Annie. Please, tell me when you are going to Hawkes." James brushed a strand of Charlotte's hair out of her face. They stood looking into each other's faces, afraid to say any more about what the day might or might not bring.

"I shall let you know," James said, then they parted.

He went to where the men had assembled.

She, fighting the wind that blew steadily, went to her cabin where she found Jack up and dressed. Before she even had time to greet Annie, Jack ran and jumped into her arms. Laughing, she covered his face with kisses. He giggled and tried to avoid her lips. When she stopped, he rested his head on her shoulder and sighed. Still wearing her cloak, she sat down and wrapped it around Jack. He seemed content to rest quietly in her arms.

"Good morning, Annie."

"Good morning, Charlotte," Annie said as she sat down opposite them.

There was a knock at the door. Betsy, the maid, who had been tidying up, ran to answer it. Emma entered with flushed cheeks from the cold wind.

"Good morning, Charlotte, Annie," she nodded to them both.

"Good morning, Lady Emma," Annie responded politely.

"Good morning, Emma. Please, join us." Betsy moved to bring Emma a chair and take her cloak. Emma sat and began to speak.

"I have already breakfasted with the countess. She is a most delightful lady. I am sorry you missed our whist game last night, Charlotte, though I know you were involved in other business. John will tell me none of it, so I expect you to regale me with all the details. This much I learned from Countess Cittidini this morning, which you probably already know, Charlotte, but I am sure Annie does not. We are stopping at Tilbury, very soon now, to bring on board three people from Devon. One is a friend of James, the other two, a couple, an innkeeper and his wife. Am I correct, Charlotte?"

"Yes."

"But why? Who are they?" Emma asked, turning now to Charlotte, who was trying to catch hold of Jack.

When Emma began talking, he had slipped his head and

body completely under his mother's cloak. Now he squirmed and giggled in the warm darkness, making it difficult for Charlotte to pay attention to Emma. Charlotte motioned for Betsy to retrieve the boy. She quickly came and snatched him away. This done, Charlotte removed her cloak and righted her dress.

"Forgive me, Emma, what was your question?"

"These people from Devon, who are they?"

Charlotte thought for a moment trying to remember a name. "One is Richard Fletcher, I believe, a friend of James's. They served in Canada together…"

"Oh, my lord!" Emma exclaimed, blushing.

"What is it, Emma dear?"

"Dick Fletcher! Oh, Charlotte, I was quite in love with him when I was a girl. You know, I used to go and visit Elizabeth and James every summer. Dick was always at the house. He and James plagued Elizabeth and me when we were children. I shall never forget the summer I turned thirteen. He was sixteen. He stole a kiss from me on the hill, near the mausoleum. I thought my heart would burst. He felt it, too, even followed me to Bath the next week. My parents were appalled and forbade me to see him again. He was not in Chagford when next I went, or ever after that. I never had an opportunity to say goodbye." Emma stopped, her eyes welling up with tears. "So, he is coming here today." She smiled and sighed. Her voice became lighter. "And the other couple, who are they?"

"An innkeeper and his wife from Okehampton. The Nortons, George and Abigail." Charlotte hesitated to say more.

"Are they traveling companions of Mr. Fletcher's?" Annie asked.

"Yes, but they play a greater role, I am afraid," Charlotte replied.

"Charlotte, for heaven's sake, why are these people coming on board?"

"They are the parents of the child Hawkes murdered."

Annie gasped and Emma shook her head in disbelief.

"For what reason? Why should they be made to suffer their loss anew?" Emma said.

"Apparently, the mother suffers from deep melancholy, Emma, as would I, if anything so unthinkable happened to Jack."

"And this will aid her recovery, do you think?"

"James thinks it might. Though at the moment, I'm not sure. He would have them hear Hawkes's confession first-hand, so no doubt is left as to who the murderer is."

"Oh, but Charlotte, to have to hear the details of such a crime and to one you loved," Annie's voice trailed off.

"As a mother," Charlotte answered, her voice shaking, "I might find solace in reliving what my child suffered. To feel that I was there and able to comfort his terrified soul. I do not know, but I like to believe it would be so."

"Death is a horrible thing, but a violent death must be that much more terrible," Emma said quietly. Annie bowed her head and began to weep.

Charlotte, realizing her thoughtlessness, knelt by Annie. "Dear one, forgive me, I should never have talked of this. You must believe that we did all we could for your mother. We were there, and I hope of some small comfort to her"

"I know we were, Charlotte," Annie whispered.

From the corner of the room came a shout. Jack leapt on Betsy as she knelt beside him and knocked her on her back. The three women could not help laughing, the serious mood broken by the picture of Jack atop poor Betsy.

"I would suggest, Emma, that you and Annie go and visit the countess. I must see how James and the others are faring. We should be in Tilbury soon. Are you unsettled about Mr. Fletcher?"

"Oh, for heaven's sake, no," Emma protested. "It was a very long time ago. All forgotten. It was just that hearing his name caught me off guard."

The ladies all stood and made ready to face the weather outside. When Jack saw his mother putting on her cloak, he ran to her side. She picked him up and nuzzled his cheek.

"You be a good lad for Betsy, Jackie. Mama will return in a short while to see that you are minding."

"I love you, mama," Jack said.

"And I love you, Jackie, more than the whole wide world." Charlotte tried to give Jack to Betsy, but he grabbed hold of her cloak and would not let go.

"Mama, stay! Mama, stay!"

"No, mama is going, but she will be back."

Charlotte struggled to stay calm as he held fast. The child was suspended between the two women. Annie stepped into the fray, taking hold of Jack's waist and tickling him. He giggled and let go of Charlotte. Annie now bundled him up into her arms. He cried angrily and beat at her shoulders. Unruffled, Annie looked at Charlotte.

"Please, you and Lady Emma should go on. I will stay with Jack. He will be fine in a minute or two."

Charlotte smiled at her gratefully as they exited to Jack's cries of protest.

CHAPTER FIFTEEN

The women were met with a strong, west wind as they stepped out on the deck. Charlotte could see Tilbury fast approaching on their port side. With Emma leading the way, they crossed to the rail, so they could watch the ship weigh anchor.

The dark, grey water of the estuary was broken into thousands of small whitecaps. Charlotte held the railing to steady herself against the wind and the roll of the ship. After several minutes, Emma spotted a boat coming steadily towards them from shore. The sailors on board also saw it and alerted James and the other gentlemen of its approach. Soon, the main deck was filled with a welcoming committee. The count and countess were in the front of the group.

Charlotte noticed James was missing. Did the innkeeper and his wife know at this point what awaited them? Charlotte was unsure. Looking over the rail as the boat pulled alongside, Charlotte caught a glimpse of the innkeeper's wife. She was a pretty young woman. Her pale skin and ruddy cheeks contrasted with the line of dark hair that Charlotte saw peeking out from under her bonnet and hood. Most strikingly, she was smiling broadly and appeared quite excited at the prospect of boarding the big ship. Charlotte's heart sank to imagine what this woman would go through in the next few hours.

Emma's hand slipped into Charlotte's as Richard Fletcher came aboard. Surprised, Charlotte turned her gaze on Emma and found she was biting her lower lip, her eyes fixed on Fletcher.

"Are you feeling ill, Emma?"

"A bit faint, I fear."

"Should we go inside?"

"No, we must stay here."

Fletcher was presented to the count and countess. He was a small man with a thin nose, which appeared to tilt slightly to the left. His eyes were dark but merry. He was handsome, Charlotte thought. Next came the innkeeper's wife, who dipped into a deep curtsey, followed by her husband, who bowed. The three were then introduced to the rest of the gentlemen. The innkeeper, a man of middling height with prominent cheekbones and a balding head, switched his cane to his left hand and gave a hearty handshake to Mr. Wilkes. He smiled as he met most of the men.

However, on being introduced to Lord Mansfield he took a step back and seemed to stiffen. "Your lordship, pleased to make your acquaintance, sir."

"And yours, sir," Lord Mansfield replied, puzzled by the man's sudden aloofness. "Have we met before, Mr. Norton?"

"No, we have not, your lordship," Norton responded in a choleric tone. Charlotte's observations were interrupted by a sharp intake of breath from Emma. She turned to see Emma watching Richard Fletcher speaking quietly to John Fuller.

"Whatever are they saying, do you suppose?" Emma asked.

"I'm sure they are discussing the progress of Edward Hawkes's confession, or perhaps how they are going to introduce James to the innkeeper and his wife."

The sound of Mr. Norton's voice rose above the rest of the conversations. Charlotte turned back to see that the innkeeper and William Murray, Earl of Mansfield, facing each other. Lord Mansfield, his face growing scarlet, seemed to be attempting to keep his temper.

"I would know the reason, Mr. Norton, why you seem so displeased with me," he demanded. "What affront have I offered you? By your own account, we have never met until now."

"You, Lord Mansfield, had the murderer of my son in your prison and you let him escape! I heard about it only after the fact, otherwise I would have hung the blackguard myself had I got my hands on him."

"If you are referring to James Clarke, I have reason to believe he is innocent and that his desperation to prove his innocence led him to dare such a bold escape."

"Innocent! He's a lunatic to be drawn and quartered," Norton fumed.

"Sir, I am not guilty of your son's murder," James said from the outer edge of the circle which had gathered around Norton and Murray.

Norton appeared stunned. His wife let out a cry and swooned, falling to the deck. Count Cesi swept into action, commanding the servants to help Mrs. Norton to her feet and accompany her to the countess's quarters. Countess Cittidini and Emma hastened to her side, speaking softly to her as she was led away. As James walked towards Norton, the count and Fletcher stepped between them.

"You bastard!" Norton shouted and raised his cane.

"Please, George, calm yourself," Fletcher pleaded, taking hold of the stick. "Hear Clarke out."

"You scoundrel," Norton hissed, turning on Fletcher. "Have you brought us here to meet him?! Never has there lived such a treasonous scalawag as yourself." Norton pulled at the stick. "Let go, I'll thrash you both, goddamn you."

John Wilkes made his way through the crowd of men and stood at Mr. Norton's side. "You are quite right to be outraged, sir. How dare you and your wife be so deceived by one whom you thought was your friend." The innkeeper looked at Wilkes as he struggled for ownership of his cane. "However, if you would but calm yourself, you might find that there is more to this situation than meets the eye."

"Speak plainly, Mr. Wilkes, and tell me what that might be."

"James Clarke is not the murderer you suppose him to be, but the guilty man is on this ship."

"What?" Norton ceased his struggle and turned his attention to Wilkes. "Where is he? Why should I believe this?" He glared at James who stood not three feet from him. "Clarke is mad as a hatter and he had my wee lad's poor body in his bloody hands. What more proof than that do you need?"

He took a step closer to James and drew himself up as tall as he could. "I will have you arrested. I will see you hang."

Charlotte stood on the outskirts of the crowd of men, but with this last threat, she began to move forward to defend James. She stopped, however, seeing James in control of the situation.

"Not today, you won't, Mr. Norton," James responded calmly. "Today, you will hear the confession of the man who murdered your son, but it shall not be me."

"Where is he, then?" Norton asked, confused by James's calm demeanour.

"He is below, in chains."

"And he has admitted to it?

"Not yet, but he will."

"Bloody hell, who is he? Some gawk off the street you're torturing till he confesses."

"No, Mr. Norton, he is a man who hates me so violently that he will stop at nothing, including murdering your poor son, to ruin my life."

As the men exchanged these words, Charlotte watched Emma, emerging from the countess's quarters and entering the circle of men.

"Mr. Norton, your wife is calling for you," she said. "Will you come?"

"I will. Please, tell her I will be there directly."

Emma thanked him and went off with the message to his wife.

Norton stood silently. The mention of his wife seemed to dispel his anger.

Looking first to Richard Fletcher, he spoke. "All right, Mr. Fletcher, I know you to be an honest man, and though I despise how you lured me and my wife here, I shall agree to see this man. You, Clarke," he continued, turning to James, "I will not let you out of my sight, for though all here may be convinced of your innocence, I am not. Since I heard how your sister had to coax you to give up my son's little body, wrapped as it was in a filthy rag, I have hated you and sworn I would see you hanged or kill you myself. So, I will not now be so easily swayed by your fancy words and fine manners."

Count Cesi stepped in, suggesting he take him to Mr. Norton's wife. "She should be told as gently as possible of the situation at hand, do you not agree, Mr. Norton?"

"Aye, I do, your lordship," he replied. He then turned to Wilkes who stood at his side. "She suffers tremendous melancholy, my Abigail. Spends long days abed, face to the wall, not speaking, just staring. Though she's not said it, I do believe that she thinks if she stares hard enough, it might bring our Henry back to life." He looked sternly at Fletcher. "This holiday was the first time that she seemed to come back to life, and the invitation to visit this ship, well, she was fairly brimming with excitement, and now this turn of events. I fear the black choler will be on her."

"Forgive me for this deception, Mr. Norton. I knew no other way to bring you here," Fletcher responded.

"Your wife, Mr. Norton?" the count urged him forward.

"Oh, aye. I will follow you, your lordship. Mr. Wilkes will you come, too? I would be glad of your company, sir."

"By all means, I shall accompany you, Mr. Norton."

Charlotte watched as Count Cesi led them to the countess's cabin. James and Fletcher followed hard on his heels, with Norton and Wilkes coming next. John Fuller brought up the rear and the other gentlemen stayed behind, shaking their heads, and talking quietly amongst themselves.

"A penny for your thoughts, Mrs. Pruitt."

She jumped on hearing a voice so close.

"I surprised you. I am sorry," Mr. Adam apologized.

"You are forgiven, Mr. Adam." Charlotte smiled. They watched as the sailors finished with the capstan, and the ship began to move its course down the estuary. Adam and Charlotte stood watching the countryside glide past.

"In this verdant setting, Mrs. Pruitt, I find it difficult to reconcile such beauty with the evil that lies below deck. When I am in the hold, I find it most necessary to separate myself from the proceedings. Looking instead at the shadows and the light, I imagine myself to be Piranesi imagining a fantastical prison."

"Why is Signor Piranesi's work so popular do you suppose, Mr. Adam?"

"He created moods, madam. His evocations are so strong, so immediate, that one cannot help but be moved. He touches one's soul with exultation and melancholy in the same instant."

Charlotte smiled. "Truly, sir, you have an artist's sensitive spirit. It is no wonder that your talents are so sought after."

"You flatter me, Mrs. Pruitt, but I gladly accept your compliment."

"If you had no boundaries on your design, Mr. Adam, what would you most like to create?"

"A garden! *Un jardin anglaise*, of course."

"Why so?"

"In it, one can come closest to giving birth to Arcadia. It lives and grows. There is the will of nature that the artist must face and master, or rather coax and tease into submission. In this living entity, I place my surprises, so that as you enter and stroll, every turn offers a new delight. Or, if you wish certain persons or events memorialized, I may do that, too, thus when you happen upon that spot you may reflect and feel in communion with that beloved and that moment of the past."

"Bravo!" Enchanted, Charlotte clapped her hands. "Thank you, dear Mr. Adam, you have lightened my heart immeasurably."

"And you are a muse, Mrs. Pruitt," he said, smiling shyly. The rain began to fall, interrupting their reverie. As they walked quickly towards the countess's cabin, they encountered Emma.

"Mrs. Pruitt, Mr. Adam," Emma greeted them. "Please excuse us, Mr. Adam, I need to speak with Mrs. Pruitt."

"Of course. Good day to you both, ladies." Adam bowed and was off.

Finding the nearest shelter from the rain, Charlotte led Emma to James's cabin. Once inside, they shed their wet cloaks and sat down.

"What is the news, Emma? Please, tell me."

"Mr. Fletcher made himself known to me. He remembers our encounter with gentle fondness." Emma beamed.

"Emma, I am so pleased for you."

"I will speak with John about it, but I have not had the opportunity to do so yet," she added quickly.

"Of course you shall, but do not let that hinder your enjoyment of the moment."

"I shan't, dear friend," Emma giggled.

"Tell me what has happened with Mr. Norton and his wife."

"Oh, dear me," Emma appeared worried.

"What is it?"

"The reason that I sought you out was to bring you a note from James. I quite forgot it in my excitement."

Charlotte tried to hide her impatience. "May I see it, Emma?"

"Oh, of course, let me just think where I put it." Emma put her hand deep in the pocket of her robe. "I know it is here." She felt several objects before she laid her hand on the paper. "Ah, *voilà!*"

Producing the note, she gave it to Charlotte.

Charlotte read to herself.

Dearest Charlotte,

The gentlemen and I are presently going to see Hawkes. Mr. Norton has agreed to accompany us. His wife shall remain with Countess Cittidini. I have my doubts that we will have any luck in drawing forth a confession. I would appreciate it if you would be ready to speak with Hawkes one last time. If he proves intractable, Charles Bonnie may have him, and we shall sail to Venice. What say you to that, my angel?

Jem

Charlotte smiled as she read the last part of the note. Would that they could escape now, in this instant.

Emma touched her arm, "You are smiling. Is it good news?"

"Both good and bad, I would say. Here, please, read it." Charlotte offered Emma the note.

Emma, taking it, looked at her friend as if to say, 'are you quite sure?' Charlotte nodded, so Emma proceeded. When she finished reading, she looked up.

"Oh my, will you face Hawkes again?"

"Yes, though I dread it." Not wanting to think about it

further, Charlotte changed the subject. "Please, tell me about Mrs. Norton. What happened when you accompanied her to the countess's cabin?"

"She was distraught, Charlotte, crying for her little boy and calling his name. It broke my heart to hear her. She could not understand why Richard Fletcher brought her and her husband here. She ranted about James being the murderer of her child and threatened to tear his eyes out if he came near her. Charlotte, I tried to comfort her and to convince her that James was innocent of the crime. She would not hear it at first. Finally, after drinking some hock, she calmed down. She spoke with the countess for a bit, which seemed to please her. Mrs. Norton asked if she might go to her husband. However, when she attempted to stand, she felt faint, and we urged her not to move. That was when I came out to bid Mr. Norton to attend to his wife. I wished him to know it was a matter of urgency. A most odd occurrence happened upon my return to the cabin. The countess excused herself, leaving us alone. Mrs. Norton was resting, her eyes closed. I heard her stir and turning towards her, I was startled to see her unblinking gaze fixed upon me. She has the palest of blue eyes. Before I had an opportunity to ask her if she was feeling better, she announced, 'I am dead to this world, but I will be born again the angel of death.' "

"Whatever did you say in response?"

"I asked her if she might not feel better after a cup of chocolate."

"And?"

"She smiled sweetly and said, 'Yes, thank you.' I rang for the servant, who went to fetch it and by that time the countess had returned."

"And Mrs. Norton said no more about angels?"

"Not a word."

"The world is mad, Emma. It confounds and terrifies me, at times."

"I agree most heartily, Charlotte. Those feelings affected me most strongly in recent days, especially when I hear stories of the Methodists, and the goings on at those open-air meetings."

The sound of the gentlemen's voices outside broke in upon their conversation. Charlotte cracked the door to view what was occurring. It was a procession of sorts, with James leading the way. Mr. Norton and Wilkes were close behind. The innkeeper's face was nearly crimson, his brows knitted and his lips in a thin, tight line. Was this expression because of his displeasure with James, she wondered, or in anticipation of seeing Hawkes?

"My lord, I have never seen a man's face with that deep a colour before," Emma remarked as she peered over Charlotte's shoulder. The rest of the gentlemen passed with sombre faces. Closing the door, Charlotte turned to Emma.

"I am resolved to follow them down. I shan't wait to be summoned."

"Why not? I certainly would, Charlotte. From what you have said, it sounds like a descent into hell. I do not understand your fascination with this business. Forgive me for saying it, but I would let the men do what needs to be done, my dear."

"I cannot do that, Emma."

"Why not? Why do you insist on being involved in this?"

Charlotte's mind was a jumble. Why, indeed, she thought to herself? Finally, she answered.

"Emma, I cannot forget that Hawkes brutally attacked me, that he nearly destroyed James, physically and mentally, and that unless he confesses, James will have to quit England forever. How can I stand by and do nothing? I will not leave it to the men."

"Charlotte, I am at a loss. Your obstinance is monumental," Emma said. "Are you not concerned at all about appearances, about scandal? I love you as if you were my own sister and shall never turn away from you. However, you must understand that if word of this horrible business were ever to circulate, you would be ruined forever." Emma was shaking when she finished.

"Emma, dearest," Charlotte said. "I am so sorry that I have unthinkingly compromised your position by drawing you into this. I shall do my utmost not to embarrass you."

"But you will not stop this business with Hawkes?"

"No, I shall see it through."

"Very well," Emma responded, her lips taut with anger as she stood to leave. "I shall be with the countess and Mrs. Norton if you require me."

"Thank you, Emma," Charlotte said to her friend's back as she moved away.

"I do not understand," were Emma's parting words.

Charlotte exited the cabin a few minutes later when she was sure that all the gentlemen had gone past. Out on deck, the mist covered her face as she walked past the open hatch to the stairwell. She stood looking out at the green, spring fields and the monotonous grey of the sky. Taking a deep breath of fresh air, she began her descent. Trying to be as quiet as possible, she moved slowly down to the deck where she had on rested on the wooden box earlier that morning. Norton's voice could be heard clearly through the hold opening.

"How am I to believe that this miserable bastard is my Henry's killer?"

"Mr. Norton, I related to you, not five minutes ago, the circumstances leading to the death of your child, how Hawkes held me prisoner on the moor, how he tortured and taunted me. Your unfortunate child was simply a means to drive me into madness permanently and to make me appear guilty of a heinous crime, which I assure you, I did not commit."

There was silence. Charlotte wished she could see their faces to understand what was happening. One minute passed, then two. Were they staring at each other? What were they thinking? In the third minute, there was another voice, that of Hawkes.

"For the love of Lord Jesus Christ, I am innocent. Please, sir help me." Charlotte assumed he was addressing Norton. "I'm a simple man. I am. I was just havin' a drink wif me mates. I thought these men was a press gang. Oh, my God, make 'em let me go, sir. I am dyin', Mr. Norton, sir."

Chills ran through Charlotte. Hawkes was the devil. He shaped his identity and truth to suit his needs. She wanted to shout, 'No, I know who he is. I know the truth!' Yet who was she to Norton, and why should he believe her?

She heard John Fuller's voice. "Mr. Norton, this man is lying. We took him the night before last as he attempted to rob a grave at Christ Church in Spitalfields."

"Don't believe him, sir. I'm a sailor. I ain't no resurrector. I never even heard of bloody Edward Hawkes afore today. Look at what they done to me. I won't confess nuffin' I ain't done."

Charlotte felt a black despair falling over her. She desperately wanted to sleep. No, dammit, she thought, I will not let him sap the life out of me. I know who he is and what he has done. "Bloody aristocrats think they can blame the poor people o' the world for all their crimes. I'm nobody's whipping boy! Mr. Norton, help me, sir."

Lord Mansfield's voice rang out, "Silence him. Put the leather strap on him." There were footsteps. Someone scurrying to find the gag, Charlotte assumed.

Hawkes called out in desperation, "Don't let him shut me up. I'm the only bloody one tellin' the truf. Mr. Norton, save me, as you're a Christian!"

"Hold his head!" Allen Peters shouted. "Grab his shoulders. Hold him steady."

Hawkes cried out, "No! Help me!"

A muffled cry came next, freezing Charlotte, making her sick. It was the cry she had held back when Hawkes raped her. Was it also the cry the baby made as Hawkes murdered him? Charlotte buried her head in her hands and wept.

From deep inside of her, a voice sounded, growing louder and louder like the rushing of the wind up a mountainside. Charlotte raised her head and, sitting up straight, said in a quiet, but resolute voice, "I will kill him today."

She stood and hiked up her skirts, then climbed the steps past the decks and out onto the main deck. Quickly making her way to James's cabin, she searched through his belongings until she found a dagger. She sat at the small table for a time. First looking at it and feeling its weight, she tried to imagine how she would use it. Hawkes was bound, so she would not have to fight with him, but where was the most effective point to stab him, she wondered?

Standing, she tucked the dagger into her pocket. She started to open the door to the cabin, then stopped, frozen. Betsy had brought Jack to play on deck. No, I cannot see him now, not as I imagine myself with hot blood on my hands. She closed the door and stood with her back against it. His voice was loud in her ears as he laughed and squealed at Betsy's teasing. Luckily, rain started to fall in a downpour. Betsy called for Jack to come and their voices quickly receded into the distance.

Charlotte opened the door, and when a break in the rain came, she ran as fast as she was able. She went down the steps to the deck before the hold where she listened to the sounds from below. There was a loud thwack and anguished cry. Charlotte instinctively recoiled.

James's voice rang out, "Say who you are!"

"Edward Hawkes," came the reply.

"Again," James demanded.

"Edward Hawkes!"

"Were you in Wolfe's regiment?"

"Aye."

"Did you know me in Portugal?"

"Aye."

"Did you kidnap and murder Norton's son?"

"No!" Hawkes spat out the word. Silence, then a loud crack of the whip and a moan.

"Did you kidnap and murder Norton's son?"

"Go to hell!"

Thwack!

"Fuck you, Clarke!"

Thwack! Thwack! Thwack!

Silence followed.

"Is he dead or unconscious?" James asked, sounding winded.

"Unconscious," came Allen Peter's voice.

"Let him down. Chain him to the post," James commanded.

When men began to speak, Charlotte took the opportunity to slip down the stairs. Absorbed in their discussion, no one saw her except James, who caught the movement of her dress out of the corner of his eye. She hid in the darkness behind the steps. The men took James into their midst. They moved away from Hawkes and closer to where Charlotte stood.

James's face was pale. He had dark circles under his eyes. Perspiration dripped from his chin as he pushed the loose hair back off his forehead.

"The man has a suicide's temperament," Mansfield said.

"I agree," Wilkes seconded. "I do believe he would rather die than give in to you, James."

Adam was the next to respond. "We are truly at an impasse. What might be done, I cannot imagine."

"My poor, wee lad to be at the mercy of such a man," Mr. Norton covered his face, bewildered.

"Get Mr. Norton a box on which to sit," Count Cesi ordered.

This done, Mr. Norton was guided to his seat by the count, who sought to comfort him. Fletcher joined them. The rest of the men stood in uncomfortable silence, looking at the floor or ceiling as the distraught man wept.

As last, John Fuller spoke. "Perhaps it would be best if we adjourned for a short while."

"An excellent idea," James agreed.

Adam and Wilkes were the first to go up, followed by John Fuller, who was guiding Fielding. Campbell looked to James, who nodded his head, indicating he should go. Count Cesi and Fletcher spoke quietly to Mr. Norton, enabling him to muster the strength to ascend the steps. They followed after him. Lastly, James turned to the guards to tell them that they should also leave.

"Hawkes has no need of your services presently."

This done, he went up and they followed. The last to leave were Charles Bonnie and Jacob Golder. It was quiet.

Charlotte listened to the creaking of the ship and the scurrying of some creatures in the darkness. She moved into the light and stopped. Now there was another sound, so soft at first that she could not identify it, nor tell from which direction it came. Suddenly, she had chills, realizing it was Hawkes laughing.

He stopped and looked at her, barely able to hold his head up.

"I win," he hissed. Pain surging over him, he closed his eyes.

"How can you possibly say that?"

"Mansfield, bloody Mansfield here, and Fielding! I should have smelled them the first time they came down here. They don't give a shit about me, but they love the fuckin' common law. Sets us apart from the Frenchies. They won't let Clarke kill me, and they'll never let goddamn Bonnie have me. A black man torture an Englishman? Hah! That's bloody heresy in their book. I know my Bow Street magistrates. And I am intimately acquainted with the bloody chief justice, Lord M." Hawkes laughed again. Slowly and with relish, he said, "Clarke is ruined. He has nothing, is nothing. And tell me, Pruitt, with all your high sentiment, is a fuck with him worth giving up everything? Will you marry him and leave your blessed, bloody England? Never see London or the lakes again?"

As Hawkes closed his eyes enjoying his triumph, Charlotte asked quietly, "Did you know Lord Mansfield has a mulatto niece by the name of Dido, whom he adores?"

Hawkes stared at her. "What?"

"His niece, who lives with him and his wife, had an African mother. I would not make assumptions about his regard for Mr. Bonnie. You might be deceived."

"You're a bloody liar."

"I would remind you that all records show you died in Portugal. That's how you wanted it, yes? So, how can James be guilty, or Mr. Bonnie for that matter, of killing someone who no longer exists."

"But I am here."

"Yes, but who are you?"

"I am Edward Hawkes."

"Yes, you have said that, but you also said you were not Edward Hawkes. Which is it, I wonder?"

"I am a man, I exist."

"You are here, yes. I am not sure you could be defined as a man. You have no genitals, and barely a penis to speak of."

"Bitch! Fuckin' bitch."

"You are certainly a foul-mouthed creature. Human? I do not think so. You show no compassion, have no concept of honour, and do not believe in God. You simply eat, sleep, and kill innocent people. Men, women, or children, it appears to make no difference. I would say the world would be better without you. I could dispatch you quickly. I have a dagger here." Taking the dagger from her pocket, she walked slowly towards him. "But perhaps I am a coward." She stopped and smiled sweetly at him. "Besides, it is my belief that you should suffer the worst possible torture before you die. This might allow you to feel, in a small way, the terror you have made your victims experience. James and the gentlemen are bored with you. I shall advise them to turn you over to Bonnie."

Hawkes's mouth gaped open. She could see him desperately trying to find a way out.

"I win." She turned to go but stopped looking back at him. "I adore Bellagio by the way. The thought of living there for the rest of my life enchants me."

"You bitch!"

"You've said that before. You are a tiresome, uneducated brigand. You cannot hurt me, Edward. You have no power now. You are nothing but an emasculated piece of dung. I have survived. You are a dead, defeated animal."

"And you are a fucking coward, Pruitt, just like Clarke. He begged to be beaten and you're anybody's whore. A perfect pair, the two of you. You were both mine for the takin' cause you're too stupid to protect yourselves. Just like your husband, never for a minute did he suspect me. I slit his throat so easily." Hawkes turned his venomous gaze on her.

Charlotte wanted to flee, but she stood her ground.

"Whore!" he screamed and spat at her. She did not move. This enraged him. "Remember, Mistress Mawk, how I spread your legs. So warm you were," he cooed. "I have a secret," he laughed softly. "I spread his legs, too."

Charlotte could not keep her eyes from widening.

Hawkes caught it. "Didn't he tell you that? He begged

for it up the arse. I made him scream and cry like a little girl. We've all had each other, eh? Come kiss me again, I'll get your cunt wet. I'll take that dagger and give you a hard, fast fuck you won't forget."

"You... are... a... liar!" Charlotte declared in as powerful a voice as she could muster. "Every word out of your mouth is a lie."

"There was only one candle lit over by little Jackie. You heard a voice that didn't belong in your bedchamber. Saw a black shape that scared the shit out of you. I tied your wrists, tied your ankles, gagged your mouth. Truth?"

"Yes," Charlotte whispered, shaking.

"Did you know I stood by your baby first? Did you know I had my hands so close to his neck I could feel his heat? So easy to snap a little neck like a twig. I have big hands," he laughed softly, thinking about it.

Charlotte's throat tightened. All her nightmares realized, she felt her arms going numb. Do not let him win, she told herself. Stay here, stay awake. She shook her head, trying to clear away the fog of terror. When she looked at Hawkes he was grinning.

"Why babies?" she asked.

"Why not? Who needs screaming brats around? Jack was lucky he was sleeping that night. Little laddie won't be so fortunate when I get out of here."

"What!? How dare you?" Charlotte could not contain her anger and fear.

"He'll be mine, just like his parents," he laughed, never taking his eyes off her.

Charlotte felt for the dagger in her pocket. She had it. Her rage building, she advanced on Hawkes.

He watched her, urging her on. "Come on, bitch, cut

my throat. If you don't, I'll get you in the dark. I'll kill you last. Make you watch Jemmy bleed to death. Turn white as marble, he will. Wash my face in his blood. Wash your face, make you eat him. Like I sliced up that kid in Portugal. Poor old Clarke, so sorry for everybody's pain. Didn't know I cut off that kid's ears and ate 'em fried.

"Oh, next comes little precious Jackie. He's a small one, won't struggle much. I'll play with him first, make him think I'm his friend, just like I did old Audley. He'll want to come with me, and I'll do him just like the babe in Devon. Snatched him right away from his brothers and sisters. Turned their backs and he was gone. He cried and puked. Didn't like riding the horse.

"I took him to the stream to wash the stink off him. Didn't like the water. Dunked him in and by God if he didn't shut up. Wailed when I took him out. Held him under. He thrashed around, eyes big, he stopped. Limp as an old man's pecker. Little bugger was still breathing when I took him out. Snapped his neck like a twig. One less, who cares? You all just fuck again, and pop, out comes another one.

"Jack'll be next. The little ones are soft outside and in." He grinned at her lecherously, then he began to chant, "Jackie and Jem. Jackie and Jem."

From somewhere up above Charlotte, there was a frenzied wail, but Hawkes continued, not noticing it. "Jackie and Jem, slice 'em up. Watch 'em die! You'll be all mine. Keep you in a cage. Have you when I want."

She was very near him now. Tears of rage streaming down her face. She held the dagger low, aimed at his neck.

He cackled and called seductively, "Ooh, Charlotte."

She took hold of his greasy hair, pulling back his head.

He laughed and purred, "Mine, all mine."

She was breathing fast, her jaw set. Just as she moved to strike, she felt herself grabbed from behind and pulled away from Hawkes.

"NO!" she shrieked. "I will kill him!"

"SHIT! FUCKING GODDAMN! NO!" Hawkes bellowed.

She struggled with the arms that held her, while Hawkes cried out, "GODDAMN YOU, CLARKE! LET HER GO, YOU FUCKING COWARDLY BASTARD! SON OF A BI..."

Suddenly, his voice was quiet.

Through her blind rage, she heard Jem speaking to her. "Charlotte, calm yourself. I am here. We have him. Hawkes has confessed."

CHAPTER SIXTEEN

"Jem?" she said.

"Look at me, Charlotte." He let her go, and she obeyed. "You did it, Charlotte. He confessed. I am a free man." He pulled her close. "You alone have saved me."

She felt lightheaded, and her heart would not stop pounding.

"You heard it all?" she asked as she took a step back from him, not able to conceive how James must have reacted to the filth Hawkes had spewed.

"Yes."

The sound of the gentlemen's footsteps coming down the stairs interrupted them. Before they surrounded her with a wall of "huzzah" and "well done", she became aware of Charles Bonnie, pike in hand, standing silently next to Hawkes. The latter's head rested on his chest, his jaw was slack. Charlotte realized that Bonnie must have rendered him unconscious. He will be all yours in a short while, if I have anything to say about it, Charlotte thought to herself.

Wilkes was the first to reach her. "An amazing display of bravery, madam."

"You have conquered the lord of the underworld, dear Mrs. Pruitt!" Count Cesi proclaimed as he took her hand.

"He is a vicious animal, Count Cesi."

"Truly, madam, he is."

"He is a savage, Mrs. Pruitt," John Fielding interjected, having just joined them. "I have known many a criminal, but none as depraved and cold-blooded as Hawkes."

The gentleman parted, and Norton, pale and trembling, moved towards her with uncertain steps. Richard Fletcher was at his elbow, ready to catch him should he fall. The innkeeper stretched out his hand to her, and she grasped it with both of hers.

"My poor, wee Henry, Mrs. Pruitt. The unspeakable acts…" he stopped, overwhelmed with emotion.

Charlotte realized that the cry she heard must have been his. "It was wrong of us to bring you here, Mr. Norton."

"No! Mrs. Pruitt, I am thankful that I am here today, as terrible as it was to hear this devil confess. I have carried a black hate in me since the day the sheriff brought the body of our wee son to us. I swore I would kill you, Sir James, if I may call you by your rightful title, for I was certain you were my son's murderer. But seeing and hearing Edward Hawkes today, that darkness has been lifted from me. You are exonerated, and I will see that Hawkes is punished royally. I pray that when I relate it all to Abigail, that she may be healed of her melancholy. May the poor soul of our Henry rest in peace now."

"I believe it will, Mr. Norton," James said.

Charlotte could not help but feel Mr. Norton's profound sadness. The assembled group honoured the memory of Henry Norton with bowed heads and a moment of silence.

Mr. Norton broke the stillness. "Mr. Fletcher, will you accompany me topside? I would speak with Mrs. Norton."

"Of course," Fletcher replied. To Charlotte, he said,

"Mrs. Pruitt, I greatly admire your courage and fortitude. I pray we have an opportunity to speak further." He followed the innkeeper to the stairs where they ascended slowly.

Lord Mansfield, taking a step forward, smiled broadly.

"I am pleased that you knew about my dear Dido, Mrs. Pruitt. Introducing her into the discourse as you did took the wind out of Hawkes's sails, eh? Hawkes erred to assume that all people have the same low opinion of Africans that he has. God made us all brothers, and my niece is the most gentle and refined creature as ever God created."

"Indeed, your lordship," interjected Mr. Fielding. "It is Hawkes that is the savage. I would never have wished for an Englishwoman to have to face him as you did today, Mrs. Pruitt. Yet his evil was matched and overridden by your goodness. It is a victory for the angels."

"It is, indeed!" added James. "As one who has done battle with Hawkes and knows the depths of his depravity, I thank God for Mrs. Pruitt's bravery and intelligence."

"Huzzah for Mrs. Pruitt!" called out Wilkes.

"Huzzah!" the group repeated.

"And thank you for winning my wager, madam," Mr. Wilkes said and looked at the gentlemen, who shook their heads at his brashness.

Charlotte laughed, filled with euphoria. She decided to move the proceedings forward.

"Gentlemen, we are done with Hawkes now. It is my opinion that he deserves to be turned over to Mr. Bonnie and dispatched in whatever manner he sees fit."

A loud, "Aye, I agree with that!" was heard from Allen Peters, who stood on the periphery of the group.

Count Cesi, standing next to Charlotte, added, "I believe that would be a most deserved ending for this villain."

"A fitting end indeed, for such a rogue," agreed Lord Mansfield, "if he were not an Englishman."

"Sir?" queried the count.

"He deserves his day in court, Count Cesi. I cannot give my sanction to anything less. He has confessed and will be sentenced officially. He will be hanged and gibbeted. There is no doubt of the outcome."

"I concur with Lord Mansfield. It is what the law demands, and his end will send a clear message to those of his kind," said Fielding firmly.

"Gentlemen, we chance his escape if Hawkes is put into prison to await a hearing," James argued. "He has too many friends in London among the criminal class who would rise to his aid. You heard for yourselves the threats he made against Mrs. Pruitt, our son, Jack, and me. If he were to gain his freedom, I have no doubt he would carry them out. You are condemning us to death by allowing this monster his rights."

General Campbell stepped forward into the circle to speak, "Why can't we compromise, sirs? We have in our midst, after all, the Chief Justice of England." He indicated Lord Mansfield, who nodded his head in acknowledgment. "As well as an esteemed Bow Street magistrate," he gestured towards Fielding. "Why not convene a special court session here on shipboard? Once sentence is passed, we can hang Hawkes, pirate that he is, at low tide as admiralty law requires."

"And we can swing his gibbet from Tilbury Point, just as they did William Kidd's," Allen Peters added. "After his body is washed three times by the tide. That is admiralty law, as well."

Looking at Allen Peters, Count Cesi remarked, "I must study British admiralty law when I return home. It sounds fascinating."

"It is, Count Cesi," Peters agreed.

Lord Mansfield scowled. "This is highly irregular, gentlemen, but taking into consideration Sir James's point, I see General Campbell's compromise as a possible option. What is your opinion, Fielding?"

"I am in agreement with you, milord. Hawkes's crimes justify a special session, though we do lose the opportunity to make him an example through public execution."

"Sir, gibbeting him from Tilbury Point may help to serve that purpose, eh, Mr. Peters?" Lord Mansfield asked, looking in Peter's direction.

"Oh, aye, it would, milord," Peters answered, proud to be included in the proceedings.

"Gentlemen," the count interjected, "since we have garnered Hawkes's confession, I shall instruct the captain to turn the ship about and set a course back to Tilbury. We shall weigh anchor there so that arrangements may be made for disposing of the body after the hearing."

"An excellent plan, Count Cesi," Lord Mansfield said. "May we use the countess's dining room as our session room?"

"Of course. Instruct me on how you would have it arranged, and it shall be done."

"Thank you, Count Cesi. Let us go topside and have a look at it." He turned to Charlotte and James. "Sir James, are you satisfied with this compromise?"

"I am, your lordship. However, I would include Mrs. Pruitt in this decision, also."

"Well, yes, of course," Lord Mansfield frowned, not

used to being corrected. "Mrs. Pruitt, what say you in this matter?"

"I would have Mr. Bonnie be the hangman, milord."

"Well, I..." Mansfield began, but was interrupted by Charles Bonnie.

"I accept your offer, Mrs. Pruitt."

Charlotte, looking at him, nodded her head in acknowledgment.

"Very well," Mansfield said, his face reddening, "let us get topside and begin. Sir James, have the guards bring the prisoner." He indicated for General Campbell to help Fielding lead the way. The rest of the gentlemen filed out to the hold behind them.

As Adam passed Charlotte, he whispered, "This scene is directly from a Piranesi sketch. Look at him," he said, indicating Hawkes's limp form as the guards began to unchain him. "I swear to you I have seen it before in one of his drawings. I feel inspired, Mrs. Pruitt."

"Mr. Adam," Charlotte chided him, "only an artist such as yourself could be inspired by such a grim scene."

"I do not choose to see that aspect, madam, but look instead at the lights and darks of the space the angles of Hawkes's face, the planes of his muscles, and the remarkable shadows that the lantern light affords."

"I stand in awe of your powers of observation, Mr. Adam. We must speak further about your ideas for *un jardin anglais*."

Hawkes groaned. Adam appeared startled. Now he had no choice but to look at the unpleasant reality of the situation.

"We shall talk more, Mrs. Pruitt, after this awful business is over." Averting his face so as not to have to look at Hawkes, he fled up the stairs.

Turning, Charlotte saw that Hawkes was flat on his stomach, his head to one side. Standing over him were James, Bonnie, Golder, Peters, and the four guards. Hawkes's eyes were shut. He moaned softly, seemingly unable to lift himself from his prone position.

"How hard did you hit him?" James asked Charles Bonnie.

"Not hard enough to kill him." Bonnie smiled, leaning against his pike.

"No, I see that. He is heavy, dead weight, though, to get up those stairs. Remove the leg irons. Let's see if we can get him to walk. Otherwise, we will hoist him up in a net." The key was produced, and the irons removed. Hawkes appeared unaware that his legs were free.

"At sixteen pounds apiece plus the weight of the chain you'd think the bastard would get up and do a jig," Peters remarked.

James instructed two of the guards to pick Hawkes up, one man on each arm. After a good deal of grunting, they got him to a standing position, but he was unable to support himself. It was clear that to move him, he would need to be dragged or carried.

"Let him go," James commanded. They did. Hawkes dropped onto the floor with a heavy thud. He lay sprawled and lifeless. James turned to Peters, "Go above and have them send a net down. Hoist him up, I am finished wasting time."

"Very good, sir," Peters replied and was off up the stairs.

James thought for a moment. "I had best go up be there to greet Hawkes. Bonnie, can you manage down here?"

"I can, sir."

"Mrs. Pruitt, will you accompany me?"

"No, my legs need a bit more of a rest before I attempt the stairs again."

James went to her, concerned.

"I am fine." She smiled at him. "It is simply the strain of the day."

"Mr. Bonnie will accompany you up the stairs."

"I would appreciate that, if Mr. Bonnie does not object."

"To be your guardian, mum, would please me," Bonnie replied.

From above, they heard Allen Peters shout, "Net, ho!" Looking up, Charlotte saw that the hatch cover had been completely removed and the net was being lowered. It came down quickly and was spread out by the guards, who dumped Hawkes's body in the middle. James yelled for them to hoist it up a few feet, leaving Hawkes dangling in air. His face towards Charlotte, his eyes closed, he made no movement.

"When I arrive on deck, we will hoist him up. Take your time negotiating the stairs. I will be waiting for you," James said, touching her shoulder.

"Thank you. I will be there directly," Charlotte replied, holding his hand to her cheek. James moved to the stairs and was gone.

Bonnie brought a box for Charlotte to sit on while she waited. She felt a great relief to be able to rest. Observing Bonnie, she noted his erect posture and self-assured air. His relaxed face was pleasing to her. The dislike she'd for him had disappeared. She noted the change and desired to make amends.

"Mr. Bonnie, thank you for your help in this business. I am truly sorry for your sister's death and your suffering."

He did not speak immediately, being overcome by emotion. At last, moving closer to where she sat, he answered.

"Thank you, Mrs. Pruitt. Since my sister's murder, I have been single-minded. I say what I think is necessary to say, when often I understand that no one wants to hear it. The colour of my skin predetermines what people think of me. Most whites would have me be invisible, not a human and certainly not a man. I will not do that, and so I am hated. Perhaps that is Hawkes's gift to me, for in killing my sister, he made me a man unafraid of ridicule or death. But then, it is a gift I could have done without."

They heard James's command from above. The net began to move. Hawkes's body remained inert. Looking at him, Charlotte experienced a sudden shock. His eyes were open, staring at her. He was awake!

The net moved up swiftly. There was the din of sailors shouting from above and the guards moving to the stairs.

Bonnie began to walk away. She reached out and grabbed his arm, crying out to him, "Hawkes is conscious. He is awake. Warn James!" Bonnie yelled up to the open hatchway, but the noise topside drowned out his cries. The net reached the hatch opening and was pulled to one side. Charlotte and Bonnie strained to see what was happening. Suddenly, there were shouts of alarm and Charlotte heard James's voice above the rest.

"Hold him fast!" To her horror, Hawkes leering face appeared over the edge of the hatch. He fixed his gaze on her, and with superhuman strength broke free of his captors, hurling himself into the hold.

"BITCH!" he screamed as he flew down. Charlotte was frozen. Time slowing down, she stood transfixed as this nightmare demon, eyes seeming to glow, hurtled closer and closer. An instant before he would have crushed her, she felt herself shoved to one side. As she landed on the deck, breaking her fall with her hands, she heard a terrible tearing sound. Struggling to sit up, she turned to see Hawkes's body, impaled on Bonnie's pike. Feeling herself caught in a nightmare, she looked to Charles Bonnie who stood looking at Hawkes.

"He is dead, Mr. Bonnie?"

"Yes, Mrs. Pruitt."

"You saved my life."

"Very likely."

"Thank you, Mr. Bonnie."

"You are welcome." He smiled as he spoke. "May I help you up, Mrs. Pruitt? If you sit there much longer, your skirts will be beyond saving."

Charlotte looked and saw that the back of her skirts had been sprayed with blood and the pool that formed around Hawkes's body was spreading out towards where she sat.

"I am able. Thank you, Mr. Bonnie." Charlotte scooted back from the blood and got onto her hands and knees. She was just coming to a standing position when James bounded down the steps.

"Charlotte!" he called out as he rushed to her. He took her in his arms. "You are unharmed?"

"Yes, thanks to Mr. Bonnie. He saved my life, James."

James looked as though he was seeing her for the first time. As though he wanted to forever burn her face, her body, her voice into his memory so he would never lose them. After a moment, he turned to Bonnie.

"Charles, thank you."

"You are most welcome."

They were joined by Count Cesi, John Fuller, Allen Peters, and the guards. They all congratulated Charles Bonnie on his bravery and quick action. Count Cesi urged James to take Charlotte out of the hold.

"We shall take care of what needs to be done, my friends. I will join you soon. Go now."

Charlotte and James made their way up the stairs. On deck they were met by Emma, the countess, and the gentlemen. Taking charge of Charlotte, Countess Cittidini insisted she come to her cabin to change her clothes and refresh herself. Thankful to be taken care of, Charlotte agreed.

As she entered the cabin, she heard the order given for the ship to be turned about. She emerged sometime later to find everyone celebrating in the dining room where a feast had been laid. The gentlemen rose, and Charlotte took her place next to James. No sooner were they seated than Lord Mansfield rose and proposed a toast.

"To Mrs. Pruitt, for her courage and perseverance in dealing with the devil himself."

"Hear, hear," the assembled group responded. Several more toasts were proposed, each more flattering and longer than the one before. Charlotte noticed that two seats were empty, but having consumed a fair bit of Madeira, she was unable to account for who was missing.

"Jemmy, who is it that is not here?" she asked him between Mr. Adams and Mr. Wilkes's toasts.

"The Nortons. Mrs. Norton was feeling unwell, but Mr. Norton said he would join us as soon as the sleeping draught took hold."

"Oh dear, he gave her thebaic tincture, do you think?"

"Most likely."

"But that is so strong."

"She's deeply distressed, I fear." James rose to respond to Mr. Wilkes toast. They all drank. When he sat, he continued his aside to Charlotte. "I believe it was useful for Mr. Norton to be privy to Hawkes's confession. However, it was Mrs. Norton whom I most hoped to help. I fear my plan has failed in that regard. Mr. Norton reported to me that this experience has only convinced his wife more firmly of my culpability."

"How is that possible?"

"In her melancholy, she sees this as a theatrical staged to delude she and her husband from the truth."

"And we are the players and you the actor-manager?"

"Exactly."

"Had she seen Hawkes's final act, she might have been convinced of the reality of the play."

"Perhaps."

"Should I attempt to speak to her, James? Might that do any good?"

"We may ask Mr. Norton if he thinks it might help. I fear it will not, however."

The count interrupted them, "Sir James, Mrs. Pruitt, you both look far too serious. Please, it is a time for merrymaking. No more long faces."

"I beg your forgiveness, Count Cesi," James apologized as he stood. "I would like to propose a toast to my dear friends, Countess Cittidini and Count Cesi, for their unwavering friendship in my darkest hours, and their shipboard hospitality."

"Hear, hear!" everyone cried loudly. The next hour was

given over to eating and drinking, interrupted only by Mr. Norton's entrance. He looked unhappy. The group quieted. He smiled wanly as he approached James, who offered him a seat, but Norton declined.

"Sir James, if I might have a word with you?"

"Of course," James said and rose.

"Mr. Fletcher, may I speak with you also, sir?" Mr. Fletcher, who was seated across the table from Charlotte, stood without hesitation.

"I am at your service, Mr. Norton." The three of them led by James, excused themselves, and passed into the antechamber, closing the door.

Emma, who was sitting to Charlotte's right, leaned over to her friend. "He did not look well at all. I do hope Mrs. Norton has not taken a turn for the worse."

Inside the antechamber, Mr. Norton was wringing his hands. "I have never in all my days had a day to match this one."

"What is troubling you, Mr. Norton?" Fletcher asked.

"My Abigail is ready for Bedlam, I am afraid. I cannot reason with the woman at all. I tried to have her take the laudanum, but she shouted at me that it was poison. She believes me now to be in league with all of you."

"In what way, Mr. Norton?" James asked.

"Oh, Sir James, she will not hear that Hawkes was the killer of our poor son, as I told you before. I tried to tell her what happened in the hold, how he confessed, how he nearly crushed poor Mrs. Pruitt. Abigail puts her hands to her ears and cries, 'Lies!' I tried to calm her, but she spat at me. Told me I was a coward for letting you live. I have never seen her in such a state. What am I to do? I am sorely afraid she will do you or herself some mischief, if she keeps carrying on so."

"Who is watching after her?" James said.

"Our manservant is with her. After all her ranting about the sleeping draught, she grabbed it from the table and swallowed it. 'There,' she says, 'I am dead now, but happy to join my Henry.' She took off her mourning ring and gave it to me. 'Make another one for your dead wife. You are the mooncalf, not me.' She stood there glaring at me until her legs gave way, and, down she fell in a swoon. The servant and I got her into bed, where she is sleeping. It will not last long enough for me to get drunk and sober again, I fear."

"I think it wise, Mr. Norton, that we disembark at the earliest convenience," urged Fletcher. "We must get your wife to a mad-doctor who may be able to ease her misery. St. Mary of Bethlehem Hospital may be the best place to take her."

"I do not agree, Richard," James said. "Being one who has suffered from a melancholy humour, I would counsel Mr. Norton to return with his wife to Okehampton as quickly as possible, where he can look after her with love and understanding."

"But I do not understand her, Sir James. I am bewildered by her black mood. I say where better than London to get the advice I need. If she is mewed up in a hospital for a time, it is better than having her scare away the trade at the inn. I know I sound hard-hearted, but I have no energy left to give her and her madness."

"What if I were to take her to Kirkmoor with me?"

James offered.

"I think that most unwise, James," Fletcher responded. "As Mr. Norton said, she might do you or your family harm."

"But dammit man, I feel I must do something," James said hotly. "The poor woman and yourself, sir, have suffered because of Hawkes's hatred of me. Though I am not the murderer, I feel a responsibility for your anguish."

"Sir James, a man of honour you are. I understand that now. I wish my wife could also. Thank you for your kindness. It was important for me to be here today, though it was near the worst day of my life."

"Mr. Norton, please communicate with me as to your wife's health. I would like to know how she's faring."

"I will, Sir James."

James turned to Mr. Fletcher.

"Richard, excuse my outburst, if you can. You have been a friend in all of this, and I would not have us part company at odds."

"Think naught of it, James," Richard waved his hand dismissively. "I am pleased that I could help, though I was uncertain of the wisdom of your plan when we first boarded the ship."

"I have to say," Mr. Norton added, "I never felt so pixy-led, gentlemen, as when I first saw you, Sir James. A man can only stand so much confusion."

"Mr. Norton, when I am restored to my place in Society and have my lands back, I hope you will come for a visit to Kirkmoor. We have excellent hunting, which I think would please you."

The innkeeper looked at James but said nothing. "You do enjoy hunting?" James asked. "I have the best hounds in Devon. Though whether my sister has kept them together, I do not know. I pray she has, if she has any love left for me."

"Oh, aye, Sir James, I would be most honoured to pay you a visit," Mr. Norton replied, regaining his tongue. "I can ride with the best of 'em. Why, if I had not become an innkeeper, I would have followed my father, John Norton, as master of the hounds. He was a legend, sir. Surely you have heard the songs about him."

"John Norton!" James said. "He was your father? Why, of course I am familiar with all the stories surrounding him. You have heard the songs as well, have you not, Richard?"

"I have indeed!"

While the festivities continued in the dining room, Mr. Norton regaled James and Richard with stories of his father and the hounds of Okehampton.

Charlotte, growing anxious with the length of time James was absent, excused herself and knocked on the door to the anteroom. James called for her to enter. She found the men in a jovial mood. At last, the four returned to the celebration.

An hour later, the ship anchored off Tilbury Point. The toasting and talking went on until the late hours. At last, everyone said their good evenings and went off to their respective cabins.

James accompanied Charlotte to her door, where they stopped outside. James kept shifting his weight from one foot to the other, looking for all the world like an awkward, young, country suitor.

"Charlotte, I must ask you now in all earnestness. Will you do me the honour of becoming my wife?"

She could not keep herself from smiling at his sudden shyness.

"Sir, I am most pleased to accept your proposal."

His broad smile and the wrinkles at the corners of his eyes made her heart soar.

"I love you, James Clarke!" she cried, throwing her arms around his neck and kissing him.

He returned the kiss. All the strain of the last forty-eight hours melted away as they held each other.

Charlotte looked into his sea grey eyes and touched his smooth lips with her fingertips. He took her hand and kissed her fingers gently. Holding the back of her hand to his warm cheek.

"Charlotte, I will love you forever. I promise."

"And I, you." All the love that they had felt in Bellagio returned in that instant.

Forgiveness washing over them both, their love was born anew. They walked arm in arm to the side rail and looked out on the moonlit river. Charlotte felt James's eyes on her and, turning to him, she saw in his face a terrible sadness.

"What is it, dearest?"

He hesitated. "Today, when I was above deck and Hawkes jumped, I felt a terror I have never before experienced. I knew he would kill you, and I was powerless to stop him." His voice trembled, "To never again touch you, to never again speak to you, my world was lost."

"We have been through so much. May God grant us some peace."

"I pray so, and that we shall be happy at last." James smiled at her. "What say we announce our marriage plans at breakfast?"

"An excellent idea!" Deciding that Jack might wake and need Charlotte, they parted company with a gentle kiss goodnight.

CHAPTER SEVENTEEN

The morning dawned crisp and clear. Charlotte was up early and off to breakfast with Annie and Jack in tow. They entered the countess's cabin to find most of the company already assembled. James hastened to greet them. He swept Jack up in his arms, smiling at Charlotte.

"Shall we tell them now?" he asked. Charlotte surveyed the group and saw that one important person was missing.

"Wait a bit, until Emma arrives."

"To do what, my dear?" Emma's voice came from behind them.

"Emma!" Charlotte smiled at her friend. "You shall find out this instant." She nodded to James to get everyone's attention.

He asked Count Cesi to direct the group to take their seats so that he might speak to them. Sensing his excitement, the count looked quizzical.

"You look as if you might burst, my friend. Are you quite all right?"

"Never better, I assure you, Francesco." James winked.

"Very well then." Count Cesi turned to the group and spoke loudly. "Ladies and gentlemen, would you please be seated? Sir James would like to make an announcement."

James looked to Charlotte and to the group as Jack

played with the ruffles at his neck. Pulling the lace from the boy's hands, he began.

"Dear friends, I would like you all to know that Mrs. Charlotte Pruitt has consented to become my wife."

There were exclamations and spontaneous applause. Jack seeing everyone so excited, clapped his hands and grabbed James around the neck. James kissed him on the cheek. He urged Charlotte to stand, which she did and there was more applause. Jack let go of his father's neck and flung himself at his mother. With his hands free, James put his arm around Charlotte. They stood happily, basking in their friends' approval. The count called for champagne. Toasts began anew, this time to the future good fortune and prosperity of the couple and their children.

At last breakfast was served. Jack finished quickly, and hopping down from his mother's lap, began to visit people individually. Annie volunteered to take him for a walk to which Charlotte thankfully agreed. After their departure everyone ate undisturbed.

Emma questioned Charlotte as to the wedding plans, wanting to know when it would be and where.

"We've not had time nor opportunity to decide those details," Charlotte responded cheerfully. "Though I would like it to be quickly done, perhaps within the next few weeks and probably at Bellagio House."

"At Bellagio House!" Emma exclaimed. "Weren't you just telling me as we were having our hair dressed that you wanted to be rid of it? You will not be married there, Charlotte Pruitt. That place is bad luck, as well as being in an unfashionable area of the town. Forgive me for saying it, but you know how my sentiments run on that subject. You will have the wedding at my house. There is more room and with all those boys running about, you'll need that. Besides which, you are already settled there. Are we in agreement?"

"I am most grateful for your hospitality. Please know that."

"I do, my dear."

"I think, however, I should discuss the wedding plans with James before I agree."

"Oh fie, he will do whatever you desire. Have a strong hand with him, Charlotte. He will appreciate it."

"Oh, Emma," Charlotte laughed, "*Je t'adore.*"

"And well you should. I am the one honest person around here, oh, besides John and James, of course," she smiled mischievously. "And sell that house!"

They both laughed, but Charlotte knew Emma was right.

After breakfast, the group assembled on deck to bid farewell to those departing. Mr. Norton and his manservant emerged from their cabin on either side of Mrs. Norton. She looked pale and drowsy as they led her to the rail of the ship. Mr. Norton shook the gentlemen's hands. He came last to Charlotte and James.

"I thank you, Sir James, for having me here. It were a difficult situation, but in the end, I will rest easier for being part of it. You come see us in Okehampton, and you too, Mrs. Pruitt. Good fortune to you both."

Charlotte smiled and nodded.

"Thank you, Mr. Norton. And you must come for the hunt at Kirkmoor," James said.

"Oh, you say the word and I will be there with bells on, sir." Mr. Norton looked happy until Mrs. Norton groaned behind him. He turned. James and Charlotte looked also. Norton's wife was staring at James, her pale eyes growing bigger as she realized through her laudanum haze who he was.

"My son," she mouthed, unable at first to put a sound to the words. Then, in a staccato cadence, she spat out, "You killed my Henry."

"We'll be goin' now," Mr. Norton said, with a weak smile. He hurried to his wife, taking her by the arm and guiding her towards the rail of the ship. The platform was swung around, and Mrs. Norton was tied in and let down to the waiting boat without incident.

James and Richard had a few words off to the side of the group. Their conversation ended with a handshake. Fletcher, crossing to Charlotte, bid her good fortune and farewell.

Emma, who had been standing a few feet behind Charlotte, stepped forward and offered Mr. Fletcher her hand.

"I hope that you will come for a visit to Grosvenor Square, Mr. Fletcher. My husband and I would be most glad of your company."

"I have business in London in September, Lady Emma. I shall call upon you and Mr. Fuller at that time, if you will be in residence."

"We will be, sir. I shall hold you to that promise." Emma smiled broadly. Mr. Fletcher looked pleased.

John Fuller appeared over Emma's shoulder.

"We may see you at Kirkmoor this summer, Richard."

"What's this?" Emma exclaimed, smiling at her husband.

John continued. "I had planned to surprise my dear wife with a visit to Kirkmoor. But now, the cat's out of the bag."

"I shall await your visit with great anticipation. You must let me know directly when you arrive," Fletcher said, looking at Emma.

"We will indeed," Emma said.

James approached them. "Mrs. Norton is getting a bit restless, Richard."

"Of course. I am on my way. Goodbye." He headed to the rail and was over the side.

"A good man, and a good friend," James said.

A sailor from the rail called out, "They're away and the next boat stands ready, Sir James."

"Thank you, I will tell the gentlemen," James answered.

"No need. We are here," Lord Mansfield said as he came up behind the group. "Fielding, with Wilkes's help, is making the final preparations for loading of the body."

"Will you return to the ship this afternoon, your lordship?" John Fuller queried.

"No. As much as I should like to partake of the festivities now that the work is done, Fielding and I have decided to go by coach back to London. However, you all have an invitation to come to Kenwood as soon as possible. We will have a grand fête, I warrant you, Sir James. I know for a fact that you and Dido would enjoy each other's company, Mrs. Pruitt."

"I am quite sure we would, Lord Mansfield," Charlotte said.

"You have not decided to call off the wedding, yet, eh?" he teased.

"No, Lord Mansfield, not yet." Charlotte smiled.

"Mama! Mama!" Jack cried with delight as he saw his mother from a distance. He broke loose from Annie and ran to Charlotte. She grabbed him up into her arms and he hugged her tight around the neck.

"Hello, lad," Lord Mansfield greeted him warmly. "Let me get a better look at you. They did not give you time to visit me at breakfast. What a head of hair you have, like spun gold. Let me see your eyes." Jack looked at him, enjoying the game. "Blue. They are indeed."

Jack pointed to the sky. "Bue!"

"So, it is lad. Good work!"

"I am ready to go, Lord Mansfield!" Mr. Fielding said as he approached the group on John Wilkes's arm.

"We are off, then," Lord Mansfield announced. As he shook James's hand, he whispered, "The lad bears a striking resemblance to you, wouldn't you say, Sir James?"

"I might be tempted to, your lordship. Odd coincidence, that." He smiled graciously. "Godspeed you to London. Thank you for your help in the business with Hawkes."

"Oh, aye, it is gratifying to rid London of such a scoundrel. Fielding and I will speak with the magistrates at Tilbury. I believe hanging the body from the Point, as your man Peters suggested, is an excellent idea. We shall see how agreeable the local authorities are. I may be able to influence their decision if they hesitate. Fielding and I have spoken with all the gentlemen who were witness to Hawkes's confession. We have drawn up a document that exonerates you of all guilt in the deaths of Henry Norton and Audley Pruitt. Come to my house in Hampstead three days hence, and I shall have the necessary documentation for you to take back to Devon. I will also send another of the same to the shire authorities to precede your arrival. I anticipate no further impediments to your reclaiming your title and inheritance."

"Thank you, your lordship."

"I have also suggested to all the gentlemen that we avoid unnecessary discussion of Hawkes's incarceration and confession. Given Hawkes's ties to the criminal world and the unorthodox way in which his confession was garnered, I think it best to be mute on the nature of this voyage."

"I heartily concur, Lord Mansfield."

"I pray that you will be able to enjoy a quiet and peaceful life with your new family, Sir James."

"I pray for that also, your lordship."

Fielding and Mansfield said their goodbyes to all assembled and boarded the boat to take them ashore. Another boat was to follow with Hawkes's remains, but Charlotte, having no desire to see it loaded, retired with Jack to her cabin to wait for the ship to weigh anchor.

The rest of the trip back to London was exceedingly pleasant. There was discussion of the wedding plans, and Emma shared with James her sentiments on the subject. James thanked her for her generosity, which seemed to please her. It was decided that in four weeks' time at two o'clock in the afternoon, Charlotte and James would be wed at 33 Grosvenor Square. There would be only a few guests. The ceremony would be simple.

James and Charlotte took a stroll on the deck by themselves. In the midst of their joy and recollections of their best times, Charlotte remembered Thomas.

"Jem, Elizabeth was sent for when Thomas was wounded. She may be in London when we arrive. He was in a very bad way. What should be our course of action in this matter, do you think?"

James's mouth tightened, and his eyes grew hard. "I

have most uncharitable thoughts on the subject of my brother-in-law, Charlotte. However, duty bids me to call upon my sister and her husband at such a time. You may do as you wish. Though if Warrender is conscious, I am sure he will ask after you."

They walked in silence, until Charlotte remembered Sir Rufus's papers.

"James, before he died, your father gave you papers that he had written. Do you remember?"

"Vaguely," James responded, trying to recall the incident. "So much was happening at the time. I have difficulty piecing it all together."

"They are in my writing desk. When I returned from Devon and thought you were dead, I simply stuffed the papers into the desk and forgot about them. Recently, I came upon them. We should at least try to review them. Your father was so insistent that you look at them."

"His writing was indecipherable, if I recall correctly."

"But we looked at them in haste. There might be something to them if we studied them more carefully. We owe it to your father's memory."

"Very well, we shall."

Standing quietly side by side, they watched the countryside glide past. Masses of early daffodils marched down to the water's edge. Charlotte wished to be lying down among them, to feel their cool stems and leaves on her skin, to be overpowered by their fragrance. James's sleeve lightly touched her arm. She felt her body grow warm and her cheeks flush. His voice broke into her thoughts.

"We have time before dinner is served. Would you have any desire to retire with me to my cabin?"

She turned to see him gazing intently at her, his lips

slightly parted, a ringlet of hair falling into his eyes.

"I do desire it," she responded, her breathing growing quicker.

He smiled. "Let us walk, shall we?" They made their way towards James's quarters. Attempting not to seem in haste, they discussed the weather, the ship's expected docking time, the flight of a passing gull. All the while, their excitement was mounting until, at last, they reached his cabin and entered.

James shut the door quietly. Charlotte grabbing his arms, pulled him to her. They kissed and pressed their bodies into each other until Charlotte grew lightheaded.

"I must sit down."

"Of course." He pulled a chair over so she could sit. She sat and smiled up at him. He knelt in front of her. "Are you feeling ill?"

"No, my love. Quite the contrary."

"You are sure?" She giggled seeing the look in his eyes and feeling his hand go under her skirts. "Because I would not want to cause you any discomfort," he murmured as he moved his hand up her leg and began to caress the inside of her thigh.

"I feel no discomfort." His hand continued its exploration. She moaned, wishing all her clothes to fall away so she could feel her body against his. "James," she whispered, "take your breeches down."

"Lottie?" he asked, not knowing if he heard her correctly.

"For god's sake, take your breeches off and sit in this chair, please!"

Obeying her, he stood up. She stood as well and helped him with the task. All the while, she kissed and stroked him.

He sat, his shirt open and naked from the waist down. She raised her skirts and sat down upon him, taking him into her. He closed his eyes, his head tilting back. She bit his neck, and they kissed open mouthed.

"Shall we have a daughter this time?" she murmured.

"Yes, and may she be as wild as her mother."

"And as wilful?"

"Yes." He pulled her dress down off her shoulders and ran his fingers over her collarbone. With deftness, he undid the ribbons that held her stomacher in place until one breast peeked out. His tongue played with her nipple, and she felt him grow inside her. She began to rock back and forth. He joined her until they came together in ecstasy. He picked her up, and together they fell upon his bed, panting and laughing.

There was a knock on the door. They stifled their laughter. "Yes?" James said in a serious tone.

Charlotte licked his ear and nipped at his neck. He attempted to ignore her.

"Dinner will be served in half an hour, Sir James."

She stroked his thigh and pulled her body close to his. "Thank you, I shall be there," he managed to say.

"Very good, sir." They heard retreating footsteps. James laid his head down, pretending exhaustion, and stared at the ceiling.

Charlotte began to crawl on top of him, but he grabbed hold of her and counterattacked. She found herself pinned to the bed with James grinning down at her.

"Thirty minutes, eh," he whispered. "Whatever shall we do with so much time?"

CHAPTER EIGHTEEN

Sailing into London later in the day, they anchored at Wapping. Emma sent for her coach to come fetch them. They shared dinner with the count and countess, Adam, Wilkes, and Campbell. Again, everyone congratulated them on their engagement. Charlotte spoke briefly with Adam, inviting him to Kirkmoor sometime in the near future.

"We shall create *un jardin anglais,* if you can take that much time away from your endeavours in London, sir."

"For you, dear lady, it would be my pleasure."

As dinner ended, Wilkes kissed Charlotte's hand.

"I applaud your bravery, Mrs. Pruitt. May we correspond? I would like to maintain our acquaintance with more regularity."

"Most assuredly, Mr. Wilkes. You must keep me abreast of your political campaign."

"I shall," Wilkes promised.

General Campbell and James talked at some length on the deck after dinner. When the boat was lowered to take Campbell to the docks, he thanked the countess for her gracious hospitality.

To Charlotte, he said, "I wish you the greatest good fortune, Mrs. Pruitt. It has been an honour to make your acquaintance."

Charlotte thanked him, and he and his valet were off. Looking around, Charlotte observed James speaking with Jacob Golder and Charles Bonnie. She excused herself, and leaving Countess Cittidini, Emma, and Annie, she crossed to where the men stood. They stopped their conversation as she approached.

"Sirs, I wish to thank you for your help to both Sir James and me. Forgive me if I have wounded you with my words or gestures. I did not understand how loyal you were and how much you both had suffered." She looked at Bonnie. "I thank you for your bravery and for saving my life. I am forever in your debt." Charlotte extended her hand and, taking it, he pressed it to his lips.

"Thank you, Mrs. Pruitt," Bonnie said.

She turned and thanked Jacob Golder, and to her amazement, he smiled.

"As my people say, *l'chaim*. Peace and prosperity to you, Mrs. Pruitt, and to Sir James."

"Thank you again, Mr. Golder." She moved to James. "I will be with Emma and Countess Cittidini when you are ready to disembark."

"I will join you, Charlotte," James said as he walked with Bonnie and Golder to the side of the ship where Adams, Wilkes, and Campbell stood ready to go. After the gentlemen departed, James thanked the countess and count again for their aid.

"Count Cesi and I shall expect an invitation to Kirkmoor as soon as you are settled," Countess Cittidini teased James fondly.

"And you shall have it, dear lady. You have my promise."

"But first," Count Cesi added, not to be outdone, "we

shall have the pleasure of seeing you wed at John and Lady Emma's."

Emma's carriages arrived and they were rowed to the docks, where they disembarked to the noise and smells of Wapping. As they slowly passed through the crowded streets by the river, Jack stood on the seat looking out the window at all the different sights, while James tried to hold his squirming body.

"Ees, Mama!" Jack squealed, pointing at a man with a basketful of eels on his head.

"Jackie, how many do you think he has?" Charlotte asked as she watched the man walk past.

"*Beaucoup, beaucoup!*" Jack replied, pointing at the basket.

"*Oui, mon petit, beaucoup.* What a smart boy you are." She smiled at him and at James. "William has begun his French lessons. Jack is very quick, he tells me."

"Takes after his father," James said.

"Pooping, Mama. Horse pooping!" Jack exclaimed.

"Your father could not have said it better," Charlotte remarked smiling at James.

James began to tickle his son, who giggled wildly.

Looking out the window, Charlotte caught a glimpse of a blond-haired man. She shuddered, drawing back into her seat. Taking a deep breath, she thought, Edward Hawkes is dead. He is not out there anymore. She breathed deeply again and smiled, looking at her lover and her son, who played happily.

How much had changed in a short time, she thought to herself. Only days ago, Jane Rourke was alive. Charlotte closed her eyes to hold back tears as Jane's face came into her mind's eye. She recalled her gentle demeanour with her children and her resolve to keep the business going after her husband's death. Now she was gone. Charlotte was the guardian and mother of her children. Life moved so swiftly at times, like a careening coach. All one could do was to hold on and hope the horses tired before it tipped over.

They left the crowded east and passed into the elegant west end. Soon, they entered Grosvenor Square and were deposited in front of Emma and John's house. Before Charlotte could be handed down, the door flew open and boys rushed out, surrounding Annie. They were full of news of their trip to Hampstead. Jack struggled to be free of James's hold, and when let go, he ran to be with the boys.

In the midst of the pandemonium, William Burke-Scott came to the door looking as if he just awakened from a nap. His long legs propelling him forward, it appeared he might knock Emma over. Luckily, he was able to stop just in front of her.

"Cousin Emma, you are back! You have been sorely missed."

"William, is the house still in one piece?"

"Of course. A trifle broken here or there, but overall intact," he said innocently and hastened on with his greetings. The last person he came to was James.

"I do not believe I've had the pleasure of your acquaintance, sir."

"Please, allow me," Charlotte offered. "William Burke-Scott, may I present Baronet Sir James Clarke. Sir James, William Burke-Scott."

"How do you do, Mr. Burke-Scott," James said formally.

"Very well, Sir James, thank you," William answered meekly, his energy evaporating at being in the presence of so formidable a man. All of a sudden, the young man's face registered surprise.

"Oh dear, me, Mrs. Pruitt, I have only just remembered, a footman came not over a quarter of an hour ago with a message for you."

"From whom, William?"

"The Countess of Chagford."

"With what news?"

"The Earl of Chagford is dead." There was silence. Everyone looked at William as if he spoke a foreign tongue.

"Did the messenger say when he had died, at what hour?" Charlotte asked.

"Very early this morning I believe. Lady Chagford arrived just last night."

"I must go to her directly," James said, looking at Charlotte.

"I shall come, also."

William interjected. "The last part of Lady Chagford's message was her request for your presence, Mrs. Pruitt. The footman said his mistress was quite distraught."

In a few minutes, Charlotte and James found themselves back in the coach and on their way to Elizabeth's house in Portman Square.

"My sister is better off with him gone." James said quietly. "I believe the man was born with malice in his heart."

Charlotte shivered, remembering Thomas Warrender sitting like a spider in the darkened room at the Old Bailey. "Elizabeth is fortunate to be rid of him, but it cannot be easy to lose two husbands."

They arrived at Thomas and Elizabeth's house and were announced. Elizabeth came to them immediately.

Charlotte and James were at a loss for words. Elizabeth was many months pregnant.

Seeing their reactions, she said, "I am to deliver in two months. Thomas and I are… *were,* so happy. I don't know what to say or think. Oh, Jemmy!" she exclaimed, running to him and holding him fast. "You are alive. How is that possible? Are you safe coming here?"

"I have been absolved, owing much to the efforts of Charlotte. I am alive and a free man, dear sister."

"Oh, Jem, such good news. I thank God for it." She embraced Charlotte. "Thank you for coming so quickly. I am sorry, dear Charlotte, for my behaviour towards you. I have regretted it from the moment the words flew from my mouth but have been too full of pride to seek your forgiveness."

"Elizabeth, we are together now. The past is forgotten," Charlotte whispered, fighting back tears at her friend's apology.

Elizabeth released her and smiled, though her eyes were full of sadness and grief. She took her brother's hand and looked into his eyes. "What a time we have had, eh, Jem?" He took her into his arms as she wept.

"Sister, let us retire to the drawing room. It will afford you some privacy." She nodded her head and led them through the door. Once inside, James shut the door to the prying eyes of the servants. Elizabeth sat with Charlotte, who held her hand.

"It is the shock, I think, of his passing so quickly that has undone me," Elizabeth confided. "The message I received simply said that he had been wounded in an attack. I understood that my presence was urgently requested, but I could not let myself believe that this would be the outcome. Thomas is dead," she said hollowly. "I loved him so, his strength, his kindness," she paused and looked questioningly at Charlotte. "Was I deceived in my view of him?"

"Dearest Elizabeth, Thomas was a complex man. Each of us has many sides. My joy was that you found happiness with him."

"Reverend Whitgate, the ordinary of Newgate, told me that you were visiting Thomas at the time of the attack. He said you were a great comfort to him." Again, she looked at Charlotte with a question in her eyes.

Sensing Elizabeth's unease, Charlotte responded, "I had gone to speak with Thomas on behalf of a friend who had been wrongly accused and condemned. Thomas offered to help. Unfortunately, the attack rendered that impossible."

"And your friend?"

"She was hanged."

"Oh, I am sorry."

"Life takes unexpected turns. It is the quickness of the turns that catches us all off guard and unnerves us, I believe," Charlotte remarked.

"Jeremy is coming down from Oxford?" James asked.

"Yes, I sent for him straight away when I arrived. I thank God I have the boys," Elizabeth said, closing her eyes to hold back tears that came with a new wave of grief.

"You are taken care of?" James asked.

"Yes, Thomas is quite thorough. Sorry, *was* quite thorough. His affairs are in good order. He wanted everything to be settled. He was assuming we would have a son. If that is so, I will be the dowager countess and our son will inherit the title. If a girl, she, like the boys and myself, will have comfortable yearly allowances and houses on his properties. Thomas even planned his own funeral. I teased him about it, but in the end, he was right." Elizabeth stopped and stared at the floor.

"Elizabeth?" Charlotte said.

Elizabeth looked up. "I must go through his papers. I need to understand how best to continue the running of the estate. I unlocked the library this morning, but all I managed to do was to stand and look at Thomas's escritoire. I could draw in detail the grain of the wood, I studied it for such a length of time."

"Would you care to rest? James and I will take care of what needs to be done."

"No, Charlotte, thank you. I have no desire to become acquainted with the intricacies of the ceiling design."

For the rest of the day, James and Charlotte helped Elizabeth greet Thomas's friends who called to pay their respects. At last, Elizabeth admitted her exhaustion and left to lie down until supper. Evening was approaching when Jeremy arrived at the house. He appeared a head taller than when Charlotte had last seen him and carried himself with a dignity beyond his years. He reverted briefly to boyishness upon seeing James.

"Uncle Jem!" he cried and ran to James, throwing his arms around him in an affectionate embrace. After that, Jeremy sat listening in rapt attention as James outlined how he came to be a free man.

After his questions were answered, Jeremy stood.

"I must go visit mother."

"Of course," James agreed.

With a sudden intensity of feeling, Jeremy said, "I am glad Warrender is dead. I hated the man. Excuse me." He quickly left the room.

Stunned, James stood for a moment, then followed his nephew out the door. Charlotte sat watching the candles flicker on the table in front of her.

"You are not dead are you, Thomas? You are here in this house, tormenting each of us still," Charlotte whispered.

James returned in a few minutes, frustrated with his inability to find out more from his nephew.

"Damn him, Charlotte, he dismissed me. Said he would take care of his mother now. Thanked me for being here. However, if we wished to leave, he would understand, he said."

"He is simply attempting to be a man, dearest. He is the head of the household now and an earl besides."

"I am the head of the family!"

"James," Charlotte began as she rose from the settee, "I am fatigued from our journey on the Thames and today's ordeal. Perhaps it is best if I return to Emma's while you have supper with Elizabeth and Jeremy. Please, calm yourself before you speak to him." She smiled at James and raised one eyebrow. "He is not your match, my dearest, you could eat him alive."

"Sound advice from my wife to be" James smiled, recognizing his peevishness. "A good sign for the future, I would say."

"May you always appreciate my counsel," Charlotte said, stepping close to him. James gazed fondly at her.

"I love you, Lottie."

"And I love you, Jem." After they embraced, Charlotte left for Grosvenor Square.

James did not return to Emma's that night, deciding rather to stay with Elizabeth and Jeremy. The next morning as he was having his breakfast, Elizabeth entered the parlour, her face pale, holding a paper in her hand. She stood staring at her brother.

"What is it, Elizabeth?"

"Thomas arranged the wager with Father."

"What? What are you saying?"

"I found this letter." She held it out to him. He took it from her. "It is a reply from Mr. Rhodes, saying that he had drawn Father into a bet as Thomas had requested and that the old man had kindly given away most of Kirkmoor on a single wager."

James read silently, his face becoming redder and redder. "Oh, this is lovely," he said sarcastically, and read aloud, *'though, truly your lordship, I do believe you're robbin' the 'spittle o this one.'*

"Why?" Elizabeth asked, "Why would he have done such a thing?"

"Out of spite. To destroy our family and me in particular. My God, Elizabeth, were you that blind to what kind of man he was?"

"What are you talking about?"

"Father saw he and Charles naked together the day our brother broke his neck."

"That's a lie!" Elizabeth cried.

"Father told Charlotte when he still had some of his faculties left."

"Father hated Thomas."

338

"Yes, and for good reason. He caught Warrender with Charles. Father saw them. Charlie was on his knees."

"I do not believe it!"

"Believe it, Mother, for besides that, Thomas Warrender married you to be closer to your sons."

Elizabeth turned, staring in horror at Jeremy, who had spoken from the doorway.

"No, no," she repeated in disbelief.

"It is the truth," Jeremy said softly, seeing his mother's anguished expression.

"Robert and Benjamin as well?"

"I don't know, but they were with him alone. I could not protect them every moment. How could I?"

"Why did you not speak to me?"

"I could not tell you. Warrender threatened to throw you out if I did." Elizabeth put her fist to her mouth.

"This was after Kirkmoor was lost?" James asked.

"Yes."

"Oh, Jeremy, I am so sorry." Crossing to him, Elizabeth tried to put her arms around him. He took her hands and kissed them but would not let her touch him further.

"I must go out. I am meeting friends at White's. I'll return soon," Jeremy said, then he was gone. They heard the front door open and shut. Elizabeth began to speak.

"Robert and Benjamin are coming up to London today. How shall I be able to face them?"

"You must show them that they are loved. I would imagine they, like Jeremy, are glad that Thomas Warrender is gone."

"You must pray for us, Jem. Pray for all our salvations. I will pray, but I am not sure God will listen. I am so ashamed!"

James took her in his arms, and she wept on his shoulder.

"We will start afresh," he told her in soothing tones. "We will all come out of this darkness, Elizabeth."

His sister nodded, and her sobbing subsided.

"I shall go prepare for the funeral," she said, wiping her eyes. "We must go to church soon."

"I asked Charlotte, Lady Emma, and John to meet us there. Elizabeth?"

"Yes, Jem?"

"I shall evict Rhodes from Kirkmoor. I will do it with my bare hands, if I must."

"I will be there with an extra pair for you to employ, if need be." Elizabeth smiled wanly.

"An excellent offer and one I will hold you to, sister."

"But, Jemmy, I must tell you that Rhodes has decimated the staff. Most of the servants are gone, I've heard, trying to find other employment. He has kept on Mrs. Rich to keep house and Mrs. Mulder to cook for him. Mr. Taggart has gone to the Colonies to be with his sister and her family, but saddest of all is Mr. Kyd, our steward." She stopped and looked at James.

"What is it? What has happened?"

"He hung himself a month ago. Mrs. Mulder told me. He was guilt-ridden about the loss of the estate and felt it was his fault."

James shook his head in disbelief. "He was a good man and not to blame."

The funeral was held according to Thomas's wishes. It was well attended by his friends and associates. There were over a hundred men there who owed their offices to his patronage. There were several women who grieved in the back pews, more for the employment they had lost in personal service to "the great man", as they called him to any who would listen, than for the man himself.

When the funeral had concluded, Thomas's remains were dispatched to Devon, where they were to be placed in the family mausoleum. Normally, Elizabeth, as the faithful wife, would have accompanied his coffin back to his final resting place. However, with the news she had received that day, she sent Thomas's remains off in one of his coaches attended by four servants.

Elizabeth decided to stay on in London for James and Charlotte's wedding and enjoy the town with her children. She wished she could stop staring at her boys. She kept hoping against hope that Thomas had not touched them, but she could not be sure without speaking to them about it, and she could not bring herself to do that. So, she watched them, to see if they acted out of character. They did not. She fell asleep praying to God for peace in her heart and salvation for her children.

Charlotte and James spent the next day at Doctors Commons procuring a marriage license. Being less than a mile from Bellagio House, they decided they would gather some of Charlotte's belongings and begin the process of closing the house. Mr. Primm greeted them at the door. Charlotte asked him to have the cook prepare dinner for them, allowing Charlotte time to decide what she would take with her.

She and James walked slowly up the stairs. She dreaded

going into her bedchamber. As they entered, she spied her escritoire and remembered Sir Rufus's papers.

"We should look at them, Jem," she said, retrieving them from the desk.

"Why? There will be nothing there of any import."

"We don't know that. We should attempt to read them, for your father's sake."

"Very well, pack them up. I will peruse them later, but it is a waste of time. The man was a lunatic at the end."

"Jem, please, look through them now. If they're useless, then put them in the dustbin."

"We're not even married, and you are nagging at me, Charlotte," James said crossly.

"Read them, sir, and leave me to my business." He began to sift through the pages, making a show of how useless it was. He quieted down and read when something in them caught his attention.

Charlotte, looking around the room, felt the pull of conflicting emotions. This place, with soft yellow walls and sunlight streaming in, had been her sanctuary. The time she spent with Jack when he was a tiny babe filled her with inexpressible joy. The thought of moments she and James had had together made her body warm with excitement.

Yet there were the dark times, too. As her mind moved there, she began to pick items up and talk to herself. James rose abruptly, crossing to the garden windows, his father's paper clutched tightly in his hand.

"What is it, Jem?" she asked, looking up.

Looking intently at her, his face distraught. "You must read this, Charlotte. My father was not the fool I thought he was. I believe he hid what was important in the middle of his chicken scratches to deter others who might have thought to read his notes." He held two sheets out to her. She took them and, sitting down at the desk, began to read silently.

To my son, James,

Dear boy, I have not served you well, but the death of your brother has forever put me in such a state of melancholy that I scarcely know myself. The circumstances surrounding your brother's untimely end are more than I can bear. I have related them to your friend, Mrs. Pruitt, who must think me the maddest of old men. Perhaps I am. I must put it down on paper before determination fails me. Thomas Warrender, the most monstrous of men, is your half-brother. What can I say to Elizabeth, who in her innocence married him?

He is not mine! No, he is your mother's son. How is that so? Thomas's father, the old earl, cuckolded me, and I never suspected. But to my defence, I was no simpleton. I was absent, having to journey to the Colonies to save my brother from the trouble into which he had blundered.

My wife, your mother, being young, was drawn into a ménage à trois *by Lord and Lady Chagford. When it was determined that she was with child, they decided that they would take it for their own, being childless. All I heard of it was that the three of them travelled to France together. What a fine opportunity for Louisa, I thought, and the earl will pay the bills.*

My lady returned from France. I returned from the Colonies. We carried on with no noticeable differences. The shire rejoiced when Lord and Lady Chagford came back with their new baby son. I prayed that we would be as fortunate and have a boy. Your brother was born two years later. I did not know the truth until your mother fell ill. Guilt-ridden, she unburdened her soul to me. Now

I do the same to you. Forgive me and live better than we did.

Yours with fatherly affection,
Rufus

"Oh, Jem," Charlotte said, shaking her head.

"What a tangled web. It's no wonder Warrender came to the end he did. Half of London hated him, I suspect."

"Perhaps it was an avenging angel who attacked him." She shivered, thinking of how different life would have been for her had he not been stopped that night.

Moving to Charlotte, James took her in his arms, and she rested her head on his chest.

"I would advise letting Mr. Primm supervise the packing up of the house," James suggested.

She felt herself lighter, both in weight and spirit.

"Thank you, Jem, of course he can. My thoughts fly in so many different directions in this room. I find myself overwhelmed."

There was a soft knock at the door. The upstairs maid peeked her head in, "Beggin' your pardon, Mrs. Pruitt, but your dinner is ready, mum."

"Thank you, we shall be there directly." She smiled up at James. "Shall we dine?"

He nodded.

"Eating is one of my two favourite pastimes," she remarked coquettishly.

"Need I ask what the other might be?" he whispered.

"If you do, I would be quite disappointed."

They left Bellagio House after Charlotte and Mr. Primm discussed closing the house and the assembling of a staff for Kirkmoor. Mr. Primm himself agreed to come to

Kirkmoor. He promised to speak with the others to see who would prefer to stay in London and who would come to Devon.

On the ride back to Grosvenor Square, Charlotte told James that she thought it best if she sold Pruitt and Byrd Ltd.

"It is too difficult to manage the business when I am out of London. Mr. Sharp is an honest man and has done well with the business in my absence, but I have no desire to come back to London on a regular basis to oversee it."

"You must do what you think is best, Charlotte. At this point in time, you have agreed to marry a penniless baronet. The business is our one source of income. I imagine you could sell it for a goodly amount, but ..."

"You think that I should continue to hold on to it?"

"No, I merely present the other side of the argument. Besides, Audley left it for Jack."

"I realize that, but he would inherit the money from the sale. Besides, you are a free man now. When you return to Devon you will inherit Kirkmoor, will you not?"

"What little is left of it. However, I believe I can regain the estate in its entirety."

"How is that possible?"

James related what had happened at Elizabeth's, concerning the discovery of the letter from Rhodes to Warrender.

"I will send a message informing Rhodes of our knowledge of his criminal activity and of my intention to press charges with the local magistrate if he does not return the property to me directly. Now that Thomas is dead, I doubt very much that Rhodes will defend his claim."

"And if he does?"

"I will kill him." James smiled wickedly.

"Jem!"

"I am a madman, after all," he responded, crossing his eyes and trying to tickle Charlotte.

She struggled to extricate his hands, but giggling made her powerless. Seeing her breathless, he stopped and began to kiss her.

"Charlotte, marry me tonight."

"What?"

"Tonight. Let us marry tonight." She looked at the odd smile that played on his lips.

"Why?" she asked, feeling uneasy.

"Because any more time seems an eternity. I want us to return to Devon to begin our life as man and wife. I want to be done with London and get the boys somewhere they can run free."

Charlotte was touched by his earnestness, but the intensity of his feeling made her wonder if he was all right.

Taking his hands in hers, she kissed his fingers. This appeared to calm him.

"You have the most beautiful eyes, James Clarke. It is unfair that a man should have such eyes."

He smiled and the skin at the corners of his eyes wrinkled.

Charlotte sighed. "Do you think we can find a vicar who would leave his tea to marry us?"

They did, though Emma protested that they should wait.

"What about the publishing of marriage banns?" she asked. "Will you even be legally married?"

James assured her that for enough money, anything was possible, and he was correct. The vicar was only too happy to oblige when Sir James promised him a large donation to the local church. Emma and John instructed the servants on how to arrange the parlour, the cook began to fix supper for all the wedding guests, and the gardener gathered flowers for the room's decoration. The boys' faces were washed. Annie, Jenny and William dressed in their finery. Elizabeth, Jeremy, Benjamin, and Robert were sent for and came quickly.

When everyone was assembled, and the parlour furniture was out of the way, Charlotte made her entrance and vows were exchanged. On being pronounced man and wife, James and Charlotte gazed at each other, lost in a world that belonged to only them. A world filled with joy, warmth, and safety, theirs at last.

The trip to Devon was raucous, with two carriages loaded with children, servants, and belongings. When everyone was settled temporarily at Scorhill Hall, James sent a carefully worded message to Mr. Rhodes. Two days later, Mrs. Mulder, the Clarke family cook, and Mrs. Rich, the housekeeper whom Mr. Rhodes had retained, came to call, saying that Rhodes had left hastily that morning, giving Mrs. Rich a letter, which she was to put in Sir James's hands.

James opened it and found the deed to the property and the agreement that Sir Rufus and Rhodes had signed. Later that same morning, James called on Squire Burney, the justice of the peace, presenting him with the document from Lord Mansfield, exonerating James of any guilt in the deaths of Henry Norton and Audley Pruitt. James spoke with him about the situation with Rhodes, as well. The squire quickly acknowledged James as the owner of Kirkmoor and reinstated his title of baronet. They shook hands. The squire welcomed James back to his rightful seat of honour in the shire.

After that, James rode directly to Kirkmoor. It had rained earlier, but the clouds parted now, allowing the afternoon sun to illuminate the spring green fields. He was home at last! Feeling exhilarated by the sunlight and his hopes for the future, he urged his horse into a fast canter. As he rounded the top of the hill, however, his heart sank on seeing how much disrepair the house had fallen into in such a short time.

Mrs. Mulder greeted him, clapping her hands together and thanking the Lord that James had returned at last.

"We ha' missed you so, Master Jemmy," she repeated over and over, tears of joy in her eyes.

"We shall have the place back in order in no time," he said, smiling at her. "I have inherited a large family, Mrs. Mulder. Will you be up to feeding so many, I wonder?

"Sir James, how can you ask such a thing? Did I not feed you and Mistress Elizabeth and yer poor brother, may he rest in peace? And look at you, such a big, fine-looking man." She laughed and blushed.

James spoke with her on whom to hire to do the repairs. He told her about Charlotte's butler, Mr. Primm, who was scheduled to arrive in the next few days. He would be in charge of running the house.

"But he will need your guidance in local matters," James told her.

Mrs. Mulder beamed happily at being given so much responsibility and agreed to help in whatever way she could.

A mist began to fall as James set off to survey the outbuildings. The stables appeared as if several horses had just escaped. Stall doors were left open and feed scattered on the floor. As he approached the kennels, the dogs began to bark frantically. He opened the door, and to his delight, the hounds looked healthy and well fed.

Walking out into the grey dusk, his eye was caught by the caretaker's cottage. He stared at it as if it had just materialized from a troubled dream. With faltering steps, he crossed the thirty paces and found himself at its entrance. The door was ajar. He stepped inside. The half-light painted the interior in shades of grey.

His gaze was drawn to the wall. The eyes reappeared where the whitewash had flaked away. He covered his face and backed away, stumbling to find the door. He struggled for breath. He was caught again under the bodies of his friends in the blood-soaked field. His back touching the wall, he sank to the floor and cried. The weight of his unspoken pain, like the weight of their bodies, pushed down on him. In his dreams, he dreaded this place whenever he came near it. He lived in terror of being swallowed up by its darkness.

Finally, he could weep no more. He raised his head and looked at the wall. The eyes had no effect on him. He stood and moved closer to them. His urge to cry, to escape, was gone. There was a stub of candle on the rough-hewn table. He lit it. Shadows danced on the wall. The ghosts were gone, and they had taken his sorrow with them. Silently, he gave thanks to the spirits he knew watched over him.

That night as he lay next to Charlotte, he felt that fortune at last smiled on him. He had struggled for so long to find his way, but now at last, his inheritance and his title were secure. He had the woman he loved by his side and more children than he knew what to do with. A smile played on his lips as he fell asleep. His heart was light, and Lady Fortune held him in her arms.

Mr. Primm arrived at Scorhill, along with many belongings from Bellagio House. It was odd, Charlotte thought, to see her life in London tied up in three wagon loads of goods. James directed the wagon drivers to Kirkmoor, following them directly to supervise the unloading. Mrs. Rich greeted Mr. Primm formally, trying to impress upon him that country folk were not without manners.

When James returned to Scorhill, he was surprised to see a handsome coach in front of the house. He entered at a quick pace and went to the parlour. Opening the door, he was greeted by Count Cesi's smiling countenance.

"Sir James, my cousin and I, upon hearing of your wedding, did not wait for an invitation to Devon. I hope we have not offended your English sensibilities."

"Not in the least, Francesco. Countess Cittidini, it is an honour to have you and the count as our guests. Or, should I say, my sister's guests."

The countess nodded her head in acknowledgment and returned to her discussion with Charlotte and Elizabeth.

"Indeed," James said to the count, "I would be most grateful for your suggestions on any renovations that we might do to Kirkmoor."

"You shall have them. Architecture is my passion, as you well know. We were at a rout only the other night at Lady Chatterton's in Portman Square where Mr. Adam was in attendance. We spent a good deal of time recalling our visit to Diocletian's palace. What an eye for detail he has."

Charlotte excused herself from the ladies' conversation and crossed to James and the count. "Is Mr. Adam well?"

"Yes, and he sends his regards to you both."

"James, we must invite him down to Kirkmoor. On the

ship, he and I talked about the possibility of his designing a garden for us."

"A garden? I was under the impression that Mr. Adam designed houses and furniture."

"That is what he has done. However, he wants very much to do *un jardin anglais*. He said it is the closest an artist may get to giving birth to Arcadia. He was most eloquent on the subject."

"When did you have the opportunity for such a discussion, madam?"

"On shipboard, as I said. Why do you ask?"

"I simply did not realize that there had been time for such an aesthetic conversation."

"James, do you suppose that there was something improper in my speaking to Mr. Adam about gardening?" Charlotte asked curtly.

"It simply came as a surprise, my dear wife," James said, trying to curb his jealous tone. "Mr. Adam would be most welcome. The garden is a marvellous idea, Charlotte."

"Thank you, James. I shall send him an invitation tomorrow."

Count Cesi, watching this interchange with a bemused smile, took this opportunity to speak,

"Perhaps we could walk in the long gallery, James? My legs are in need of stretching after our long ride today."

"Whatever is your pleasure, Count Cesi," James responded, watching Charlotte as she crossed back to join the ladies.

During the next few weeks, spring came full blown to Dartmoor and brought a flurry of activity to Kirkmoor. James, Charlotte, and the children moved in and got settled. Robert Adam arrived, and with his advice and the count's eye, the grounds began to take on a neoclassical look. There were long discussions around the dining room table as to where the ha-ha should be placed, and exactly what the folly should look like. James sometimes wished he had not agreed to the renovation, and especially not *un jardin anglais*. It seemed to him that whenever he walked into the parlour, Charlotte was talking with Robert Adam on this or that bend in the pathway through the garden.

Early one morning, James lay awake, watching Charlotte sleep. Where in the past he would have admired her beauty, now a jealous anger took grip of his heart and mind. He imagined Charlotte wrapped in a sensuous embrace with Adam. The man took her as James watched, her body shuddering in pleasure, her lips parted, her breathing fast.

In anger, James raised his arm over the sleeping Charlotte. Opening her eyes, she moved quickly to the side as he brought his fist down.

"James!" she cried and jumped out of bed, horrified. James looked at Charlotte's shocked expression. He wanted to reach out to her, but jealousy overcame him.

"Have you given yourself to Adam?"

"What? No, I have not!"

"You are with him constantly."

"James, that is not true."

"But you cannot deny that he fascinates you."

"I am simply attempting to help with the garden's design," Charlotte said, defending herself.

"The garden!" James fumed.

"Yes, James, please listen to me. With a beautiful garden, I believe I can overpower the melancholy influence of the moor. The moor is always looming over all of us, but now with the flowers, the pools, the trees, we will be able to look out on beauty."

"I have seen how you give all your attention to Adam. How you laugh when he is clever and nod when he is profound."

"James, please, you are imagining all this."

"I beg to differ." He rose abruptly. "I am going to the moor. To me, it contains true beauty, not this man-made or woman-made nonsense." He moved quickly out of bed, leaving Charlotte concerned at his behaviour.

James rode out with his hounds to the glen that he had loved since his childhood. He sat by the brook that ran through the clearing.

Charlotte followed him there. She watched as the dogs tried to get his attention. They pushed their noses under his arm and licked his face. He shooed them away, commanding them to sit and be still. The dogs came running to her as she approached.

James, seeing her, stood and greeted her unenthusiastically. "Charlotte, why are you here?"

"Because I have been a fool."

"I do not understand your meaning," he responded, pain playing around his eyes.

"I have loved you for over ten years, but in that time, I have continually pushed you away. I am a fool. I am here to beg your forgiveness."

"You are my wife; I am your husband. We are together," he said.

"Please, James, hold me in your arms. *Je t'adore.*"

Looking at her beautiful face and her beckoning eye, he could not remain aloof. He reached out and pulled her to him.

"Why do we hurt each other so?" he asked sadly.

"I do not know," she said softly. Her eyes closed as she rested her body against his.

They spent the afternoon in the glen. Bird songs filled the air. Even the dogs seemed happy to sleep. As they made ready to mount the horses, James took Charlotte's hands.

"The garden is a wonder. Forgive my jealousy and anger."

"I am very happy with it, Jem, but this place is the true Arcadia." She looked up at him. "Are you glad that we are wed?"

"Yes, truly. And you?"

"I am."

"Would you give me a tour of the garden in the morning?"

"I would be most happy to." She answered. They rode back, content.

The next morning, James, taking a turn in the garden with Charlotte, was pleased by what he saw. He later congratulated Adam on its beauty and ingenuity of design. As the summer came to an end, the garden was completed. James and Charlotte planned a grand fête, complete with fireworks. All the gentry of the shire were invited. John and Emma arrived a week before the festivities. Richard Fletcher came the next day.

The evening of the party, James took the opportunity to give a special thanks to Adam and Count Cesi for their help in the renovations of the grounds. Two days later, the count and countess said their goodbyes, leaving for London, and from there to Venice.

Winter was cold and wet, but on the rare day when they were able, Charlotte and James would walk the garden paths, arm in arm. April arrived, and Charlotte received the sad news that Mary Mungris, the housekeeper at Whitestone in Rosthwaite, was gravely ill.

"I must go to her, James. She has always been like a second mother to me. It would be wrong of me not to be with her now."

James did not disagree with her, but he dreaded their being apart. He chose not to tell her of his feelings. He helped her prepare for the journey, teasing her occasionally that she would miss riding to the hounds in a fortnight.

"Even Mr. Norton is coming. He is bringing with him a most remarkable fellow, he says, who is now master of the hounds in Okehampton. 'He's an older man,' Norton wrote, 'who has a way with dogs that is a wonder.' Think what you will miss, Charlotte."

"You tempt me so, Jem. How could I miss such fun? The furiously barking dogs, loud, ill-mannered people riding badly and drinking heavily. Not to mention cold, soggy fields to ride over. All are truly delights not to be missed. Unfortunately, dear husband, I shall have to forgo them all."

It was decided that Charlotte would take only Jack with her. Annie would accompany them to help with the lad and be a companion to Charlotte. They would take Betsy, two footmen, the driver, and a few other servants to help.

"We shall be falling over each other at Whitestone," Charlotte remarked on realizing how many people were going and how much packing they would have to do.

The sun shone brightly the day before they were to embark. The morning was exquisite in its warm temperature and clear blue sky. James was sitting by an open window when Charlotte awoke.

"We must go to the garden," were his first words to her.

Groggily, she sat up and asked him to repeat what he had said.

He moved to her eagerly, like a small boy. "Behold the morning, Charlotte, it is a gift from the angels. Please, rise, we must go out and walk. I want to hold you in my arms and kiss you. Do not tie up your hair. Let it flow down your back. Oh God, you are the most beautiful woman in the world." He sat on the edge of the bed and embraced her. Letting her go, he continued. "This elation that I am experiencing, I remember having only once before. It is a remarkable feeling."

Before Charlotte could ask when this was, he continued. "It was the first time I beheld the golden dome of the Hagia Sophia in Constantinople. I had been at sea, and we arrived in port at sunset. The light was extraordinary."

"Jem, are you feeling feverish?"

"No, Lottie, I am very well. I simply love you. Come wrap yourself up. We are going out!"

Charlotte laughed, watching him hunt comically for her shawl.

He grimaced in mock frustration as he looked under the bed and behind the chairs. At last, he shouted, "Eh, voilà!" when he saw it at the foot of the bed.

She giggled harder as he wrapped her in it and gathered her up in him arms.

"James, please, put me down," she begged, barely able to catch her breath from laughing.

"I shall not. You are my prisoner and I am carrying you off to my castle." He carried her to the door and began to open it.

"You will wrench your back, Jemmy!"

"Quite right. Put your shoes on and walk, wench."

"I will not. Now go away and let me dress. I shall be ready quickly."

"Very well, but do not put too many clothes on. I will just have to take them off of you."

"Oh, for pity's sake, leave this room at once. Wait for me by *l'orangerie*."

"Fine, I shall be the one eating fruit. Do not go to the garden without me."

"I love you, James."

"And I you, Lady Charlotte." He smiled broadly as he turned to leave.

Sensing his ardour was sincere, Charlotte took his advice on clothing. She dressed in a loose-fitting country dress she had worn at the count's chalet. When she arrived at *l'orangerie*, he took her by the hand and walked swiftly to the folly, which was a replica of a Grecian temple.

At the steps, he halted and turned to her. Kissing her, he whispered in her ear, "I am the happiest of men."

Then, he swept her up in his arms and entered the temple. There, on the smooth marble floor, he had spread blankets and pillows for them to recline on. Gently, he laid her down on the impromptu bed. He sat down next to her. He took her hand in his and brought it to his lips. She pulled him down to her side. They kissed long and deep. Their lovemaking was passionate and joyful.

Later, they strolled through the garden hand in hand. "This truly is a beautiful place, Charlotte. Are you pleased with it?"

"I am, Jemmy. I walk here without experiencing any of

the dread and isolation that before weighed upon me in Devon. The garden contributes greatly to my peace of mind." She stopped and faced him. "But having you and the children here makes a tremendous difference, too. I cannot find the words to express my love for you. When I see you, when I touch you, when you turn your attention to me, I am complete. Yet it is more than these moments. I adored you from the first instant I saw you walking down that street in Bristol."

"Why, is that so?" he responded, trying to look serious.

She saw a smile play across his lips. "I am in earnest, James. Do not make light of my thoughts."

"I was simply thinking how handsome a man appears in a well-tailored uniform."

"O fie, and you did. But I am trying to articulate a more significant idea. I wish to discover the source of the connection that one person feels for another, especially when it is an enduring bond. Why was I so drawn to you? Why do I continue to adore you?"

"Perhaps it is as the Greeks thought," James suggested. "That the gods could toy with a human's existence, making him act out whatever was their whim. The East Indians believe that we live many lives, so I am told. Who knows what the truth is, Charlotte? I do not pretend to have the answers. My turn at madness taught me that what we call reality is a fragile thing. I will never know, for instance, if the old man on the moor existed. To me, he was as real as you are, but perhaps he was an invention of Hawkes, or perhaps he was my own creation."

"James, please, I was talking of love. Pray, do not mention Edward Hawkes, especially not in the garden."

"Forgive me." He looked at her with great earnestness.

"I believe, dear wife, that we were meant for each other, and whoever's design that was or is, I thank him or her most gratefully."

"And I believe this day is too beautiful for me to be cross with you for anything."

"Thank you, madam, for the reprieve."

"You are most welcome, sir. Perhaps we should visit our temple once more to thank the gods who have put us together on this earth." She smiled at James seductively.

"I believe your suggestion has great merit. Let us make haste, lest they change their minds."

That evening, there was a going away party for Charlotte, Jack, and Annie. The family, some close neighbours, and even the servants assembled to dance and eat. Late in the evening, as the festivities were ending, Charlotte happened to see Annie and William whispering to each other in *l'orangerie*. Smiling to herself, Charlotte thought that love was in the air.

The next morning dawned clear and dry. The carriage was loaded, and the horses made ready. James and Charlotte embraced.

"I do not know if I will be able to be without you, Lottie," James whispered to her. "You may find me on your doorstep some morning."

"I will not tarry, my love, but I must see Mary."

"Charlotte, I know that this visit is most important. Please, take whatever time is necessary. Just remember we need you. Don't fall too much in love with the fells again."

"I shan't, though to tell the truth, I have missed them. Would that I were a poet and could express the beauty of those mountains."

"Or that I were a painter, Lottie, that I might fill our

house with their images so that you could be content here."

"Forgive my restlessness, James."

"I love you, every trait."

"I wonder, will you always?"

"For as long as I live."

"And I, you."

He handed her into the carriage. She watched as he picked up Jack and hugged him. The boy responded in kind; his small arms wrapped around his father's neck.

"I shall see you soon, Jackie. Be good for your mama, son."

"I will, Papa. *Adieu.*"

Charlotte noticed Annie and William off to the side of the carriage, saying their goodbyes. There were tears in Annie's eyes and William's face had a serious expression. This, Charlotte noted, was a situation to be talked about on the journey. Though quite how to do that, she had not the faintest idea.

Soon, everyone was on board with Sam and Ben, the footmen, riding on top. Charlotte, Jack, and Annie waved out the windows as the carriage drew away from the house.

Chapter Nineteen

Because of the newly installed turnpike roads, the journey was costly, but smoother than in the past. On the way, they stopped in Bath. It was there that Charlotte shared with Annie the story of the first time she met James. Annie nodded her head knowingly, as Charlotte spoke of being so infatuated that she could not eat or drink. When Charlotte told the story of the ball where Harvey Shelbourne spilled punch on Samantha Toland's dress and James first noticed her, Annie sat transfixed.

Leaving Bath, they carried on to Oxford, Coventry, and Birmingham stopping for the night at inns along the route. The next leg took them to Manchester, and then to Kendal where Charlotte spent the day doing business with weavers who were buyers of Whitestone's wool.

The last days of the journey began cold and grey. After crossing over the Dunmail Raise, the sky cleared, and they saw the thick snow on Skiddaw's peak to the north. In Keswick, they stopped at the coaching inn for the night where Charlotte remembered arguing with her brother years before. Sending word for Mr. Duddon, Whitestone's overseer, to bring the ponies, Charlotte and the others ate at the inn while warming themselves by the fire before retiring for the night. The next morning when Mr. Duddon arrived, they were all ready to mount up. Jack, riding in the saddle with Charlotte, clapped his hands happily.

Soon, the Jaws of Borrowdale narrowed around them, dark and foreboding, as they crawled slowly down the old packhorse trail. As they entered the middle valley, the afternoon sun illuminated the early spring green of the valley floor. The snows of Great Gable glowed to the south and the river Derwent flowed merrily alongside the trail.

Charlotte's heart rejoiced. She was home. Looking at the fellside, Charlotte pointed, "Jackie, see, there is our house. Do you see the big house up there?" she said excitedly.

Whitestone rested isolated on its hillside above the village. Before the ponies reached the village, they turned eastward on the pack horse trail to Watendlath. Charlotte pointed out to Jack the Herdwick sheep in the fields, their blue-grey fleeces shining in the sunlight.

It was lambing time. The ewes rested, watching their babies frolicking on wobbly legs. Jack giggled at one black lamb in particular with a white star on its head gambolling in the high grass. After crossing over the river on a narrow stone bridge, they began their ascent. The first half was a gentle, steady climb on the deeply rutted trail. Jack squealed with delight as the road became steeper, and they had to lean forward to help the pony climb the hill.

Charlotte was filled with a mixture of excitement and dread. As the house grew closer, she wondered if she could face seeing Mary Mungris in such a state, but at the same time, she prayed she was not too late. The windows of the house reflected the gold of the late afternoon sun. She loved this place. She felt complete here. It was as if she was being welcomed back by a lover whose gentle, enchanted embrace made her forget there was a past or a future.

When they reached the level ground covered in small, white stones in front of the house, Charlotte handed Jack down to Annie. She dismounted at the same time that Sally Poole, Mary's daughter, came out to greet her.

"Oh, Lady Charlotte, welcome home," Sally greeted. She was red-eyed from crying. Still, she attempted an awkward curtsy but had to stop midway overcome by tears. Charlotte put her arm around Sally to comfort her.

Jack, let loose by Annie, headed for the steep hillside. Moving as quickly as she could, Annie gathered up her skirts and chased after him, hoping to catch him before he tumbled over the edge. Charlotte held her breath, then breathed easier when Annie was successful in stopping Jack. She ushered Sally into the house.

The kitchen was warm and inviting. The slate floor was covered with new rushes, and a fire burned in the hearth. On the wheel-spit, two joints of mutton turned, and water boiled for tea. Charlotte sat down with Sally in the inglenook.

"Oh, dear Lord forgive me, Lady Charlotte, this is no way to greet you. But what a night! Mum was out of her head and spitting up blood. When she came to her senses, she started carrying on about dusting. I had told her yesterday that you were expected, but she hadn't even seemed to notice until she started in about the dusting. She hasn't uttered a word today. She's a little bit of a thing now. Hardly eats."

"I would like to see her, Sally. Shall we go up?"

"You wouldn't be wanting your tea first?"

"No, thank you."

"Very well. It's best not to wait."

Sally lit two rush lights, giving one to Charlotte. They left the kitchen and walked down a short hallway to a winding stairway leading up to Mary Mungris's room. The door was ajar. Sally pushed it open further as quietly as she could.

Charlotte saw the dark, carved bed that Mrs. Mungris had slept in ever since Charlotte could remember. The figure in the bed was so small. She could not fathom how this was the same robust woman who so delighted her as a child.

"Mama, Lady Charlotte has arrived. Do you hear me, Mama?" Sally stroked her mother's arm, but the woman did not acknowledge her daughter's voice or touch.

Charlotte fought back tears, speaking softly to Sally.

"I should like to sit with her for a time. Would you look after Jack? He seems able to get into mischief so easily. I know Annie must be at her wit's end."

"I shall go find them." Sally smiled, seemingly glad to leave the room.

Leaning over, Charlotte kissed Mary on the cheek. She was struck by the scent of the old woman. It was Mary's smell. Charlotte immediately felt comforted by it. This truly was the person she had always loved and who had so doted on her. She sat on a small wooden chair next to the bed. Mary's eyes were closed, her breathing shallow and fast. Thankfully, she did not seem in pain. Mary's weathered hand rested near her face as she lay on her side. Charlotte studied her hand with its wrinkles and mottled, brown spots.

Charlotte began to sing the lullaby that she loved as a child. The old woman opened her eyes. She had a look of concern on her face but did not speak. Stopping, Charlotte touched her hand to comfort her.

"Mary, it's me, Charlotte. I have come to see you."

The woman looked at her uncomprehendingly. Her consternation seemed to pass, and she closed her eyes.

"Dear Mary, I hope you can hear me and understand that your care for my family meant so much to me. I know my grandfather thought there was never a better housekeeper in all of Cumberland. He could be such an irritating man, and you were always able to soothe him when he was in a choleric humour. My mother always spoke so highly of you. You were a mother to her from the time my grandmother died. Thomas and I would have blown off the fells long ago, but for your care.

"I shall miss you. I have been far away of late, but you are always in my heart, dear Mary. How will I raise Jackie without you to advise me? Please, stay close to us if you can. I know God will have you at His right hand, and He is wise to do so. I love you."

Charlotte's tears fell as she spoke these last words. She swallowed, trying to regain her composure. As she wiped her eyes, she realized Mary was looking at her and smiling.

"Mary?" Charlotte whispered hopefully, but the woman's eyes closed.

When Charlotte returned downstairs, Sally was setting out dinner in the parlour on the long, oak table Charlotte's grandfather had made. The fire blazed as they ate their mutton. Charlotte asked Sally to join them, but she insisted that she had to make certain that Charlotte's servants were taken care of first.

"I will set them all to work in the morning," she said, "but tonight they should be fed and made to feel at home."

The rain pelted the windowpanes, and the wind howled

so loudly that Jack came and clung to Charlotte's skirts. The foul weather continued through the night. In the morning, when Charlotte went to walk to the glade above the house, she was driven back inside by the cold rain.

As the household waited to see if Mary Mungris would recover or not, Charlotte surveyed Whitestone and decided on the different tasks that should be attended to when the weather cleared. She met with Ned Duddon, Whitestone's overseer, who tended her flocks and shipped the wool and the finished wool products to Kendal. They determined the number of lambs that would be sold after the spring lambing was finished.

After a fortnight, Charlotte was able to move the servants into action as the clouds parted and a respite from the rain was granted. The inside of the house was painted. The lime work on the outside was done and missing slates on the roof replaced. New rushes were cut and dried for the lamps and to cover the floor in the kitchen. Washing was done and hung out in the warm sun to dry.

Charlotte planned an outing to the valley with Jack and Annie to survey the sheep with Mr. Duddon. As they were leaving, Sally, with the help of two servant girls, moved Mary downstairs and out into the air. Mary, bundled in blankets, slept sitting up in a chair by the kitchen door. Her loud snores punctuated the air as Charlotte and the others walked down the path.

The valley smelled of thawing earth and flowers. Jack was allowed to hold one of the new lambs under the supervision of Ned Duddon. He patted it softly and nuzzled its neck, then released it to its concerned mother.

As Jack played in the meadow under Annie's watchful eye, Ned approached Charlotte and asked if he might have a word with her.

"Of course, Mr. Duddon."

"Lady Charlotte, I have been in your family's employ for many years, since I was just a lad, if the truth be told."

"My grandfather always spoke of you with great regard," Charlotte responded, "and knowing that Whitestone is under your care has been of great comfort to me, as well."

"Lady Charlotte," Mr. Duddon plunged ahead, his face red from being praised, "I need to be leaving Whitestone. I have a brother who has gone to the Colonies and has written asking me to come. It's an opportunity for my family to have property of our own."

"Mr. Duddon, I encourage you to pursue this path if you are moved to do so, though I will sorely miss your good work." Clearly relieved to have told her, Ned Duddon promised to give her time to find a new overseer.

When they returned up the fell, Charlotte sat by Mary's side for an hour, while Jack and Annie walked up to Yew Crag. Charlotte breathed in the fresh air and raised her face, eyes closed, to the sun. She turned her attention to the vista before her, looking out over the shimmering green of the valley to the rust-coloured bracken on the opposite fellside. She smiled.

"This is what heaven must be, I do believe," she commented quietly to the sleeping Mary. "I cannot imagine a more beautiful place. Not even my garden, which I do love, can compare this sweet scene. My great-grandfather was a very wise man to choose to settle here."

As the air began to get cooler, Sally and the servants took Mary back to her bed, leaving Charlotte alone to view the sunset. She wrapped her woollen cloak around her, listening for Jack and Annie's return from their explorations. Someday, she thought to herself, she should like to live here again. She heard Jack some distance off. He was running down the hill and shouting at the top of his voice just as her brother, Tom, had done.

Time passes so quickly, she thought. Jack rounded the corner of the house and catapulted, laughing and breathless, into Charlotte's arms. Annie followed several yards behind him, endeavouring to walk with some semblance of dignity in the clogs that Sally had lent her.

Soon, they were all in the house and washed for tea. Charlotte broached the subject with Sally of Ned Duddon leaving for the colonies.

"I shall have to find a new overseer for Whitestone before I leave for Kirkmoor. I wish to ask, if you and your husband would consider overseeing the house and lands for me here?"

Sally's face brightened. "Oh, Lady Charlotte, I will speak with my Hugh. He has our flocks and the farm, but Whitestone has always been my home. My father was here thirty years and my mum forty-five. I am so honoured that you would ask. I will send a note off to Edward this very instant." She excused herself and hurried off to write a note to her husband telling him the news.

When Charlotte rose the next morning and beheld the blue sky, she determined that Jack, Annie, and she must have an outing to the fells. Having no desire to visit where her brother had died, she recalled Sour Milk Ghyll having breath-taking views and happy memories. She ordered that the farm cart be made ready. Baskets of food were prepared, and she asked the two footmen, Sam and Ben, to accompany the group on ponies.

They passed down through the valley with Charlotte driving the cart and followed the path by the River Derwent through Seatoller. With Thorneythwaite Fell on their left, they ambled south to Seathwaite, stopping at the farm at the end of the road to bid the farmer good day. Charlotte asked if they might leave the cart there while they walked up along the ridge to the ghyll. He agreed.

The farmer, Rafe Cockbain, was the son of the farmer who had assisted Charlotte's mother and grandfather the day her brother died. She remembered Rafe's face, his red cheeks, and angular nose. He was two feet taller and several stone heavier now, but it was the same person, of that Charlotte was sure.

The trunks of the trees glistened as they picked their way across the large, round stones where a stream rushed out of the fells. The path became steeper as they neared the first plateau. Here, they rested for a few minutes, then began again. It took them an hour and a half to reach the ridge. William and Ben walked behind Annie and Charlotte. For the steeper grades, Ben carried Jack on his shoulders, while Sam struggled with the heavy baskets.

The group made their way along the summit to the ghyll. The sound of the rushing water was still distant when Charlotte's attention was caught by the song of a lone cuckoo. It echoed off the rocks, beautiful and haunting. She stopped to listen. Even Jack, who had been singing loudly, halted and looked to see where the bird might be.

Charlotte noticed all the wildflowers bursting from the rocks, the dainty, white strawberry, the purple violets, and the pink primroses. Their vivid colours were striking against the blue-grey of the granite. It is the exquisite beauty of the large and the small that I love here, thought Charlotte.

As they moved on, the roar of the water drowned out the birdsong. The ghyll was overflowing with the runoff of the melting snow. It thundered over the precipice and flew in sheets of spray back up into the air. They clambered up the fellside to a grove of trees where there was a small, flat clearing. There, they sat with the baskets and devoured their food. Charlotte knew that somewhere close by, her grandfather had had his plumbago mine. He had sold the precious, black wad in Keswick, making enough money to build Whitestone.

The ghyll had widened during the fifteen years since she'd been there. Charlotte remembered the beck as much smaller, as well. Now, it was a torrent that hurled itself over into the breach. After eating, Charlotte walked down to the edge of the cliff to watch the water falling. She longed to be a bird, perhaps a skylark or meadow pipit, spreading her wings and leaning into the wind. What a joy it would be to rise into the air and ride the currents!

Jack's cry brought her back to the present. Turning, she saw him straining to be free of Ben's grasp. Moving quickly, she took his squirming body into her arms and calmed him while the luncheon baskets were retrieved from the ground. She carried him for a bit, pointing out the red admirals that danced from thistle to thistle. William nearly caught one, but it escaped, leaving him to pick the sharp thistle out of his palm.

Charlotte helped Jack gather treasures to put in his little basket as they walked back to Seathwaite. He found smooth, white pebbles and multi-coloured bark. The finest discovery, however, was a large, blue-black raven's feather.

On returning to Whitestone, they found Sally in a terrible state. Her mother had fallen into a deep sleep.

Nothing they tried would rouse her. Charlotte, attempting to comfort Sally, got her to drink a cup of tea and sit before the kitchen fire.

At last, though she dreaded it, Charlotte mounted the stairs, her body suddenly tired and heavy. She opened the door to Mary's room. The elderly woman was still. Charlotte shrank back, afraid that she was dead, but looking more closely she saw the slightest movement of Mary's chest. Charlotte stepped forward and put her ear to the woman's nose.

There was a feeble breath still. Going back to the top of the stairs, she summoned one of the kitchen girls and gave her instructions to bring extra rushes for the lamps.

"Tell Mrs. Poole that I shall sit with her mother for a time. She should rest now and between us we shall watch Mary through the night. Ask Mistress Annie to please look after Master Jack." The girl took her leave and disappeared quickly down the stairs.

Going back into the room, Charlotte sat by Mary's bed. She bowed her head and prayed. When she finished, she lifted her head in time to see the room infused with the pink light of dusk. Looking out the window, Charlotte could see the fells glowing red in the last light of the day. She took hold of Mary's hand, pressing it to her lips. She placed it back across Mary's bosom.

Later in the night, when Sally came to relieve Charlotte, several rush lights had already burnt down. As Charlotte stood up to leave, Mary let out a long sigh followed by a deep rattle. Both Charlotte and Sally froze, unable to accept what they knew to be true. At last, Sally fell upon her mother's chest.

"Mama! Mama!" she cried out.

The old woman's head lolled to one side, and her mouth fell open. Shuddering, Charlotte put her arm around Sally, helping her to sit in the chair by the bed. She righted Mary's head and closed her mouth.

"God bless you, Mrs. Mungris," she whispered softly. The wind began to blow down the fell, sounding with a moan that died out only to return again. The windows rattled. Charlotte patted Sally's shoulder gently as the woman wept beside her mother's body.

The next day was taken up in the preparation for the funeral and burial. In the midst of all the activity, Hugh Poole, Sally's husband, approached Charlotte. Bowing formally, he asked for a few minutes of her time. She led him into the parlour where she sat at her grandfather's table. She invited him to join her, but he chose to stand. His gaunt face and deeply set eyes gave him a stern appearance, but this was softened by the burr in his voice. Charlotte noticed how large and strong his hands were, a consequence of his being a shepherd and a farmer, she imagined.

"Lady Charlotte, Mrs. Poole wrote of your offering us a position. We would be most proud to accept it."

"Thank you, Mr. Poole. Sir James and I shall be very pleased to have you and Mrs. Poole overseeing Whitestone. We shall discuss the duties entailed in a day or two, when all these sad proceedings are at an end."

Hugh Poole did a long, slow bow and left the parlour. Charlotte sat watching the fire burn for some minutes, musing on how quickly time passed. She recalled when Hugh Poole was a skin-and-bones shepherd who chased up the hill in front of Whitestone, his long staff in hand, as he searched for a stray ewe or lamb. She would greet him with a cheerful hello, which he returned with a grunt and a side-long glance. She thought him odd, but Mary had spoken highly of him over the years. He was a hard worker, she said, and took good care of Sally and the children. Charlotte was glad that he had accepted the position of overseer of Whitestone.

Shivering and wet, people began gathering at the house the next morning. The earliest to arrive collected in the kitchen close to the fire. Mary Mungris was beloved in the village, so by the time everyone was assembled, nearly thirty men and forty women stood inside and outside the house. They ate cheese with bread that Sally had baked the night before and drank the ale provided. Some were weeping, others spoke quietly, recalling the good works of both Mary and her husband. The body had been set into a coffin painted black and covered with a fine cloth from London that Charlotte had brought.

The men began singing a funeral psalm as the coffin was borne with difficulty down the steep and slippery fellside. Hugh Poole's shoulder bore much of the weight of the coffin as one of the front pallbearers. Sally and their children were just behind with Charlotte. The women wore their red cloaks to shield themselves from the strong gusts of wind that blew down the fellside. As the procession filed through the village, still singing, more people joined. Sheep and horses looked up from their grazing, presumably curious to see so many people together. The songs ended, and they moved on with only the sounds of feet to mark their passing.

Briefly, the foggy mist that had descended on them lifted. A shaft of light set a field adjacent to the churchyard aglow. Just as quickly, it was extinguished as they met the vicar at the church. Charlotte was surprised by his diminutive size, but his oration proved worthy, and the ceremony was fittingly solemn.

As they committed Mary's body to the earth, the rain began to fall in torrents, causing people to leave at a quicker pace than seemed appropriate. However, Charlotte thought afterward that she would have been wiser to join them, for by the time she arrived at the Pooles' house, she was soaked to the skin.

Sally and Hugh had a small, well-kept cottage in the village at the town's end, which now filled with the bereaved. Charlotte stayed on a short while until the crush of people became too much for her sorrowful heart and wet body. She retreated, a solitary figure, back up the hill to Whitestone.

The next day, Charlotte was sick in bed with a high fever. She began to shake uncontrollably as her fever mounted. At one point, she fell into a fitful slumber only to be awakened by her own moaning. In her delirium, she imagined herself pregnant again as she had been with her last sickness at Whitestone. Annie kept Jack away, and Sally, though exhausted herself, watched over Charlotte.

Three days into Charlotte's illness, Sally decided to send a letter to Sir James. Annie agreed to help her compose it. Its conclusion was unhappy but true.

You never know, Sir James, what course such an ague may take or how quickly.

At dawn the next morning, Ben and Sam, the footmen, were dispatched to Kirkmoor with the letter.

CHAPTER TWENTY

After ten days of sweating and delirium, the fever broke. Though extremely weak, Charlotte was able, with help, to come down to the parlour for broth, bread, and butter. Jackie ran to his mother and climbed in her lap.

"Mama! Mama wake, Annie!" He took his mother's face in his small hands. "We go Lodore" He jumped off her lap and began spinning around the room. "Lodore plash." He threw himself on the ground in imitation of the swirling waters.

"Come, come, Jackie," Charlotte called him.

He stopped, still lying on the floor, and looked up at her.

"I want you to come here, Jackie," Charlotte said with as much energy as she could muster.

He stood up and looked at his mother.

Annie took Jack's hand and led him back to Charlotte. He climbed onto her lap again and rested his head on her breast. She held him and closed her eyes.

"Jackie loves Mama," he whispered.

Later that morning, she sat by the door of the kitchen in the same chair where Mary had rested. The warm air and the sweet scent of the wildflowers on the hill did much to revive her spirits. She prayed that James was on his way.

She hoped she would receive word from him in the next few days.

Three days later, a letter arrived from James. The postmaster of Keswick, on seeing that it was from Sir James Clarke, carried the letter himself the nine miles to Whitestone.

"Not wanting," he said, "to leave it to lesser hands."

Charlotte thanked the man and asked Sally to provide him with refreshment. She opened the letter with trembling hands.

My dearest Lottie,

I wish to hold you in my arms, to feel your body against mine, to hear your laugh, to see the flash of anger in your eyes when we disagree, to see you hold Jack in your arms. I will, I swear, never let you out of my sight again, my sweet wife. You know that I love you beyond all else. I pray that your fever has abated and that you are daily regaining strength.

Elizabeth has her baby, and it is a boy. He is to be christened Charles James Warrender, the Earl of Chagford. So, she will be the dowager countess and remain in residence at Scorhill. William, Jenny, and the boys are all well and send their regards.

I am, at this hour, awaiting my traveling companion. As soon as he arrives, we will be off.

The hunt at Kirkmoor was a success. My hounds have not lost their love of the chase, which gladdens my heart. I am much obliged to Mr. Norton for introducing me to the master of the hounds at Okehampton. He brought a most excellent pack with him. This same gentleman is the one I am waiting for this morning. He has asked to accompany me to Cumberland to see for himself the quality of the northern dogs.

Ben and William, in their haste to deliver the news of your health, came the fastest route to be found. They shall guide us back over the sands of Morecambe Bay in order to reach you quickly.

Look for me over Honister Pass, my angel. I shall travel day and night to be at your side.

As I finish this, my companion, Silas Tomkyn, has arrived and is ready to go. We are off. I pray we arrive before this letter, but if not, know that we are not far behind.

With all my love and devotion for you and Jack.

Your loving husband,
Jem

Charlotte held the letter to her heart, smiling at the thought of kissing Jem and holding him in her arms. But his news of coming over the sands of the bay terrified her. She had heard of the treacherous quicksand swallowing up travellers. She prayed that he would come to her safely.

Seven days after the fever had abated, Charlotte spent the morning sitting in front of the house, staring into the distance. This day or the next must surely bring James's arrival, she thought. She longed to see him, to feel the strength of his arms around her and hear his soothing voice.

Closing her eyes, she slept in the midday sun and dreamt of flying high over the rooftops of Rosthwaite. Dipping and soaring on the warm breeze, she saw James in the distance by the churchyard on a white horse. He was dressed in a red uniform with a grenadier's high hat. She was running to greet him, but he did not acknowledge her. He rode on, looking straight ahead with a sombre expression. His face was so pale. She was frightened.

She struggled to fly again, but the breeze became a

howling wind, and she toppled head over heels in the churchyard. Landing in a muddy pile, she raised her head, only to realize that she rested on Mary's grave. Moaning, she fought to wake herself.

At last, her eyes opened. Breathing was difficult, her chest hurt, and her eyes were hot. Not again, she thought, I cannot be sick again. Calling out for Sally, her voice was thick and raspy. She stood up, wanting to move into the house, but she fainted on the kitchen doorstep.

Much later, she awoke in her bed. The walls of her room glowed pink. Looking at the window, she saw the whole sky glowing in that same shade. Annie sat at her bedside, and on seeing Charlotte awake, she took her hand gently.

"We have sent for the doctor in Keswick, dear Charlotte. You must rest and gather your strength. Jack is fine. Ben is looking after him."

"Ben?" Charlotte asked.

"He arrived this afternoon, bringing word from Sir James. He should be arriving tomorrow."

"And I in my bed," Charlotte groaned unhappily.

"You will recover. You are the strongest woman I know."

"A true Amazon. Yes, so I have been told." Charlotte coughed and flinched at the pain that shot through her lungs.

"No," Annie laughed. "I meant nothing of the sort."

The doctor came, huffing and puffing up the stairs. Charlotte would learn later that when the doctor was first told that the patient was in Rosthwaite, he hesitated, but on being told it was Lady Charlotte, he lost no time in mounting his horse. After examining her, he suggested bleeding as a cure, but she would not agree to it. It was finally decided that China tea and barley water would help ease the pain and get the patient on the road to recovery.

"You must rest, Lady Charlotte. Do not tax yourself," the doctor instructed.

"But I must return to Devon with my husband."

"Not for at least a month, I am afraid. You would risk damaging your health permanently." The doctor was paid handsomely for his advice and given supper and a room for the night.

James did not come the next day, nor the next. On the third day, rising from her bed, Charlotte wrapped herself in her shawl and sat at her window looking over the valley. All her fears were heightened by ill health.

Annie found her, sitting slumped, staring at the distant fells. Charlotte looked at her, hollow eyed.

"I am so afraid that James has met with some dreadful accident. Why did I come here, Annie? I should never have left my beautiful house, my garden." Annie went down on her knees and grasped both of Charlotte's hands.

"Please, dear Charlotte, do not trouble yourself. Shall I send Ben out to Honister Pass? He will bring us news. I'm sure of it."

Charlotte agreed. She watched from her window as Ben made his way down the fell on horseback and off through the village. He was gone an hour and a half when he returned at a gallop.

Annie ran noisily up the stairs and into Charlotte's room.

"Sir James is very near," she announced breathlessly. "He is just coming down the trail past Stonethwaite."

This news inspired Charlotte so much that she threw

off her shawl and began brushing her hair. She had to stop her toilette briefly when she was overcome with a coughing fit. This passing, she managed to put on a loose-fitting dress. Wrapping herself again in her shawl, she came haltingly down the stairs and walked out into the spring afternoon.

She spotted James below in the village. Eagerly, she watched him as he turned his horse to the east and began his ascent up the hill. Her heart raced as he set his horse into a canter. He saw her and began waving his hat in the air. Joyfully, she waved back.

And then he was there. Quickly dismounting, he grabbed her up into her arms.

"Oh my god, Lottie, I was so afraid I had lost you. I cannot be without you. You are my life, and I will never allow you out of my sight again." Charlotte held on to him, taking in each of his words as if they were a life-giving elixir.

"Jem, when you did not arrive two days ago, I had such trepidations, but you are here. I praise God."

His clogs resounding on the slates, Jack came running out of the door with Annie right behind.

"Papa!" He wedged his way in between his parents and hugged his father's legs.

"Jackie!" James cried and lifted his son into the air. "Look at my handsome Jack. Oh, I have missed you."

"Papa! Papa!" Jack shouted putting his arms around James's neck. The little boy pulled his father's head towards his face and hugged him. As they turned to go into the house, Charlotte noticed another horse and rider coming up the packhorse trail. She touched her husband's shoulder.

"James, do you know this man?"

"It's Tomkyn. I completely forgot about him when I

saw you." He waved to the man who waved back.

"Who?" Charlotte asked.

"Silas Tomkyn, the master of the hounds from Okehampton. I believe I wrote to you about him. He has come along to see the Cumberland hounds that I have praised so highly." The man's white hair flowed down his shoulders from beneath his tricorn hat. He wore a dark brown, woollen coat and an olive green waistcoat. Charlotte recognized the horse as one of James's prized hunters.

"He rides the chestnut?" she asked.

"Yes, his own mount could not have made so strenuous a journey. As it was, our poor horses nearly sank in the sands of the bay. Luckily, our guide moved us to more solid footing before we were overtaken by the tide. We had to stop for a day, while a storm blew in the pass. We started up yesterday, but the hail drove us back. Poor Tomkyn needs a hearty meal after our adventures."

"I will have Sally put on beefsteaks for tea."

Silas Tomkyn came to a halt in front of James and Charlotte. She was struck by the tremendous eyebrows perched over his deeply set eyes. He peered down at her like an eagle surveying its prey. Instinctively, she took a step back.

"Did I leave you in my dust, Tomkyn? I do apologize." James laughed. The old man smiled.

"Damn my eyes, Sir James, I haf niver seen a hound so speedily take after hare as you did on seeing this hillock. The scent of yer lady, eh, sir?" teased the old man, winking at James.

"You are a rascal, sir!" James retorted, not at all affronted.

Charlotte was taken aback by the familiarity the man

displayed but decided to say nothing.

Tomkyn dismounted with some stiffness in his legs. When he stood on the ground, he was shorter in height than Charlotte. He bowed his head slightly as he greeted her.

"Good afternoon, Lady Charlotte. Forgive an old man's rudeness, if you can. I am most pleased to make yer acquaintance."

"And I you, Mr. Tomkyn. I bid you welcome to Whitestone. Do come in."

"Thank you, your ladyship." Tomkyn said, taking off his hat and bowing a little deeper.

Charlotte noted his prominent cheekbones and ruddy complexion. His nose was large and sharp at the tip. His hair, though white now, had probably once been blond. His deference made Charlotte decide to reserve her opinion of him, though if truth be told, he made her uncomfortable.

As they sat for tea, James reported that the boys and Burke-Scott were all surviving. Annie smiled at the news of William. The conversation turned to the hunt at Kirkmoor. Silas praised James's prowess as a rider and hunter a few too many times for Charlotte's taste. She smiled politely, but at last, fatigue overtook her, and closing her eyes, she rested her head on James's shoulder.

"Come, dear wife, allow me to carry you to our bed," James whispered softly.

"I would be most appreciative if you would, dear husband," Charlotte said, not opening her eyes.

James gave Jack a hug. He asked Sally to find a place for Silas.

"I will return in a bit, Jackie. Shall we go for a walk in the moonlight?"

"Yes, Papa!" Jackie replied happily. "Just you and me."

Silas, watching the happy scene, commented, "A son is a father's joy. There is no replacing that, Sir James." Charlotte noted the sadness in his voice.

Carrying her easily up the stairs, James sat down on the edge of the bed with Charlotte still in his arms. Cradling her like a child, he rested his face in her hair. She pushed her head gently into his chest and breathed in his scent. They sat this way for some time, having no desire to move.

At last, Jack's cries for "Papa!" could no longer go unheeded. James laid Charlotte down and tucked the covers in around her. He brushed the hair from her face. She took his hands and kissed them. Smiling, the lines by his eyes wrinkled, and Charlotte sighed.

"Rest, my Lottie," he whispered.

"I shall." She closed her eyes and listened to his footsteps on the stairs. She drifted to sleep with sounds of Jack and James's voices outside.

Though James was attentive to Charlotte's needs as she recovered, he spent a good deal of time out riding with Silas, visiting neighbouring villages to inquire after dogs. Hugh Poole introduced them to the masters of the hounds in both Keswick and Grange.

Now, Charlotte found herself sitting outside the house watching ominous clouds gather in the west as she waited for James to return. Annie joined her, and they talked happily on several subjects until Charlotte mentioned Tomkyn. Annie's good mood vanished. When pressed by Charlotte on this change in her countenance, she reluctantly confided that Sally, just that very morning, had said her husband could not abide the man. Charlotte asked if any reason was given.

"Mr. Poole says Mr. Tomkyn laughs too much," was

Annie's response.

The men returned just as the storm broke. James was in fine spirits when he strode into the parlour and kissed Charlotte.

"What an excellent day we have had, Lottie. I look forward to you being able to join us. I cannot say enough about Cumberland hospitality. The people in the south could learn something from the graciousness of these yeomen."

His enthusiasm made Charlotte forget about her conversation with Annie, but later in the evening as they were playing cards, she had reason to remember it. The subject of children was brought up and Silas mentioned tersely that his son had been lost at sea. Only a few minutes after that, Charlotte happened to glance at Tomkyn. A look of anger on his face made her shudder, but in the next instant he was all smiles and laughter.

When she and James retired for the evening, she broached the subject of her unease with Tomkyn. James responded that he felt none of that for Silas.

"I feel as if I have known him for a long time," he chided Charlotte, saying that she was jealous of the time he was spending with his friend just as he had been jealous of her and Adam. "And did I not admit the error in my judgement?" He raised his eyebrows and smiled at her in his most charming manner. She did not pursue the subject.

July came with warm breezes. The evenings had grown long now. James, with Tomkyn's help, assembled a fine pack of hound pups to take back to Kirkmoor. One morning, James put all the dogs in a temporary enclosure in front of the house. Hearing their barking, Jack came outside. He squealed with delight when set in the midst of the licking, tail-wagging dogs.

Awakened by the sound of the dogs and Jack, Charlotte arose feeling queasy, but it passed as she did her toilette. After taking a cup of tea and a slice of bread for her breakfast, she and Hugh Poole discussed which lambs were to be sold at market and how much wool was likely to be sent to Kendal. The rest of the day, she planned preparations for returning to Kirkmoor, though secretly wishing they could spend the summer at Whitestone.

That completed, she walked outside to find Jack showing the treasures he had found on the outing to Sour Milk Ghyll to his father. James was remarking on the silken sheen of the raven's feather and the beauty of the smooth, white quartz pebbles, when Silas suggested that Jack show them the place himself.

"I would like to gather up some of those stones meself, Master Jack. Will you show me where to look, lad?"

Proud to be addressed in this manner, Jack responded, "I show you." Seeing his mother approaching, he ran to her, "We go, Mama?"

Having overheard the conversation as she approached, Charlotte thought she would like to take in the view one more time before they journeyed back to Devon. "I think it is an excellent idea, Jack." To Tomkyn, she said, "Would you ask Sally to prepare our baskets, and Ben to get the farm cart ready?"

"At once, Lady Charlotte," Silas answered. Charlotte noted his smile appeared forced but chose not to remark on it.

Jack began to jump about excitedly at the idea of the excursion. James gathered him into his arms and started to dance a jig himself. Smiling, Charlotte shook her head at their gaiety.

"Such a pair you are!"

James danced over to Charlotte and, grabbing her waist with his free arm, he twirled all three of them around and around. Charlotte laughed at first, but quickly became sick to her stomach. James stopped, concerned at her pale face.

"Lottie, what's wrong?" She sat down and held her head. He knelt beside her, releasing Jack, who sped away to find Annie. At last, her stomach somewhat calmed, Charlotte raised her head and smiled weakly. "I believe we are blessed with a new Clarke."

James sat back on his heels in disbelief. "You are with child?"

"I do believe I am, Jemmy. Our frolic in the folly at home has proven to be fruitful. I pray my fever will not hinder the baby."

"You should rest. Going up to the ghyll will be too strenuous."

"No, my dearest husband. I wish to see it one more time. I love the heights. I promise, I will not overextend myself. Do not deny me the pleasure of being with you and Jack.

"I can deny you nothing, Lottie." He looked lovingly at her.

In no time, the dinner baskets were ready. It was decided that the party should include Jack, James, Charlotte, Annie, Silas, Benjamin, Hugh Poole, and his two daughters, Dora and Catherine. Sally had insisted that her husband accompany them in case Charlotte should need to return before the others. Charlotte smiled when she saw Hugh brought along his shepherd's staff. She imagined him once again bounding across her path after wandering lambs.

As they came down the hill in two carts and entered the village, the sound of the Rosthwaite fiddler drew them to one of the farmer's doors. Jack jumped down with Catherine and Dora at his side. They joined the other children, dancing and merrymaking, until urged by Charlotte, they boarded the cart once more.

It was nearly one o'clock when then reached the Seathwaite farm and were greeted by the owner, Rafe Cockbain, and his wife, Molly, who were just sitting down to dinner. They left the carts and horses in the yard and began the trek up the fell. Jack chased after two swallowtail butterflies, but Catherine called after him.

"Mind the dust on their wings, Jack. Do not hurt them. Poor, sweet butterflies." Jack soon stopped his pursuit, more from loss of interest than from Catherine's admonitions.

"Children are blest indeed, don't you agree, Lady Charlotte," Tomkyn wheezed as they began the ascent to the first plateau. "They have no thoughts for the past or the future. Master Jack is free of care, wouldn't you agree?"

"I pray so, Mr. Tomkyn. Though he has been moved so many times in his young life, I wonder."

"Aye, my poor son had a hard life, losing his mother when he was young. He survived into his manhood, but he still died young and tormented."

Charlotte found Tomkyn looking at her from under his shaggy brows. His cold, blue eyes gave her a chill. She stopped.

"Are you ill, Lady Charlotte?" Silas asked with concern.

"No, I need only to rest. Pray, carry on. I will follow." The old man obeyed, hurrying to catch up with James. Hugh Poole and Benjamin, who were bringing up the rear with the baskets, stopped to see if Charlotte needed help. She instructed Benjamin to go on.

"I have a question or two to ask Mr. Poole."

When they were alone, Charlotte told Hugh that she had heard of his misgivings regarding Silas Tomkyn. Poole said nothing at first but walked on with Charlotte.

At last, he admitted, "Lady Charlotte, little I know of the outside world, but that man carries a darkness with him where're he goes. Jessie, my dog, d'inna care for him, growls when he comes past. Jessie knows."

"But he is master of the hounds. Why do they respond to him, do you suppose?"

"Hounds have no sense that I can tell, Lady Charlotte. Jessie is a collie. She knows her sheep, and she knows her people."

They were now beginning the steep ascent, making talking difficult. Hugh walked close by Charlotte. As she pulled herself up the steepest section leading to the ghyll, Charlotte decided she must speak again to James about her apprehension concerning Tomkyn. Perhaps they could send him back to Devon with the hounds in the next few days, maybe even on the morrow. She sensed that it was imperative to be rid of him, if only she could break the spell he had cast on James.

They approached the roaring waters of the ghyll and were blessed with a panoramic view of the valley to the north and the fells to the south and east. Annie asked Charlotte for her permission to walk on some distance with Benjamin and Hugh Poole to observe an eagle's nest. Charlotte warned her to watch her footing, and she was off with a smile. Dora and Catherine sat with Jack, who was already opening one of the baskets. Silas found a rock near the children to perch on and seemed content to rest there. Charlotte caught up with James, who was marvelling at the vistas.

"I do understand your fascination with this place, Charlotte. It is perfect in its combination of valley, water, and fell."

Charlotte hesitated to break in on his thoughts but feared to wait to find another opportunity to speak to him.

"Jem, when you arrived, I told you of my fear that you had met with some accident. That dread I felt has not left, rather it has only grown. I know the source of it." She hesitated to go on, but James looked at her expectantly, so she proceeded. "It is the presence of Silas Tomkyn." James raised his hand slightly as if to interrupt her, but she continued. "Please, let me finish. I understand that we have spoken of this before, but I believe now, even more firmly, that he is a malevolent presence in our midst."

James asked calmly, "On what do you base your fear, Charlotte?"

She hesitated to say that several others felt as she did and that even Poole's dog abhorred the man. This last, she knew, would set him to laughing.

"I can only say that the more I speak with him the more uneasy I become."

"What has he said that so upset you?"

"It is not what he says, but rather the expressions of rage I see on his face from time to time. His eyes hold no human warmth."

"How is it that I find him quite the opposite? With me, he is all mirth."

"I do not believe his smiles or his laughter," Charlotte replied heatedly.

"My dearest, I trust your feelings," James said, not wishing to upset her. "I will send him back to Devon post-haste if it will ease your heart."

"It will, James. Thank you for understanding." She moved to him and kissed his cheek.

"The hounds are bought. There is no reason for him to tarry." James glanced around and found Silas Tomkyn sitting with the children near the top of the cataract. He motioned for the old man to join them. Silas rose awkwardly and moved to them with a stiff-kneed gait.

"Yes, Sir James?" Tomkyn said as he neared James.

"We would speak with you, Tomkyn, about our plans for returning to Kirkmoor and your part in them." The man stopped, his eyes narrowing, though he continued to smile benignly.

"Sir James, you do not plan to cast me out from such happy company so soon?" To Charlotte, he said, "Lady Charlotte, have my rough manners offended you? I would make amends wit' you if tha' be so." Charlotte did not respond.

James intervened. "Nothing of the sort, man. The hounds are ready to travel south. You will leave tomorrow, Silas. Benjamin can accompany you."

"But, Sir James, what o' yer desire to visit the masters of the hounds in Chester and Oxford? Have you forgotten yer hopes for gathering the best hounds in England?" Tomkyn moved to James's side, causing Charlotte to have to step back from her husband.

"There will be time to do that later, Silas."

Silas smiled expansively. "Oh, aye, time is of little concern for you, Sir James. You are a young man with a young wife." Here, the old man wrinkled up his face, trying to curb his feelings. "But for me, with these white hairs…"

"Come, do not be melancholy, my friend. There will be time aplenty, I warrant you."

James's speech was interrupted as an eagle crying from overhead plummeted past them down the cliff face to its prey below. The group was silenced, awestruck by the power and speed of the bird.

Tomkyn moved past Charlotte, muttering, "How surprised a hunted man must be when he is finally caught, eh?" Startled from her thoughts on the eagle, she only half heard what he whispered, but his tone got her attention.

"What did you say, Mr. Tomkyn?"

"It was of no consequence, Lady Charlotte," the old man responded, shuffling back towards the children.

"There. It is done, my dearest. He will be off tomorrow."

James took hold of Charlotte's hand and led her towards the top of the ghyll. Here, they stood watching the water plunge over the edge and collide with the rocks far below.

"When we are back at Kirkmoor, I shall show you all the parts of the moor that I hold dear. Would that please you?"

"It would, and it would please me to walk in our garden again, and perhaps even lie naked in the folly on a summer's night." James kissed her lips deeply. Charlotte closed her eyes, enjoying the warm touch of his lips. Their reverie was shattered by a scream.

Horrified, James and Charlotte saw the old man dangling Jack by one arm over the edge of the cliff. Tomkyn, a wicked smile on his face, shouted at them.

"Did ye know I am a man who believes the Bible when

it says an eye for an eye?"

"Tomkyn, do not harm him. Put him back on solid ground," James called out, terror in his tone.

Charlotte's heart pounded loudly in her ears.

"Do not hurt him, Sir James?!" the old man scoffed. "Did you give my boy a chance, I wonder?"

"Please, give him to me," Charlotte cried as she took a step towards the cliff.

"How can an old man refuse a poor tearful mother?" Tomkyn replied bitterly. "But you are not an angel of mercy, lady, from what I have been told. No, indeed, you played a major role in my Edward's murder. Tell me you did not."

His words were gibberish to Charlotte. All she could see was Jack hanging, terror-stricken from the old man's hand.

"Hawkes!" James spat out the name like a curse as he realized the identity of the monster that held his son in an iron grasp.

The old man smiled broadly and brought the boy back in front of him where he held Jack tightly against his body.

"Well done, Clarke, but I am puzzled you did not remember me from the moors, boy. What a kind old gent I was, eh?"

"You!"

"Oh aye, t'was me. But now I have a score to settle for my Edward." So, saying, he pulled his hunting knife from its sheath. "A fine, soft neck has Jackie," he cooed to the boy.

At the same instant Charlotte screamed, "NO!" James rushed forward, wrenching Jack from the old man's grasp and flinging the boy to safety. Charlotte ran and grabbed

Jack. With him in her arms, she stumbled back awkwardly, to get out of the way of the two struggling men.

James fell on Tomkyn, trying to disarm him. Charlotte saw the knife flash as the two men rolled dangerously close to the cliff edge. Fortune, in that moment, turned her back and the blade found its way just under James's ribs. Shocked, he sat up and looked in disbelief at the knife.

The old man scrambled to his feet, triumphantly pulling the knife from James's body. He kicked the wounded man back to the ground. Tomkyn hesitated, looking back and forth between James and Charlotte and Jack. He cocked his head, as if deciding whether to strike James again, or attack his wife and son.

In that instant of indecision, he did not see Poole and the others return. Poole, not knowing what had transpired, was in a state of confusion. Charlotte handed Jack to Poole and grabbed the staff from his hands. Rushing forward, she hit Tomkyn squarely in the chest. Off balance, the old man staggered backwards. She gave him no time to recover, but hit him again, driving him over the edge of the cliff.

Dora and Catherine became hysterical and started screaming. Jack was crying and struggling to get free from Hugh Poole. For his part, Poole attempted to calm his daughters and maintain control of the terrified little boy. Annie, shocked, roused herself and took hold of Jack. Benjamin simply stood, unable to move.

Charlotte knelt beside James at the edge of the precipice. She put her face next to his.

"It's over, Jem. You are safe," she whispered, fighting back her tears. She tried to embrace him but felt a dampness next to her skin. It was his blood-soaked clothing. She held him. "We must get you home and care for your wounds."

Suddenly, James's body started moving towards the cliff edge. Looking up, Charlotte saw Tomkyn's hand grasping James's leg. The old man had managed to find a foothold as he fell. Climbing back up, he had grabbed James and was dragging him closer to the brink.

Charlotte grabbed the staff again. While she desperately held onto James, she beat at Tomkyn's arm. Finally, he lost his grip on James's leg. With nothing to hold on to, he fell screaming to his death on the rocks below.

She took James's head and shoulders into her arms. Blood seeped from the wound and spread in a widening pool over the rock covered ground. He looked at her, his face pale. She kissed his warm lips and held him. He closed his eyes.

"Oh, dear God, no." she said, shaking her head.

Poole came to her aid. "Lady Charlotte, hold this tight against his wound." He offered her his folded coat, which she took and did as he instructed.

"Ben, run to farmer Cockbain's house. Get help, boy, now!" Ben shook off his stupor and ran, flying down the mountain.

James opened his eyes. "What happened?" he whispered.

"Tomkyn stabbed you. He fell down the ghyll. He is dead," Charlotte told him.

"I'm cold," James said quietly. He winced as he tried to take a breath.

Annie, who had all the children in tow, offered her shawl for James. Charlotte took off hers as well and covered him with both. Poole knelt down by Charlotte.

"Help is coming, Sir James. We will get you down the fell. Lady Charlotte, Molly Cockbain, the farmer's wife will help ye and I will fetch my Sally, as well, to look after his lordship."

"Hugh, please, send Ben for the doctor in Keswick."

"I will, Lady Charlotte, as soon as he returns," Edward assured her.

"And the authorities, Hugh. We must notify the authorities of what happened."

"Aye, Lady Charlotte. I will see to it."

In a short time, Ben, Rafe Cockbain, and several farm labourers arrived. Gently, they lifted James onto a hastily made litter, all the while keeping pressure on the wound by pouring honey on it and covering it with clean cloths. They carried him to the Cockbain's farmhouse below in Seathwaite.

Rain began to fall as they brought James into the kitchen. Molly, a large, ruddy-faced woman insisted that he be put in their bed and led the group down the hallway to the bedchamber. Charlotte did not protest. She helped settle James and ministered to his wound. After that, Charlotte gladly accepted a cup of tea from Molly.

"Please, your ladyship, sit down." Molly guided Charlotte to a chair beside the bed. She covered Charlotte's shoulders in one of her own shawls. "Here young master, sit by your mam." She placed Jack on a stool in front of Charlotte.

Annie and the girls stood in the doorway. Charlotte finished her tea and handing the cup and saucer back to Molly, thanked her for her kindness.

"You are most welcome, Lady Charlotte. Rest now, if you can, and I will see to the girls."

As soon as Molly, Annie, and the girls were gone, Jack crawled into his mother's lap. She gathered him close to her.

"Oh Jackie, I love you so, my dear one." He held her tightly.

"Tomkyn hurted me, Mama."

"He was a bad man, Jackie."

"I'm scared, Mama. Will he come back?"

"No, he is gone forever, dearest."

Jack looked at his father. "Is Papa asleep?"

"Yes, and you should rest now, too. Shall I sing you a song?"

"Yes, Mama."

Charlotte began a lullaby that Mary Mungris often sang to her when she was a child. Soothed, Jack rested his head on her breast. He fell fast asleep. Charlotte listened to Jack's soft, steady breathing for several minutes until James groaned. Charlotte pushed forward out of her chair and carried Jack to the foot of the bed where she laid him down gently. She covered him with Molly's shawl. She pulled her chair closer to James and rested her head near his, trying not to disturb him. He did not wake. His breathing was shallow and his face pale, but he rested, seemingly without pain.

CHAPTER TWENTY-ONE

Charlotte awoke. James was moaning, his face wet with perspiration.

"Dear God, please, do not take him from me," she prayed. "Please, please," she whispered.

She spoke soothingly to James, and he settled back into quiet sleep. His son slept at his feet. Leaving the room to seek out Molly, she found her just entering the kitchen from outside. Her head was covered with a shawl, and her face was wet from the rain. She had an armful of plants torn out by their roots.

"I've got just what his lordship needs," Molly said. "Take me a bit to get them ready." She gave Charlotte a bowl of water and rags to help ease James's fever. "I will be there directly, Lady Charlotte. You cool him off for now."

Jack continued to sleep soundly while Charlotte gently wiped James's brow. His breathing calmed as she spoke softly to him. Molly entered and, going to James, carefully took down the bedclothes, lifted his shirt, and removed the cloth she had placed on the wound. Charlotte saw that the wound looked less inflamed and swollen. Molly applied a generous amount of honey and placed a poultice of crushed leaves and herbs over the wound.

James moaned.

Molly instructed Charlotte to help her wrap a bandage loosely around his body to hold the poultice in place.

James moaned again and closed his eyes tightly against the pain as the women moved him.

That done, they covered him, and Molly left the room. Charlotte began to softly wipe his forehead and the tension slowly eased in his face.

Later, Sally Poole came into the bedchamber and, touching Charlotte on the shoulder, indicated she should lie down beside James and rest. Grateful for the help, Charlotte did as Sally bid. The rest of the night, Charlotte was occasionally aware of Molly and Sally ministering to James.

The next morning, the doctor arrived, accompanied by the constable. Trees toppled by the night's storm had slowed their progress to the farm. While the doctor tended to James, the constable talked with most everyone who had witnessed Tomkyn's attack. Rafe came in from outside and reported that he and some of the other farmer's had had found Tomkyn's body at the bottom of the cataract where it had lodged between two boulders. They'd brought it back in a farm cart and put the body in the barn. The sheriff was satisfied that no foul play was involved in Tomkyn's death, and that it was most definitely self-defence on the part of Charlotte and James. He did not even take the trouble to speak with Charlotte. She learned later, after the men had gone, that Molly refused to allow the constable to enter the bedchamber.

"He had no business bothering you, Lady Charlotte. The very idea that he needed to question you was ridiculous. I told him so in no uncertain terms. His mam and me are good friends. 'Leave Lady Charlotte alone', I said, 'or yer mother will be after you.' He will not bother us again I can tell you."

"Thank you, Molly, for your good care of us."

"And the doctor? What did he say?" Molly asked.

"That what you are doing is correct and proper, and it will heal James faster than any of his medicines."

"He said that, did he?" Molly asked, cocking her head to the side.

"No, not exactly," Charlotte said with a small smile, "but I would say it to you. Oh, you should have seen the doctor, Molly. He puffed himself up with great importance as he examined the patient very thoroughly and finally, said, 'All is in order, Lady Charlotte, all is in order.' I thanked him, he bowed most grandly, and gave me a bill for his trouble."

The next few days, Charlotte apprenticed herself to Molly as they worked to bring James back to health. On the fifth day of the vigil, Charlotte was sitting next to James as he slept. She was drifting off to sleep with her head resting on the bed when she felt the touch of his fingers on her hair. Surprised, she looked up and found him smiling at her.

"Lottie, I love you," he said, taking her hand in his.

"Oh, Jem and I love you."

"Have you saved me yet again? You must tell me what went on. I remember Tomkyn had Jack and that we fought, but after that, all is a jumble."

Charlotte recounted what happened as James listened quietly, still unable to raise his head from the pillow. After a few minutes, his eyes closed, and Charlotte stopped talking. She caressed his face, and finally fell asleep beside him.

James was able to begin drinking broth and eating a

small amount of bread the next day. It was warm outside, so Jack and Charlotte took a walk and brought James flowers they had picked in the meadow by the farmhouse. He was sleeping when they came in. They sat very still and waited for him to awaken. Sensing their presence, he opened his eyes. Jack broke into giggles on seeing his father's delight at the bouquets.

The following morning, James was able to walk a few steps with help, and soon after, it was decided that he was strong enough to return to Whitestone. As they prepared to leave the Cockbain's house, Charlotte thanked Molly again and again for her help. The large woman embraced her, and both cried on parting.

A few weeks later, the doctor pronounced James ready to travel. Preparations were completed for the journey south. The morning they were to leave for Kirkmoor, a dense fog lay on the ground. As it began to lift, Charlotte asked James to walk with her and Jack up to the top of the hill. Though James's strength was returning, he still needed to go at a slow pace, so Jack ran ahead of his parents up the hill on the path to Watendlath.

A ray of sunshine pierced the clouds and shone on Jack as he climbed. Suddenly, bursting out of a stand of trees, a white stag quickly advanced towards Jack. It halted very near the boy. Jack froze. Charlotte and James stopped as well, afraid a sudden movement might startle the animal. The stag, luminous in the bright sunlight, gazed at the boy.

Jack slowly stretched out his hand to it.

"Careful, Jackie," Charlotte whispered.

The stag hesitated.

Charlotte tensed, ready to run and pull Jack out of harm's way.

After a moment, the deer simply turned away from the boy and disappeared at a trot down into a nearby ghyll.

Jack watched it go. He ran to his parents, shouting, "Mama, Papa, did you see? Did you see the white deer?"

Charlotte smiled. "We shall take it as a sign of good fortune, Jackie."

"I be lucky?"

James squeezed Charlotte's hand and interjected, "Aye, you will, son. You're my Lucky Jack from now on."

"Lucky Jack. Lucky Jack. I Lucky Jack." he shouted as he ran down the path towards the house.

"I hope it will always be so," Charlotte said.

"For all of us," James added, touching Charlotte's growing belly.

They stopped. James put his arms around Charlotte, and they kissed. Standing quietly, they watched Jack as he met Annie, who had appeared by the side of the house.

"We will be happy, Charlotte. I promise you," James said as they waved to Annie.

"I will hold you to your word, sir," Charlotte said, smiling fondly at him, and they walked down the hill to the waiting ponies and the road south.

EPILOGUE

In a tiny chamber at St. Mary Bethlem in London, Abigail Norton sat on the edge of her small cot weeping, her wrists chained together. Facing the wall, she argued with her dead son, Henry.

"My little one, I will hear no more about it. You know I could not fight your father. The drug they gave me would not allow me to think straight, let alone argue that I was sane."

She paused and listened to the voice only she could hear. After a moment, she shook her head.

"I do not believe that. Your father could not love me. Else why would he abandon me here so many weeks ago? He may have even given permission for the tortures these doctors inflict upon me."

She frowned, remembering the beatings, the spinning chair, the freezing cold baths, the induced vomiting, and the purging of her bowels. It seemed almost inconceivable that her once-beloved husband could be so cruel. Yet, he was different since…

Abigail looked at her shackled wrists and clenched her fists.

"No, my little one. I will not believe his lies. It was Clarke who killed you dead. I know it, and no one, not you nor your useless, cold-hearted father will convince me otherwise. I will find a way. I will fly from here.

"Help me, Henry," she pleaded, looking up at the cobweb-filled junction where wall and ceiling met. "Help me transform into a spider, a bat, a fly. Help me transform and be revenged on he who murdered you and he who put me in this hell hole.

"God or the devil, give me wings."

COMING SOON

The
Spider's
Smile

THE SHADOWS OF ROSTHWAITE
BOOK THREE

by

COLLEEN KELLY-EIDING

ABOUT THE AUTHOR

Colleen Kelly-Eiding is a member of the Screen Actors Guild, American Federation of TV and Radio Artists, and Actors' Equity. Her husband is an actor, as are their two adult daughters. Theatre, acting, and above all, storytelling, are part of her family's DNA.

Colleen was in the first class of women at Kenyon College in Ohio when the school went co-ed. She studied drama and political science at the University of Manchester in England. She received an MFA degree in acting from the University of Minnesota, and has since been an actor, director, casting assistant, 3rd grade teacher, and audiometrist.

Favoured by Fortune has been occupying Colleen's imagination for a quite a long time. After both daughters graduated college and were out on their own, she and husband Paul became empty nesters. The time seemed right for Colleen to bring young Ms. Pruitt, our heroine, to life and let Charlotte tell her story.

During her time in Manchester, Colleen fell in love with the country. When she returned to England to do research for her novel, she was beyond elated. She interviewed a curator at the Victoria and Albert Museum, spent time researching indictment records from the 1760's at the Guild

Hall in London, walked the route that the carts of the condemned travelled from Newgate Prison to the Tyburn Tree. Visiting the tiny village of Rosthwaite, located in the beautiful Borrowdale Valley in the Lake District, where much of the action takes place, helped give context and inspiration to Colleen.

Colleen continues to act for stage and film. She studies sculpting and ceramics. And enjoys traveling to Comic Cons around the world, where her husband is a frequent guest.